AN INCH OF PAIN WITH
A SLICE OF RAINBOWS

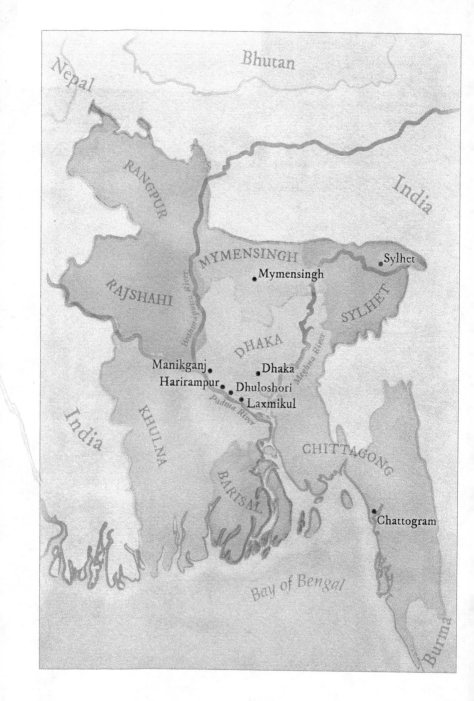

EAST BENGAL (BANGLADESH)

An
INCH OF PAIN
with
A SLICE OF
RAINBOWS

Nuzhat Shahzadi

Cover art: Rubaiyat Khan
Book design: Sara DeHaan
Map: Doug Nelson, DCNMaps.com

Publisher's Cataloging-in-Publication Data

Names: Shahzadi, Nuzhat, author.
Title: An inch of pain with a slice of rainbows / Nuzhat Shahzadi.
Description: Fairfax, VA: Nuzhat Shahzadi, 2020.
Identifiers: Library of Congress Control Number: 2020912620 |
ISBN 978-0-5787214-9-1 (paperback) | ISBN 978-1-7353520-0-8 (ebook)
Subjects: LCSH Family—Fiction. | Bangladesh—History—Fiction. |
Women—Bangladesh—Fiction. | Self-realization in women—Fiction. |
BISAC FICTION / Literary | FICTION / Historical / General | FICTION /
Cultural Heritage | FICTION / Women
Classification: LCC PS3619.H3493 I63 2020 | DDC 813.6—dc23

To my mom
who inspired me with her impossible zest towards life,
her astounding, feisty spirit...infectious love...

To my dad
who loved us unconditionally...

Contents

Preface   *ix*

PART I. 1930S AND 40S

   1. There is a river   3

   2. Rioting in my heart   35

   3. Sweet-salty times   53

   4. "Mistress of gloom"   59

PART II. 1950S AND 60S

   5. Awakening   73

   6. Senses and sounds; colors and contours   85

   7. Build me a dream...   91

   8. Becoming a woman   103

   9. A taste of Heaven and Earth   113

 10. The girl with beautiful eyes   123

 11. Sequence of events   133

 12. The white of lilies, the pink of lilies...   139

13. . . . Made with heartaches and heartburns   163

14. Whatever it takes   177

15. One cup of worries, one drop of Manna   189

16. A brother of standing   199

17. Departure   205

18. Sisters for life   213

PART III. 1970S AND 80S

19. We lived through the war!   231

20. Salad days and re-awakenings   245

21. Kingdom in the clouds   255

22. Woke up on the wrong side of your love   303

23. "Will you make me something beautiful for you?"   315

PART IV. CONCLUSION—JANUARY 1985

24. Silk sheets and diamonds   351

25. A good plan, ripples of revelations   365

26. Shadows and mirrors   393

Acknowledgments   397

About the Author   399

Preface

This book is a work of fiction though the contexts are grounded in reality. If any character in the book resembles anyone in real life — it's unintentional.

Growing up, I loved to listen to stories and read whatever I could find in print. I spoke and played with the characters of those stories in my dreams. My brain kept on storing anecdotes and tales and narratives, which eventually became my creative-bank, helped me to craft my thoughts as I took to writing.

I also came across countless amazing people in my childhood, and later in my adult years while I travelled across the globe as a UN Humanitarian aid worker. They were ordinary, unassuming, and very human.... I found abundant resources in frank smiles, or a stoop, or in eyes with deep sparkles, or the age ravaged faces.... The lives of these people inspired me to tell their stories. I felt an urgency to share what I stumbled on, what I knew. I found immense joy in discovering the extraordinary in commonplace, in everyday lives. This humbled me.

I took robust creative license to give life to characters based on my deeper exchanges with individuals from diverse circumstances — some intensely fascinating, while others belonged to the fold of everyday existence. In the book they are not portrayed as I met them in real life. I invigorated my imagination and lavishly used an array of fragments from different personalities to create a character. She or he is a mixture, cocktail blend of many shades, countless traits...unrecognizable in entirety — representing a quintessence of the human spirit. I believe, the fear of exposure sometimes imposes unnecessary restrains — and that defeats ingenuity, the power of a writer. My style may work or may not. I leave it to the readers to decide.

I have tried to be truthful regarding the historical contexts as narrated in the book. It was a lengthy process of listening to credible voices that lived through those times and persisted. I have also attempted authenticating their testimonies with reliable sources through thorough research to avoid misinterpretations, to the best of my abilities. For the time-period I lived through as described in the book, I followed similar steps but also tried to recount each occurrence from my perspective, that I felt, encountered and witnessed at any particular time — as a little girl wrapped in my tiny universe, listening, observing unobtrusively the situations unfolding around me, or as an adult as I embraced life and kept walking through it.

NUZHAT SHAHZADI
September 2020

PART I.
1930S AND 40S

CHAPTER ONE

There is a river

I.

It's early morning. The soothing breeze rustles the coconut leaves. In this small village at the edge of Dhaka, life is languid and calm. People call it Laxmikul, which in the Bangla language means lucky land.

Sanu Bibi gets up from bed, as always, before the rooster announces daybreak in its brassy, boastful crowing. Bengalee women, especially when young, are thought to be immodest, unwomanly if they laze late in bed. Mother stirs slowly under the quilt. Her bad knees and backache keep her up through the night in old age. Sanu tiptoes outside. She unlatches the chicken coop and heads towards the pond.

Nothing very exciting ever happens here besides weddings, births, or fights between two groups over land ownership. The land is like gold here—it holds the potential of many, many fertile crops, wrapped in promises of good days. Land is life and livelihood for most people.

Laxmikul village is miles away from the hustle and bustle

of busy towns, a tiny spot hidden by intersections of countless rivers as marked on the map. An occasional bullock cart or a rusty bicycle on the hard dirt road that serpentines around the paddy fields, the school-tin sheds, and the local bazaar can be considered diversions sometimes. On summer days, the sun beats down mercilessly, stifling the landscape. The green paddy fields spread for miles and miles—as far as the eye can see—etched with the blue of the sky reflected on water and merging into the vast horizon.

It's almost summer. The dewdrops glisten on the damp grass. The green of the trees is mirrored in endless waters encircling the landscape in unbroken monotony. In the distance, young rice crops dance with the wind, audaciously happy. And Sanu walks into the immaculate morning.

She has turned eighteen—too old to remain unmarried by the moral standards of this tiny village! Alas, no one has "snatched" her yet, as the older women say, meaning she hasn't been desired enough by a man to propose for her hand, though a prospective groom has very little role to play when it comes to his marriage. His family and relatives are the match-makers and decide on his behalf.

Sanu comes from a respectable and wealthy noble family, as Mother likes to call them. Landownership and trade have contributed to the family riches over generations. So the search for a deserving husband to match her aristocracy continues. This match is crucial—it has to be right. It's not easy. A daughter of this family can't be married off to a commoner, any low-bred peasant. Sanu nowadays feels a tiny bit ashamed because she's the only one among her friends still unmarried. Most of them have children by now. They try to tell her naughty stories about their husbands, life with their in-laws...about the sudden tremors felt in adoration when a baby moves for the first time in the womb. Sanu feels awkward at such talks while the others giggle and fall on each other in mirth.

The morning coolness is welcoming as she wades into the subdued stillness of the pond, undoing the reflection of coconut trees on the serene water, trapped in a glassy canvas enmeshed in deepest emerald. The rains are only a few weeks away. The south breeze carries the unmistakable scent of rain.

During the rainy season, Sanu's sisters, like all other married women, will be visiting with their children. A married woman can visit her parents only once a year. That's the custom in all noble families. Usually, trusted elderly male servants chaperone them as the husbands stay back home to take care of domestic and financial matters. They don't have the luxury to laze with in-laws. Unless there is a wedding or funeral or a significant family matter where a son-in-law's presence is absolutely essential, they opt out of the yearly visits.

As the monsoon waters flood the shores, the boats start to glide in, carrying the women to their motherland. Sanu longs for such times. With the rains, the water level rises, drowning the strip of land between the pond and the river, making it easy for the boats to be anchored right outside their home's front yard under the palm trees. Sanu can almost hear the rich, throaty songs of boatmen drifting in the air, bringing home the dear and near ones after a long, dreary wait.

Mother at those times is busy cooking many kinds of mouthwatering sweet delicacies and rice cakes. Sanu has to help her, though she longs to be near her sisters, hear their stories of love and laughter—the suffering and heartlessness they face in indefinite proportions in measured lives of belonging forever to their husbands' worlds....

In the evenings, the children are sent to bed early. The young mothers sit on mats in the inner yard while the magical moonlight floods the tin roofs, the treetops, the vast strip of the silent, deep waters. The accounts of their lives sound like fairy tales to Sanu. She never has visited anyplace so far beyond this village where she was born.

The women from the neighboring houses are welcome to join in. Her sister Tota is fun and full of bawdy jokes. She's also popular for her melodious voice. She sings trendy songs that tell sad stories of unrequited love—of a young bride who longs to visit her parents...about a girl who has given her heart to an unattainable suitor. Her silky voice is arresting, casts a spell, embracing the silence of the night in pathos that brings out an inexplicable emotion in Sanu. Her eyes get heavy with unshed tears as she keeps listening.

Mother usually cautions them to lower their voices, but she is more lenient with her married daughters than with Sanu, possibly because Sanu is unmarried. The sugary aroma of rice pudding lingers long in the air. The coconut leaves tremble with the wind, casting uneven shadows on the women. As the moon slowly fades, they laugh and sing in catchy tones as if there is no tomorrow....

Sanu's thoughts are broken by birds chirping. She has been lost in daydreaming and is late today. Mother is going to be very upset. A modest Muslim Bengalee woman should never be seen in wet clothes by anyone, not even by maids. That's unacceptable. She hurries towards home.

Sanu finds Mother ready for morning prayer. She is visibly cross. The reason is clear. Phuli Bibi, Sanu's eldest sister, has again refused to pray, claiming she is menstruating. This is her usual ploy to avoid getting up early. Sanu, like all others, grew up knowing it's forbidden for a Muslim woman to reach out to God or touch the Holy Quran when she menstruates—she's not allowed to go near the granary, is barred from entering the vegetable or fruit gardens. She's meant to stay away from mainstream life. A woman in her period is like a contagious grenade ready to burst into endless shrapnel of bad luck should she come in contact with anything tangible or sprouting life or has the potential to...a calamity personified. She's banished from the house of worship and gets a week's escape from the Divine and the life around her—seven days of solace. She can't share the same bed with her husband when she bleeds. Her body is considered to be napak—unholy, not fit for any offerings to living beings, nature, and the ultimate Supreme. This is a known fact, unequivocally accepted by everyone in this village and among all faiths.

When Sanu began menstruating, she was educated about it by older women in the household and accepted the regulations, as did every other woman around her. She understands the frustrations of being limited this way. But a woman who bleeds must play by these rules. No one can get away from them. Her Hindu friends share the same fate, and so do those from other religions that she is aware of.

Menstruating Hindu women aren't even allowed to enter the kitchen or temple, bathe, or wear flowers in their hair. They are considered useless and are forbidden to participate in any regular sphere of life. Menstruation is labeled as unclean in the Christian faith too. It's treated as shameful, possibly because femaleness is considered to be inferior to maleness, as women of Bengal learn from childhood. Everyone Sanu knows has no complaints about this. Her Buddhist friends accept the point of view that menstruation is a natural physical excretion that women have to go through on a monthly basis. However, the common belief is that during this time, women tend to have a weaker emotional balance and need religious support more than at any other time. In reality, they are kept out of the temple and branded as impure, filthy. Hindu beliefs have possibly influenced Buddhist practices in some cultures, including in Bengal... and all these discussions are too much for Sanu to comprehend. To her it's easier to follow the norms than question them and get into trouble like Phuli.

Phuli refuses to conform to the norms and creates war with everyone. This vexes Sanu, but she doesn't know how to help her sister, sweeten their mother's anger, and smother the wagging, gossiping tongues constantly finding fault with Phuli. It's a heavy burden on Phuli. But she isn't afraid to confront age-old common wisdom. She believes that the destiny of women across religions somewhat binds them in a fabric weaved in fear—a dread so strong, so perverse that it attempts to deny their infinite potentials and violate their freedom. This unwarranted paranoia, deeply prejudiced, and possibly among others has inflamed the motivation to subjugate and control women through the ages. It's not that women didn't understand this, but they knew it was more meaningful to take care of their families than protesting futilely. They went their separate ways with laments and sighs against injustices buried in their hearts, and their resilience grew stronger with the passing of the days. To Sanu, all these ideas are too much!

Phuli is outspoken about the benefits of praying. She even jokes about it openly. "God must be a he," is her usual line of attack.

"Look at you, Sanu! You're so shameless. Praying every day for a handsome husband? A moron? Maybe try praying six times." She loves to tease constantly. Sanu understands the undercurrents somewhat but doesn't voice her thoughts aloud.

Phuli thinks the Almighty has failed women in every possible way. What blasphemy! Sanu is horrified. But Phuli suffered immensely in her husband's house—a story that's hard to forget.

2.

Phuli was married at ten and sent to live with her husband in a village on the other side of the Padma River. She wasn't allowed to visit her parents before she became sixteen because of some misunderstanding at the time of the wedding between her father and her father-in-law. They locked horns like angry bulls in profound hostility because their fragile, macho egos were challenged.

Phuli's father, popularly known as Boro Mir, or head of the Mir family, a feudal lord by all means, refused to bow down and comply with the demanded apology because a bride's father is considered lesser in status in Bengalee culture. The conflict heightened. No one considered how it would impact Phuli.

Phuli paid the ultimate price. She couldn't see her family for six long years. Lack of an apology shaped her destiny. Such is the rage of Bengalee men in power.

Finally, through many interventions and mediations by elders from both sides of the family, Phuli was brought back home. The long, lone years were over. It felt like a pardon from life imprisonment. Six years away from her home, from her family, and from the familiar waters, trees, and flowers was brutal. She never returned to her husband's house because she didn't want to. Boro Mir agreed to it. No one could talk him out of his decision. So that ended Phuli's married life.

Phuli stayed at her parental home in secure freedom, completely ignoring the pitiful looks and waves of gossip targeted towards her. People were afraid to openly criticize her because of her father's position.

At home, her life went back to the former routine, but somehow, somewhere it wasn't the same anymore. She landed in an irreversible situation and eventually was resigned to it. The story of her short-lived married life she kept buried inside forever.

~∂

Phuli doesn't know what a man's affection means, or motherhood—to conceive in love and hold a baby in her arms. Her husband worked in Kolkata and came home barely once a year for a week or two. That was the only time she saw him, usually very late at night. That was the brief conjugal life she had known. It has been years now. She doesn't have any fond memories of her husband or the time she lived in his household. With the passing of time, the memories dulled. Some re-membrances pop up in a flash sometimes, though. One brutal recollection remains very vivid even today—the rude shock she got the day after the wedding. As was the custom, she was supposed to have waited to be assisted by her sisters-in-law and maids—for bathing, fixing her braid, wearing kajol or kohl to blacken her eyes, the normal activities to get ready for the day. Before the female entourage invaded her privacy, Phuli decided to oil her hair as it had gotten tangled in the hustle and bustle of the wedding rituals. The clumsy hair was extremely annoying.

"Oh my, my! The new bride is oiling her hair herself . . . with her own hands!" said an older woman. Phuli was caught red-handed in the act perceived to be disgraceful by a one-night-old bride. All others laughed quite mercilessly at her shamelessness.

"Shall I use my feet instead?" Phuli retorted. She didn't understand why they were mocking her. The women were greatly offended at her outrageous response. She was labeled as immodest right away.

She was summoned by her mother-in-law, the ultimate matriarch, who, like others of her kind in Bengalee house-holds, is commonly empowered to make rules and decisions in the women's world and especially entrusted to chastise stray daughters-in-law.

"Notun bou [new bride], this kind of behavior is not acceptable in our house. You don't answer back like an inso-lent, low-class woman! I thought your mother had brought you up better. My mistake." She was angry. Phuli was at a loss for words. Her misbehavior, added to her father's unapol-ogetic conduct, was marked as an insurmountable defiance.

"You listen when spoken to," was the harsh warning, dipped in an icy-cold, scathing voice. Phuli was only ten and didn't understand her error. She had yet to learn the rules. She wanted to melt into her mother's arms and cry and cry.

Phuli was allowed to be with her husband only when everyone, including the maids, had gone to bed, almost at midnight. The room had a semi-double bed against the window with a darned, wrinkled bedsheet thrown carelessly to conceal its harsh bareness, two flat pillows, and a small table with a jug and a glass sheltered under a hand-knitted crochet cover. Most of the space in the tiny room was swallowed by the bed. It required exquisite mastery to move around in the minute unclaimed space without making a noise or hitting one's elbows against the tin walls. It was a fucked-up hole.

A kerosene lamp left on the dirt floor gave less light and more shadow; the tightly shut windows banished the tiniest fraction of air in the sweltering heat. The body burned much more in the hot, airless room as a complement to the unbearable heat than in passion. She had to get up long before the call for morning prayers, long before the household woke up, and leave the bedchamber stealthily. The very trace of her time with her husband was to be buried in the light of the day. That was the custom a modest woman had to follow to avoid being branded as wanton.

The man used to give her made-in-Kolkata cookies to eat—which she usually refused—ruffle her hair fondly, and touch her...bruise her...in an attempt to crush her soul and body. During his stay, he repeated the same acts religiously every night. Phuli was advised by the womenfolk to cherish the excitement of those nocturnal bouts, to accept the responsibilities of a good wife. She detested them, though. The smell of the salty-syrupy cookies hung unspoiled, mingled in the moldy air of the nocturnal bedchamber days after her husband returned to his workplace.

Dear husband's visitations were actually spread between

hanging out with friends, fishing with them, and spending time with his parents and relatives. Phuli was always the after-thought, it seemed. They never discussed anything, never com-municated in any way. She hardly saw him during the day. At the time, it didn't matter so much. He had no love, ani-mosity, or latent anger towards Phuli. He simply endured her existence but mostly ignored her. Some nights he would disap-pear for a long time. She wasn't even aware of his presence in the room when he came to bed to sleep unless she woke up in submission to his desires. He slept late, and by that time Phuli was up and busy with household chores. No one thought this wasn't normal. No one made any effort to make her belong to her husband's life. She lacked the knowledge and the art. In the last two years of her stay in that household, the man didn't even care to visit. Looking back, Phuli now thinks he might have had some romantic affiliations in Kolkata. A lover? Maybe... or affairs with bad, dirty women? Well, women who sell their bodies must be called dirty as customary, though Phuli couldn't ever agree with it wholeheartedly.

During the bathing times at the pond, some women talked about those "evil" women in Kolkata who were experts at stealing the innocence of men, who gave bad diseases to men. They wore red color on their lips, darkened their eyes with kohl, decorated their braids with bold flowers to entice sus-ceptible souls! They were bad but beautiful with bodies like razor-sharp knives that could cut through naive hearts. Their eyes reflected the lights of dancing stars. Their skin glowed and was as soft as butter that melted at an ardent touch. They spoke with a thousand melodies in their voices and laughed like the unbound flow of the Padma River. Who could con-test such crafty adversaries? They were full of beguiling antics to cast spells on unsuspecting males. That's what Phuli understood.

The Kolkata of that time was different. Things were changing. People were changing, and so were their lives. It was a time of restlessness and uncertainty, caught between desolation and hope as countless voices were becoming louder and louder in anti-British protests. There were plots and counter-plots hatched across undivided India to rid the subcontinent of the Brit forces, their influence and rule. The East India Company, under the guise of which the British operated nearly two hundred years on the Indian subcontinent, was loaded with anarchy and corruption—was brutal and hungry for power, trying to keep control over a vast population through a rule of force and savagery.

It was almost the last leg of the British rule. Kolkata was the hub of business and work, the epitome of culture and social climbing. Native men mostly worked in low-paid jobs, flocking to this magical town from all over Bengal and other parts of India. They came to find their destiny from near and far. At their low wages, they could afford only a few days' break in a year to reunite with families who resided back in distant villages. Life was dreary. Men had needs, unmet desires—those were the rules of the game, an open secret that no one talked about or moralized on. Money changed hands; bodies were sold and bought in the dirty, damp, semidark backstreets of Kolkata. To many, such transactional physical intimacy was immoral, grave paap—a cardinal sin. These ladies of the night, as popularly known, traded their bodies. What did they do with the money they earned—buy cheap jewelry that had the power to sway hearts? Sweets to eat? Or betel leaves to have red mouths and glittering teeth to become more fetching? Phuli wondered. Her fantasies knew no bounds. The men must be dirty to lust over such women.

In those long, lonesome, dreary months of her husband's absence, her mother-in-law and the others blamed Phuli. They taunted her. She was made liable for all the glitches in her marital existence. They convicted her as the sinner for the crime she did or didn't commit. She failed as a woman, not being able to keep her husband attracted to her. She wasn't aware of any deceit or skills as how to perfect this craft. No one had a kind word for her, to guide her. She was so alone those years...and finally desired her husband's presence, more so to restore her tarnished status. It was ironic that in such desperation she thought of her husband often and as an ally.

At the end of the day, every evening, the stars filled the lonely sky with a dusty glow. The same stars shone in the skies of Kolkata, in her own village. Her heart grew awfully lonesome. "Oki garyal bhai, koto robo ami ponther dikey chiya rey.... Ki kobo dushker o kotha...[Oh my beloved, I keep waiting.... How shall I speak about my sadness?]." A popular folk song about the anguish of a Bengalee woman trapped in her yearnings, in loneliness, played round and round in her head. Phuli secretly tried to communicate with her husband. But she was caught and the letter destroyed after harsh rebukes by her mother-in-law under the instructions of her father-in-law, who was consulted due to the gravity of the matter.

"It's not good to try to be a khanki. Pray. Keep your mind away from evil thoughts." Her mother-in-law called her a prostitute.

"No woman in our household has ever written a letter to be mailed to Kolkata. This is wantonness." Her voice was stern, acid-coated. Even the maids giggled at the absurdity of the situation. What wife in her right mind would stoop to such undignified lowness?

Remarriage was taboo in respectable families in Bengal. It happened in the lives of commoners, peasants, and maids. So no one talked about it. At sixteen, Phuli became a living widow. She didn't get a talak or divorce. She deserted her husband and became a woman of an uncertain status—not a

widow, not a divorcee or abandoned by her man, but a defiant—a new, unheard of nameless entity altogether!

3.

Sanu changes out of her wet sharee. The six yards of cloth
craftily worn to cover the entire body, creating an illusion
of modesty, sometimes can reveal as much as it attempts to
conceal, subject to the intention of the wearer. She begins to
pray. Her long, damp hair moistens the prayer mat at her
feet. It's unfortunate that a suitable man can't be found for
her. Her two brothers-in-law are also trying, Mejo's and Tota's husbands. Mother says that when the flower of marriage
blooms and God gives permission, only then her marriage can
happen.

In noble families, the bride-to-be is never introduced to the
groom's family before the marriage talks are concluded. Family members arrange the marriage. The final decision comes
from the male heads of the families concerned. The nobler the
girl's family in heritage, wealth, and achievements, the more
the amount of bride price money offered for her. If she happens to be pretty, it's considered a bonus, good luck for the
husband.

Ploys are attempted to learn about the girl while the matchmaking continues. In such cases, old beggar women from the
would-be groom's village are bribed to find out about the girl's
looks as they are allowed to enter any household by pleading
for alms without raising alarms and then report back. Sanu
has faced such situations. Mother was extra-cautious so that
strange beggar women couldn't sight her when they came to
beg. Sanu had to pay the price, of course—take cover in the
kar, a space built as storage, situated between the tin roof
and the ceiling of a residence hut. In summer, that's the hot-
test place on earth. Once Sanu had to stay there a whole day.
Modest Muslim Bengalee girls have taken cover in such situa-

tions. Sanu understands and so do others. That's the custom. Period.

Sanu has already been declared the prettiest among the sisters by the most ruthless senior matriarch critics in the extended families. Word about her beauty is already out there, in gossip and gatherings, at weddings and funerals. Her long, bountiful, dark, waist-length hair hugging shapely hips is common knowledge. Her large jet-black eyes under dark arched eyebrows set on a paan leaf or heart-shaped face stir envy among many. People talk about her freshly churned butter–toned skin that glows in a soft, endearing radiance, ready to charm. But her destiny remains unchanged, waiting for a hero to walk her into a new world where hopes grow, love dominates....

On most evenings, Sanu embroiders by the hurricane lamp's light till bedtime to keep busy, or she reads storybooks. She is fond of fairy tales where the impossible happens. Routinely, Phuli sits outside near the jackfruit trees enjoying the cool of the evening, though she is repeatedly told to remain indoors after dusk falls. In this place, life stumbles in dense darkness till the morning sun seeps in, awakening essences in the brain—that's how Phuli's days and nights are defined. Modest women stay indoors at nighttime. But who listens? Phuli always has her way...from the day she declined to return to her husband's house. She refuses to follow the basic rules that women abide by to be normal, accepted, and the absolute wholly-holy woman. Nothing has been able to change her so far.

$\sim$

Mother drapes herself in a large cotton shawl, muttering under her breath. She's going next door to have a letter read. Maybe it's from Sanu's brother from Kolkata or one of the brothers-in-law. Sanu can read Bangla, but it must be about her marriage, so Mother doesn't ask her. Her faith in Phuli isn't strong, so she is excluded. Mother can't read or write Bangla. Like most trusting Muslims, she learned only Arabic script in childhood in order to read the Quran but without understanding the meaning of a single syllable.

"My bad luck. Why would such shame befall this family?" Mother keeps grumbling as she gets ready. She is referring to Phuli's situation: abandoned by her husband, disowned by his family, barren—worthless.

Sanu cringes at such times. Her heart reaches out to her ill-fated sister, who has every right to protest. Only Mother doesn't seem to realize how it hurts. She has become quite intolerant since Father died. The burden of Sanu's situation has added to her frustration and despair, and possibly embarrassment.

"Who would want to do anything with us?" Another subtle hint about Phuli.

~

They eat an early dinner as always. After washing and cleaning up, Mother speaks out. She is visibly excited. The sisters wait in anticipation as she takes her time—slowly prepares betel leaf and sliced nuts from the distinctive containers, adds lime solution, and throws the concoction into her mouth. Now it's ready to be consumed. She chews the stuff with lazy relish for some seconds and then spits out a lava of red saliva in the pitchkari—the brass spit holder. Anxiety eats up the sisters.

"A letter has come from Tota's husband, our own Dhola Kazi. He has arranged Sanu's marriage. Only thing..." she pauses. The younger women hold their breath, all alert. "The groom's a bit old. Not that much, actually. What's in a man's age, anyway, huh?" Mother hesitates very slightly and spits again. "His first wife died some years ago. But he comes from

17

a very high-class, rich family. The older the groom, the more cherished is the bride. That's what my mother used to say." She tries to soften the blow, perhaps. "He's very interested to marry into this family. Whoever it is, I'll go ahead with this proposal," she adds with finality.

"But Ama, you can't sacrifice Sanu! How can you even consider it?" Phuli's voice is low but firm in protest. Her face is hardened.

"Phuli, don't interfere in what you don't understand. Bekub women speak before they think." Mother spits again, with more aggressiveness this time, calling Phuli stupid without any qualms.

"Look, look at her face! She's a child, Ama!" Phuli suddenly draws Sanu close, turns her face to the light. A bewildered Sanu tries to free herself from Phuli's iron grip.

"Go to sleep, Phuli. Don't annoy me further. You've done enough." Mother sounds stern and then moves towards her bed, a sure sign of dismissal. To many, Phuli is a constant reminder of bad luck and may have contributed to the delays in Sanu's marriage. Good families try to avoid scandals.

Bhaijaan, as they call their only brother, works in Kolkata and is the oldest, followed by Phuli, then Mejo, the sister who is comfortably married with a big brood of kids and who lives very far away in the town of Mymensingh in the north-central part of East Bengal. Her visits in recent years have become infrequent because of the distance and financial implications. Tota is the fourth born, and Sanu after her is the youngest.

Bhaijaan, after graduating from the prestigious Aligarh Muslim University, got fully involved in politics besides his nine-to-five job. He is also a follower of Gandhi and strongly believes in the rights of the people of India to be liberated from the tyranny of the British Raj. His free time is spent mainly in campaigning and mobilizing people to participate in nonviolent protests called by Gandhi. He hasn't been able to pay attention to the needs of his family. Even then, Mother isn't very critical of her only son.

Sanu remains wide awake through the night. Her heart beats faster at the news. She can't sleep—can't sleep!

4.

Sanu was born after Phuli's return from her husband's home. At the time, Phuli was too consumed with her own life to focus much on what was happening around her. She was trying to adjust. It was a hard struggle. The place she left behind at ten had changed considerably. There were new brides, many births, some deaths, and some girls she knew were married off, living in faraway villages.

Mejo got married right after Phuli's return, so Tota was the one who mainly assisted Mother with the care of infant Sanu. There were maids to help and also relatives who lived in the joint family, but somehow Tota just took over. Then tragedy hit.

Boro Mir died very suddenly while he sat on the veranda one evening smoking hookah—a tobacco pipe with a long, flexible tube that draws the smoke through water contained in a bowl, very popular in Bengal. When the servants found him, he was long gone. The body was cold, but the hookah was still warm.

Tota and Sanu share a special bond. They are very close, though the sisters see each other only once a year since Tota got married. Sanu was barely three at the time. Tota loves Sanu with a fierce protectiveness and tries to take away all her pain. She is never afraid to rattle her own world to help her little sister.

Tota prays for better luck for Sanu. She hopes her sister gets a kind husband who will value her, love her, and treat her as family. She wishes Sanu would find a welcoming home with in-laws and be blessed with many children.

Tota's children are her universe, her solace.

5.

Tota's life has been quite eventful. She got married when she was almost labeled an old maid like Sanu, but she couldn't have been more than twenty in reality. She was ripe and about to dry out, as people said behind her back. The Mir girls were jinxed where luck in marriage was concerned. Finally, Dhola Kazi was found for Tota. As was the norm, neither his mother nor Dhola saw Tota before he wed her.

Dhola's mother, Amina Bibi, was eager for this match because the Mirs were a reputable family. Dhola was an orphan. His father had died in Kolkata during the great plague in 1899, four days after contracting the disease.

That was a scary time as the plague devastated the beautiful, buzzing town. Houses became barren; streets were silent. Life came to a screeching halt as the deadly disease took its toll. People fled Kolkata, and those who couldn't succumbed to death in volume. Death came swiftly and was inevitable. There were dead bodies piled up everywhere on deserted roadsides. More people, however, died in Patna and the coastal town of Bombay.

The stench of death haunted the towns, overpowering the smell of daily life. Dhola's father died alone, at the beginning of a promising future, in his room at night in a men's mess (hostel). His dead body was buried in Kolkata. People were too afraid to transport a plague death. He didn't have time to see his son of only two weeks and take farewell from his wife, Amina Bibi, who was barely fifteen. She came to live with her father after being widowed.

Dhola was brought up by Amina Bibi with little influence from his maternal grandfather. He completed his primary education with difficulty, a bit of a handful to manage being an only child and a thoroughly spoiled brat. In the wickedness of his adolescence and unruly ways, he gave his mother many reasons to be disappointed and reduced her to constant tears. Protecting him from the wagging gossips of the idle village community became her major occupation during Dhola's growing-up years.

Luckily, at an early age, he was introduced to the family business as his grandfather was in poor health and tied to the bed, waiting to die. Dhola's sole maternal uncle had no interest in work and lived off the family income. Most of the time he was away from home over long periods, attending or organizing folk theaters, wrestling matches, or football games, always in pursuit of idle pleasure. In a way, he welcomed Dhola's association in the business, which meant a confirmed, regular source of shared profit without the headache of sweating over hard work. Initially, Amina Bibi managed the finances, keeping her distance from prying public eyes till Dhola was ready to take over. Traditionally, women and money didn't mix well and was not encouraged. Dhola's concentration started to grow, and eventually he began to expand the business that was bestowed on him.

Luck was in Dhola's favor, and in a few years he made a fortune, which was the envy of many. In his twenties, Dhola prospered so much that he started buying land, adding to the already-inflated business gains. It was high time to find a gentle, good woman to be his wife. All he needed was a spouse with breeding, beauty, and class.

Respectable families of Amina Bibi's choice were not too eager to form marriage alliances with young men such as Dhola—orphaned, poorly educated, guardianless, and self-made with a history of a disorderly past. As his position was not lucrative among prospective brides' families, he had to agree to pay a high bride price in the bargain by selecting Tota due to her heritage and family wealth, though she was much older than the accepted norm for a bride.

~○

Tota had always been the levelheaded girl. Her flawless, water-lily-pale complexion, much cherished, was marred by her protruding front teeth, which made her look extremely plain, unlike her sisters, who were paragons of beauty. She was aware of her shortcomings and accepted them with sensibility. Her intelligence, kind heart, and inner beauty of the soul mostly went unrecognized. Possibly lack of appreciation eventually turned her into a cold, hard person outwardly. She had difficulty expressing her emotions for fear of exposing her vulnerabilities. She shielded her pain with aggressive ruthlessness and denied access to it to anyone trying to get close to her.

One look at her face as she stepped into her new home, Dhola's mother felt she had been cheated in the deal and never forgave Tota. Dhola met her for the first time in the bridal chamber, and his mind was filled with distaste. He expected a beautiful bride like the wives of many of his cousins and close friends. He couldn't love Tota but used her body with a vengeance. Tota submitted to his cruelty without protest. She didn't question anything. If she suffered, she did it alone without any outward display of emotion or complaint. The children came one after the other, the three boys and Sabaa. Her world was filled up. Her loneliness was curbed significantly. She found consolation in taking care of the family, in slaving away countless days and nights in routine duties around the house.

Dhola gradually began to look around in other places for fun, as Tota believed, but she could never prove anything. The very idea was distasteful, tormenting. However, she didn't object to it or confront her husband. She wanted a home, a father for her children. She didn't want to go back to her mother's house like Phuli, who was ridiculed behind her back, or to be pitied like Sanu, though people were more sympathetic towards her.

What else could a Bengalee Muslim woman do?

~⊃

Amina Bibi would find different ways of tormenting Tota. She also would do the same with her own brother's wife, Pori, who was Tota's age. In earlier years, they lived as an extended family. Later they moved to their own houses.

Amina Bibi controlled the kitchen and managed the household. She would never give the young wives enough to eat. They were allowed meals after the whole household, including the servants, had eaten. There wouldn't be enough left most of the time, and they would go hungry day after day. They wouldn't dream of reporting this to their husbands, and even if they did, the men would never react. It was Amina Bibi's domain. That was the accepted reality.

Sometimes while they cooked, the fragrance of freshly steamed rice and daal (lentils) would hit them crazy. Some days, Amina Bibi would step outside of the homestead for an early dip in the pond or to wash some of her favorite clothes while the cooking was being done. The maids were normally engaged in sun-drying the harvest heaped in the granary, cleaning, and sweeping the big yard, while cooking was left to Tota and Pori. On such occasions of Amina Bibi's temporary absence, Pori would cajole Tota to take a helping of the freshly cooked food. They would quickly ladle a portion on a plate and go behind the kitchen hut. One kept guard while the other ate. If Amina Bibi found out, she would make a big noise, shaming and reprimanding the young wives in front of the entire household. They were terrified of her. The two of them would continue to giggle throughout the day after such missions were accomplished, only to be chastised by disapproving looks from Amina Bibi, who was unaware of the cause of their mirth.

6.

Dhola at the time worked mostly in Kolkata, as the printing business operated from there. He visited the family in the village once every six months. His mother would fill up his ears with damaging stories about Tota, bordering on lies and misconceptions. Dhola never protested or said anything in support of Tota. He didn't reprimand her in public. The punishment would come at night, inside the four walls of the sleeping hut, in silence, witnessed only by the two of them. As Dhola cruelly crushed her body underneath his, Tota's soul would break and bruise in the forced way her husband took her body and wrung his joy out of it. She knew it would be futile to try to defend herself against Amina Bibi's accusations. Dhola, even if he didn't believe the lies, would do whatever he wanted to discipline Tota. He practically ignored her throughout in every instance, to the delight of his mother.

Dhola thought of punishing her more. He decided to remarry—a girl of his own choice this time. This was the ultimate defeat for Tota. For the first time in her life, she confronted Dhola.

"You can't remarry. You can't bring my shoteen...a second wife in this house. I won't let that happen." Her calm, firm voice startled Dhola.

"You're no good. I'm a man. I need some joys in my life. You have given me nothing." He wanted to brush her away. Tota's face distorted with restrained emotion. Her eyes flashed with a fire Dhola had never before witnessed in his mostly docile, submissive wife.

"You have your fun all the time. I say nothing! I knew all along what you were up to. I have seen your noshto-nojor [dirty eyes] but tolerated them," Tota spat out.

"What nojor are you talking about, silly woman? Have you lost your senses?" Dhola barked back, but his eyes held a hint of amusement.

"Don't do this to me. You have children. Don't hurt them," she pleaded as Dhola looked past her in dismissal and didn't respond.

"You bring another woman in this house over my dead body. I'll kill myself before that." Tota walked away with her head held high in finality.

~

The preparation for Dhola's wedding continued with full steam. The tailor passed by several times for measurements for his new outfits. New bedding and mosquito nets were bought. Orders were placed for embroidered quilts. The handymen began repairing the roof of the bungalow hut in the corner of the inner yard beside the tall jackfruit trees, allocated possibly to be the residence of the new wife. The maids exchanged secret glances as they absorbed the activities that kept them constantly on their toes with no time to gossip. Amina Bibi's gait was filled with jubilation as she hurried to and fro from the inner yard to the outer yard, giving instructions, supervising the work of the laborers who were fixing the partitions or cleaning the vast grounds covering the homestead. She was all smiles as she chewed betel leaves and nuts with women of neighboring houses, happily puffing on her hookah. There was immense curiosity about what was about to happen, and soon. They talked in whispers like conspirators because of Tota's constant presence somewhere in the background. In silence, Tota persisted.

The passing days became a torment to Tota inwardly. Dhola started sleeping in his bangla ghor—his hut in the outer yard—totally avoiding any intimacy with her. Except for meals, he hardly stepped into the inner yard. Even then the food was served by his mother while Tota stayed in the shadows. He was deliberately shunning any contact with her. There was no communication between them. The environment around Tota was closing in. She was asphyxiated by this ugly ambience of secrets and ignobility.

Tota locked herself in her room. No one could make her open the door. The children cried for their mother. Amina Bibi got worried. It was no idle threat. It was a situation of discomfiture, but Dhola chose to ignore it. At the back of his mind, he was sure that Tota would give in. The news got out. People were afraid of Dhola, so they didn't flock to his house, but their curiosity and gossip became intense. The maids looked troubled and whispered when they bathed and did laundry in the river. Word spread fast. Four days and four nights passed. Tota didn't come out of the hut. Sabaa and her brothers were distressed. In the Bengalee household, children do not voice their emotions or concerns. They don't exchange ideas with adults. They are meant to listen and watch in silence, speak with politeness when spoken to, so they were powerless spectators like the others.

It's rare among noble Bengalee Muslim men to keep more than one wife at a time, unlike in Arab countries or in some Muslim cultures. But it does happen here sometimes, especially when a woman is barren or is proven to be unfit as a wife due to mental or physical illness. In some rare cases, if a man fancies a younger woman, under the pretext that the first wife needs assistance in managing domestic matters, he takes a second wife. It's a cover-up but acceptable.

Sharing a husband with another woman is the basest existence a woman can ever think of. Fighting for a man's attention is an extremely humiliating position for a woman, as if she is being stripped naked of all dignity and publicly renounced. It declares to the world that she is useless, and so her man wants another wife. It's not what a woman would desire at any time. Even death is nobler than this indignity of a shared life. Tota knew it well.

Amina Bibi always maintained that they were cheated in the bargain negotiated over the bride price paid for Tota. They were deceived with a low-quality bride. In her mind, Tota deserved to be punished for not being beautiful like her sisters and mother, more so because of her stoicism in the face of all negativity, her strength to tolerate it, and her stubborn aloofness, untouchable by anyone unless she allowed it. Amina Bibi felt Dhola's actions were justified and rejoiced in any indication of Tota's degradation.

Finally it was the day! Dhola's new life was ready to unfold. He wore his finest clothes. His happy whistles echoed through the thin tin walls as he dressed the turban on his head. It was his wedding night. He should look his best. This time he had seen the would-be bride himself from afar, a beautiful sixteen-year-old girl with a body like the young lotus stem, fresh, exhilarating as the brilliance of virgin dewdrops in final submission on the greens at dawn. His body became alert with excitement as he looked at the girl. He wanted her. His mind was intoxicated with allure into the nameless land of all-consuming delights. He thought of the taut, firm breasts underneath the red sharee waiting for the wedding night. He couldn't forget the thick lips and the sway of her hips, all ready to be offered at his altar of unrepressed desires. His mind was made up. He began fantasizing... bawdy thoughts countless times, lying sleepless even when Tota was nearby.

With great languid care, Dhola applied shurma (kohl) to his eyes, as is expected on such occasions for men, massaged sweet-scented oil into his hair, and wore a strong, intoxicating atar (perfume) proclaiming his masculinity.

All preparations were made. He was ready to leave the house. It was going to be a small wedding party. Two of his older cousins, one close friend, and the matchmaker would join him. They were waiting for Dhola at the village market, close to his betrothed's father's house.

He stopped in front of Tota's hut and stood there. There

was absolute silence inside. He looked at the door intensely for a long time. The servants came looking for him as it was getting late. Suddenly, Dhola threw his turban on the ground.

"Bring an axe! Hurry!" he shouted to the servants.

As his mother, the maids, and several female relatives watched in terrified silence, Dhola broke down the door with swift blows of the axe. He found Tota lying limply on the mud floor, lost to the world. Dhola stepped inside and, in a quick sweep of his arms, lifted up Tota's senseless body.

As he brought her outside, he whispered, "Tota, Tota, open your eyes. I'm here. Don't die.... I'll never marry again. Never!"

The women poured water on Tota's forehead and fanned her. She stirred slowly. After a long time, she opened her eyes. Amina Bibi held a glass of green coconut water to her lips. It was almost like the first day Tota had entered this house as Dhola's bride. The entire scenario was reenacted one more time. Sabaa and her brothers crowded over her, too young to understand the complexity of the situation but glad to have their mother back.

"Dhola isn't going to bring another woman here, ever," Pori whispered in her ear.

Tota slowly sipped the cool coconut water and decided to live as Dhola's only wife, joyless but in dignity. Even then, her life with Dhola remained unique.

7.

Though Dhola disliked his in-laws, he allowed Sabaa to be shipped off to her grandmother's place whenever it was feasible, for many reasons. Dhola's own upbringing had much to do with this decision. Being brought up in his grandparents' home by his widowed mother didn't add much to his nobility in the eyes of society. They thought he lacked something—gentility, possibly, even though he made so much money eventually. No matter what, the Mir family was considered to be of a high class because they could boast of wealth and lineage handed down from one generation to the next. Dhola was critical of them about many things, but surprisingly he wanted his daughter to be associated with them so that her aristocracy wasn't questioned at the time of her marriage.

Deep down, Dhola was also worried about the toxic environment brewing at home where his own mother and Tota were engaged in constant conflicts, sometimes in long verbal battles. Tota was becoming rebellious as the years progressed and started to fight back. Dhola didn't want Sabaa to become like them with the negativity that these women regularly hurled at each other. He had high hopes of Sabaa marrying into a noble family one day and believed she deserved being groomed in a decent atmosphere. He didn't trust the relatives from his own side, who fared much less successfully in wealth, elegance, and social standing.

Dhola was certain that Sabaa would stay loyal to his teachings of what a woman should be, what she could want, a daughter committed to his total endorsement, an unwritten prescription. He took a calculated risk... but in his arrogance, Dhola totally ruled out that the three wacky women could have any power to corrupt Sabaa's young mind, that he could eventually lose control over her judgment. Sabaa, alas, carried almost 50 percent of her mother's genes, which Dhola failed to recognize at the time. To him, lineage was through men only.

Sabaa got accustomed to the fun visits to her grandmother's house from an early age. She was always chaperoned by an elderly female relative and maids on such trips under the care of a trustworthy male servant who had been in service to Dhola's household for years. His duty was to ensure Sabaa's safe passage to her grandmother's and back home in Dhola's big boat sailing on the tumultuous waters of the Padma.

~◡

Sabaa is close to both her aunts, Phuli and Sanu. And the women dote on her. In return, she loves them. Visiting them is always a fond occasion. In their unusual bizarreness, they are incredible—that's how Sabaa's young mind defines them.

Sabaa's favorite attraction is an expedition to the roof storage area of the main residence hut. And Sanu is the guide, always. Together they often climb the steep wooden ladder, mindful of the cloistered space that opens into the realm of forbidden treasures... Sabaa loves to fantasize. Under the low ceiling, trunks, baskets, and bundles store collections, bursting with jewels and clothes, never ever used, like the hidden troves of ancient kings guarded by three women.

Sabaa's life is surrounded by numerous fascinating anecdotes about her mother, her two aunts, and her grandmother. Sabaa is in awe of these women, mystified by their uniqueness. They are unlike any others she knows. They are Amazons—brave, attractive in their somewhat uncanny, special ways.

Sabaa particularly loves the tale about how they once slaughtered a sick cow. At her request, her aunts repeat it often amidst much laughter. A cow is very precious in a Bengalee family. It is killed only at times of festivals. It doesn't make sense to let a cow die even in sickness before the meat is sanctified with proper slaughtering procedures. Otherwise, it's meaningless wastage! The Hindus, however, worship cows and nurture them as deities. They are happy to consume cow's milk and dairy products. Cows are safe with Hindus—they treat these animals as their own mothers, unlike Muslims, who lustily wolf down beef at any chance.

The story goes that one evening Phuli, Sanu, and their mother took things into their own hands as a big cow from the herd fell ill. These women had never been popular among their relatives who are also their neighbors. They are relentlessly criticized by most as they live quite independent lives without full male protection. The only son of the house works many miles and many rivers away in Kolkata and has no control over the females in his household.

So these women didn't want to involve anyone. They didn't go around begging for male assistance. The three of them overpowered the sick cow and slaughtered it with a sharp knife in their inner yard in the twilight. Under the light of the hurricane lamps, they carved the meat, stored every edible piece by boiling it or sprinkling it with salt, and cleaned up the mess—the blood, skin, horns, and hooves of the dead animal—and buried the carcass in the backyard near the swamp. They cooked some meat for dinner under the stars and ate and laughed and sang through the wee hours of the morning—the champions who rose and roared to protect their free spirits, the three witches of Macbeth, as Sabaa later labeled them when she read translations of Shakespeare's works in her teenage years.

Growing up, Sabaa considered the cow slaughtering as a heroic act since Muslim Bengalee women aren't allowed to even slaughter a chicken. It's not acceptable in the religion. Only men can kill animals to feed their families. But there is a loophole that proclaims if a woman fails to find a man after searching in seven households, she can go ahead and do the deed. Very strange norm! So usually men are hunted down to assist.

Later, when she was old enough to grasp the intricate contexts, Sabaa realized she had been embraced as a direct surrogate of these women, hoodwinked into their cult early in life. She accepts this with mixed feelings. Her aunts shared many interesting stories of their lives and continuously encouraged Sabaa to challenge boundaries that decent little girls weren't expected to cross. She never could forget about an instance when they coaxed her to sing and dance at their neighborhood school function. Sabaa's confidence evaporated as she eyed the large audience. In great panic, she ran off the stage after messing up the lyrics of a popular song. There were applause and laughter from the kind audience, but even then she was very, very embarrassed. Her aunts, however, congratulated her on her feat, her courage, and made sure Dhola never learned about this incident.

Sabaa eventually grew up into paradoxical ideologies in two households—her father's and the house of her grandmother and aunts, where she is a constant visitor.

8.

The streak of brightness in the morning sky is welcoming. Sanu wakes up. Even the ghastly night has passed after Ama broke the terrible news. On the way to the pond, Sanu almost comes face to face with Mia, distantly related on her mother's side. He is not supposed to be here at this ungodly hour. Sanu covers her head properly with the edge of her sharee and quickly walks past him. In a brief glance while in passing, she catches his eyes. There is definitely something there that she can't fathom. In a flash he is gone. Her whole body trembles like a drifting fallen leaf caught in a stormy whirlpool. She almost collapses on the bank of the pond. The brief encounter with Mia has shaken the life out of her.

Years ago, when Sanu was barely thirteen, Mia had tried to write poems about her. Someone had ratted him out or gossiped about it, and he was harshly reprimanded by the family elders. It became the talk. Women chatted about it when they gathered at the pond. Mia was only seventeen but was guilty of composing love poems, expressing his romantic dreams about Sanu. It was an offense in a close-knit Bengalee community. At that time, this very news thrilled Sanu; it was a significant matter. She would have loved to read his poems, but they were possibly destroyed under the instructions of the elders. It was also at this time that she was told she had become a woman and was restricted from meeting male relatives unless very close through blood ties.

Sanu had thought time and again about the reasons for becoming the inspiration of Mia's poems. The opportunity never occurred to ask him. As if she would have done that! A modest woman would rather die of shame first than be so forward with a man. Only Phuli can be so direct and outrageous.

Often, Sanu plays with the idea of intimacy with Mia. Especially on long, sleepless nights, these thoughts warm her heart. The lanky tall frame, the head full of dark hair, and the charm of his smile on a pleasant face haunt Sanu. When he speaks, his Adam's apple becomes slightly more visible and catches the eye as the words form on his lips. The piercing, deep-set, sharp eyes under the broad forehead combine with his magical voice and can indeed turn heads, though Mia is unaware of the effect he has on others. He stands out in a crowd.

During many harvest seasons, she heard him sing as the cows kept stampeding and thrashing the freshly cut paddy while husking at the approaching dusk. The bells on their necks never stopped ringing as they moved round and round in unison, creating an orchestra with the chirping of the crickets, the glow of the fireflies, and the vast calm of the night. The sweet incense of the husked paddy mingled with the melodious tune of Mia's voice transformed the nights into ethereal magic.

At such times, in the inner yard women also sang songs that carried the message of joys that the new crops would bring to the village. The promise of abundance of rice in the storage, some cash to afford a little luxury, for things desired glowed on their faces. On such starry nights, the hearty laughter of men accompanied by love songs definitely broke many hearts—of young girls and new brides, for sure.

Sanu, like most women from the neighboring households, remained awake during the entire night of paddy husking. She liked to watch the maids cleaning the rice from the last traces of rice hulls with the help of kula, the flat trays made out of bamboo chips. They labored hard under the brightness of many hurricane lamps lighted with kerosene oil. The women's yard, partitioned by dry jute canes, always maintained strict pardah, or privacy, separated from the men's courtyard. At such times, even from a distance, Sanu could hear Mia's tunes infiltrating through the partition. The subject matter of his songs were usually about a heartless beloved who didn't respond or keep promises made through eye contact, someone for whom the soul and body cried every moment, in sleep, dreams...each waking second.

Sanu's eyes stung with tears as Mia's voice drifted through such moonlit nights....

CHAPTER TWO

Rioting in my heart

I.

Mother constantly talks about Sanu's wedding. Any day, the matchmaker, along with relatives of the groom, will be visiting to fix a date for the event. Before that, Mother intends to invite Sanu's cousins' wives to talk to her, as customary, to enlighten her about the responsibilities of a married woman. They are sure to come laughing, fixing their buns, with little ones in their arms or suckling on their tender breasts. They will speak about many things — right from what to expect at the in-laws' house, how to keep them happy and to maintain grace and dignity . . . and then, of course, how to steal the love of the husband, bewitch him for his own good.

Since adolescence, Sanu had dreamed of a gallant knight who would love her and walk her into a land of unknown yearnings. In some strange way, the knight always takes on the image of Mia. So she constantly scolds herself for being immodest and recites the Quran to free her soul of all evil longings, to banish Mia from her wicked mind, to keep herself steadfast to her virtue.

But all her efforts are totally disrupted when the stillness of the night suddenly is pierced by Mia's rich voice: "*Jalai aa gela moner agoon nivaia gela na, bondhurey....* Oh my beloved, you ignited the fire of passion but refuse to quench the flames of love."

He invades her sacred world often by repeating these lines over and over, possibly to taunt her. On such nights, Sanu has difficulty falling asleep. As she leans her head on the windowpane, tears moisten her bosom, soaking through her blouse. It doesn't end. The untold pain continues, haunts her through the silence of darkness.

Once, Phuli discovered her and was surprised by the muted tears. She didn't ask anything. There was an unspoken understanding between the sisters.

2.

Sanu's wedding day is fast approaching. "The groom is old and has been married before"—people keep talking about it; the gossips fan the flames of inventiveness. Does he stoop? Cough at every instance...? Burdened by aches and pains as are the elderly relatives she has witnessed? Can he be the husband she dreamed of all her life? These very thoughts freeze Sanu's heart. The man must be old enough to be her father, as she has gathered from the whispers around her. He has grown-up children. Oh! What can she do?

Her sister Tota's husband Dhola is the matchmaker from their side. He's a tyrant, a man of uncertain temper, and gets angry at the slightest or no provocation. No one dares to mess with him. He could have threatened to send Tota back, packing her off for good if Mother had hesitated to agree to this match. On the other hand, Mother is also anxious to get Sanu settled in her husband's home. She wouldn't be able to die in peace if Sanu remained unprotected, unmarried. Mother feels lesser as a parent as she hasn't been able to get Sanu married off yet.

At eighteen, Sanu has become a liability. She is almost treated as a spinster. It's so humiliating, more so for Mother. Sanu wishes she were a swan and could glide away with the new floodwaters into the sea...or fly far into a new horizon of warmth like the hot steam that oozes out when rice is boiled...or nestle into the *oomph* that awaits hidden inside the folds of a blanket on a cold wintry night. She wants to hide from everyone, never to be found again.

The days and nights torment Sanu. She can't eat and is tortured further when she tries to sleep. Phuli is the sole witness to her agony. Mother has chosen not to notice. She keeps busy with preparations. Soon Bhaijaan will arrive from Kolkata. Sanu longs to share her anguish with him. She doesn't know how to talk to an older brother about marriage or even what to say to him. It's immodest, disgraceful for a woman to discuss her own marriage with a male guardian. She doesn't understand why God has made women so bashful. She has been given a soul, a spirit, a life, but not enough voice to express her wishes, to fight for fairness. Thousands of needles seem to pierce into her every second. She wants to scream out her lungs in protest! She would be happy in the arms of a commoner whose body has the sweet smell of a mix of sweat and soil after a hard day's labor in the field...who could touch her heartbeats with a look...cradle her against his rib cage all night in ceaseless passion. Sanu catches gazes of sympathy. They pretend to look away. Terror riots in her heart, paralyzes her body.

3.

Sanu wakes up at the sound of a crow crying its heart out. She has overslept and didn't get up for prayer. Not even Mother woke her up today. She has been excused from Mother's rigid rules as it is her *holdi kuta*—a ritual that assists the bride to prepare for her wedding. Her hands will be decorated with intricate designs of flowers and leaves with *henna* dipped in tea leaves, and her body will be massaged seven times with turmeric paste mixed in fragrant oils. The wedding usually takes place a day or two after this ceremony. The turmeric massage continues till then.

Only married women are involved in making preparations for this ceremony. Unmarried girls are not allowed to touch the turmeric paste as the common belief is that would for sure delay their marriage in future. Widows and deserted and divorced women are banned entirely. They are forbidden to handle bridal affairs, the bride, and her trousseau. They can watch from a distance. A woman without a man is bad luck even if it's the mother of the bride. Such women are bad omens as their lives are considered unfruitful, meaningless, and failures without men as protectors and masters. However, the bride's mother is allowed to participate in some specific rituals. The widowed grandmothers usually partake in singing and dancing.

Seven married women begin grinding fresh turmeric tubers. The piquant scent of turmeric encircles the backyard, reminding everyone of the upcoming festivities. The women sing popular tunes while busy with their chores, mixing them with giggles. They laugh without any reason, with minimal cajoling—it's a joyous time! They talk about their own and other past weddings. The lyrics of the songs border between romanticism and explicit bawdiness, but this is adequately tolerated and has the full endorsement of society. Most Bengalee spiritual and love songs have carnal connotations because passions are accepted to be mystical and divine. The conventional tradition and expression of sentiments in sensual metaphors and folklore are contradictions to practiced Islamic norms. But it's a paradox that Bengalee culture thrives on.

Sanu will be massaged with grounded turmeric, as is the practice, till the wedding day morning. It's believed the yellow hue of the crushed turmeric adds a glowing effect to the skin.

Light-skinned women are usually considered to be pretty in Bengal, a result of genes implanted as casual offshoots during invasions by Aryans, possibly, through the ages. The Aryan race is a synonym for the Indo-European heritage and has been accepted as innately superior to other racial groups on the Indian subcontinent for ages unknown. In the nineteenth century, the term *Aryan* was adopted as a racial category. The concept of beauty, especially for women, as such has a lot to do with the identification with Aryans—light complexion, height, facial structure, straight and high nose.

While the rigorous turmeric ritual continues, a bride-to-be is forbidden to eat fish to keep evil spirits away, and refrains from being seen by the men of the house, even by her father, brothers, or uncles. She is treated like a princess.

Sanu hears the children's voices outside, playing and laughing, totally unaware of what lies ahead for her. Her two sisters, Mejo and Tota, have come with their husbands and children. The entire household is engaged in merrymaking. The aroma of condiments and sugary delicacies drifts in the air. Five robust goats are ready to be slaughtered. Chickens in cages are piled in one corner of the yard, to be killed anytime. Beef is never served at weddings of the wealthy. It's associated with aches and pains, coughs, and digestive issues. And of course, Hindu guests would find beef extremely offensive. Many things have to be considered at such a huge event. The whole village has been invited, hundreds of people. The groom will be served with at least fifty items right after the wedding has been officiated. He is expected to taste everything with his entourage, usually comprising close friends. It's a prestigious challenge for the bride's relatives, especially sisters-in-law, to serve as many items as possible. They have been preparing the feast for days.

Two humongous fish draped in red fabric have been sent over from the groom's house along with dozens and dozens of sweetmeats and yogurt packed in painted clay pots. Big baskets filled with fresh betel leaves and nuts are also sent, along with dry dates imported from Arabia, the holy Prophet's land, and an essential part of the ritual. Sweets are to be relished by guests, family members, and servants, and betel leaves are to be consumed till all are exhausted. The bellies of the fish are filled with silver coins as tips for the maids who will cut and cook them.

The maids place water-filled large brass *kolshi*, or pitchers, in the four corners of the yard where the male servants have earlier pitched banana plants. A stage has been made on the mud floor with leaves of coconut. The roof of the stage is adorned handsomely with palm leaves and marigold flowers. As expected, at this ritual altar, Sanu is resigned to forfeit her life to save the honor of her noble family, save her mother from the shame of indignity.... Sanu has no other option.

4.

Tota is accompanied by her three sons and daughter, Sabaa. Sabaa has just turned eight. With curiosity and questions stifled in her sharp eyes, Sabaa follows the reigning bedlam. She senses the strained air, notices the forced smiles hanging on Phuli's lips, uncertain emotions on Sanu's pale face. Sanu is distant. Phuli is otherwise engaged. A silent urgency is eating at the entire household, so unlike times in the past. Nothing is normal anymore.

Fond memories of swimming in the pond with Sanu, the ecstasy of chasing tiny red fish in shallow waters in the early morning breeze, breaking into goose pimples, and so many adventures they had together over the years keep coming back. Sabaa wants badly to go back to their regular routine...to play with Sanu's silky hair, feel it against her cheeks, and inhale the covert fragrance of the flowery hair oil while listening to the stories Sanu usually tells her from popular folklore... to fall asleep against the soft comfort of her body. All that's forgotten, is gone, now banished as unnecessary luxury.

~

By noon the house is crowded with relatives and neighbors. The yard becomes muddy with people rushing in and out, footsteps of servants running errands. The maids pass food to the male servants from the inner house. They are restricted to cross into the threshold of the inner yard meant only for women. There is a fusion of tension and excitement in the air. The groom and his entourage are coming in three big boats. They are expected to arrive by late afternoon. They will be offered refreshments on arrival, and after *Magrib*, or the evening prayer, the marriage ceremony will begin.

Sabaa watches Sanu. Sanu has been crying since morning and has not touched any food or water. It's normal to refuse food—attributed to bashfulness and good upbringing. No one is bothered. She is bundled up under the quilt on her bed, face pressed against the pillows. Sabaa overhears the sisters speaking in whispers.

"My sister, I don't want this marriage.... Stop it, please stop it...?" Sanu's voice is distorted with emotion, hoarse.

"Why were you born a woman?" Phuli's eyes flash in rage. She is angry at herself, angry with Sanu and the load of nothingness in their destiny of zero gain, heavy with only losses.

Sanu pulls Phuli's hands towards her and places them on her heart. Her lips tremble with unspoken words. Her voice doesn't have any power to break out anymore. The sisters look at each other in silence. The painful tears flow unbound. They hug and cry for themselves. They cry for the other.

~

The firecrackers announce the arrival of the groom. The entire household is on the alert. The best has to be offered to the bridal party; otherwise, the whole village will be defamed. Neighbors and relatives split up their responsibilities according to their age and status. Everyone is expected to lend a hand in managing the situation. They are more than polite— rather, extremely humble in their devotion to please as hosts.

Suddenly Mia's voice floats in. He prompts the servants to be faster, guiding them through the mayhem. His deep voice penetrates all restrictions, knifes in through the *pardah*, raids the inner yard, crashing against the tranquility of the residence huts. Sanu's body goes very rigid and then trembles. Her heart is in turmoil, like a feather, weightless, flying with a stormy draft. A chilling agony shoots through her.

The groom and his people eat and rest well for a while. As the sun goes down, evening prayer is performed. The marriage ceremony has to begin now. Sanu is slumped on the bed, moistening her pillow with tears. She has had so many dreams about her wedding night—the groom in her thoughts always transformed into Mia, virile, stout, keen, and loving, not burdened by age and wasted in familiar intimacies of previous marriages.

The maids scurry around carrying hurricane lamps, carefully polished for the occasion. The last-minute preparations linger on. Women concentrate on chores that must be finished before the ceremony begins. Shadows of approaching evening crouch stealthily, encasing the huts.

A large china bowl is brought into the room, filled with equal portions of milk and water. Mother sits close and holds both of Sanu's hands in hers and dips them in the liquid. Prayers hang on her lips for Sanu and her husband so that they are inseparable in body and soul, never to part again, like the mingled milk and water in the bowl. Though Sanu wants to wring her hands free and run out of the house and leap into the deepest end of the pond, she obediently sits beside her mother as the ritual demands—powerless, defeated.

"They're coming! They're coming!" The alert is on.

The *imam*, or priest, accompanied by two elderly male relatives of the groom who are to act as the witnesses to this marriage, is heading to take Sanu's consent. Her brother is the witness from her side. The priest, in front of these witnesses, will ask three times if she agrees to this marriage, and after she affirms, the proceedings to officiate the marriage will continue. Then is the signing of the *kabin nama*, the legal marriage document. Sanu's brother will sign on her behalf, as is the norm. At night, the marriage has to be consummated.

"Yusuf Ali, son of the late Hashmet Ali, is marrying you, Sanu Bibi, daughter of late Mir Kashem, with a *moharana* of taka one thousand. Do you agree to marry this man?" Everyone gasps at the amount of the moharana. Sanu's bride price is exorbitantly high! The imam repeats himself in a monotonous, bland, toneless voice. There is a hush in the room. It's crowded and hot. Almost all the women from the village have come to see the *nikah*, or wedding ceremony, though only the senior female relatives are allowed to sit close to the bride while the others watch through windows and peep through numerous holes in the tin walls. No one wants to miss the drama.

The groom will have to pay the agreed-upon moharana to his wife in case of a divorce only if it's proven that she's not at fault and has been obedient to her husband at all times. If things go smoothly and the husband dies before the wife, she will have to withdraw her claim by forgiving him formally for being unable to pay the money before the dead man is buried in his grave. However, the widow inherits a share of his property according to Muslim inheritance law.

The women cover their heads modestly in front of the imam and his company. Sanu, with her head bent, sits motionless. It seems like ages. The elderly women gently nudge her. "Say yes," they whisper in her ears.

Sanu sits still, lifeless, frozen. Time passes. The imam becomes impatient and repeats himself once again. Sanu says nothing. The bridal red silk sharee heavily embroidered in gold threads covering her head rustles, suffocating her. She gasps for air. A cousin's wife puts a handkerchief in Sanu's hand. She hardly holds it, and instantly it drops to the mud floor. Women around make room for the imam to see. This indicates that the bride has agreed to the marriage. She can't be shameless and voice her consent publicly. Once this event is over, there will be lots of laughter and teasing, reflecting on how soon consent had been given on different wedding occasions, which bride took less time, proving an impatience to get married. That's considered to be immodesty.

The handkerchief act is repeated twice more while the priest watches with emotionless dead eyes. Then he says, "Amen," and leaves with his team. They are all satisfied; the bride is in agreement and of her free will has accepted this marriage. Now they head out to take the groom's consent, and Sanu then will legally and eternally belong to Yusuf Ali. Sanu gives out a muffled cry and falls back on the bed.

The women rush towards the partition that divides them from the men's yard. They watch the groom's ceremony from afar. They hear the groom finally saying, "Amen." Everyone repeats, "Amen."

The women spectators run back to Sanu. The good news spreads. Now she is, indeed, a married woman. Nothing touches Sanu anymore. She freezes into silence.

5.

A big tray covered with a red silk drape is sent from the men's yard. Mia carries it in. The tray contains ornaments for the bride. One of the cousin's wives, senior and powerful in status, receives it from Mia. She will oversee the next steps. She is followed by a trail of curious women at her heels. Everyone is dying to see the contents of the tray. She pushes them away endlessly to make her way.

Inside the room, she removes the cover. The jewelry glitters in the lamplight. There's a hushed silence. It's a known fact that the groom is rich, but here is a fortune. They stare into a limitless trail of bangles, armlets, waist ornaments, necklaces, tiaras, anklets...an array of gold, diamonds, ruby, emeralds!

Women come forward to help Sanu get ready. She's totally unresponsive. She sits very still. This is understandable. Sanu is a bashful, modest girl. Her behavior is in total harmony with the custom. In low tones, the women admire the ornaments.

"The groom didn't look that old, actually. Age may have weakened his loins, but his power is in his money." Some go as far as being this hopeful while others giggle in hushed voices in the background. Shadows keep forming in distant corners of the room under the confinement of feeble hurricane lights.

"Look how lucky you are," begins one woman and, holding Sanu's wrists, puts the bangles on. There are too many bangles, different in make and design, that adorn her swan-like flawless, smooth arms. Sanu looks at them for a few seconds with her head erect. Then to the horror of the women, she takes off the bangles and throws them out of the door and into the open yard. A silence falls. Then someone picks up the bangles from the dirt. Maids begin to peep. With a dry smile, the cousin's wife ties armlets on Sanu's upper arms. Sanu waits patiently and, once it's done, repeats her act...and keeps repeating it! Maids hurriedly recover the ornaments from the mud, horrified, bemused. Like others, Sabaa watches from the sidelines, stunned and scared. Tota comes running.

"Sanu! Sanu! What are you doing? People will start to talk. Oh, my sister! What have we done...?" Her laments die in whispers and tears. Sanu doesn't respond. Her palms are cold, lips parched. Her cheeks bear the stains of dried tears.

The older male relatives are informed. Tota's husband,

Dhola Kazi, with their uncles at his heels, enters the inner threshold. He is not a man to put up with nonsense. He doesn't have time for women's audacity, which he terms stupidity. As they step in, some jewelry falls at their feet.

"Enough!" roars Dhola. "This foolish woman wants to defame me in front of others. This is a ploy to insult me in public. That's what she wants. I'm not going to put up with this humiliation. If this woman doesn't come to her senses, I'll kill myself rather than be a laughingstock." Dhola can be melodramatic when the occasion arises.

In fury, he impulsively picks up a machete lying limp on the ground and, shaking with rage, rushes towards the nearby bamboo plantations, threatening to take his own life. A small crowd of men and children follow, trying to dissuade him. Even at such a critical moment, Dhola crafts a grand demise.

Dhola is famous for his hotheadedness and unruly temper. His in-laws are usually petrified of him. Women and servants move away in panic. Sanu's mother rushes with great haste to stop him. Tota runs after him, too, to prevent him from committing a rash act! Sabaa is dumbfounded at the commotion that grips the house of wedding. Madness reigns, throttling the jovial mood. Some women with frail minds start crying. People wait, holding their breath for the drama to strike. Tota laments out loud while following him behind others. In a moment, the entire festive scenario changes into sinister theatre. Sanu becomes alert; she hears the alarmed voices outside. She knows she has to act fast. Everything depends on her now.

"Stop him. Oh, stop. Tell him...I'll do what he wants," she whispers, choking. Sanu's words are taken to Dhola with the speed of lightening. The men pull him onto the porch adjacent to the inner yard. Someone brings him a chair. Another fans him.

"Bring him a glass of *sharbat*, quick!" says Sanu's mother in a trembling voice. In a second the beverage arrives, sweet and cold, made of crushed almonds and pistachio mixed in sugary milk, believed to be calming. Dhola tosses the glass into the yard in fury and gets up, refusing the offer of apology and peace by his mother-in-law.

"This is all Ama's fault. Couldn't train her daughters properly. Look at this household! One daughter back at home...couldn't lead a married life...and the other? Almost became an old maid but for me! And the treatment I get? I ask you, am I not the son-in-law of this house?" Dhola barks. "For insulting me like this, I can divorce Tota right now. Tell me what will happen then? Wouldn't it serve them right?" His angry voice cuts through the sudden hush that falls. Spectators nod in agreement. Bhaijaan holds onto Dhola's feet tightly to calm him down, melting in humility, in an act of apology.

People side with Dhola. What an insult to the son-in-law. How daring! The Mir women have become arrogant. They call the shots, living independent of male protection and at every instance breaking norms with no qualms.

"They think they're above criticism, above societal control," someone whispers.

"Tell Sabaa's mother to get ready. I won't touch any food or drink in this household where the damn women make the rules. I'll never step in here again. We'll leave after midnight." There is finality in Dhola's voice. The chaos dies down as suddenly as it began.

6.

The groom and his team are served dinner. Fifty items of delicacies are offered. He's expected to try everything. This is also one of the tests of proving his manhood to the womenfolk on the bride's side. The servants fan him with a big six-foot-long silk fan, attached with strings. It was brought from Rangoon by Sanu's father when he had business over there during his younger years. The cool air dries up the beads of perspiration on the groom's forehead. Despite all precautions, some of the commotion did reach him. He's anxious to return home.

The journey back must begin right after the *Eshar* prayer, which is performed when the night is still young. It takes three hours to reach Yusuf Ali's home by boat. It's a big, magnificent vessel, with sturdy sails and twelve boatmen. The sails will catch the wind and speed up. The women try to feed Sanu once more. She doesn't respond. She sits like a beautiful statue, bejeweled, in a trance....

The groom is taken into the women's yard. It's the final closure of the ceremony. His male entourage hands him over to the women at the point where the two worlds separate. The joyous mood begins to bounce back. Women start singing as they lead him by his hands towards the interior of the house where Sanu waits for him. A different group of younger women bar his path. The way to the bride isn't so hassle free. He is supposed to buy his passage to get in. The women giggle and haggle, teasing him for money. The groom has to prove himself here as well. If he gives in easily, he will appear to be weak. His prestige depends on how little the women can bag from him. Usually, after the bargaining is done, the groom pays extra amounts to show his generosity and win over the women. The unmarried girls and young brides buy bangles, and sweets, and betel leaves with this kind of extortion money, reminiscing on how hard it was.

"Look what these dumb females are doing! Don't waste time! Stop this idiocy this instant!" Dhola spits on the dirt floor as he yells.

The merrymaking stops as suddenly as it began. The groom is quickly taken to Sanu's room. Sharbat is offered to Yousuf Ali. He barely touches it. He feels tired. It has been too much for him already. A mirror is brought in. Sanu and her husband are huddled under a red, lacy scarf. The mirror is held in front of them underneath the cover.

"Look into the mirror. See each other for the first time in

your lives. A moment to remember," whispers a woman in charge of the ceremony. Strands of Yousuf Ali's escaped silvery hair from under his turban glimmer in the lamplight as well as his tired eyes. His faintly wrinkled face and stooped shoulders cover most of the mirror.

"What do you see, *daman mia* [Mr. Groom]?" asks someone in jest.

"Is it a rose? A new moon?" another woman teases.

It's customary for the groom to compare his bride to a thing of beauty, something romantic that people will remember and talk about for years to come on different wedding occasions. Sanu's eyelids tremble; she's unable to open her eyes. She feels the man's presence beside her, can now smell the masculine odor, a hint of his body slightly touching hers.

"Hurry up, now." Dhola's voice is heard from outside. The spell breaks.

Mother comes forward as all rituals have come to an end. She takes both of Sanu's hands in hers and places them in Yusuf Ali's palms. "I give her to you," she whispers, her voice distorted by tears. "Protect her from shame and defamation. Give her a home under your feet."

In a gesture of respect, the bride and groom, assisted by female relatives, touch Mother's feet and those of the other elderly. Before stepping out, Sanu faces her mother one last time before she embraces her newfound identity. They hug, and for an instant her reserve breaks. She clings to Mother like a child, as she used to when scared. Mother looks into Sanu's eyes...a pool of pain and despair. Oh, what has she done?! Then it's over in a flash. It's only for a brief instant. Sanu disengages, is herself again. She steps outside into the cool of the night like a queen, in her ravishing beauty and sparkling jewels.

The boat is ready. The maid who's to accompany them helps her into the boat. The boatmen shout instructions, and slowly it pulls away from the bank...into the waves...into the lonely night. Is this what Sanu wanted—to visit a distant land? She throws herself on the wooden floor of the boat. Her whole body shakes with passionate tears wringing out her very soul with it.

7.

At midnight the boat reaches Sanu's new home. Despite everything, she had dozed off. The womenfolk come forward to welcome her as the boat anchors. They are servants, whose families have been living in this household for generations. Relatives wait in the main house. With their aid, Sanu steps into the inner yard of a magnificent large mansion made of brick and marble with countless rooms and hollow passages buried in its womb. The light from the hurricane lamps reflect on the cold, hard walls of the house looming under a moonless sky threatening with gloomy clouds. Women in beautiful attire and jewels come forward with sweets, flowers, and *mangaldeep*—flames lit on tiny clay burners to bless the bride and welcome her to her new home. Their eyes, laden with sleep, look curiously at Sanu.

"I have four children," says Yusuf Ali. "Two sons, two daughters. All married. They have given me nine grandchildren...between the ages of two and fifteen," he adds with pride.

A piece of a sweet is offered to Sanu. She almost chokes on it. Someone keeps fanning her in the background, though it's not very hot—more as a courtesy and a display of respect.

"*Salaam, noa amajan* [new mother]," greets a deep voice as a pair of hands in a sign of respect touch her feet enclosed in soft, silk sandals. Suddenly, in an instant, Sanu's position has been elevated. She has become the mother of adults much older than herself. Someone tilts her face upwards for others to see. Her ornaments tinkle softly, a note sweet to the ears.

"What a beauty!" gasps a female voice. Sanu opens her eyes.

The face peeping back into her eyes is buried in surprise, full of understanding, sympathy. Her stepdaughter smiles at her. Sanu sees her new stepchildren, the husbands of daughters, wives of sons, and older grandkids who have been eagerly waiting. Toddlers are fast asleep, oblivious to Sanu's life-changing moment. The oldest son is in his late thirties while the youngest daughter is about twenty. Something inside of Sanu dies that night.

8.

Yusuf Ali and Sanu are taken to the bridal chamber. The night is almost over, frozen in a lethal, impenetrable darkness of silence. Nothing stirs, not even the ardent frogs, no breeze outside. Sanu is consumed by a feeling of foreboding as thick as the earthy walls of a newly dug grave. In a couple of hours, the roosters will begin to crow. The call for Fazr—the morning prayer—will soon tear up the stillness of the night. The silk spread on the big four-poster bed rustles as Yusuf Ali climbs on it. He puts out the lamp before that. It's better, bearable in the dark, thinks Sanu.

"Sanu, you're so beautiful," whispers her husband. "Alas! I'm an old man. I may not be fit for you. I will try my best to make you happy." His breath becomes raspy.

He quickly disrobes her and climbs on top. She feels the pressure of his hardness against her. His shaky hands grope all over her rigid body and find the tautness of her breasts. His hands are cold on her warm body. Is this called *marriage*? Is this what other women have been whispering about? She doesn't want him. His body is merely a weight that presses her down, incapable of igniting her. With every thrust, her whole body is engulfed in endless spasms of pain. What a surrender...what a way to step into the threshold of marriage, to become a *real* woman.

~

At dawn the maids find her crumpled in her blood-spotted clothes and bedspread stained with Yusuf Ali's amorous passions. They fail to hide their giggles as Sanu's face is aflame with embarrassment. Also, it's now proven that she is a modest virgin. They will gossip and laugh as they wash her shame in public in the river amongst so many others watching, which will also be labeled as her virtue, her talisman proof of chastity broken on the bridal bed. By evening, it will be common knowledge and the talk of the village—her virginity and loss of virginity, in the same breath. People will heave a sigh of relief that all is normal and as expected.

CHAPTER THREE

Sweet-salty times

I.

Tota returns to Kolkata with Dhola and the children the day after Sanu's wedding. Though mother and Bhaijaan managed to pacify Dhola's anger, he was anxious to leave. Too much indulgence at his in-laws' house has never been a comfortable thing for him. In any case, Sanu's wedding eventually ended smoothly. Dhola was satisfied.

In 1942, when Sabaa was four years old, Dhola rented a house and brought his family to Kolkata. Amina Bibi didn't join them but didn't stop Tota either, as Dhola needed someone to cook, clean, and care for him. That was important above all. She was OK to loosen her iron control over Tota for the benefit of her son. Except for regular visits to Harirampur village with the entire family, Tota is finally free of Amina Bibi.

Life is very different in Kolkata, though Dhola's behavior hasn't changed much. It's interesting even if one stays indoors.

They live on the top flat of a double-storey building constructed with red bricks and grey stones. Dhola rented it for security reasons as he keeps late hours at the printing press. Their floor has several rooms built around a vast, open, roofless terrace in the middle. A hanging balcony overlooks the road on the front side, easily accessible from the bedrooms. The two bathrooms are away from the living quarters, at the far end of the terrace. Green creepers with scented pink flowers spiral around the steel fences of the balcony and the somber granite pillars on the ground that support it.

Tota and the children are by themselves mostly with two maids, one young and the other elderly, who can run outside errands without a chaperone. Dhola doesn't trust the male domestic help available in local pools who could be recruited at a cheap salary.

The house is gated, built on a big compound full of ancient tall trees, near a busy main road, and so it's a safe location for a young family. The edge of the compound is encircled by a shallow, slim pond that usually dries up in winter, but it's a hot bed for mosquito breeding during summer, harboring every raindrop. The landlord with his large family lives on the ground floor.

After the children go to bed, Tota usually sits on a stool on the balcony and watches the mobile life on the road: busy commuters, the outline of the trams in the distance, the rickshaws and buses, voices blended in a strange out-of-tune chorus, sounds of movement—vibrant, animated fragments of many lives tied together in a juxtaposition of parallel momentary existence. The headlights of passing motor vehicles sweep over the house, frequently lighting up the trees in the dark—craft a mystic air—impenetrable, forlorn. At such moments, Harirampur village seems too far away, too distant, in another life.

2.

Tota loves going to the zoo, and so do the children. Kolkata's zoo is very famous. It houses many animals in large cages: lions and giraffes from Africa, the royal Bengal tigers from the Shundorbon forests in East Bengal, elephants from Kerala, bears from China, and exotic birds in flamboyant colors from distant lands. Dhola isn't against such outings with the children. He normally hires a horse-driven cart for the entire day, and Tota, the children, and the maids climb inside the hooded part, fortified with snacks and drinks to eat at a picnic spot inside the zoo. Dhola sits in the front beside the driver, commonly known as the *coachwan*. The two robust horses shit and fart several times in the thirty-minute journey, constantly swinging their tails that grow a tussle of long hair at the very end to drive away the flies attracted to their hind side due to the frequently released odors. The children are too glad to sit inside with Tota to stay as far away as possible from the smelly horses.

Sometimes Dhola takes Tota to watch Bangla talkies or cinema shot in black and white. It's a common source of entertainment in Kolkata. They also love the local folk theatre or opera known as *jatra* performed live on an open stage. The word *jatra* means *a journey* in Bangla. It's a form of popular folk musical containing spontaneous songs and dance sequences sneaked in to ensure audience attention. Loud orchestra music and melodramatic dialogue deliveries are essential characteristics of jatra. The stories are based on Hindu mythology and historical romances derived from the lives of kings and queens. Young men play female roles wearing heavy makeup, artificial high boobs and wigs of long, dark tresses. They look really beautiful as women.

Jatra has its roots in fifteenth-century India. It gained popularity in the eighteenth century. During the British colonial times in the nineteenth and early twentieth centuries, jatra was also used as a voice to popularize political themes. Over the years, jatra became modernized.

In some of the staged stories, Tota can find traits of her own legacy of shame, somewhat echoed in the intriguing lives of Sita, Parvati, Rukhmini, and Rani of Jhansi, the Hindu female deities and nobles subjected to intense catastrophes due to dire situations — abductions, defamation, abandonment, cruelty, and death, mostly caused by actions of men who controlled their destinies. These stories bring back the memory of the curse that follows her family....

Tota's maternal uncle was a *zamindar*, or a feudal lord who owned over 70 percent of the land in his own village and the neighboring villages. He was a benevolent man and fairly treated his subjects, who lived on and farmed his lands. A few, however, cultivated their own fields. Some others were businessmen who traded in goods, real estate, etc. All were liable to pay reasonable yearly levies to him from their yields. He also had business in Kolkata. Some say he had dealings with the British East India Company, which made him an extremely wealthy man; one would need months to count all the gold coins he had.

The zamindar was highly respected in the region. All his daughters were married off early. His only son survived him and inherited his immense wealth and title at a young age.

Inheritance, bad company, gambling, womanizing, and boozing made the young zamindar erratic and oppressive. He had a roving eye for pretty faces. At his command, his henchmen abducted whomever he fancied to his heavily guarded *bagan bari*, or garden bungalow. Police were in his pocket, and so were many other influential people. No one had the courage to protest.

A widespread story was that his only daughter was widowed at sixteen and returned back to his house. She was sad

and lonely. The upper floor of a teakwood two-storey bungalow that overlooked the Padma River at the edge of the inner
yard was allocated as her residence, where she lived with her
maid. She spent most of the day watching the fierce waves
and sailing boats. At night she got restless looking at the silent
waters. Then something happened....

One fine morning, it was made public that the daughter had
been sent back to live with her dead husband's family. No one
heard about her anymore. But there were whispers, and the
whispers grew. Rumor had it that the daughter, in her loneliness, had fallen in love with a farmhand, undesirable between
a respectable widow and a low-bred philistine...and she got
pregnant.

Before her shame became exposed, the zamindar summoned his henchmen. One dark night when the moon was in
lunar eclipse, she was strangled and her dead body thrown in
a deserted dry well in a nearby bamboo forest owned by her
father. The farmhand simply vanished.

~~

Meanwhile, the zamindar's wife died. His three sons married
and had a houseful of children. Then tragedy struck—his
sons and their families drowned when their boat capsized on
the Padma while they were returning home after attending
a wedding. Only the sick daughter of the youngest son and
his wife who stayed behind were spared. To the villagers, this
was divine justice, a result of curses of the oppressed. Tota
and her sisters were young girls at the time. Their father had
cut off all contact with the zamindar.

The zamindar's downfall began soon afterwards. His business in Kolkata collapsed. In 1940 the great famine hit Bengal, followed by floods and failed crops. He was in debt and
started selling off his land cheap, at the price of water. One
morning he fell from his horse while very drunk and died of a

broken neck. By the time all his debts were paid off, nothing was left; even the big house was auctioned. So one night his son's widow and granddaughter silently left the village. Many years later in Dhaka, a relative told Tota that the widow worked as a cook at a single men's boarding house. The curse had trailed her.

Tota believes the curse has followed her family as well.

Though Tota would have liked to live in Kolkata forever, the riots of 1947 eventually force Dhola to return to Harirampur village with the family.

CHAPTER FOUR

"Mistress of gloom"

I.

Sanu misses her mother, Phuli. The big house with its stone steps feels strange, creepy. Its walls are so impersonal, icy cold. Gusty winds blow from the river and chill her heart. Her stepdaughters and the sons' wives are very kind to her. They seem to realize and understand Sanu's pain, her desolation and loneliness. Nights are long. The days bear no meaning. Tears dry up on Sanu's blouse-hugged bosom, and fresh tears well up. Her soul feels imprisoned in this house. Sometimes, suddenly in the middle of the night, she wakes up startled. "...*Jalaiya gela moner agun*...." Mia's rich voice glides in with the moonlight! She wonders, *Was it a dream? A hallucination?*

Sanu slowly gives up on living. She only breathes but forgets to live. She only follows what she is told to do, dragging along, limp and lifeless.

Yusuf Ali doesn't understand Sanu. Her silence infuriates him. He gives her lavish jewels, clothes, and whatnot. He has never seen her react to anything. She never looks at him, even in the privacy of the bedchamber when he seeks intimacy. Her eyes remain downcast, focused on the floor. At first he thought it was shyness, but now he feels it's defiance. A silent wrath builds inside him, though he consciously tries to push it aside.

He begins to spend most of his time in the outer-yard bungalow, meeting with people, conducting his daily business, napping sometimes. He also eats lunch out there and comes to the inner house only for dinner and to sleep. It's his deliberate way of protecting himself from the unnatural feelings that try to rattle his heart at the sunset of his life. By avoiding Sanu's company as much as possible, he finds refuge. He doesn't want her to invade the quintessence of his being and vanquish his mind, now feeble with old age. He's afraid of the power she has over him, but isn't aware of it herself.

Sanu is so graceful, barely a child. He feels proud to be able to possess her—if only he could reach her soul. Sometimes out of frustration, Yusuf Ali keeps himself totally aloof, doesn't touch her or talk to her. Sanu never complains, never makes a move. He forgives her. She accepts him without a word. He lusts after her body with new vigor, biting her lips and breasts, and bruises her. Sanu endures in total silence.

It amazes Yusuf Ali that she isn't yet pregnant. They have been married for some months already. He has seldom spared her of wifely duties at night. She lies limp in his arms each time he takes her. Violating her is a one-way street. He's OK with that as long as Sanu doesn't resist him. He would have liked her to be more animated, human, when he touches her. She remains like an ice goddess, always. If only she were to become a mother, she would possibly change. He thinks of ways to win her over.

He gives her bundles of money. She doesn't touch it. She doesn't fancy it at all. Her eyes remain vacant of any excitement, any emotions. He brings heaps of clothes—silk, lace, cotton—to attract her, offers the goods at her feet in worship. Sanu remains indifferent, unaffected.

"Even a wooden doll would react to the jewelry, money, and gifts I pile at your feet. What's wrong with you?" Yusuf Ali exclaims in surprise, laced with frustration. Sanu doesn't respond.

2.

Normally on most mornings, after the ritual of bathing and praying is over, Sanu walks around the garden in the backyard to pass the time. She watches the household waking up, hears the maids' hurried footsteps on the beaten dirt yard, carrying wheat flour, eggs, rice, and vegetables to the kitchen from the storage at the main building. The sounds of the morning transform this house. Different kinds of food have to be cooked, and fast. The kitchen is an open straw-roofed shack without walls, built in one corner of the inner yard where six big clay stoves are side by side, constantly aflame till dusk sets in and dinner is eaten right after the nighttime prayer is over.

The male servants who work in the fields leave the house when the sun barely breaks out of darkness. They eat leftover rice soaked in large earthen bowls of water to prevent fermentation in the heat. They devour the watery rice with chili, salt, and onion—no fancy eating as they have to hurry to work.

Steaming white rice, daal—a soupy preparation of lentils—and vegetable curry are for the schoolchildren. The rice is so soft that it melts in the mouth. The taste hangs onto the lips. There are many children in this house. Sanu doesn't even know their names properly. Some are Yusuf Ali's grandchildren; some are relatives' kids who live in this big house as its integral part. For generations, relatives have lived in this household and enjoyed its hospitality.

Soft hands make flat bread, or *roti*, egg omelets are piled up on large trays. Tea is boiled for hours in thick milk and chunks of homemade molasses—sweetened deeply for adults. Sanu usually skips breakfast. Sometimes she waters the jasmine plants and picks the fragrant white flowers. She doesn't wear them in her hair anymore, not since she came to live here. The garden also grows pale pink roses and marigolds, darkened into orange shades by the blazing sun.

Sanu doesn't like the house. It's unfriendly. It's a magnificent mansion. The main building is called *dalan*. Adjacent to it is a cluster of individual abodes, tin-roofed with brick walls. Each contains only one spacious room with inner partitions for privacy, normally occupied by one family—relatives with close blood ties who are a part of the joint family, daughters when they visit, and close kin who stay for a long duration as guests. These residences are built in the inner yard so that close male relatives have easy access.

The steps, the hallway, and the narrow, short corridors of the main building are made of white sparkling cold marble brought in by big, slow boats from Kolkata, Sanu learned from the maids. It takes about a month to transport any kind of raw construction materials from such a distance. The floors of the living quarters are made of expensive mosaic; each room has a different attractive floral design.

There are some lodges in the outer yard where Yusuf Ali has his bangla ghor, or bungalow, while the others are occupied by male guests and distant male relatives. His two sons and their families live in the main building, as does he with Sanu, occupying the largest room with a huge roofed balcony facing the river.

Routinely in the morning, the maids hand over the breakfast trays to male servants who work in the outer yard, to feed the residents. Sanu is fascinated by this well-managed, smooth operation. In the inner yard, women eat after the children leave for school and the men depart in pursuit of daily business. Women take their time and eat to their fill. The same process is followed for other meals and evening tea with snacks, which are usually sweet rice flour dumplings cooked in molasses and heavy cream, and *kheer*, or rice pudding stewed in milk and grated coconut. Sometimes biscuits and sweet raisin bread are bought from the *bazaar* for a change. The air becomes heavy with the appealing aroma of these delicacies, exciting the stomach with an ardent, frenzied appetite.

After breakfast the regular household chores begin: cooking the meals, cleaning, washing, and sun-drying pickles and stored grains. There are too many maids. They need to be guided, managed, and supervised. Someone is always responsible to administer these chores with a steady hand. No one ever came to seek Sanu's opinion; no one needs her guidance, though practically she is the mistress of this house. As Yusuf Ali's wife, she is entitled to a position of authority.

In the dry season, the children walk to school, which is about a mile away. In summer, the monsoon waters flood the roads, and the children are ferried in boats by servants. There are at least ten boats for daily use at those times. Some boats have roofs, mainly for use by women and family members, while the others are dinghies, which are for going to the market and running daylong errands. So far, Sanu has never gone out of the house.

Rumor has it that Yusuf Ali was initially contacted with a proposition of marriage of his nephew, Robi, with Sanu. He decided to look into the matter as Robi's guardian and found out about Sanu's beauty, youth, and appeal. A sister-in-law who hailed from Laxmikul village confirmed Sanu's unearthly loveliness, respectability, and virtues. His mind was made up. After being a widower for five years, he had been considering remarrying but hadn't been successful in finding the right woman. Now was his chance to intervene, take control of destiny. He would find a good woman for Robi later. He wanted Sanu for himself; his choice was clear. Though this news was kept secret, it leaked. Eventually it became popular gossip. Women continue to talk about it at the pond while bathing and doing dishes and laundry, and at lazy hours followed by late meals in the afternoons. The maids talk about it too. It starts to circulate with tremendous speed, juicy chatter as people realize Sanu's beauty and youth are tied brutally, forever, in a loveless marriage with an old man. Marriages between older men and younger women are quite common in Bengal, but the triangle with Robi keeps the talk alive, adds spice to the story as he lives under Yusuf Ali's roof. Somehow it reaches Sanu's ears as well.

It is a distasteful revelation. Sanu wishes she had never heard it. When she first met Robi, she couldn't talk to him or look at him but was aware of his powerful masculinity, strong body, rugged face, stout arms. She was conscious of his deep, throaty laughter, and his low, husky voice. He had almost *become* her husband! Goodness!

Shivers run through her body whenever she hears him now. She tries to think of what life could have meant in this icy stone house had she been married to Robi.

3.

Robi manages a big store at the Sadar Bazaar, or the great marketplace, about twenty minutes' distance from the house by boat. Yusuf Ali has handsomely invested in the store. It sells all kinds of coveted goodies directly transported from Kolkata. The supplies are replenished quarterly as demand for the goods is high. Robi's is the only store that offers so much variety, so many choices, such an abundance of options. The sharees are high-quality *muslin, jamdani*, and delicate silk, hand-embroidered with gold, cotton, and silver thread. The prayer mats are made of soft *makhmal*, a velvet material famously woven in Persia. Then there are china plates and dishes, mirrors, different varieties of fragrant soaps, hair oils, shoes, umbrellas, costume jewelry, combs engraved with semiprecious gems, and expensive perfumes made in England, France, and the Arabian countries. It's the best store in the entire region. People come from far and wide to buy and to see the extravagant displays of merchandise mostly meant to cater to the needs of the middle class and wealthy.

In her daydreams, Sanu finds herself lying in Robi's arms, cooking for him, taking care of their child born in passion...on moonlit nights gliding in a boat with him invading the stillness of the waters burdened with milk-white lotuses...early mornings waking up in adoration of his spent love. Sanu has never exchanged one word with Robi since she has been in this house, but in her mind she builds a million moments of a shared life together. Sometimes she thinks her mind is becoming corrupt, wanton with lusty thoughts. She is a married woman. She has a husband even if he is someone she doesn't cherish and has failed to love. Her heart waits for familiar footsteps in the evening. Her pulse races at crashing speed as she picks up Robi's voice in the inner yard. Her soul is crushed under the weight of shame. She's his uncle's wife!

Krishna in the Hindu religion is a deity, worshipped by ardent devotees, and is famous for his love for his maternal uncle's wife, Radha. According to Bhagavat Gita (the Song of God), the Hindu sacred book, they were cursed to be separated for one hundred years, though passionately in love. Their eternal illicit love has become immortal and has been worshipped through the ages. Many famous love songs in Bengal are based on this unforgettable love and echo the pathos of the passions of Radha and Krishna, the love between two unequals—a god and a woman married to his uncle.

"*Tomai rid majhare rakhibo chere dibo na....* [Will keep you enclosed in my heart, not let you go, let you fall.]" The tunes of their spiritual love songs echo in the paddy fields and bazaars, and in the voices of boatmen as they row across vast unknown water terrains. Sanu thinks of the lovers, incestuous but true. She places herself in the image of Radha, the uncle's wife of her lover, Krishna, who is very much like Robi. Her heart continues to burn in indescribable anguish.

~

The days come and go. Months pass. Sanu doesn't seem to belong here. She doesn't connect with anyone. The household has accepted her the way she is—aloof, silent, lost in her own universe. They keep their distance and empathize with her. The women, especially wives of the stepsons, are not hostile towards her. She commands respect among them, but there's no cordiality. The bond hasn't developed. Living among so many, Sanu leades a completely separate life of solitude. She has no friends, no foes. The only person who has some close contact with her is her husband, but the physical intimacy is his choice, forced upon her. She doesn't desire it. She finds no joy in it. They hardly have any conversations beyond brief broken sentences, never exchange any views or chat about inconsequential goings-on.

As the days pass, Sanu becomes more and more listless. She dreams of her mother, of Phuli…of the beautiful moonlit night at home…the green paddy fields under the rainbows that shoot out of the thick clouds after showers during the monsoon. She longs to go home. She feels trapped in this stagnant, dead life. The women watch with understanding. Possibly, they witness the dying of her soul, slowly, very slowly with the coming of every new day.

Sanu falls sick. The *Kabiraj* who is the local healer fails to cure her. He takes his leave, suggesting that she should be treated in Kolkata by a *gora*, or white doctor, which is unheard of. Everyone is worried. If this continues, they fear that Sanu might not live long. Yousuf Ali's married daughters are summoned. They arrive with their children, concerned for their stepmother. Finally, the older son talks to his father. Sanu's brother in Kolkata is notified of her condition.

Sanu fervently waits day and night for Bhaijaan to come to get her. She is afraid of dying before he arrives. It's a week's journey from Kolkata. One night she calls her stepsons' wives and requests that her dead body be sent back to her homeland for burial. Sanu's behavior terrifies the household. There's the smell of death in the house! The silent, cold marble stairs and walls harbor an ominous air.

Bhaijaan arrives. He has come straight from Kolkata. He managed to send out a brief note to Mother about Sanu's condition before he boarded the steamer that brought him to Yusuf Ali's village. After refreshments, when he finally gets to see Sanu lying helpless, wasted, his heart breaks into a million pieces. He's shocked to see the frail body languishing on the bed, has difficulty recognizing her. He can't control himself any longer and wails...for his baby sister.... Oh, what has everyone done to this golden doll?! He makes up his mind. She shall go home with him.

This news reaches Yusuf Ali. He's very angry. This is not the way a wife's brother should behave. A brother can make a request, seek permission, but can't dictate any course of action regarding a woman who lives under her husband's roof and custody. But Bhaijaan is adamant. He wouldn't leave without taking Sanu back with him. There's a lot of sympathy in the household for Sanu, the beautiful goddess-like woman whom no one could fathom, no one could reach in the real sense.

Yusuf Ali's sons intervene, and finally he gives in but with one condition. If Sanu leaves the house that night, her brother should sign a paper forfeiting any claim of mohorana. This also means Yusuf Ali may divorce her at any time if he decides not to bring her back, or this departure could even be considered a virtual divorce, eventually subject to interpretation by the community elders or imams. Bhaijaan gets a jolt but straightens up quickly. He has come to take his little sister home for her to die in peace. He signs the papers.

The fragile bond breaks and Sanu is let loose, ultimately from a fate that didn't bring her any solace, any joy... a soulless existence, a submission enforced on her.

Almost the entire village swarms towards Yusuf Ali's house to see Sanu's departure. They want to be the first ones to witness the unfolding drama. She may not come back, ever! She may not survive this illness that feasts on her young, vibrant body and consumes it from the core. Women wipe away their tears. The stepsons' wives touch her feet as if it's the final parting. Only Yusuf Ali doesn't come to the inner house. Sanu's eyes search for him. She feels this would be the last time ever to look at the face she has tolerated for months.... The face that she learned to live with though could not love... the man who gave her an identity as a married woman, saved her from the indignity of dying an old maid. In her heart she knows she will never meet him again. This is goodbye. Nothing is said to him, no farewell taken.

Sanu would have liked to see her husband one more time, thank him in her own silent manner. He housed her for six long months; she feels gratitude. In a feeble voice, she asks everyone present to forgive her, as is customary. That's all she is able to do.

Finally, she is carried into the boat. The mounting waves increasingly strike against its hard wooden frame, rocking it with a hunger to move on. The sails pick up the rough breeze and surge forward as soon as the anchors are up. The journey home begins.

As the sails steadily catch the wind, Sanu begins to feel slightly better. She asks for water. She's now able to swallow. She falls into a heavy, dreamless sleep after a long, long time. The boat glides ahead breaking the waves, steadily, silently — purposefully.

4.

Hours pass. Sanu is semiconscious most of the time. She doesn't know whether it's day or night. After almost an infinity of riding on restless waves, the boat enters the familiar waters of home. The faint fragrance of water lilies and wild blossoms, overpowered by the savory scent of spicy curries and condiments mixed with the smell of inert moist earth, fills the air. The waters of home feel soft and smooth, welcoming against the hull, against the oars.

The boat is anchored in the backyard. Maids hurry and carry Sanu to the inner house. She sees Mother and Phuli anxiously peeping at her face. She smiles at them, reassuring them she's alive. There's the sound of firecrackers and many voices in the background, as if a celebration is in progress.

"What's that noise? What's happening?" Sanu says in a frail tone.

"Mia just got married. The household is welcoming the new bride," Phuli answers.

Sanu turns her face away and closes her eyes. A stabbing pain consumes her heart.

PART II.
1950s AND 60s

CHAPTER FIVE

Awakening

I.

Sabaa feels lonely, especially these days. She is almost twelve. She senses her body, her emotions are changing. Some days are happier; other times she's weepy, angry, defiant. She wishes she had a sister with whom she could talk, laugh, share secrets, and play with dolls. Tota has put restrictions on her movements recently as she's growing up. That's normal here. No more dips in the new floodwater and bouncing with the dancing waves. No more running after butterflies. No climbing the mango trees in the front yard to pick the ripest, sweetest, juiciest fruits from the highest branches. She has to stop being herself, though it's very frustrating. She's not a little girl anymore. She has become taller. Her body is gradually announcing curves and grace. Onlookers pause to give her better scrutiny. All these signs force more restrictions on her carefree existence.

Her two older brothers have their own lives — school, football, boating, and fishing. Their world and hers are divided.

They can do many things that are banned for her. The younger brother, Elias, is still a breastfed baby, sickly most of the time. Sabaa takes care of him when Tota is too busy. He's a good diversion.

Though Dhola is a strict father, the older boys enjoy greater freedom. He doesn't interfere too much in their everyday lives if their grades in school are good. They are even allowed to organize village jatra, or folk theatre, performed by local boys, mostly their friends, as well as football matches or wrestling games with rival teams from adjacent villages. Some families, though OK with sports, aren't comfortable with jatra. They think it could spoil the boys eventually. Dhola has no such qualms and believes in the *boys will be boys* theory.

Luckily, the brothers are kind to Sabaa, though they maintain some distance from her at all times, as expected. They speak with her as needed, play *caram* or *ludo* on idle afternoons, and sometimes chaperone her to visit relatives who live close by. They're like any other Bengalee brothers.

Since puberty, they have moved into the outer-yard residence huts, but they have easy access to the inner house as necessary for meals or any contact with female family members. Dhola doesn't approve of boys getting too involved in the women's world and ensures his sons are more engaged in outdoor activities besides their studies. Their interactions with their mother are restricted to mundane activities and revolve around eating meals, care given in sickness, laundry, and attending family events and celebrations. They're not encouraged to share their feelings or problems. They're not expected to have more than everyday conversations or engage in gossip that goes beyond routine issues. Even under such constrained norms, the bond between the mother and sons continues to be strong in affection, not so much in expression. Tota feels a deeper closeness to her three sons. She understands them, though reciprocity is limited. They're like the regular guys who don't surpass expectations and are present in her life in a comfortable way. With Sabaa, she's bewildered at times.

Sabaa misses school and her friends. Her schooling ended when Dhola brought the family back to their village, Harirampur, from Kolkata three years ago. At the time, her grandmother Amina Bibi, whom she lovingly calls Dada, remarked that Sabaa was ripe as a watermelon, ready to be married off even though she was only nine!

Dada is good at citing local proverbs to make a point, and she does that very often. Some are hilarious, but they can shake up perceptions.

There isn't much to do here in this backward village that remains submerged underwater during the monsoon for almost seven months, cut off from the rest of the world. Sabaa wonders how this tiny place fits into the greater layout of the universe—no bazaars spilling over with stores that offer incredible extravagances from different parts of the world or talkies to watch, not even a park, unlike Kolkata, where they used to visit when Dhola had free time. Bengalee women aren't expected to go on outings without proper male chaperones, even in Kolkata. There were other Bengalee families who lived nearby—Muslims, Christians, and Hindus—who used to visit them at home regularly with children. She loved playing with them. Pickles, signature dishes, and condiments were shared and relished. Kolkata never slept. It was always on the move in its vibrancy, diversity, daily wonders, and maddeningly sweet mayhem. She deeply misses the enchanting city of delights!

Sabaa completed primary schooling in Kolkata before they migrated to Harirampur. Dhola at first actually wanted her to continue with her education, though it was unheard of in this conventional community to send a *sheyana*—a mature girl or "a girl growing boobs," as commonly understood—to study with boys. Not a single girl of Sabaa's age was enrolled in the only high school in the village whose main patron was Dhola himself.

The school is more than three miles away from the house. In the dry season, the walk in the scorching sun is unbearable. In the monsoons, boats are the only means of transport on good days, but frequent heavy rains and cyclones are usual and disruptive to normal life. Starting a dispute with the established norms and his mother, who disapproved of education for girls outside of the home, were also dissuading factors Dhola had to consider seriously.

"Is your Sabaa going to become a *jodge-barrishter* [judge barrister]? What?" Dada had raised her brows, mixing the English words in her broken vocabulary as she challenged her son while taking a puff at the hookah.

"Our headmaster can teach Sabaa at home. Hire him. He'll be glad to earn some extra." So the issue was finalized once and for all. Picking a battle with his own mother wasn't the wisest of actions. It's best not to quarrel with the crocodile with which one has to share the same waters, Dhola had learned early in life.

He would have liked Sabaa to be accomplished like the white British women, the *memshahibs* he had come across in Kolkata and watched in the talkies. They worked as doctors and lawyers, helping their own people. Such noble work! In a bizarre contradiction with himself, Dhola was sort of a romantic where his daughter was concerned. He was proud of Sabaa and wanted her to outshine the other females around her. But this wasn't Kolkata where people weren't so quick to criticize and condemn if norms were bent. In this retrograde village smothered by superstition, religiosity, tradition, and constant struggles with malaria, cholera, and flooding, it became his duty to protect his daughter from the harshness of the outside world.

However, he ultimately settled for home education for

Sabaa. In his heart, Dhola knew Sabaa could have become *someone* had she gotten real opportunities. Anyway, the seventy-year-old headmaster was engaged five days a week to teach her English, Bangla, mathematics, and science, three hours each day. Dada and Tota lavishly fed him a meal after each lesson was over. For religious studies, the family imam was hired.

Sabaa loves solving mathematics problems and is interested in literature... and so she continues to study through home-schooling. Learning becomes her passion. She is tutored at home till she is finally married off at twelve.

2.

Tota tries to understand her daughter, but she is too busy most of her waking hours with countless chores to give her sole attention to Sabaa. She is extremely watchful of Sabaa's needs but doesn't know how to be her confidant or hold her attention. She teaches Sabaa to cook and make pickles, but Tota isn't very skilled at crocheting, stitching, knitting, or embroidery. She knows just the basics. Sabaa picks up intricate needlework from neighbors' young wives. She has become quite clever with her acquired proficiencies and produces with perfection. It makes Tota very proud of her daughter. Sabaa's feats are like Tota's own victories. Sabaa has knitted sweaters for Tota and Dada, which both women wear on winter days with pride.

Tota isn't a great reader either, possibly because since she has been in this household pursuing mundane responsibilities, creating comfort for others, managing her own pregnancies, and taking care of her children after their birth, along with handling Dhola, his mother, and the constant presence of guests, she barely has any time for herself beyond the compulsory daily five prayers and reading the Quran, sometimes....

Reading seems to be a luxury. Before she got married, Tota

did read some folklore, fairy tales, and stories of saints and popular legendary heroes. When her children were younger, she told those stories to them whenever time permitted.

Sabaa reads voraciously, mainly translations of literary works of famous writers and poets: Pearl S. Buck, Hemingway, Tolstoy, and Rumi as well as Bengalee talents Tagore and Nazrul. However, D. H. Lawrence is her favorite. Whenever they get a chance, her brothers remember to pick up books for their smart little sister from Bangla Bazaar, the local book market in downtown Dhaka, famous for its voluminous collections, situated close to Dhola's printing press. Friends and family also bring lots of new publications directly from Kolkata. Often she exchanges books for shared reading with female relatives with literary interests.

Sabaa is quite mature for her age as she is cloistered mostly in adult company. She has an entourage of friends. Only a few are her age-mates while most are older women who love to hear the stories after she finishes reading each book. Whenever she is confused or needs clarifications, she takes her questions to her private tutor. The old headmaster is only too happy to explain passages from novels and lines from poems patiently to his young student. He's the only one in her world with whom Sabaa is able to discuss literary matters.

Her status elevates her among her listeners, as she's always ready with new stories. She walks them into a different world outside of this tiny village into a coveted land where the characters become heartstring-tugging favorites. Her friends gather frequently on lazy afternoons when she narrates from her recent readings. As they attentively listen to her narratives, Sabaa introduces the universe of Paul and Gertrude Morel from *Sons and Lovers*, her favorite novel, or *Anna Karenina* by Tolstoy. Dada beams with pride as she sits with others, taking full credit for Sabaa's intellectual accomplishments.

In the background as always, Tota continues to be busy with her usual household labor, carefully storing or drying the huge piles of grain under the sun with the help of the maids, or making pickles to fill uncountable jars and bottles for the entire year's consumption. Sometimes oblivious to others and in complete silence under the pretext of being occupied with her tasks, Tota stands behind the circle of Sabaa's audience, keeping an apparent distance. Dada doesn't welcome Tota to join this scholarly group. In her mind, Tota is a philistine, not intellectually sophisticated enough to understand the value of literature. Tota, however, takes pride in Sabaa and wants others to discover her daughter's wit and intellect. So she makes her peace. She concentrates on her unrecognized manual work with dogged diligence, though at times her ears pick up Sabaa's voice, entirely dedicated to her tales.

She loves it when Sabaa recites lines from *Sons and Lovers*, translated in Bangla: "*Shudhu lamp-post taar pichoney andhokaar, shomoggro ratri jeno shekhaney.* [There was only this one lamppost. Behind was the great scoop of darkness, as if all the night were there.]"

After every recitation, Sabaa elaborately explains the meaning and the deeper implications. Tota's ears hang onto each word in awe along with the other listeners, honored that Sabaa is her very own. At just twelve, Sabaa has become really smart! Tota knows she isn't competent to engage Sabaa's clever mind beyond routine interactions and so candidly withdraws behind the offering of her unconditional love that she displays by taking good care of her daughter.

Sabaa sometimes gets frustrated. She longs for a warmer tie with her mother but doesn't know how to initiate it. Tota is always too ready to please her, overtly attentive, slaving away to get Sabaa's appreciation. This bothers Sabaa. She doesn't want to be considered superior to her own mother in any way.

She craves a normal relationship where Tota is the parent, assertive of her rights, not so humble, like a doormat melting into almost nothingness.

It took Sabaa years and years finally to understand and interpret Tota's devotion, her undying admiration folded gently in the vastness of her love.

3.

Sabaa's school in Kolkata was walking distance from their house. Their elderly maid walked her every day to school. She was actually Sabaa's partial nanny. Those days, *nanny* was not a commonly understood term. This maid took care of Sabaa's clothes, made her bed, and cleaned the room she shared with other female relatives who visited from time to time. A separate room for a little girl or a grown unmarried woman was unheard of. Why would a girl need a room by herself? She should always be protected and feel cared for if she lived with others. She would also learn about sharing and adjusting. After all, when a girl is married, she will have to compromise and give in at every step in her husband's house and possess an unselfish nature as expected. Her needs and wishes should be the least important. Her happiness should be tied to making sacrifices for others. That's the norm for a girl born in a respectable noble family. Otherwise, what's the difference between her and a common peasant maid? Sabaa was coached accordingly.

Kolkata was volatile at the time. Sabaa remembers how Tota used to be nervous if she was delayed at school for any reason. The situation had begun to change quite drastically from 1946. The British were finally getting ready to move out of India. There were hushed talks about Gandhi in households, even among women. The Quit India movement was launched in 1942 with Mahatma Gandhi at the helm, the leader who made nonviolence his principle to inspire people to dream and live together in harmony. People's lives were constantly torn by racial violence, suspicion, hatred, betrayal, and rage. Hindus and Muslims, the two key players, being put against each other by the cunning of the British as well as by their own leaders and other interested actors for personal gain, resulted in further viciousness. Integrity became rare in the heat of the political environment.

During that uncertain time, Dhola seriously considered returning to his own village with his family for safety. Tensions were growing stronger every day. Riots between Hindus and Muslims were beginning to break out in several towns. Voices of all Indians echoed united in the Quit India slogan, and the movement was gaining momentum amidst hostile racial contexts. The leaders of each majority group were speaking in fiery tones to put pressure on the British Raj to leave.

On one of those days, Sabaa attended a march with other children from school to the Victoria monument, where political leaders addressed the agitated crowd. Thousands exploded in fury. It was the middle of the hot, moist summer. The scorching sun heat up the speakers' passion for freedom, for their rights. Sabaa didn't understand most of what they were saying, but it was great fun! She had never been on the street like this before. The cars and buses passed alongside but of course slowed down to allow the children to march by. Sabaa, with others, also raised her tiny fist in protest and chanted at the top of her lungs, "*Bharot Charo!* [Quit India!]" The words didn't mean anything to her, but she felt the excitement in the air. That day she was late from school. Her nanny waited an extra hour to walk her home.

At home, Tota was fearful and listened to Sabaa's exciting tale of joining the procession to save India. On that day, Dhola decided it was time to return to their village situated in the eastern part of Bengal, proposed to be included in Pakistan after all political arrangements were finalized.

"Sabaa's mother, get ready. Start packing immediately. We're leaving Kolkata," Dhola alerted the household to Tota's surprise and relief.

Dhola's printing business was doing very well in Kolkata. Going back to East Bengal meant selling the property and business. It was a worrisome time. Uncertainty loomed in the air. People were migrating from one location to another based on their religion, as the possibility of splitting India into two countries was becoming a reality. The only option left was to exchange his business and the three houses from which the printing work operated with a Hindu businessman in Dhaka who wanted to move to Kolkata, which would soon become part of the Hindu-majority India.

In three months, the property exchange materialized. Dhola and his family escaped the worst communal riot in history, which spread like wildfire in many parts of undivided India. Finally, two countries were officially born on 14 and 15 August 1947—Pakistan and India, created based on religious faith: Pakistan for the Muslim majority under Mohammed Ali Jinnah as their leader, and India under the leadership of Jawahar Lal Nehru, mainly as a Hindu-majority land.

Pakistan had a unique situation. Its two parts, East Pakistan (East Bengal) and West Pakistan, were separated by more than one thousand miles of Indian land between them. India bordered East Pakistan on three sides. Twenty-four years later in 1971, it separated from West Pakistan after a fierce battle—a bloodbath—and became an independent country known as Bangladesh.

After partition, Kolkata remained the capital of West Bengal, whereas Dhaka became the capital of then-East Pakistan or East Bengal. Though Bengal was divided on the basis of religion, the culture the Bengalees shared remained unified across the borders.

Bengalees speak the same language, belong to the same race, love the same poet (Tagore), and practice many common rituals and festivities. East Pakistan's allegiance to Bengalee culture remained a bone of contention among the West Pakistanis that ultimately led to life-changing political scenarios as the years unfolded.

CHAPTER SIX

Senses and sounds;
colors and contours

I.

Dada makes sure that Sabaa acquires the etiquette fit for the daughter of a *Khandani*, or virtuous family. As is the custom, the neighbors' daughters-in-law are now allowed to educate her about womanly issues, which focus on adult matters laced with sexual connotations among several domestic matters. Sabaa feels shy and somewhat embarrassed being exposed to the graphic expressions on such occasions, but openness about basics is village culture. These young wives know so much about women's lives! Sabaa's whole body trembles inwardly in anticipation of what might lie ahead.

Sabaa is also very much tuned into music, especially from old Hindi and Bangla films and folk and spiritual songs known as the *Baul gaan*, in addition to Tagore's songs. Dhola mostly favors folk songs and plays the discs on a battery-run record player, as the device is popularly called, a present to him from his eldest son, who bought it in Dhaka. As time passes, Dhola gradually hands over the management of the printing business to him.

The record player contains a multiple-band radio. Dhola usually operates it when he wants to listen to songs. Everybody else around enjoys it as well. He plays it at a high volume so that the sounds penetrate the partitions of the inner and outer yards. Neighbors walk in to listen with him while the music rolls on. In the evenings, Dhola tunes in the news channel, again turning the volume very high for the benefit of other listeners. In the entire village, besides Dhola, only a handful of houses own radios, but no one has a record player.

Sabaa finds it difficult to socialize with friends as much as she would like because they don't live close by. The daughters and women of noble families do not walk over to visit relatives and friends. They are carried in palanquins, or *palki*, in the dry season and in hooded boats in summer when monsoon waters submerge every strip of land visible. Four stout male servants carry the palki and work as boatmen as well as needed, along with odd jobs around the household and the barns.

The visits essentially happen during festivities: weddings, pregnancies, baby showers, births, ear piercing for female babies, circumcision for Muslim boys, the *Poita* ceremony for Hindu Brahmin boys. In addition, visits are undertaken during the two *Eid* festivals every year as well as at funerals and any family reunions around visitations of relatives after the harvest season when people celebrate good yields from the farmland. People's lives are eternally and absolutely entangled with the paddy fields in this tiny village. However, only the wealthy can maintain servants for palanquins or rowing the boats.

Muslims celebrate *Eid ul Fitr* after thirty days of fasting. It's subject to the sighting of the moon. *Eid ul Azha*, the second Eid, is celebrated two months and ten days later, right after *Hajj*, the holy pilgrimage performed in Mecca, attended by millions of devout Muslims from all over the world. Cattle are slaughtered as an integral part of the ritual. The meat is distributed among the poor, relatives, and friends. One portion is kept for the family. The feasting and merrymaking continue a full week during each Eid. People who work in towns return to the villages to be with their families. For many lucky ones, these are the only times they are reunited with their families.

New clothes are worn during Eid. Dhola makes sure that fancy sharees and accessories are brought in from Dhaka for Sabaa, Tota, and other relatives. Colorful handloom-woven clothes are bought from the local market for servants and the poor and are distributed among them before Eid prayers. Sabaa loves her new clothes. She usually receives several items. The best time is when, after bathing, they wear new clothes and sit down to eat together on the mat on the floor of the main hut. The maids eat with the family. On Eid days, all are treated as equals.

Sabaa and women of the household are also allowed to watch *pooja*, observed by Hindus. The goddess *Durga* is widely celebrated in East Bengal. Clay statues of Durga are made by local artisans with care and diligent craftsmanship for months in each village and town. Durga is the goddess of power and strength. She encompasses the essence of salvation and sacrifice, and is worshipped as the mother of bounty and wealth, beauty, and knowledge.

Durga pooja happens in autumn when the monsoon waters recede. Sabaa and her family watch the ceremony sitting in palanquins along with women from other respectable households. The women very modestly peep through the white-lace curtains of the palanquins as the valiant male servants stay on guard. Each palanquin can hold two people.

To Sabaa, Durga pooja is associated with the vivacious array of colors and the symphony of music, spiritual songs, drumbeats, and thousands of voices...the incense of flowers mingled with the burning of *dhoop*, an herbal essence with a pleasant sandalwood scent. It's also the taste of sweets made of dairy that cling to the mouth even after consumed, crowding in village fairs where handicrafts are sold, the hullabaloo of endless actions—an air of joyous carnival transcending madness into magic.

Chaperoned by elder female relatives, Sabaa loves to walk through the narrow aisles of the village fair spilling with local merchandise spread on the ground. She buys if she fancies anything. The atmosphere is packed with the sounds of footsteps, haggling, and laughter.

And finally, the immersion of the clay statue of the goddess Durga in the river on the tenth day, amidst tears and wailing of pious Hindus, ends the festival on a melancholy note. That's the saddest part and an intrinsic component of the ritual—the sacrificial profaneness of ecstasy grounded in the realm of sorrow. Sabaa's heart also cries with them. It's like witnessing your own mother being thrown to the hungry, fierce waters.

2.

As common in wealthy households, Sabaa's playmates at home are daughters of maids whose families have been working in the household for generations—poor, powerless, peasant women. Many of them are widows or have been deserted by their spouses. They live with their children in the household. Boys up to the age of nine are allowed to sleep in the inner house in the hut delegated for maids. The daughters live here till they come of age. Then the master of the house, who is considered the benefactor, marries them off to fitting suitors. They are allowed visitations during festivities and illnesses. Their husbands are mostly employed in households of close relatives and friends, or they work in the bazaar or with the boats that keep them away from the village for months. The boys from age ten join the field hands and learn the basics of farming. Schooling for the servant class is unheard of. Most remain nonliterate till they are buried.

Sabaa's friends are fully conscious of her social status as the daughter of the master of the house. So most of the time when they play *ludo*, hopscotch, or word games, she's allowed to win. They admire her for her beauty, intellectual capacity, education, and her art of narration. They swim together in the pond and race to pick the whitest water lilies at the farthest end of the water's edge. They oil and comb her dark, waist-length hair and braid it in trendy styles, decorating it with jasmine flowers. They are always ready to serve her with loyalty and affection. She is recognized as a kindhearted, easygoing person, so an everlasting friendship develops, and trust is built as they grow up together.

After the midday meal, they sit on coconut leaf mats and embroider together. Gossip and modestly dirty jokes are common at this time. Sabaa gets the latest updates from her friends since they have more mobility. They are sent on errands to the neighbors' houses within walking distance. They also spend much time at the river close to the house doing laundry or washing utensils with ample opportunity to trade stories.

In the remote Harirampur village, nothing much happens. The tide rises as the moon dances with the waves of the Padma, and the boats sail on the treacherous waters at daybreak. Sabaa senses the footsteps of change in the demure bosom of this remoteness; her heart knows change is going to come....

CHAPTER SEVEN

Build me a dream...

1.

Sabaa watches Dada and Father whispering quite often these days. Tota isn't allowed entry into these conspiratorial exchanges. Sabaa fails to understand Dada, a kind person by nature but harsh to her mother. Dada simply won't include Tota in any important matters. At the beginning of each month, Dhola gives Dada the monthly household allowance, and she manages everything. She even decides what Tota needs—clothes, bangles, fragrant bathing soap, talcum powder, and Tibet Snow, the face cream emboldened by a stiff, concentrated scent that Tota loves so much. Dada isn't very generous in addressing Tota's needs timely, though, which creates conflict every month. Dhola refuses to intervene in women's affairs at home. In the feminine world, Dada rules!

Dada allows Tota to cook only for the servants, a large force who work in the fields and need coarse, simple nourishment, not for the family unless some particular circumstances demand Tota's involvement. Dada herself cooks the family meals with the assistance of the maids—delicacies that her son, grandkids, and guests crave. She thinks Tota is too clumsy to be trusted with these culinary perfections.

In the past, it was common knowledge that Dada wouldn't even allow Tota to eat three times a day, and the amount of food offered at meals left her hungry. Dada and many mothers-in-law like her believe that if women, especially young wives, eat too much, they invite misfortune and poverty into the family. It's customary for women of noble families to eat less. Women of class put food in their mouths with civility and distinction, and are satisfied with scanty portions. Low-bred women stuff their bellies with grubby fingers, gobbling down voraciously. Tota and many like her strongly disagree with this norm, possibly established to break the daughters-in-law.

There always has been some sort of undercurrent between the two women. In the initial years after Tota entered this household, she held her peace at every cruelty. But with the passing of years and motherhood, she has become less cautious, so there are frequent flare-ups, strong retorts resulting in bitter quarrels that Dada always wins—wailing, beating her chest, shouting abuse and obscenities, telling the whole world of her sacrifices and sorrows of widowhood at fifteen. At such times, Sabaa's heart bleeds for her mother. But she is unable to intervene.

Dada governs everyone's lives. That's how it is. In quarrels, although she is mostly wrong, the relatives and neighbors side with her. She belongs here. She's a real tyrant, a matriarch with loyal followers. Tota is always an outsider. She has come from another family, another village. Solidarity comes first, but she's Sabaa's mother, and her mind always sides with Tota.

2.

Sabaa dutifully embroiders intricate designs of flowers, leaves, birds, and butterflies on tablecloths and bedspreads using colorful silky threads. At the time of matchmaking discussions, these handicrafts will be displayed, demonstrating her artistic skills necessary for an accomplished woman of class. Sabaa has also embroidered *bhulo na amai* (forget-me-not), a popular theme of the time, on pillow covers, crisscrossed with patterns of roses and jasmine. All preparations continue at full steam to get her married off.

Dada came back to live at her father's house after being widowed. Unlike most women, she didn't choose to be with her in-laws as her father was endowed with land and highly valued assets. He passed away while Dhola, her only child, was still in school, followed by his sickly wife. Dada had only an older brother.

Though uneducated, Dada has a shrewd business sense and managed their father's huge land and properties after his death. Her brother was the executor in name only and accepted Dada's judgment. She took over the entire management of their finances and fates. The finances definitely flourished.

It was a known fact that Dada controlled the life of her only sister-in-law as well. Gradually, her brother separated some properties from her watchful eyes and lost heavily by investing in unwise ventures. At one point, Dada disassociated her own finances, and very little was left under the joint agreement. She kept managing her portion with some hired assistance and eventually handed it over to Dhola. It gave him a solid footing to navigate into the business world when he came of age.

Dada's husband was from Dhuloshori village. She always wanted Sabaa to be married to a native from there. She still knew a few respectable families in Dhuloshori and begins exploring possibilities with relatives and informal matchmakers.

"I want a jewel for my only granddaughter. The best. Nothing less," Dada announces to Dhola. That's when her attention is drawn to Ishmail, the meaning of whose name is *God listens*.

Ishmail is a meritorious student and comes from an educated family, though financially constrained. He just got admission to the medical college. His father remarried after being a widower for some years and started his new family with his own monetary woes. Ishmail aspires to be a doctor and needs financial support to continue with his education. In his desperation, he is ready to marry for money to pursue his goal. Many wealthy families begin offering their daughters in marriage with the promise to bear the costs of his medical education. But his aunt, who has brought him up and is his real guardian, is looking not only for tuition money but also a union with a noble family. Dada decides to give her blessing to Ishmail and agrees to pay all expenses. Dhola approves.

At nineteen, Ishmail lands at a crossroads to choose his destiny. His youthful mind is propelled by noble proletarian passions to serve the communities living in the have-not class of the society—the lost, the forgotten, and the ignored. He becomes an ardent admirer of the ideology of emphatic innovative thinkers, including Karl Marx, the world-renowned revolutionary socialist whose work reflected the ordeals of the oppressed, and Shukanto Bhatyachariya, the famous Bengalee poet who voiced the agony of poverty and the indignity of ever-present injustices. From childhood, Ishmail has been touched by the desperation of the helpless and has vowed to ease their suffering. In the fiery yearnings of his innocent youth, he doesn't care about the costs of personal renunciation in order to endow his life in commitment to the cause of the needy. The medical profession to him seems to be the best way to help others.

He, as such, finally succumbs to the ultimate altar of sacrifice to fulfill his dreams and jumps headlong and blindfolded

into the mercenary bargains offered by Dhola, in total ignorance of what Sabaa has to offer or who she really is. The
negotiations are finalized to Dada's delight. All parties agree
to move forward with marriage talks.

3.

Sabaa and Ishmail aren't expected to meet before the marriage ceremony is complete. The two family elders have come
together a few times over the monetary negotiations and other
logistics associated with the wedding. Sabaa is awestruck at
all the stories she has heard about Ishmail. Her whole village
has praised Ishmail and his intellectual faculties. Boro Ma,
Ishmail's aunt, is a reputable beauty herself. She has been his
emotional anchor, his key caregiver, like a parent even when
his biological mother, her younger sister, Nafisa Bibi, was still
alive. In essence he has always considered and preferred Boro
Ma as his mother. In the wee hours of the nights of malar-
ia-infested fever, sharp spasms of earaches, colds, coughs, and
tummy infections, she was ever present, sitting by his bed,
massaging him with warm mustard oil soaked in garlic cloves
to ease the pain. Her lips would tremble in silent prayers, re-
citing verses of the Quran and making *Mannat*—a vow to
sacrifice an animal in the name of God—for the remission of
her Ishmail's afflictions, his quick recovery. Once Ishmail got
well, she would have a goat slaughtered to protect him from
evil eyes. Every time he opened his eyes in those dreary, feverish nights, Boro Ma's loving face, her kind cold hands on his
scalding forehead, would bring momentary solace. In sickness
and health, pain and joy, he sought her more than his own
mother.

His mother passed away in her early twenties when Ishmail
was in grade seven. They lived in the same household since
the husbands of the two sisters were also biological siblings.
Ishmail fulfilled Boro Ma's hunger for a son as she had only

three daughters, who were older than him and were married off while he was still in school.

~

The beggar women begin to flock to Dhola's house. Finally, after much conniving, some of them get a glimpse of Sabaa's beautiful face. In a flash, it becomes public knowledge that Sabaa is prettier than Boro Ma. Boro Ma beams with pride at the news and distributes sweets for their good luck. It's as good as getting a princess and half of the kingdom in the bargain!

4.

In 1950, on a lovely spring night when the stars are ablaze with silvery fire, Sabaa becomes a bride. Tota wipes her eyes as the imam pronounces, "Amen." Sabaa is a child bride, a child wife to Ishmail, at twelve. Sanu, Phuli, and their mother have come for the wedding. Dhola fetched them in his big boat. Sabaa couldn't think of getting married without them!

Dhola stresses that as Sabaa is a child, the newly married couple should get to know each other gradually and maintain a brother–sister-like platonic relationship till Sabaa is physically ready to be a wife. It's a common custom of the day, such *Aaqd* weddings. So it's officiated with the agreement that the marriage will be finally consummated some years later. No eyebrows are raised; no criticisms flow. However, the newlyweds, Sabaa and Ishmail, don't even get to look at each other. No one thinks it's necessary. They remain strangers in marriage—faces unknown to each other. Not even photographs are exchanged. The household breaks into festive rituals.

~

After all chaos dies down, the women sit under the starlit sky, adorned by soft moonlight. They relax on a large mat on the ground in the inner yard. The maids bring a brass tray of *paan* along with betel nuts, lime, and fragrant *masala* made of cardamom and fennel seeds coated in sugar to add flavor to the betel leaves. Tota takes over. She prepares paan and passes them over to the others. This is the way to unwind after a hectic day. The lamps in the residence huts are dimmed or blown out. Tonight, after all is done, everyone is fatigued with pleasure, filled with fun. The maids sit alongside the edge of the mat and chew paan like the rest.

"*Daman era shaat bhai shaat ghorar showari....* [Groom and his seven brothers are proud riders of seven horses.] *Damaan bala daat rey anar er daana rey....* [Groom is very handsome; his teeth sparkle as the gemlike seeds of pomegranate.]" They sing wedding songs—Phuli, Tota, Sanu, neighbors, and the maids. The songs are dedicated to the groom, full of praise of his grandeur and physical beauty. The melody drifts around the household as the night deepens.

5.

Ishmail goes back to Dhaka the next morning with fresh designs and the fragrance of henna leaves clinging to his palms. Though he tries hard, he can't rub off either the orange hue or the deep, subdued scent of henna. He returns to his classes, burying a feverish desire to catch a glimpse of Sabaa's face. He doesn't even dare to voice his wish. He's a married young man at nineteen, a first-year student at the Dhaka Medical College who wasn't even allowed to meet his bride.

Ishmail is outwardly shy. Though his friends have come to know about his marriage, he's unable to discuss it with them. The emotions are too heavy, new, overwhelmingly intriguing. He is an extremely private soul and prefers to keep personal matters reserved, shut off from public eyes. During the day, in busy times in classes, and in brief polite interactions with classmates, he manages to hide behind an unbreakable, bulletproof shield of discretion. In the evenings, he discourages any conversations with his dorm roommates and aggressively takes refuge behind the pages of his medical books with a fierce devotion.

6.

Ishmail has always been a loner. He was brought up between two women, his mother and aunt, Boro Ma, to whom he was more attached emotionally from childhood. He had little interaction with his own mother while she lived as, from the age of seven, he attended a convent school in the hilly small town of Darjeeling in West Bengal, India, hundreds of miles away from home. His father worked there with a British geological company. There were no good English medium schools in those days in their village or even in Dhaka city. All schools used Bangla as the primary medium of instruction, and the teaching standards were low. His father understood the value of a good education in British-ruled India, especially for a Muslim boy should he want a challenging, more deserving destiny than his forefathers in a world where Hindus were becoming highly educated, were in control, and were preferred by the British Raj.

After school, Ishmail spent most of his time in the bungalow-type dwelling built on top of a low hill, invaded constantly by clouds infiltrating through the open windows, with four other adult males—his father, a distant uncle, and two others from around their village who worked for the same company in Darjeeling. It was common for wives of working men to stay back home while the men shared rented residences in locations of their employment.

Life was easy and carefree but lonely. He didn't have much time to hang out with friends. Back to the house right after school was the unwritten norm. The rules in the house were flexible otherwise. In the evenings, visitors came for a game of chess, carrom, or cards, in which Ishmail sometimes participated if his studying was done. Steaming cups of tea with sweet, nutty cookies were served several turns as the games continued. Some evenings, the guests were invited to stay for dinner, which they mostly accepted. During the shared meals, snippets of harmless jokes and reflections on newly released talkies dominated the discussions while they ate. Sometimes politics would enter into the exchanges. Ishmail was a silent observer and listener. The adults made sure that he got a proper share of the meal and ate well. He loved to eat with them, though he couldn't follow most of their conversations.

The house wasn't too messy. The food wasn't too tasty, as they weren't endowed with exceptional culinary skills, or served on time because the men sometimes cooked late or ran out of requisite ingredients that needed to be fetched immediately. Those times, Ishmail helped by running to the nearest store to pick up a bag of potatoes or onions or any condiments. It was a favorite errand he was too happy to undertake. The ten-minute walk uphill to the tiny kiosk at the edge of a cliff amidst rows and rows of green pine trees, and walking back alone in semidarkness on the narrow, serpentine tarmac road piercing through the heart of the deep forest seemed a real, good adventure.

∽

The color of henna fades from his palms eventually, but a feverish excitement enslaves his soul. Something new stirs deep within him. The unknown face of a girl overpowers his concentration, reduces him to confusion. The intensity of this emotional havoc seizes his inner spirit.

7.

Sabaa's life returns to normal after the *Aaqd*. Dada begins giving her life education, which basically includes codes of good behavior at all times with the spouse and his family. She cites proverbs to highlight her points. Sabaa has to stifle her giggles as she looks at Dada's serious face while receiving her counsel. Sabaa longs to run into the deepest depths of the green, green paddy fields...with outstretched arms in an audacious attempt to touch the ends of the rainbows...but her life has changed too much. She's married! She misses swimming in the new floodwaters and looking for the water lily roots closeted under the shallow waves. The servant girls who are also her best friends are now treating her with open difference and added respect. Suddenly she has acquired yet another status. Sabaa has been their friend all along but at the same time also maintained a balanced position as the daughter of the house. It's a must for girls from noble heritage to learn how to behave with compassion and dignity towards servants.

Sabaa feels a strange, inexplicable unrest gripping her heart. Nothing has changed outwardly, but something has changed, definitely. It's hard to define. A typhoon of feelings has fired her up in strange ways. Sometimes she sits near the bamboo bushes adjacent to the backyard of the house and stares into the water that encircles the homestead. She sees her reflection.... Her face stares back at her. According to Dada, she is blossoming as the water of marriage has touched her, giving her fullness and elegance.

She can't concentrate, is forgetful and irate. She doesn't find interest in the regular life brimming around her. Reading becomes joyless. Somehow the faceless face of Ishmail haunts her, day in, day out. Nights are the worst. She lies awake, motionless in bed, careful not to wake up Dada, with whom she shares the bedroom hut. In her mind she relives every moment of the day of her wedding.

"Pity he won't see you!" "What a waste! You look stunning!" her friends whispered and giggled. Sabaa had tried to stay modest, not to join in, but couldn't stop the smile that broke out on her rosy-pouted lips, ending in charming dimples.

"Oh...that smile is enough to break the poor guy," the whispers taunted, to her amusement.

Sabaa is the youngest among her friends, with zero romantic experience of any kind. She hasn't had the time or opportunity to meet anyone of the male gender. Her emotional connection so far has been with the heroes she reads about in books. They visit her in her daydreams at best. Nights used to be bogged down in innocent deep sleep, but that has changed now.

Sabaa becomes the center of gossip. Women talk about her when they are at the pond and at family gatherings. Their curiosity is titanic and knows no bounds. They talk about Sabaa's captivating appeal, her charm, and Dhola's wealth. They craft a future that awaits her with Ishmail. There is envy, and there is admiration. Sabaa is too unblemished, her life too perfect to be true. Some think she takes after her aunt Sanu, is as flawless in beauty....

Though she tries, she can't remember most of what happened that night. Too many things raided her emotions. She has a vague memory of being led by an older relative to the waiting group of elders who accompanied Ishmail to the ceremony. She had respectfully touched their feet and in a minute was hurriedly brought back to the inner house. Ishmail was somewhere sitting in that room.... She felt his presence, also bashfully tried to catch a sight of him from the corner of her eye. Maybe he tried the same, but the elders blocked all views! Does he think of her as often as she does of him? Sabaa wonders. There's no way to find out. He's too far away in Dhaka. Legally they are married now. She belongs to Ishmail, and in a strange way he is hers!

Without meeting him, without any contact or even knowing him at all, Sabaa falls violently in love with Ishmail!

CHAPTER EIGHT

Becoming a woman

I.

The medical college is closed for a few weeks in summer. Ishmail is invited to spend his first vacation at his newly gained
in-laws' homestead. The celebrations begin. Many kinds of
rice flour and dairy concoctions, sugary dumplings dipped in
thick milk and laced with almond paste and raisins are prepared. Special sweet yogurt in earthen pots famous for its
thick, creamy texture and mouthwatering flavor is ordered
from the village bazaar. Spices are dried under the sun along
with pickles made of green mangoes, olives, and limes. The
hurricane lamps are polished and kerosene jars are stored,
and embroidered bedspreads are washed and aired crisp.
New pillows are made.

Tota takes special precautions so that the fragrant white
rice is husked on time, dried, and kept ready to be cooked.
Goats have been fattened for months to be killed for the occasion. Dhola's head farmhand alerts the fishermen to supply all
large, fresh daily catch throughout the duration of Ishmail's

visit without fail. They will be rewarded with more than the market price. The *jamai* (son-in-law) is coming home. He's the one and only that Dhola will ever have. All preparations must be immaculate.

Sabaa dyes her palms with henna and her feet with the red hue of *alta*. Dhola instructs his oldest son to send a pair of handwoven silk and muslin sharee for Sabaa from Dhaka. Her brother picks saffron- and lavender-colored pieces with elaborate patterns of flowers and leaves on the wide borders embroidered with multihued delicate yarns. Muslim women avoid designs of birds and animals or images of any living thing on their attire. Only images of nonliving objects are acceptable.

Sabaa knows she won't have any private moments with Ishmail, but when he is invited into the inner house to eat, she will be allowed to sit beside Dada, facing him with a hand fan, demure and aloof, pretending to drive away the flies by politely waving the fan. She and Ishmail may steal some glances, some secret smiles to last them till the next vacation. She's excited and curious as this will be her first face-to-face meeting with her husband, but she knows no words are to be exchanged. It's not expected and not permitted.

Ishmail arrives. Along with all the women of the household, Sabaa peeps through the bamboo partitions to finally get a glimpse of his face. He is not handsome but has a serious, dignified, intellectual look. He has been coached at home to be the jamai. A jamai has to follow certain ethics and ground rules—measured laughter, immaculate etiquette, untouchable pride, and fathomless dignity. Ishmail plays it to the hilt and secures the expected endorsements from his father-in-law's household members.

Despite all the codes and rules, Ishmail hopelessly falls under the spell of Dada and genuinely begins to love her and his girl-bride, who sits in the background in a bundle of clothes. Occasionally he catches a peep at her pretty face, slightly moist with sweat in the humid weather, a glance held a fraction of a second longer or a quizzical look from her dark eyes targeted towards him. He is unable to decipher the meaning, but it feels heartwarming. It smells of romance, unknown to him so far. It lures him to have wild dreams at night, and strange, unknown heart-throbbings at daybreak.

He goes back to the medical school with renewed vigor and encouragement, feeling high and low. He is inspired to read romantic literature and writes love poems that remain confined in his notebook. He composes long, lovelorn, passionate letters, never mailed, which pile up and consume much of the empty space of his small tin suitcase painted with lotus flower designs in loud colors. In his unadulterated world, Sabaa reigns.

2.

The brief encounters with Ishmail touch Sabaa's soul. A new kind of emotion enslaves her, eats at her constantly. She is sad and forlorn. Her mind isn't under her control anymore. Her body feels alien. She longs to share this with Dada but doesn't find the right words. She can't open up to her friends either. Tota is too occupied with never-ending chores to notice much. Sabaa longs to talk to her mother, but at the end of the day, Tota is so exhausted, she melts into sleep as soon as all work is finished, right after total surrender to the divine on her prayer mat. The slow months roll on....

One night, Sabaa suddenly wakes up, her body shaking as a warm liquid flows between her thighs. There are bloodstains on the bedspread. Her body freezes with an unknown fear. She calls out for Dada. Dada picks up the lamp. She examines the bedspread and then looks at Sabaa. The glow from the lamp lights up her face. The decades-old wrinkles look deeper, close, within grasp.

"Dada! Look! What's happening? Dada?" Sabaa is terrified. It's so sudden. She did receive some hints about such happenings in passing from her counseling, but no one explained it in detail. It was sort of hush-hush and giggles. She had no idea what it meant at the time, the intensity of the dread it could create.

Dada whispers, "You're a woman now. This blood is the juice of new lives that are yet to come from you. You're ready to bear fruit."

"What fruit, Dada?" Sabaa cries out in panic, unable to understand the riddle.

"Don't be afraid. It happens to all women. It's a blessing and a curse that we learn to live with," Dada adds. "You have to be very careful from now on. How you behave will be reflected on your body. It can bring you the burden of disgrace if you're careless," she says in one breath. "Your body is meant only for your husband. This blood is to produce babies."

Sabaa has too many questions, but all she gets is an explanation embroiled in more riddles and puzzles that confuse her. She doesn't understand Dada's references about dishonor or how babies are produced. In the semidarkness of the kerosene lamp, Dada creates a mystical atmosphere filled with the taint of forbidden secrecy. Sabaa shivers involuntarily at Dada's raspy whispers, the profound darkness that hangs in the corners of the room, impenetrable, impossible.

Dada shows her how to make pads from old clothes and wear as protection to hold the menstrual blood. Staining one's attire is considered scandalous.

"You can never make a pad from a man's clothing. If you do so, his life will be cut short." Sabaa fails to understand how that could be possible, but Dada doesn't care to elaborate further.

"It's gunah [sinful]," Dada cautions. "You have to avoid fish, eggs, and meat for five days. Otherwise, your blood will have a bad odor. You don't want that. Wash your pad and let it dry in a corner, a dark place where no one will notice. No need to display your lojja [shame]. Always keep your lojja close to your bosom," she further advises. Menstruation is a shameful thing, Sabaa learns early in life like all Bengalee girls.

Sabaa gets additional education on menstruation. Everything points towards how this is going to make her life more complicated, lesser, because menstruation is reprehensible and at all costs to be concealed. This doesn't boast of the glory of passage to womanhood but contrarily underplays the potency of bearing children, is vilified with soft condemnation for becoming a full woman. That's how Sabaa interprets it.

3.

Sabaa wakes up to the sound of songs. She has slept late after the startling, traumatic entrance into adulthood. She is told that her in-laws have been informed and they would be coming in the evening. It's their right to know that their son's wife has become a woman and is now ready to protect their lineage as expected when the time is right.

The maids grind rice as they sing. They exchange meaningful glances, stifled mirth as Sabaa steps outside into the yard. She blushes involuntarily as she walks past them, pretending not to notice that she's the main object of their interest. There is a general air of cheerfulness permeating the daylight, settled comfortably on the homestead, the water's edge, and the vast green terrain beyond.

Delicacies made of fragrant white rice flour will be ready for the guests by evening. The pleasant scent of freshly ground rice floats around. Sabaa is baffled by the contradiction of celebrating her bleeding that's meant to be confined, an issue to be shrouded in lojja. Now the whole world will know about her menstruation. What will Ishmail think? Sabaa wants to die in shame.

~◡

As dusk falls, two big boats anchor at the front yard. Voices and hurried footsteps echo around the homestead. Boro Ma, with her three married daughters, their husbands, a large brood of children, and servants, arrives as expected. Women alight with clay pots filled with sweets. Some carry red sharees, loudly proclaiming the color of Sabaa's menstrual blood. Lojja, lojja—she blushes as sweat beads form on her upper lip. Her cheeks are on fire. The maids carry rattan baskets overflowing with betel leaves, hordes of coconuts, ripe mangoes, hefty bunches of bananas, tall cuttings of sugar cane tied with robust ropes, molasses of different kinds, pots spilling puffed rice. They also bring long strands of jute fibers dyed in a dark red hue as a tribute to her bloody mess. Women begin to hum *geet*—popular folk songs—as they enter the house.

Sabaa wears a new sharee and sits on a low stool in the middle of the yard. Female neighbors and relatives come in and join in the singing. The men are housed in the outer yard *bangla ghor* or Dhola's living room. Everyone is expected to participate in the merrymaking and consume the food with guests. Dozens of hurricane lamps light up the inner yard. Some women start dancing. Dada joins them. She loves a good dance and popular geets. The maids hurry, carrying scalding cauldrons of spicy fish and chicken curries. Some continue to stir their cooking, still steaming on the stoves, while others run around the yard doing errands. The house turns into a carnival.

Dhola keeps busy with the male guests. At one point, some of the close male relatives also join the celebration in the inner yard. Dhola stays back in the bungalow. It's not his place to participate in young people's fun, especially as he is the father. The brothers-in-law grab this opportunity to exchange naughty jokes, skirting on sexual hints and language. Sabaa doesn't understand much and keeps her gaze fixed on the floor in perplexed awkwardness as the men and women laugh at shared bawdy interactions. She wants to escape into the safety of her room. But Dada's intention is to introduce her into the real adult world. Though Sabaa is not expected to participate in the talk, she will be learning a lot about the dynamics of mature behavior in which men play an important role.

The relationship between Bengalee women and their brothers-in-law is unique. It's mostly friendly, fun, flirtatious, and frivolous. Sexual allusions dominate the discussions, and jokes are shared; repartee between the parties is common. It's part of keeping the relationship interesting, alive. Sometimes, in some cases, especially when a woman's husband is absent from home for a long time, complications arise as closer intimacy than desired may develop with her brother-in-law. It happens but is strongly disapproved of and denounced harshly.

Tota is busy, sweating in the heat of the earthen stoves, feeding the hungry flames, stirring the cooking, and directing the maids. On this special occasion, Dada relaxes her iron-fisted rules and allows Tota to cook. She is more interested in taking part in the festivities than getting buried in unappealing domesticity.

Tota isn't expected to join the merrymaking, but she is happy to be permitted to be in charge of the mechanics. Her responsibility is to ensure the large regiment of guests and the household are served on time and relinquished to the gluttonous joys arranged for their palates. Later, after all chores are over and her hard sweat has dried, she knows she will get a chance to sit with the women from Ishmail's household and exchange pleasantries over hookah and betel leaf consumption. After all, she is the mother of the girl who is the person of interest in this grand gala.

∽

Sabaa's world of men comprises mainly her father, three brothers—limited interactions with them from time to time—and occasionally some connection with Dhola's and Dada's cousins, men in their sixties and seventies. Dhola, being the only child, has only a handful of blood-tie close relatives. Sabaa didn't get to know her Mejho aunt's boys because they never visited. Dhola isn't fond of them either, and so, apart from briefly meeting them at her grandmother's house only a few times, there has been no contact.

Regular male–female communication isn't so common in the culture, though more so in rural areas. Men and women live side by side in a parallel life and mostly connect only when there are specific needs. Even among siblings, regular exchanges between the two genders become more restricted as they grow up. Tradition and the separation of females from the outside world possibly influence their relationship.

Sabaa, however, thinks that she and Ishmail will be different. She has read so many novels in which men and women express emotions, laugh together, share their inner thoughts, and care about each other. In some strange way, she loves her father. He is a dependable provider as a parent, though she questions his role as a proper husband to her mother. Bubbles of mutiny sometimes erupt in her blood when she sees how Tota is reduced to next to nothing in this household. She doesn't understand her mother's acceptance of the lesser position. Sabaa is also surprised that Tota doesn't reproach Dhola and carries on in her existence with dogged devotion. She has created her own mechanisms to survive, has found her niche, her usefulness in this household. Stubbornly, Tota plunges ahead and silently pursues her own way to protect what she values. Outwardly, she seems docile regarding matters surrounding Sabaa's marriage because she wants the best for her daughter and abides by the circumstances that ensure this goal. This means taking a step back on every occasion to let the smooth flow of events to mature. Accepting Dhola's and his mother's decisions actually led to the fulfillment of her own wishes and kept peace in the house. So she occupies herself with the most mundane tasks.

4.

Sabaa's father has always been proud of Sabaa and her brothers. Though she wasn't sent to school after returning to Harirampur, Dhola supported her intellectual cravings. Often she found her father very human. Since he started doing well financially, Dhola has offered housing to poor male relatives and paid their schooling expenses. These teenage boys reside in the smaller bungalows in the outer yard within the boundaries of the homestead. In addition to studying, sometimes they do grocery shopping, pick fruit from the garden adjacent to the house, lend a hand in the vegetable patch, or occasionally take the boat out to the bigger market in the next village junction to pick up medicine, batteries, or whatever is needed. They also chaperone older women of the house on various occasions. Though distantly related to the family and not total strangers, they are not allowed to chaperone a younger woman if she is alone, as is the norm. A young woman can't be seen in the company of a male not closely related.

Dhola also often acts as a benefactor. At weddings he has been seen footing the bill for food or jewelry for the bride that the poor families can't afford. Critics say that Dhola uses his money to strengthen his hold over people, flexes his wealth to buy loyalty, a power play to establish his control over the village. However, some disagree with this. At the end of the day, people do benefit from his generosity. Hence the gossip and the praise run parallel, trying to define Dhola, sort of an intriguing man, unmistakably baffling.

5.

The new moon comes. Ishmail writes to Dada regularly. Sabaa has to read them out loud to her. Dada never attended school. She can read the Quran but not Bangla. She doesn't understand one word of Arabic, though, like most Bengalees, she is expected to recite the verses without realizing the meaning of the words in totality. She recognizes the Arabic alphabet and has memorized what she's learned. Tota and Sabaa are no different. As is customary, they have an overall understanding of the summary of what the verses preach but not the specific meanings of each Arabic word.

In every letter from Ishmail, the last couple of lines are meant for Sabaa only, love offered in covert disguise. She doesn't read them aloud. Dada is vey intuitive. She follows Sabaa with her eyes as she reads, doesn't miss the signs of the slow blush that creeps onto her cheeks.

"Is that all? Did you read everything? I think there are some more lines—you skipped?" As Sabaa finishes reading, Dada isn't satisfied.

Sabaa keeps her face expressionless and pretends to be offended. "Dada, if you don't trust me, go and get someone else to read it. I'm done with you." She shoves the letter back into Dada's hands.

Dada gives in and cajoles her. Both are aware of the affectionate playfulness—very acceptable in the Bengalee culture between a grandparent and a grandchild. Both know that Sabaa is going to smuggle some personal lines for Ishmail in the response letter from Dada in her beautiful handwriting.

CHAPTER NINE

A *taste of Heaven*
and Earth

I.

In 1947, after the British formally left India, the country was divided into two independent nations—Pakistan and India. Pakistan had two provincial wings, East and West Pakistan, centrally governed. A thousand miles of Indian territory separated the two provinces. Bengal was divided into two parts—East Bengal became East Pakistan, whereas West Bengal remained as a state in India. Culturally, East Pakistan (East Bengal) was much more aligned with West Bengal.

Right after the birth of Pakistan, there was a demand from East Pakistan to declare Bengali or Bangla as one of the state languages of Pakistan, along with Urdu.

On 21 March 1948, Governor General Mohammed Ali Jinnah, in a civic reception in Dhaka, forcefully proclaimed that "Urdu, and only Urdu" would be the official language of Pakistan. He delivered a similar speech attended by students at Curzon Hall of Dhaka University on 24 March. At both events, he was faced with strong protests. Before he left Dhaka on 28

March, on radio he reasserted his Urdu-only policy. The seed of discontent and defiance was sown among the Bengalee nationals, and the struggle for Bengali as an official language grew intense, as it was the mother tongue spoken by the majority of the population.

On 30 January 1952, Bengalee organizations collaborated to form a broad-based All-Party Committee of Action (APCA) with Kazi Golam Mahboob as convener and Maulana Bhashani as its chairman, two prominent political figures, and with two representatives from the Awami League, Students League, Youth League, Khilafate-Rabbani Party, and the Dhaka University State Language Committee of Action.

Throughout the month of February, this committee held protests. On 20 February 1952, the government enforced Section 144 of the Criminal Procedure Code prohibiting processions and meetings in Dhaka City. This order generated agitation among the students. On 21 February, a general strike was observed throughout East Pakistan. At noon, a meeting was held at the campus of Dhaka University. Students decided to defy the official ban, and processions hit the streets to stage a demonstration in front of the Provincial Assembly in Dhaka. Police tried to break up the protesters with tear gas shells. Students fought back by throwing bricks at the police. The riot spread to the nearby campuses of the medical and engineering colleges. At four p.m., police opened fire in front of the medical college hostel, killing five people: Salauddin, Jabbar, Barkat, Rafiquddin and Salam. The first three were students of Dhaka University. Many students and members of the general public were arrested. News of the killing spread like wildfire, and people rushed by the thousands towards the medical college premises.

On 22 February, thousands of men and women gathered at the Dhaka University, Medical College and Engineering College areas to pray for the victims of the police shooting.

After prayers, when more than thirty thousand people started a mourning rally, police began firing at the unarmed procession, killing several people, including a nine-year-old boy and an activist, Sofiur Rahman. Police also fired on the angry mob that burned the offices of a pro-government newspaper. Four people were killed. As the situation worsened, the government authorities called in the military to suppress the protests.

Meanwhile, bowing to pressure, the chief minister of Pakistan, Nurul Amin (a Bengalee native), made a motion recommending to the Constituent Assembly that Bengali should be one of the state languages of Pakistan. The motion was passed unanimously.

On 23 February 1952, a general strike was spontaneously observed despite the resolution by the Provincial Assembly. The police crackdown continued.

On 24 February, the government gave full authority to the police and the military, mostly comprised of West Pakistanis, to control the situation in Dhaka and normalize the city within forty-eight hours. During these forty-eight hours, police arrested almost all the student and political leaders connected with the language movement.

APCA called for a general strike on 25 February to protest the government's actions. The students of the medical college erected a "Shahid Minar" (Martyr's Memorial) overnight at the place where Barkat was shot to commemorate the sacrifices of the students and the general population. (Shahid Minar later became the rallying symbol for the Bengalees.) On the same day, Dhaka University was closed down indefinitely.

Industrial workers in the town of Narayanganj (situated on the outskirts of Dhaka) observed a general strike. In the face of oppressive actions by the government, the movement slowed in momentum in Dhaka, but it spread widely throughout East Pakistan. On 26 February, police destroyed the Shahid Minar monument. A protest followed, and the protesters were severely beaten by the police. As a sign of protest, black flags adorned students' halls and educational institutions, markets, shops, and public places. It became a movement of the people, spearheaded by students with support from local political parties. In the face of police brutality and arrests, unrest and the students' movement continued.

In 1954, the Constituent Assembly resolved to grant official status to the Bengali language. Bengali was adopted as an official language of Pakistan along with Urdu in Article 214 (1) when the first constitution of Pakistan was decreed on 29 February 1956.

Like all Bengalees, the language movement changed the lives of Sabaa, Ishmail, and their families forever.

⟡

Dhola abruptly returns to the house from the village bazaar considerably disturbed. He comes back without finishing his business there.

"There has been shooting in Dhaka near the medical college. Many students died as the military opened fire," he tells the scared women of the house. Dada wants to know the reason. "The West Pakistani government wants Urdu to be the only official language. We have to forget Bangla, learn to speak and write Urdu," Dhola says, exasperated.

"But Bangla is my *buli* [language]." Dada is puzzled. What Dada understands so simply isn't understood by the West Pakistanis. And they pay heavily for their stupidity and arrogance as the years unfold.

"Many students have been arrested. Some died on the streets, some possibly on the way to hospital.... So many rumors! No one knows the truth...." Dhola's voice trails off with worry.

They have to get news of Ishmail and his two older sons, who now study in Dhaka. It would take three to four days

to get a response from a telegram. Chances are that with the
ongoing turmoil, it may not even be delivered. No one knows
whether Ishmail is still in the hostel or has moved out to hide
in some safer location. The military has targeted the university area. They have been attempting to break up the protests
by shooting randomly and killing students. His sons reside in
their old town residence, far away from the scene of distur-
bance. They should be safe.

In the evening, people flock to Dhola's front yard to listen
to his radio. The BBC Bangla service is the choice. New batteries have been bought from the bazaar store. Dhola increases
the volume to the maximum as the women listen from the
other side of the partition in the semidarkness of approaching dusk. There is anxiety among the listeners as almost everyone has family members in Dhaka. BBC reporters explain the
political situation of the country. The language movement history of East Pakistan, aka East Bengal, is unique...

2.

The country is paralyzed with shock and fear. The blood of
the fallen students matches the color of the crimson *krish-
nachura* flowers in bloom all over East Pakistan. People are
horrified as the military of a sovereign nation opened fire on
its own citizens, the students. The jails are filled with protesters. The situation in Dhaka continues to dominate discussions
everywhere. In the village school, the senior students hold a
ceremony in solidarity with the movement. All of East Bengal
roars in resistance to protect her mother tongue.

Sabaa's brothers arrive four days into the trouble. They
hopped into a boat along with fellow villagers because downtown Dhaka is away from the university area and on the edge
of the river with easy access to the water transportation system. They were lying low till the political situation calmed
down to venture out of the house. They tried their best to con-

tact Ishmail but weren't successful in locating him as the city is under constant protests and curfews. The university and medical college areas are the focus of all the trouble and are the target of crackdowns by law enforcement authorities. However, after delaying their journey in the hope of finding Ishmail, they give up and have to leave since the personal safety of young male adults has become an issue. The police and military are arresting them without any justification from anywhere beyond the locations of unrest. They are using fear and brutality as weapons of subjugation.

Dada takes puffs on her hookah without stopping. She smokes heavily when upset. Sabaa's heart is wrenched with anxiety. She can't cry out loud; she can't talk. A heavy rock seems to sit on her chest and stifles her breath. She finds no joy in anything. Ishmail occupies her thoughts. What if he is arrested, is hurt and needs her? What if he has been fatally shot? Maybe she will never see him again. She remembers scenes of the parting of young lovers from sad movies she has watched in theaters in Dhaka, and her eyes sting with muted tears. She feels the whispers going around, the concerned looks. Fear torments her. Suddenly, the familiar world seems distasteful, intolerable.

Finally, Dhola gets information that it's safe to travel to the turbulent city and sends two of his servants to Dhaka. They will look for Ishmail and return with him. The journey will take three days and three nights in the boat. They will be crossing the Padma, which is like a tigress even before the monsoon begins. The waves swell when there is a depression in the Bay of Bengal, the largest bay in the world, which forms the northeastern part of the Indian Ocean. It's bordered mostly by India and Ceylon (Sri Lanka) on the west, East Pakistan/East Bengal on the north, and Burma (Myanmar) and the Indian Nicobar and Andaman Islands on the east. If they are unfortunate, a seasonal cyclone might strike without any notice, with the possibility of capsizing the small boat—Sabaa has learned about all these facts from her geography lesson. If the servants find Ishmail unharmed, he will be here in a week. Sabaa spends her time in prayers along with Dada and Tota.

Tota understands her daughter's suffering, her pain. Sabaa is just a girl, afraid and confused like all others caught in the midst of this turmoil. Sometimes after the evening prayer, she sits with Sabaa silently or oils and combs her long hair. Her mother's soft, gentle touch soothes Sabaa. But Tota can't take away Sabaa's agony entirely.

Sabaa now realizes seriously that her destiny is tied with Ishmail. The marriage is for real, not child's play, though she has stayed with her parents, unlike other married girls who have to live with their husbands' families. Without Ishmail, life seems to have lost its spark, its charm aborted, denied from being fruited. She thinks of the brief stolen glances, the precious moments she had with him at the guarded mealtimes under Dada's watch. The slight quiver of his chin before his face broke into a wide smile, the intellectual look in his eyes behind his glasses, and the casual strands of hair leaping over his eyes keep haunting her. She can't even conjure up his exact features as the times with him were extremely short, fleeting moments of euphoria, shyness. He attracted her in an inexplicable way, but then, he is the only man who belongs to her solely, whom she has been connected with romantically so far.

3.

There are noises and commotion outside as dusk falls. Voices are heard, elated and somber. The entire household is on alert. The servants have returned from Dhaka. Footsteps rush hurriedly towards the outer yard. Maids drop their work and peer through the cracked partitions. Sabaa watches as Ishmail alights from the boat.

"He's alive! He's alive!" Sabaa's heart tries to break out of her rib cage. She is unaware of what she is doing. The world swings, and in a flying race, she is beside him, almost in his arms. She is not ashamed; she is not modest anymore. She knows her destiny is entwined with that of her young husband. No one reprimands her; no one calls her shameless or wanton. Ishmail holds her close, very much moved. Together they fall in step with the others.

Tota, Dada, and the women who have gathered at the commotion wipe away their tears of relief. In this village, people cry over simple matters, are sentimental over trifles that easily touch their artless hearts. Servants watch the drama, motionless.

That night, Dada orders the maids to prepare the bridal chamber for the young couple. The new bungalow hut in the inner yard is opened up. This is kept for special guests and rare occasions. Its entire floor is made of teakwood. The entrance door has fascinating designs of flowers and leaves carved on its wide wooden frame, intricately fitted on glass that forms the background. The large windows are made of hardened timber panes and groan with feeble pain when forced open, unleashing the sweet, soft, musky smell of the smothered stagnancy of closeted air. On windy nights, the unlatched windows catch the southern wind that fills the room with a comfortable coolness. The double bed, covered with a hand-embroidered quilt and overlaid in numerous pillows, is adorned with jasmine petals for the night. In the corner, kerosene and *hazak* lamps are kept dimmed, all prepared. Two decorated hand fans are left on the small bedside table that holds a jug of water and two glasses. Dada doesn't forget to place Rumi's book of poems on the table—a gift to her from Ishmail last summer.

During his earlier visits, Ishmail had occupied Dhola's bangla ghor in the outer yard with its comforts and splendors facing the Padma. On sleepless moonlit nights, he watched how the waves transformed into a mystic glory as the hours advanced. He found inspiration for countless love poems by gazing at the river on such nights, being aware that somewhere in the inner yard was his beautiful wife lying in her bed, separated by a few heartbeats away, guarded by the heartless rules of the house. It's different this time. Now he is permitted to become Sabaa's mate in its full implications.

After bathing, Ishmail eats the delicacies at dinner, prepared in haste but with care. The fish is cooked in lotus stem and thinly sliced red potatoes dipped in hot spice. Two kinds of lentils in thick gravy doused with green chilies, turmeric, and garlic paste, and stir-fried young banana flowers served with soft, fragrant steamed rice create culinary ecstasy after the long day. Dinner is eaten in the light of the hurricane lamps. Right afterward, he is ushered to the outer yard to talk to Dhola in detail and meet the entire village, which has gathered to listen about the happenings in Dhaka. Women stand beside the partition. Many of their men are still stuck in Dhaka. Finally, after more than an hour elapses, Dhola signals that the meeting is over. A servant has already been dispatched to inform Ishmail's family members about his safe return. Everyone hopes that the situation will cool off in the upcoming weeks.

Sabaa waits with a pounding heart for Ishmail, sitting alert on the flower-adorned bed. Her pulse races at breakneck speed as she hears his footsteps, and after a brief pause, she catches the sound of the door being latched from inside. The bed slightly quivers as he sits on one side, very near her. Sabaa feels like fainting, not out of fear but from intoxication by his proximity. It has been a long wait of twenty-four months for this moment. Ishmail speaks in a low whisper and turns her face towards him with his slightly shaking hands. Sabaa looks at him directly from such a close distance, for the first time locking her eyes with his—a kind face with a clumsy set of teeth and intelligent deep-set eyes imprisoned behind thick glasses give him a scholarly look. A high forehead faintly damp with beads of sweat, a broad hairline, and a headful of thick, wavy oiled hair shine in the light of the lamps. In Dada's presence, in the past, her demure looks towards him missed the details. The quick, secretive glances formed incomplete images, which now get fully furbished. For the first time, she sees him as a person, as her husband, invincible, and not someone created in her fantasy.

His rugged body in a medium frame indicates a delicate balance of strength and softness, which she likes. Ishmail had an accident as a boy while playing football. The ball had hit his mouth with brute force. The village doctor somehow managed to save his teeth, which after healing looked forever tumultuous. Sabaa doesn't see his physical shortcomings. She hears his deep voice. She likes his masculine closeness and the warmth. They talk for the first time, but it seems as if they have been conversing their entire lives.

Ishmail tells her about his life in the medical college, his studies, and some jokes that are commonly shared among friends that make her laugh hard, unabashed. He doesn't feel shy with her either. Words form spontaneously on his lips and pour out. He feels confident, and the talking continues till the wee hours of the morning. Ishmail is also a good listener and listens to Sabaa as if his life hangs on every word she utters. No one has ever given so much attention to what she says. There's no awkwardness between them.

The night owl cries in the distance. Sabaa shivers and moves closer to Ishmail. The frogs begin to invade the silence of the night, croaking in the pond and muddy puddles at the edge of the homestead. A trapped firefly circles around the bed, twinkling tiny flecks of light. Time seems to halt.

Ishmail holds Sabaa's hands and pulls her close to him. She hears his heartbeats racing recklessly against hers. He undresses her and loves her gently. That night, Saaba offers her virginity as a gift to her young husband.

CHAPTER TEN

The girl with the
beautiful eyes

I.

On a July morning in 1956, Dada brings out the little bundle
in her arms and hands it over to Ishmail. As the still unset-
tled eyes of the baby girl try to focus on the face of the new
young father, he declares, "I'll call her Dhrubo-Tara, my pole
star...the girl with starry, beautiful eyes." The tiny thing
wriggles and yawns as he holds her carefully. Eventually her
name gets shortened to Tara.

Sabaa lies back on the hard wooden bed and heaves a
sigh of relief. Finally, she can have her freedom. The last few
months of pregnancy, Dada and her mother were totally reg-
ulating and dictating her every move. The discovery that she
was pregnant was scary and joyful at the same time. Dada
instantly took over and restricted her food. She was to eat less
so that the baby stayed small. Low-weight babies were easier to deliver, as was the common belief. Sabaa's young birth
canal was too narrow for a big baby. Ishmail disagreed. Medical science advised a pregnant woman to eat extra for her

own strength and the growth of the fetus. He had sent some vitamins for Sabaa, but Dada seized the bottle and threw it in the pond. She knew how to keep her granddaughter healthy during pregnancy without filling her up with useless modern drugs.

~⁀

During pregnancy, Sabaa wasn't allowed to pick up anything heavy or do hard work. She was forbidden to bathe in the pond. She couldn't keep her long hair loose in the evenings. Dada would braid it to avoid evil eyes. She had to stay inside the house before dusk fell and keep all windows closed at night to keep away the dark forces, whatever they were. The heat and humidity were unbearable. The maids took turns fanning her and washed her soft, small feet in rose water. They massaged her back with fragrant pumpkin oil as she lay on the bed, and they fed her lotus seeds and juicy pieces of watermelon so that her belly remained cool, the growing fetus unperturbed.

In the light of the hurricane lamps, some nights, when less tired, Sabaa read and reread the translated versions of Omar Khayyam or *The Good Earth* by Pearl S. Buck, Ishmail's gift to his wife. Every time he came to spend a holiday, he was sure to bring Bangla translations of books for Sabaa as well as recent publications in the native language. Sabaa started liking Tagore's works, especially the novel *Shesher Kobita (The Last Poem)*. She memorized most of it and recited it to her bewitched female fans whenever they requested and to impress Ishmail.

"Read me lines from Khayyam," Dada would sometimes request.

On his vacations, Ishmail read to Dada. He also explained the meaning of the poems to his earnest listeners—two women from two generations. Dada dimpled as she grasped the romanticism expressed in the love poems. But such occasions were becoming rare because in his free time, Ishmail also had to attend to sick villagers and meet with various respectable people from among Dhola's acquaintances and relatives. Though he had not yet graduated, people expected him to provide remedies for their illnesses. In their minds, he was as good as a doctor because in this village, there were only the natural healers and homeopaths.

Pregnancy had been an ordeal and had transformed Sabaa forever, turned her from a girl into a woman. The snapshots of those months remain etched in her memory, always. During the sixth month of her pregnancy, Dada and Tota had organized *satosha*—a baby shower for Sabaa. The women relatives cooked *phirni*—rice pudding and *pitha*—sugary rice dumplings with dried milk inside as stuffing—as they sang lewd love songs. They dyed Sabaa's feet in red hue, and she was draped in a new red-bordered white sharee as was customary for such an occasion. They decorated her palms with henna, and she wore matching new red glass bangles. Her long hair was knotted in a tight bun and adorned with a garland made of jasmine flowers.

The color red has a special significance in Bengalee culture. It's auspicious and symbolizes both sensuality and purity. It's also a color of celebration and is closely associated with marriage, birth, beauty, and happiness. The bridal sharee hence is always red—the transition to a new life wrapped in a happy shade.

Dada made sure that a number of little boys were invited to the baby shower. After the meal, she played the popular traditional game of guessing the gender of the unborn baby. She arranged sweet rice dumplings in a large china serving dish, placed it on a stool at the opposite end of the yard, and instructed all the children to run and grab the treats as fast as they could. The girls were quicker and outmatched the boys.

They were the majority! Dada counted heads and was upset. It meant a girl for Sabaa. A bad omen. Boys carry the family name. The firstborn should always be a boy, like her Dhola.

In a corner of the inner yard close to the main house, a separate room was built with raw bamboo walls and the floor covered in palm-leaf mats for the birthing. Delivery was considered *napak* — unclean — so it couldn't happen in a residence hut. Sabaa's heart sank. She didn't want to live in that room. It had a low roof, narrow windows, and a solid door. Dada tore the borders of all her sharee and made two pieces out of each. One she was to wear as a sarong and the other to cover her bosom and upper part of her body. Usually, quilts were embroidered with threads taken out of the borders of a sharee for general use. Threads from clothing of a menstruating new mother would make it unclean — that was the common belief. So she was to be kept away from all household stuff to keep them *paak*, or sacred, while she menstruated after birthing.

Sabaa was transferred to the bamboo house in the last month of her pregnancy and not allowed to go out of her room except for toilet needs or for bathing. Tota and Dada took turns sleeping in the same room on a separate mat beside her. One elderly maid slept just outside the door in case they needed anything at any time during the night. It was an imposed seclusion that all women were bound to go through during the last months of pregnancy. The maids brought cool water from the pond and bathed her as she sat on a wooden stool behind the bamboo house, too heavy and tired to move.

"I don't like it! Why are you keeping me prisoner? Dada! Are you listening?" Sabaa revolted, screamed, and threw her sandals and the pillows against the wall. No one reprimanded her. Her insolent behavior was ignored. Young pregnant girls are allowed some tantrums. After all, Sabaa was about to bring so much joy into the household!

When the pain finally came, she gasped for breath. Tota

held onto her hands as she screamed and scratched, tossed, and turned. The merciless pain of childbirth tore through her young body.

"Ma, ma! I'm dying!...The pain is killing me!...Am I dying?..." Sabaa cried again and again for hours. Out of sheer fatigue, she would doze off for a few seconds, but with the return of the piercing pain, she resumed the screams.

She could feel her mother's warm teardrops on her forehead, bathing her face. Is this what Tota went through when she was born? When her three brothers were born? Her brain reeled over and over again with the same question while she agonized under the crumbling pain. What was keeping the little life so long inside her? Driving her through this excruciating, throbbing torture? Sabaa almost burst her lungs screaming so hard. Nothing was soothing; nothing could ease her suffering.

After a long, long time, when her body was limp with exhaustion and damp with sweat, her tears dry and her back exploding, there was a sudden, startling, unstoppable motion within her. An agonizing, tearing pain shot through every inch of her body. And then came the heavenly relief. Just like that, in an instant, everything was over. The suffering stopped. The world became sane again. In the background, she could hear an infant crying. She turned onto the other side of the mat and fell asleep.

2.

"She's a lioness." Ishmail's voice brings Sabaa back to the present. He places the baby beside her. His eyes seek hers momentarily. Instantly, Dada pushes him out.

"No! No! It's not good to be too close to the new mother. You must observe forty days' separation from her. No seeing her before that, no touching."

Dada knows no mercy, firmly loyal to the inflexible rituals and norms. Sabaa's husband is forbidden to come near her till she stops menstruating, which possibly will continue for over a month. Dada is a sentinel keeping guard on Sabaa. Her three brothers watch their tiny niece through the window. They are also denied access to the room. They would have liked a nephew, though. They feel helpless about a baby girl, not sure what their roles are with her, but they nevertheless welcome her, love to watch her while she sleeps or wakes up hungry. It's a new experience, a strange bond.

Sabaa's kid brother, Elias, is much more intrigued by the new life in this house. He spends most of his free time sitting outside the window, waiting for his niece to wake up so that he can get a peek at her face. Sabaa's heart goes out to him. Whenever Dada is out of the room, she holds the sleeping baby close to the window. He carefully touches Tara's soft, tiny cheeks through the bamboo bars in the window.

3.

Sabaa has been continuously hungry since giving birth. The first few days are crucial for the new mother. So Sabaa is given small portions of steaming rice, turmeric crushed with mint leaves and herbs, and ground *kali-jeera*, or black cumin seeds mixed with mustard oil and garlic paste. According to Dada, these foods will help Sabaa to heal faster and have to be eaten at every meal. Her insides are raw and torn. Fish and meat would give her diarrhea, which can be fatal. Gluttony would bring disaster. But an ever-consuming hunger haunts Sabaa day and night. She feels she could now devour the entire world; nothing can satisfy her ravenous appetite.

In the evenings, the maids rub warm garlic-soaked mustard oil on her belly so that it heals faster. The sweaty heat dampens her clothes and the bed. Dada has wrapped a piece of old cloth tightly around her midriff to flatten her abdomen. It squeezes her so much that it's hard to breathe at times. Dada also places a clay stove at the doorstep. Only selected people are allowed to enter. Whoever enters has to first warm their hands and feet on the stove, kept alive twenty-four hours with glowing charcoals. That's the custom. It keeps the evil away and possibly germs. As extra protection from paranormal forces, Dada also puts a key under Tara's pillow, which is made of a piece of old cloth rolled up in a circular shape so that her head turns out round. It's a common belief that the dark forces keep away from objects made of iron chips. Bengalees love to weave a fog of fantasy around a new infant and the environment.

Dhola isn't too excited by the arrival of a granddaughter. A grandson would have fit his dignity better. It punched a hole in his immaculate macho pride, but he makes sure that the baby receives all the necessary attention and care. A birth is always an occasion of joy in this village.

Once in a while, Dada shows some extra kindness and bends her restrictions. Just before the approaching dusk, she opens a window one last time for the day to allow Sabaa's brothers and Ishmail to have a look at Tara. As her proud father and three uncles watch her, fascinated, she smiles in her sleep. Tara, the girl with beautiful eyes, begins the first days of her life in Dhola's homestead.

4.

Tara was delivered by Hawa's mother. That's the name by which their traditional midwife is known. *Hawa* in Bangla means *wind*. Her hands in action are light and efficient. She delivered Sabaa and all her brothers in this house. Hawa's mother has an aura about her. She's a frail-looking woman in a small frame with abundant stamina. She's not literate, is hard of hearing, and is toothless but chews crushed betel leaves and nuts all day long. She may have lost her teeth to bad oral hygiene rather than to aging. When she speaks, the inside of her red mouth, stained by betel leaves, catches the eye. So far, not a single baby has died under her birthing care. Hence, she is in great demand in the village. Had Sabaa produced a boy, her delivery fees and tips would have hit the ceiling. Dhola is a generous man and pays well when it comes to providing services to his family. This time she will get a new sharee, a cotton shawl, and one hundred *rupees*. Like most village women, she doesn't wear any petticoat or blouse underneath her sharee in this hot, humid climate and will forgo charging that to Dhola. She may be able to coax him out of some additional money, though, to buy a pair of shocking-pink-colored plastic flip-flops that she has seen in the stores in the bazaar.

Hawa's mother knows that Tota will hand over something extra from her own savings later. With the help of trusted maids, Tota sometimes sneaks rice from the granary and sells it among needy village women at lower prices than the market and on credit or partial payments. There is always a constant demand for it, and Tota's secret trade, built on mutual benefits, flourishes without Dada's knowledge as all transactions are done when she is out on her rounds to her neighbors' houses for a good gossip over a cup of tea, quite often after the midday meal.

Sabaa hates the food given to her so far. She quarrels with Dada after a few meals. It's time to say goodbye to herbs and the distasteful diet. Tota tries to calm her down. She promises to cook her favorite dishes when her raw insides are healed properly and able to handle spicy food. Even dysentery is fatal to a woman who has just given birth. So under such circumstances, food has to be eaten with caution. Sabaa drools at the thought of steaming rice and ilish fish curry cooked in coconut cream with water lily stems in a bed of hot green chilies.

However, on the sixth day after delivering Tara, Dada serves Sabaa a feast, as is the custom, because it's her *choi-sha-tura*—a ritual, a celebration of a new mother's strength and achievement, and to appreciate her fertility. In total, seven dishes are served—the head of a large fish, leaky gourd curry, small fish cooked with finely chopped onions and potatoes, three kinds of mashed vegetables, and *mishiti doi*, or sweet yogurt. The watery curries are believed to help in producing milk.

Tota has labored all morning to prepare the festive food for her daughter, who has given her the best gift, the tiny Tara!

CHAPTER ELEVEN

Sequence of events

I.

A lot happened in the meanwhile. Bhaijaan left Kolkata in support of the "Quit India" movement in early 1947 and started Gandhi's handloom weaving endeavor in the village, as his legacy. A large group of young men joined Bhaijaan and became passionate about patriotism, preaching nonviolence as the key principle to peace, prosperity, and healing. The sound of handlooms in the outer yard was constant company to the women of the house. The months rolled on, and finally Pakistan and India got their independence from the British. But Bhaijaan continued the weaving initiative with the youth.

Then Bhaijaan fell ill. Before any diagnosis could be made, he died after suffering from five days of a high fever. It was a big blow. Tears fell; laments were stifled. His mother, Phuli, and Sanu were stunned by the tragedy, and he was laid to rest under the big jackfruit tree near the bamboo bushes at the end of the outer yard. When she got the news, Tota travelled by boat for a day in the rough monsoon raging with savage waves on the Padma River. The boatmen had to stop and take cover several times to be safe from thunderstorms, which delayed the journey. The funeral was over by the time Tota reached there as the dead body could not be preserved in the hot, humid climate for too long. Her heartbroken wails could be heard from the riverbank, from the dirt road to the mosque.

The relatives watched Tota with empathy as she threw herself over the newly dug grave of her brother. They understood her anguish and cried with her. Sister Mejho was unable to come. Her pain was enclosed in the words she wrote in a letter addressed to her mother and the sisters. Sanu's tears were boundless as she read it out loud. It was a sad time.

The house became emptier without the familiar sound of the handlooms and Bhaijaan's presence. There was a routine, some purpose in life when he was around. The three women's lives lost their rhythm, which moved around the only man of the house. He was dedicated to his work, married to his passion to influence young minds. His heart didn't get a chance to know the love of a sweetheart; he moved on before he could give time to any romantic thoughts.

Mother was beyond repair in grief. After her son's death, she spoke very little, moved about less, slept poorly, and her desire to live was lessened. One morning, Sanu found her body cold and motionless. She had died in her sleep.

Tota attended her mother's funeral with Dhola and their children. The burial took place at dusk after the evening prayer.

2.

The house is more desolate, more silent these days. The two women, Phuli and Sanu, guard their home, the graves under the jackfruit trees, and their family valuables hidden safely in the rooftop storage. They sell the cows and lease out the farmlands to landless peasants, agreeing in exchange to a bargain of half of the crop yield.

Sanu is still young, still beautiful after all that has happened, but broken and subdued. Her life is wasted on dreary tasks. She busies herself with mindless chores — makes pickles with Phuli, cleans, cooks, and reads sometimes, which breaks the monotony of emptiness. Yusuf Ali never tried to contact her. In the eyes of the law, she is considered divorced as her husband hasn't paid for her upkeep for years. Three years with no contact between couples is enough to annul a Muslim marriage. Sometimes remorse catches up. She questions her decision to abandon her husband. As long nights lie cushioned under incessant rains — the raindrops hit the tin roofs and create steady melodies out of intrinsic, familiar sounds — Sanu stays awake trying to count each drop. The purposelessness of her lost life and the yearning to cling to it bewilder her some nights. In her relationship with Yusuf Ali, there was only profound sorrow and plenty of solitude. So she had no choice but to give it up at one point for sure. Very slowly, sleep comes, and she drifts to a land of fathomless darkness. Life seems vacant, barren of any promise of hope....

Sabaa's visits are rare these days as she is being groomed to become a good wife to Ishmail and a responsible mother to Tara. Tota is also very busy with all the changes but is committed to continuing with the summertime visits. Sanu lives for those times.

3.

Mia lives in Dhaka, the big city. It takes more than a day in a motorboat to reach there. He visits once a year with his family. He has one daughter and one son. Sanu has met his wife, Ruby, and their children. They don't visit Sanu. Ruby is plain, down to earth, and seems to be a sensible person. Sanu doesn't feel any animosity towards her. She longs to hear Mia's voice carrying those love songs over the waves.... She doesn't dare talk to Mia, though sometimes her heart is heavy and longs to seek out his eyes, especially on lonesome, lazy afternoons or starry, maddening evenings when the breeze is high and whistles against the tin roofs. A kind of restlessness seizes her at those times. A tender valve in her heart remains infected forever with thoughts of Mia buried deep, beyond any trace of the outer universe that she shares with others. She tries not to think of him. The magical moments are all gone, all wasted. She lives in a world of isolation, tied to emptiness, and he is a married man with a family.

Mia doesn't sing anymore. The lyrics are lost. The enchanting voice has abruptly halted in midair.

4.

Tota's life is whole with her children, son-in-law, and now a granddaughter. She hopes to see more grandkids, especially grandsons, in the future and dreams of a life with caring daughters-in-law when her own sons marry. She wants to be a better mother to them—unlike Dada, a bitter lesson learned from her own life. Tota's contentment is scrawled in thin lines of subdued heartaches for sure. But all along she has controlled negative emotions, weighing them against what was within her grasp, and she has tried to be satisfied. She calls it destiny.

Years ago, when she stepped into the threshold of Dhola's house, she decided to make a life for herself in a passionless marriage. She accepted her fate and stubbornly refused to look back. Sanu, however, still remains a concern. With everyone gone, Sanu is the sole guardian of their home once alive with countless voices and thousands of footsteps. Phuli, Mother, and Bhaijaan now lie peacefully in their graves. The house rouses daily in bare quietness. Mejho doesn't visit anymore. Now it's only Sanu and Tota, the sisters in entangled destinies of untold pathos.

~⤳

As the children grew older, Dada tried to take full control of them. In her own way, she is quite fond of her grandchildren, though she hates their mother. Sabaa is the apple of her eye, and Dada means the world to Sabaa. No one asked Tota when Sabaa's marriage was arranged. She was hurt but also happy at the same time to get someone like Ishmail for her daughter.

Tota senses Ishmail is rational and caring, unlike Dhola, who is uncultured and ill tempered. Sometimes in his fury, he hurls things at her and publicly criticizes her, calls her brainless. If he thinks the rice is too soft or too hard or the curry too spicy or oily, he simply throws the food right into the yard as a spectacle for all.

Some days he just goes out of the house hungry and angry. This happens often. It pains Tota when her husband wrecks every attempt she makes to please him. However, at one point, much, much later in life, she just doesn't care anymore and is not the least bothered by the insults he tosses at her.

Dhola isn't the least bothered by Tota's pain and enjoys her humiliation. Tota copes with his angry episodes with calm composure to hide the constant indignities, steadying herself to face the maids especially. When the children were younger, at such times they usually took cover behind haystacks at the back of the homestead, Sabaa crying silently all the while. Tota knew from the start that her life with Dhola would never improve. Her children gradually filled her emptiness.

Tota hasn't been able to make any friends because her mother-in-law disapproves of idle gossip and chatting. However, Tota is allowed to visit her family but only once a year for a month. Her waking hours are spread out between mend-ing, cleaning, and other manual work. Her only break is caring for her fruit garden at the back of the house just near the tube well water pump used for drinking water by the household and the entire village. Dhola allows female villagers to collect water from his house, and they have free access to it anytime.

Tota grows papaya, mango, grapefruit, jackfruit, rosewood, and custard apples. She also has a patch of okra, pumpkin, and eggplant, always rich in yields. String beans and bitter gourd creepers give lush produce. Flowers are trivial, worthless to her. Life with Dhola forced her to concentrate on sensible things — flowers are fancy. She knows she isn't beautiful enough ever to catch Dhola's eye with flowers in her hair.

~⌒

Tota proudly maintains her garden. Her children love the juicy fruits. It gives her immense satisfaction to share the harvest with family and neighbors. Eventually, Tota gets more and more into prayer as the years progress — her only solace, her sole refuge.

Dhola has nothing to do with her anymore. She's now totally useless to him. Her body is sagging; very faint lines and wrinkles have begun to appear on her face and neck. The protruding veins are louder under the skin on her hands, very visible. Her mind is also weary...

And she continues to plunge ahead, wrapping her sensitivities in a stoic shroud.... Tota creates a world of her very own — *sacred, secluded, and secret.*

CHAPTER TWELVE

The white of lilies, the pink of lilies...

I.

Ishmail finally completes his residency. He has been searching for employment from the first day of his residency with
the hope of finding something suitable on completion. It's not
easy. The economy in East Bengal/East Pakistan hasn't been
prospering as expected. Many fresh medical graduates like
Ishmail face the hiccoughs of a transition to the job market.
His family is still taken care of by Dhola. It hurts Ishmail's
pride to be so much in debt to Dhola for everything in his life.
This financial handicap challenges his manhood, makes him
feel inadequate to Sabaa.

Dhola initially had agreed to set up a drug store for Ishmail
and further sponsor the cost of establishing his medical practice. But now he doesn't show much eagerness. He voices that
Ishmail's father should contribute as well, a parental responsibility that should be borne by a real man. It's an impractical
justification as Ishmail's father hasn't been involved at all in
the finances of his son's life. Dhola accepted all responsibility
from the day Ishmail married Sabaa.

Ishmail's father, Isaq, has aged. He remarried after Ishmail's mother passed away when Ishmail was in school. His income is just enough to support his second family with two minor children. In addition, he also supports the upkeep of Ishmail's only younger sister, who has been living with a close relative since their mother passed away. Ishmail was never welcomed by his stepmother, so he didn't get to know his half siblings. He's disappointed in Dhola, who is fully aware of Isaq's situation. Secretly, Ishmail had expected more from Dhola, had relied on him to find his footing in the world right after he attained his medical degree.

It annoys Ishmail immensely to be of poor means. He finds it distasteful to even converse on the subject of finances with his arrogant father-in-law. A thorn of resentment at Dhola's heartlessness keeps pricking at his heart, at the unjust way Dhola treats his only daughter by depriving her of monetary assistance that he so easily has the power to bestow. Rightfully, Sabaa has claims on her father's property. Ishmail tries to reason that he doesn't want Dhola's money, but at the same time a deep, repulsive, stale bitterness wells up inside him, unspoken, as dark as the clouds in a thunderous sky before a heavy spell of showers.

Ishmail continues the job search for months, discusses it with relatives, weighs possible options, and finally decides to set up his own home with his young family in Manikganj—a tiny, godforsaken subtownship where the cost of living is comparatively inexpensive and also offers the promise of growth of his medical practice with tenacity, gradually.

Harirampur village soaks in the morning drizzle, forcing the waters of nearby rivers and ponds to break their banks. Everything is set up for the journey. The boat is anchored in the backyard. Sabaa at last is about to leave her parents' home and begin her own life with Ishmail and their two girls. In the light rain, one of Dhola's cousins carries little Zahra covered in a towel, saving her from the sharpness of the stubborn spray. Zahra is only thirty days old, Sabaa's second daughter, another disappointment to Dhola.

Zahra is going to her new home with the others, totally unaware of the importance of this transition. Tara is slightly over a year old. She is fascinated by the big boat and the exuberant realization of being allowed to sit in it. Now and then she touches the water with her tiny fingers, looks with amazement as the water breaks into ripples followed by ripples. The young maid, accompanying them as her nanny, holds her tightly to prevent her from falling overboard.

Tota's heart wrings with aching at the upcoming separation from Sabaa and the grandchildren. She is going to miss the toddler Tara and the tiny Zahra. It will be tough on Sabaa, but luckily Ishmail's Boro Ma will join them for the first three months to assist. Years of conditioning at Dhola's household has taught Tota self-control. She knows a woman's place is in her husband's home, to bring up her own family. Letting go of her only daughter is heartbreaking, but that's the tradition. This is the first time the realization dawns on her that Sabaa is married, that she belongs elsewhere.

Tota buries herself in endless tasks for Sabaa's upcoming departure, the only refuge she knows to process her sadness. She makes sure that the tiffin carrier is filled with plenty of steaming rice and the spicy ilish fish curry cooked with plantain and hot green chilies, freshly plucked from the garden, that Sabaa loves so much. Tota also packs a large bowl of *phirni*—rice pudding cooked with dense milk and a generous addition of homemade molasses. This is Ishmail's favorite dessert.

Tota loves Ishmail for the person he is but more so as he is taking a part of herself away to a new home many rivers away. She hasn't had many chances to share private moments with Sabaa, though she has kept an alert eye to be there for her soundlessly, in the background, as her daughter was claimed by many others and numerous tasks all these past years. Her love for Sabaa has been expressed in meeting her physical needs—food, the comforts of daily life, care in sickness. It has been a robust, uncrafty kind of love that doesn't overcrowd the bond with meaningless sentiment and verbose expressions. Tota secretly wipes her tears and continues with the last-minute preparations with a heavy heart.

Time to say goodbye. Sabaa hugs her mother and finds it heart-wrenching to let go of her. The parting takes on a different meaning this time. She's going away finally; she doesn't belong anymore to her parents' house. She has to be forced away from Tota's bosom as the tears keep falling.... Sabaa climbs inside the roofed boat. Dhola already blessed his daughter with dignity when she touched his feet prior to the last-minute parting scene. Dada makes Sabaa promise to write once a month as they part. The three figures stand in unison as Sabaa's boat pulls away from the bank and sails into the buoyant waters—three different people from three different universes, all weaved into the intricate fabric of Sabaa's world.

Tears blind Sabaa as the landscape becomes hazier and slowly gets swallowed by the horizon. She keeps looking back at the lonely figure of Tota still standing against the fierce waves, alone on the riverbank, lips moving in silent prayer while the others withdraw.

2.

Manikganj is a small town. The narrow-slivered roads, very much like blood vessels stemming from a diseased heart are bumpy, broken in places, a combination of tarmac and muddy strips. The main road snakes through the bamboo bushes and deep, thick, overgrown stretches of abandoned fruit gardens, embracing ill-constructed culverts and patches of green, endless paddy fields somewhat losing their way into the infused blue of the sky. Once in a while, an old jalopy belonging to the municipality sputters along the road on some aimless errand. Tiny, rickety horse-drawn carts pass by, carrying visitors or the hospital staff, wedding guests, attendees of social events or celebrations. The very sick are also transported in the carts as the dilapidated, dismal sole town hospital, orphaned by lack of financial sponsorship, has no ambulances, modern equipment, or life-saving drugs. Oppressed by absolute impoverishment and the misery of apathy, the hospital itself seems to be in need of resuscitation to take its next breath.

~⌒

Ishmail rents a tiny bungalow for his family within walking distance of the hospital, which also houses the only pharmacy in town. The bungalow is situated on one corner of the municipality, strewn with overgrown plants, outlined by a thick boundary of bamboo bushes on two sides, a vast, empty, green open field in the front and a large water-lily-infested pond at the back, trailed by an endless deserted swamp of grassy land. Morning glory and soft ivy greens crawl from the bank of the pond towards the bungalow where Tara loves to track down strange snails, shouting out her little lungs in mirth every time she spots one. It has a picturesque appeal that initially attracted Ishmail to lease it at a nominal monthly rent. He never regrets his decision the entire time he lives there. It's the only home he has known in a long, long time until life claims him to the farthest end of the country in search of a more challenging, secure future several years later.

It's a different life in Manikganj town. Ishmail gains the respect of the residents. He establishes his practice out of the small decrepit, worn-out pharmacy. It is housed in one corner of the main hospital building, painted in faded dull yellow, lavishly buried in moss. The skeletal bricks keep staring bluntly from the depths of a long-lost cement coating. Incessant rains craft constant puddles to fill up the numerous unsuspecting holes around the grassy entrance. The destitute, desperate villagers from the outskirts clamber all the way to this hopeless, stale hospital with hopes of medical miracles, to get yet another shot at life, caught between fear and optimism. Word of mouth spreads fast, and they come by the dozens to the young doctor when no longer able to resist long-neglected ailments. Ishmail builds his chances of a flourishing practice by banking on the needs of these sick and weary, with a sincere desire to save them.

Ishmail also makes house calls to see patients in their own communities, cycling miles away. The land is spoiled by the stubborn green of the crop fields interwoven with countless ditches preying on the sanity of travelers. He cycles alongside sudden ponds bursting with unnamed fish, brushed with limitless lavender of hyacinth blossoms, and housing colonies of mosquito larvae. Daytime is somewhat manageable with skillful maneuvering, but on moonless nights without streetlamps, the precarious road becomes a formidable reality as he plods on his long, lonely journey towards home.

People from every tiny shack flock around him as they hear the bells of his approaching cycle, a parting gift from Dhola to ease his practice rounds. Some are sick; others come to observe the marvel. Ishmail is kind to all and inquires after their general health. Usually someone brings a wooden stool for him to sit under the shade of trees while another one fans him. They try to spoil him with a king's reception. It's suffocatingly hot with drenching humidity throughout the year in this land of lush vegetation. The dogs stand nearby to be chased away with pebbles if they veer too close. They don't bark but watch in loyal silence, wagging their tails as a mark of participation.

Ishmail listens to all complaints, examines every patient, and calmly repeats his advice. From his bag he also distributes medicine that he gets as free samples at the pharmacy. Sometimes he pays for the drugs from his own pocket to save lives, which creates a hole in his meager earnings. He knows what it's like to be poor. Women are mostly shy when he checks their blood pressure. Children and adults watch awestruck at his equipment. They stand in a circle and stare, mesmerized, seduced by his academic proficiency, and end up placing their indefatigable loyalty in Ishmail's *daktari*, his medical skills.

The townspeople begin to like and trust him. They admire his courage to settle down in this township, which holds few attractions, comforts, and pleasures, rather than Dhaka city with its greater charms—markets, libraries, parks, and talkies in the theatres. Career development is much more ensured there if one gets the right footing. Very few would take such a risk to build a life in this backward place. They feel ever grateful to Ishmail for choosing them over Dhaka's seductive powers, irresistible to the young, new generation.

As the months roll on, Ishmail's popularity rises steadily. He is repeatedly invited to social meetings and receives requests to speak at prestigious events. He is greatly valued, his sincerity appreciated at every moment. But the money from the practice is barely enough to keep body and soul afloat. The people are the poorest of the poor, and cash is scarce. Though destitute, his patients are not heartless. They bring fruits, vegetables, grains, eggs, fish, and whatever they are able to as payoff in kind. Occasionally, chickens are also included. They carry the goodies in cane baskets to his doorstep. Sabaa and the girls are amused and accept the offerings with much graciousness. The girls love to keep the chickens as pets. It's not easy to get them to agree to kill the birds for meals. Sabaa thinks it's cruel not to inform her daughters before a chicken ends up on the table. The discussions are mostly to cajole them.

"Tara, the hen has come to our house to be your friend, to play, to be your food buddy. You like to eat chicken legs, right?" Sabaa tries to explain to her stubborn daughter.

"No," Tara says. Always defiant...

"No," Zahra imitates her older sister. She's a year old now and learning new words every day.

"Chicken meat will make your aba cycle faster. He has to help sick people. He loves meat. You love him, yes? What do you say, Zahra?"

The negotiations continue, and simple bribes are promised to finally get Tara to agree to the martyrdom of the unfortunate chicken, a rare treat for Ishmail and the girls. Zahra doesn't realize the connection between the live and cooked chickens. Her attention span is claimed shortly by a crawling snail or a butterfly circling near them.

3.

They eat ilish fish cooked in mustard paste with lotus stems and rice at countless meals, as these are the cheapest options that they can afford. Each time the food tastes equally novel, unique, impeccable in its appeal. The savory charm of ilish curry dominates the culinary exoticism by miraculously boosting the appetite at every contact with the tongue. None of them are stressed over the limited choices or unhappy at the simplicity that life offers. They are not even bored. Eating as a family is much more endearing, they learn, as each day passes.

Sabaa tries hard to improve her cooking skills. One time it

gets too spicy, next time less salty or too salty, or overcooked. Ishmail has no objections. He laughs away his young wife's complaints and laments about her small failures in trying to do bigger good.

"Listen, Sabaa, I'm giving you nine out of ten for curry today." His voice is a mixture of equal levels of honesty and playfulness as he grades Sabaa's skills almost every time she wants feedback. He never goes below eight, though. She passes with honors marks every time.

"It's your wife you're rating. You're too generous," Sabaa normally remarks.

"I'm more for filling my tummy.... I recognize the hard, honest intention behind the cooking." Ishmail sounds truthful. Sabaa accepts it as the justification sounds fair enough.

She is relieved that her efforts are duly valued. She remembers Dhola's violent outbursts to her mother's cooking, sometimes on no genuine grounds, subject to his mood of that particular moment. She is glad that Ishmail is so unlike Dhola. Ishmail is a person who not only fathered her children but also someone who is a true companion, someone she loves, respects, and depends on, shares her life with—always can talk to without any reason or necessity arising out of responsibilities or rationality.

It's a hard life for Sabaa, living in constant want, but she doesn't like to ask her father for money. She is a very proud young woman. She takes pride in Ishmail's education, smartness, and honorable profession. In her letters to Dada, she speaks of how good life is—about the girls growing up and Ishmail's importance in this small town. She can't talk about her poverty. She has started to patch the clothes that she wears at home. Ishmail's shoes have also gone through one round of patching. The only thing that bothers Sabaa is when she can't give two *ana* (cents) to the maid to buy one orange every day for Tara. The little girl loves oranges.

In her letters to Dada, she tries to create a happy snapshot of her life in this distant township. Her recent note reads:

My dear respected Dada,

I hope all's well back at home. Is your knee ache better? Don't forget to get a daily oil massage to ease the pain. I think you need to smoke less hookah. Doctor shahib tells me smoking can hurt.

The girls are growing fast. Zahra speaks some words now. I'm teaching them at home—not only the alphabet and numbers but also songs and dancing. I'm also knitting a sweater for you. It's deep green in color—like the grass in our compound. It'll be finished before winter. Not easy to get wool here, so our subregistrar's wife got some from Dhaka. She's a nice woman and teaches me many things. Reminds me of Maa.

When will you visit me here? It's a very small town—full of mosquitos but also the home of many wildflowers and incredible water lilies. Our house is buried deep in plants and trees. I don't know all the names. I like it here, Dada.

It rains most of the time, so I embroider a lot as I have nowhere to go. We also get fresh ilish fish caught from the Padma and are never too tired of eating it. Doctor shahib promises to take us all to see you as soon as he has time. He's very busy but remembers you. He sends his salaam. Please keep us in your prayers. I miss all of you, Dada.

Ever yours, your loving granddaughter,
Sabaa

P.S. My salaam to Baba and Maa. I'll write to them separately. How're the mangoes coming this year? Is the kali cow with calf?

Ishmail likes to circle the town and the villages on his bicycle as he makes his regular rounds, ringing the bell for the cows to move from the road or to alert naughty kids who love to suddenly emerge at the bends. He rings it more vigorously as he enters the home grounds. Zahra is a toddler now. She runs to the door whenever she hears her father. He rings for her. She won't allow anyone to go near him as he steps indoors. He belongs to her for the first few minutes till her attention is engaged elsewhere. Tara is self-willed and surprisingly independent for her age. If she is busy in her play world, she ignores Ishmail till she is ready for him.

Ishmail has taken over full responsibility of his family and is able to extend more caring since they came to live in Manikganj. The girls adore him. In the privacy of his own home, he now has plenty of time to talk to Sabaa, laugh with her, voice his innermost thoughts without the prying eyes of Dhola's cramped household. He doesn't have to share her with a houseful of people anymore. Both feel liberated from the chains of past cluttered lives stacked with people and endless occurrences.

On many idle noons splashed by unceasing rains, they listen to Tagore's songs on the old secondhand radio bought from the local flea market. With leisure, he explores her flawless, lush body with passion, unfolding to the couple, as newest discoveries while the girls are lost in naps under the care of the maid.

"I like the way you laugh, Sabaa...unbridled, so uncommon." Ishmail admires Sabaa's spontaneity.

"Dada always scolded me for being loud. When I turned eleven, she stopped me from bathing in the river, but I often tricked her. Maa knew but never gave me away."

"You're a wicked, wicked girl! Caught red-handed!" Ishmail strokes her neck as he speaks. Sabaa melts in laughter.

"I'm glad you're who you are.... I didn't get to meet you when our marriage was arranged. Look what I got! A princess."

"A poor princess. Why wouldn't Baba give you any money? He's all for his sons. All his talk about his love for me is lip service, not honest, I know. I knew that," Sabaa blurts out, her emotions showing.

"We'll do what we can. I want to give you and our girls a respectable home. Let's not talk about your father. He's a very tortured, calculating man." Ishmail measures each word before speaking. Sabaa takes a few minutes to think in silence, then shrugs.

"OK, no more about my father. Doctor shahib, I love you, our simple life, my patched clothes, and your many-times-mended shoes." She laughs again, uninhibited, and rests her head on his shoulder.

4.

Sabaa has never witnessed her mother and father ever discussing anything at all—no important family issues or any mundane matters, gossip, stressful emotional revelations. They never held discussions about their children. They never even sat down side by side on any occasion or at any idle moments. They are two individual spirited souls bound by a relationship that was crafted by others as essential but possibly more so as a necessary evil to fulfill the norms. Dhola continuously unleashes unbounded anger towards Tota, as far as Sabaa can remember. The rest of the time he is indifferent and doesn't attempt to establish any contact with his wife. That's all there is in her parents' joint existence under the same roof.

With Ishmail, the relationship, their connection is so different that the novelty overwhelms Sabaa. The revelation of touching another soul is astonishing, beyond any expectation. Their daily conversations are infused with unspoken camaraderie, shocking spontaneity, the ecstasy of intimacy in the sanctity of a home they share. The joy of simply listening and speaking in unabashed fearlessness at any time on anything, even if it borders on naïveté and ignorance, completes Sabaa as a woman, as a person in her new home.

On some long, airless evenings, the discussions are artless, ordinary but novel, with hints of interest in their simplicity...

"Cooking ilish fish with plantain again for dinner. No surprises. OK, Doctor shahib?" Saba asks casually.

"I love it with mustard much more," Ishmail comments while taking time to get ready for patients, whose rare visits have been wounding the purse.

"Mustard is approved." An instant agreement—no conflict, no resistance.

At other times, the conversation flows on an entirely different track. When Ishmail is in a romantic mood and wants his young wife to grasp the creative urgency bubbling in his brain that needs to burst out, he wants her right beside him.

"Sabaa, why so much time in the kitchen? We can survive on rice and omelets. Come to me. I want to read Tagore's love poems to you."

Sabaa loves these exhilarating moments. She drops everything and listens spellbound as the voice of her husband introduces her to an unreal dream world where the sky is bluer than azure, the water dances in sparkles of sapphire, the boatmen whistle while spreading the sails to touch the silvery clouds.

Ishmail's deep voice penetrates the subdued, pervasive stillness outside—the solitary bamboo bushes, the tall trees motionless on a windless day, the clouds dark and heavy on a weary journey to the earth's arms:

The morning sea of silence broke into ripples of bird songs;
and the flowers were all merry by the roadside;
and the wealth of gold was scattered through the rift
of the clouds....

We sang no glad songs nor played;…
we spoke not a word nor smiled;
we lingered not on the way.
(Translation)

She especially loves to listen to the poem entitled "Lost Time":

Thou hast taken every moment of my life in thine
own hands.
Hidden in the heart of things thou art nourishing seeds
into sprouts,
buds into blossoms, and ripening flowers into fruitfulness.
I was tired and sleeping on my idle bed
and imagined all work had ceased.
In the morning I woke up
and found my garden full with wonders of flowers.
(Translation)

5.

During the monsoon, the pond overflows its banks and merges with the swamp and paddy fields. The entire landscape is taken over by the gushing surge of new waters, swelling up in the rains, enriched by faraway rivers breaking their banks under the pressure of tons of foaming water. Waves after waves are created and spill over, consuming the vast flatlands. The houses are on higher ground and remain above the water's reach. Boats belonging to neighbors are anchored around their compound, tied to the hanging roots of trees.

Most nights it rains. Some nights the moon shows up, pushing away the blanket of bitter clouds to the farthest end of the sky, out of focus, and tosses its magical rays towards the earth. The landscape is bathed in pale enchanting brilliance.

On some such nights while the girls are asleep, Ishmail takes Sabaa out on a boat because she loves night outings, and this is all he can afford. He rows slowly, careful not to disrupt the emboldened silence that drops in right after the sun sets. The small waves break against the hull and fade into the lily pads—pink, white, and yellow, fascinating in their uniqueness, dancing with the waves, brushing up against the rough wooden body of the boat as it heads towards the paddy fields, drowned under the mild waves. The scent of lilies and wild blossoms sits heavy over the water under the dimly lighted sky and in the slow, soft, stirring breeze.

Ishmail stops rowing and sits beside Sabaa. Together they witness the engrossing beauty of the mounting night around them. His heartbeat voicelessly sings with Sabaa's. He holds her close in the embrace of his arms. His mind composes incessant verses of love, of urgent longing for oneness with the creator of so much splendors in nothings—trifles, as in great things of excellence.

The immaculate white of jasmine flowers in Sabaa's hair stands out in the faint moonlight. Ishmail can separate the distinct scent of jasmine from the mixed burden of the wild incense drifting in the air. He is thankful once again for this simple life, for the love he has found. They sit transfixed, soaking in the soft stillness of the night, awestruck at the magnificence of nature spread out effortlessly, the magical water lily jungle swaying with the rising current.

6

Ishmail regularly consults Sabaa on domestic matters, regarding neighbors, colleagues, and life in general. He wants to hear her views. Her opinion is valuable to him, which Sabaa finds immensely gratifying. It adds to the sense of importance she has in her own family, so unfamiliar in Dhola's household. Ishmail brings stories of his outside life to their home threshold.

"You know what happened today? Our police chief sent

a request. He wants me to write a false medical report showing the injured attackers are actually victims. Can you believe that?" Sabaa waits to hear more. "These hoodlums got hurt as villagers fought back, defending themselves, their land. Police are in the pocket of the powerful. It's so wrong! So corrupt!" Ishmail's voice erupts in anger as he shakes off dirt from his shoes after a long, rainy day of making house calls. He had to bike almost fifteen miles back and forth in the sudden summer drizzle.

This is another example of immoral local politics, another incident of fighting over land, which is a common occurrence around this township. The powerful community leaders try to influence the legal system, to bend it to their side. Police and government officials favor them as it's unwise to pick a fight with people in power. It's very hard to stay neutral while living in a close community in a tiny township! Ishmail finds this unethical and tries to push back.

"You've to be careful. You can't afford to make enemies. Maybe meet with Shikdar shahib separately and explain? As a doctor you can't lie. You've got to be neutral to serve everyone, no?" Sabaa advises.

Shikdar is the muscled community leader. He supports power plays in land disputes and forceful occupation of lands by his loyalists but at the same time aspires to be recognized as a benefactor. He is approachable and, strangely enough, can be rational on occasions.

"I think you're right. But such dishonesty! I'll try. Not easy, I know," Ishmail agrees.

Though Ishmail tries to avoid it, he becomes somewhat involved in this highly partisan issue. Land is life in Bengal. The fight for land ownership begins at home with one's own kin and community and against the raging rivers as priceless fertile crop fields are lost to erosion, leaving a man destitute and powerless to combat his destiny.

One night during the wee hours, Ishmail and Sabaa are awakened by the noise of stones thrown at their house. Some stones hit the tin roof, making eerie, hollow sounds; some shatter the front windows. Sabaa is bewildered and trembles in fear. The girls thankfully sleep undisturbed. After a few minutes of rowdiness, the stoning stops.

"This is a tactic to scare us. I'll meet with the police chief in the morning. I'll inform Halim shahib as well. He's a politician. People listen to him," Ishmail assures Sabaa. He is quite shaken at this attempt to intimidate him.

Saaba fears the ruthlessness involved in the fight for land. There have been soft warnings to caution Ishmail in the past. He goes out for house calls at night. She worries for his safety. Lawlessness over land is common, and police sometimes turn a blind eye to save their own skin. And of course, partiality rules. Sabaa is aware of village politics and how lies and manipulated gossip may be used to hurt Ishmail because he can't be broken, pulled into the influential corrupt circles. In this town of "nothing ever happens," things begin to brew. However, Ishmail's consultations with town elites and the unanimous acceptance of the invaluable services he has been providing to the communities override the calculated risks of his defiance. Hence, gradually, the threats slide down, but the interested parties decide to keep an eye on Ishmail without causing any direct harm to him and his family.

In the evenings, when he comes home early or has no patients to attend to, which happens frequently during the months of thunder when the clouds hold the rains, Ishmail relaxes in Sabaa's company. Their whispers and soft ripples of laughter spill over into the firefly-plagued backyard, the almost impenetrable silence overpowered by the mating calls of the monsoon frogs exploding their lungs out to subdue the sounds of the rain. Sabaa is happy and content, basking in the adoration of her caring genius husband, much esteemed by his patients and influential residents of this township.

The two girls are growing fine. They learn with Sabaa as they are too young to attend the school far away from home. The main road sometimes is almost impassable during the monsoon, which continues for months.

In her leisure hours, Sabaa teaches dancing to the girls. "*Holud Gadar phul, ranga Polash phul…einey dey haat theke, einey dey madh theke, noiley radhbo na badhbo na chool….* [Bring me marigolds, bring me flame flowers…from the market, from the fields, or I won't braid my hair, I won't cook….]" Their happy chorus rings through the house.

Tara is skillful, and her steps match Sabaa's. Zahra is clumsy and falls on her back as she tries to maneuver the moves. Amidst unrestrained laugher, the mother and daughters keep practicing. When they perfect it, they will dance for their father.

The days drag on undisturbed. The months fly by fast. Sabaa's life seems fulfilled and flourishes into a contentment she never thought was possible. Every morning and till she lies limp in sleep at night, her lungs inhale the scent of bliss to their fill. Ishmail's love completes her.

7.

For the past few months, Ishmail has been spending a longer time at the pharmacy where he practices and is constantly late for dinner. The girls are drowsy right after they eat and asleep when he finally returns home. Sabaa waits for him every night, awake, alone in the dim light steadily emanating from the low-voltage electric bulb, guarding their dinner as it grows cold with every futile minute sneaking away.

The long, dark nights gather over the bungalow, the tiny waves of the pond, the encroaching lush green carpet of the unkempt ground as Sabaa keeps waiting. Overpowering heat hisses from the swamp, from the greens. Ishmail claims work keeps him busy as the number of patients has increased gradually because of his hard work with the community. In addition, there have been seasonal outbreaks of ailments as well. They moved to Manikganj over a year ago. Ishmail's time is gradually claimed by his patients and others. These days he miserly spends his time playing with the girls or reading to Sabaa—a regular ritual, their in-house entertainment after the day's work. Sabaa recognizes the demands of her husband's work, but she misses their moments together. She longs for him, especially when the lazy drizzle beats against the roof, the rows of trees, the stooping bamboo bushes outside, and falls in steady monotony on the morning glory patches, now a fierce dark green growth in the monsoon. Sabaa gets forlorn. She feels a chill rising in her heart.

~

Because of his literary talent, Ishmail is frequently invited to recite poems at cultural events and sometimes is one of the chief speakers at social functions. His captivating eloquence inspires people. They like to listen to him. Sabaa feels proud of her husband's achievements. In this tiny place, word of mouth travels fast, and while sitting at home, she gets some of the gossip from her maid, local visitors, or the elderly vendor who sells fruit, carrying the goods in a large basket on his head. They talk about Ishmail, the young, committed doctor. They are full of praises—about his kindness and accomplishments. A sharp sweetness nestles in her heart and keeps growing as the world speaks in her husband's favor.

To match Ishmail's intellect, Sabaa continues to educate herself at home. She is determined to widen her knowledge. This also fills her empty hours somewhat and protects her from whining inwardly about Ishmail's absence. Her lack of formal education bothers her, makes her feel small. She would have liked to have finished schooling and attain a degree, become accomplished and the most deserving consort to her educated husband. A handful of women whom she came across in Dhaka, mostly Hindu, have degrees. The only way open to her in the past was to voraciously read—the works of eminent Bengalee literary talents, translations from other cultures, magazines published in Kolkata, especially when Ishmail was toiling at the medical college.

Doubts about her own worthiness begin to gnaw at Sabaa's confidence. Sometimes she wonders whether Ishmail finds her intellectually inadequate. In her universe with him, she is mostly an ardent listener while he is the speaker who brings in new and exciting tales of the outside world. He tells her stories about the political situation in the country, global scientific facts, and trends—even narratives related to his medical profession. He is well versed and articulates ideas with a natural flair. He also listens attentively to whatever Sabaa has to share, greatly values her perspective. But her proficiency is limited, theoretical, learned from whatever she finds to read. Her contribution to their conversations is marred as she inhabits a shell, a narrow world prescribed by the restraints of the household.

She wants to surprise him, so she toils hard to strengthen her intellectual capacity. It's impossible and humiliating as well to try to go back to regular schooling at her age, being a married woman and a mother of two. She wishes if somehow she could sit for the matriculation exam, her self-esteem would be boosted. She could study with a private tutor to prepare for it. But she is too shy to bring this up with Ishmail. Then there's the issue of finances. However, she enlists Ishmail's assistance in borrowing books from his learned friends. Money is scarce to spend on new books.

This sense of inferiority haunts her, follows as her shadow

throughout her life. Years later, Sabaa laments the missed opportunity of not attempting to pass the formal exams during her endless free time in Manikganj, to continue in college further and put an end to her feeling of intellectual inadequacy forever....

~◦

So far, Sabaa has visited her parents only once with Ishmail and the girls, primarily to be with ailing Dada. Dhola at that time bought their return tickets and also gave an envelope with some money to Ishmail. So the financial damage due to the family's travel was recovered, and the rest of the cash was used in household expenses.

After that, her three brothers and parents visited her to check on her new home and new life. Dada couldn't make it as her arthritic condition escalated. Dhola liked the house and the grounds. Along with some wooden chairs and necessary household items for Sabaa from the local market, he also bought two goats for his granddaughters, to be later slaughtered or sold for profit. Their visit made an additional dent in the young couple's finances. But at their departure, Tota secretly gave Sabaa a bundle of cash from savings from her covert trade, which has expanded with time. Tota now owns several cows leased out to poor peasants. In return, she collects a 50 percent share of all profits from the sale of milk and calves while the cows remain her property. Dhola eventually had found out about her business but decided not to intervene, to Tota's relief.

Sabaa regularly writes to Dada and Tota. Dhola in his letter has stated clearly that it would be best for them to try to concentrate more on their new environment before further visits can be made, on both sides. It's hard but it's essential. He has sent servants several times bearing presents for them—lavish supplies of freshly husked rice, fruits, vegetables, mustard oil, homemade pickles, molasses, and clay pots stuffed with sugary delights. He also sends money regularly as gifts for his granddaughters, which comes in handy at times of need, which are constant.

Boro Ma has visited a couple of times, which meant additional expenses. Ishmail had to borrow money to pay for her transportation costs. She likes Sabaa and teaches her recipes that Ishmail is fond of, tells her stories of his childhood. She adores her granddaughters and doesn't ever utter a word about desiring a grandson, unlike so many other older relatives and friends who have an indirect assumption that Sabaa is at fault for not producing a boy. Ishmail is very thankful for this. She is not like a typical mother-in-law to Sabaa—critical, hard to please, redundantly judgmental. Her friendship and love are the best gifts she extends to her young daughter-in-law.

Since she got married, Sabaa has found it easy to communicate with Boro Ma, speak with her anytime without reserve. The older woman's infectious affection has created a rare rapport between these two women, binding them forever till the day she passes away a decade later.

8.

Life continues. After completing regular chores, reading, and embroidery, Sabaa has too many vacant moments to kill. Her life is cloistered in this tiny bungalow clasped in everlasting green and the unbroken rain, day in and day out. As she waits to hear Ishmail's footsteps in the evening after all is done and the girls are in bed, old thoughts return.

A strange twinge of suspicion snaking its way inside her heart keeps gnawing—creates senseless anxieties. Though she can't pinpoint any instances of genuine faults that Ishmail is guilty of, her qualms come and go, casting uneasy shadows. She faces a real dilemma in her inexperience, in her current friendless, solitary world. She has no one to communicate with who would understand the turmoil that pierces her serenity, which is gaining momentum as time passes. She can't discuss this with Ishmail. She trusts her husband but feels sidelined when he gets engrossed in his world of work, the daily demands he navigates through. *Am I still appealing to Ishmail?* She can't banish this thought. *Does he love me as he used to? Value my loyalty? What if I'm not good enough for him anymore?* The questions keep popping up.

In the packed presence of many—his patients, friends, neighbors—Sabaa has to fight for Ishmail's attention. An eye-opening discovery that sits thickly on her mood—becomes oppressive. The feeling of incompetence over her scanty exposure to the outside universe keeps haunting her. Humans are creating history, engaging in breakthroughs in science and politics, protecting and reshaping the world by ending wars, defining peace talks, attempting to conquer vast indomitable space, and discovering the amazing underworld that lies in the folds of the fathomless depths of oceans... and she doesn't belong to any of it. That troubles her. In this dreary place, fatigue in intimacy is easy; life is bound to turn into odorless boredom sooner rather than later. It's a fatalistic challenge for her that she fears.

To tame her thoughts, she religiously bends over the narrow lines printed in the tiny font of the daily newspaper crammed with potential revelations, more in forceful exasperation than curiosity. But on some lonesome nights, a tsunami of tears drowns her—often.

CHAPTER THIRTEEN

...Made with heartaches
and heartburns

I.

Ishmail has a new disciple, who shows a keen interest to learn. It's Nurse Kamala, a recent addition to the hospital. He likes to help her and spend time explaining and teaching professional matters whenever there's an opportunity. They discuss patients, drugs, and how to improve the overall health situation of this town with its existing obstacles. Kamala is an ardent pupil and eager to learn medical facts from the zealous young doctor. She genuinely wants to improve her caregiving counsel and follows his guidance.

It's refreshing for Ishmail to be able to discuss professional problems with someone who understands and has a keen hunger to learn from him. In a place like this hellhole of inadequacy and unlimited limitations, it's uplifting, an engaging diversion.

Kamala raises eyebrows with her rather hearty laughter when she is genuinely amused and the habit of humming popular songs in a subdued tone even at work. She expresses her opinions flat out and up front, which is a novelty in a rather conventional place like this but is also perceived as too bold, not a praiseworthy quality in a woman. She isn't afraid of challenges or to engage in uncomfortable conversations. She's quite a revolution in this tiny township.

In every way their equal, sharing this workspace, Kamala is kind of an enigma, an ebullient presence who can't be ignored and the only woman coworker in this all-male workplace besides a couple of temporarily employed cleaning maids, who shy away into the background, overburdened by their dreary tasks.

Men like Kamala's independence and can talk to her without inhibitions, more so because she is a nurse. She seems to belong to the men's world but is the wrong gender. Anyway, they don't mind too much. Her presence is paradoxically welcoming and cautioning at the same time. Women, of course reserve special views about her.

Kamala lives in the hospital quarters alone, without a maid. So interested neighbors and idle gossipers have sparse information to use as weapons to either blemish or honor her. She makes home visits to check on the sick on the rural outskirts in a horse cart, the only mode of transport on the nearly impassable broken roads. People live in constant poverty. Most are farmers or small-time earners. They normally feel intimidated in the alien hospital environment where their street-smartness comes to no use. They don't understand the language of medical sophistication or the strange unfamiliarity with which they are dealt. They live in a desolate world of little means, narrow optimism, small joys, shackled in malnutrition, burdened by disease and suffering. They like to be comforted by someone whose hands they can hold, with whom the price of shame of their ignorance is low—and they can ask the most naïve questions without any dread. Kamala fits the bill. She's greeted by the young and the old with open arms—into their simple hearts. She's perceived as one of them.

While out on one of her rounds, she comes to the house to be introduced to Sabaa, as common courtesy demands. Kamala is in her midtwenties, slightly older than Sabaa. The first things Sabaa notices about this plump, youthful woman are her penetrating, deep-set, well -proportioned, slightly slanting, innocent jet-black eyes and a disarming, pleasant smile in a deeply tanned face. They talk about the town, its people, the regular challenges. Sabaa likes Kamala's easy, carefree nature. The girls are shy at first but soon start to snuggle close to her. Their curiosity and Kamala's smiles win them over. She has a way with them. She can't stay too long and takes leave after tea.

"Do visit again," Sabaa says genuinely. "You have admirers here." She points to the girls, who stand in the doorway beside her to see Kamala off.

In a few months, Kamala earns the approval of the residents—the rural poor and the elites. At the same time, she becomes an object of intrigue in this tiny township, which is not accustomed to having a single, independent young woman in their midst, who has traveled from a distant town to work all alone. This isn't common, not natural, has no precedence.

2.

As the months pass, Ishmail's admiration for Kamala deepens. The work they do together as colleagues is comforting. It also gives him an opportunity to discuss his philosophies with her. She listens ardently but is ready to differ if her views oppose his, unlike the women he comes across who usually agree in veneration or because of lack of knowledge on the topics he brings up. Kamala's banter is refreshing, her ideas thought provoking. She is well read but also a shy, secret writer. Her enthusiasm for literary pursuits is contagious. Ishmail can't escape it. He convinces her to share her covertly treasured verses and offers to honestly appraise her poems and creative efforts. After work hours, the two zealous, inspired souls find ways to connect on the pretext of revolutionizing the literary world with their boundless, innovative energy.

Ishmail fishes out his own writings from an old heap and reads them out to Kamala, who listens spellbound. Not so often, she has some words of suggestion or edits some verses and phrases that he finds clever, fascinating. He starts to write again with new vigor, endless love poems, of feelings that remained unawakened, unstirred, buried in the humdrum of the regular existence of recent years.

The earnings from patient-chasing hasn't improved much, so Ishmail explores possibilities for a stable income as the family expenses keep multiplying. The girls are growing. Sabaa deserves a better life, a total divorce from these endless meager, penny-counting wants. She has never uttered any resentment or lamented the daily miseries that arise out of unceasing insufficient funds.

A distant uncle advises Ishmail to check out the prospect of joining the army. There's a great need for doctors. The salary and benefits are lucrative and the risks are low. The duty stations would be in West Pakistan initially, but the family is allowed to join after the first two years of mandatory training. It would be good cultural exposure for the girls and a relief to Sabaa, as well as a smart career move for him. A new world would open up, and it might not be a bad thing altogether. Ishmail toys with the idea and strongly considers it.

3.

Sabaa becomes more fetching as full-blown womanhood hits. Her grace and dignity, warmth, and calm presence of mind amaze people around her. However restless she is inwardly, she camouflages it craftily, keeps it locked inside, pushed away from the public eye. She's aware of the challenge she faces with Ishmail's growing intimacy with Kamala, but she's also confident that this is a phase that her young husband is going through in this desolate place, peddling in poverty and extreme hardship, laden with pessimism in whatever he wants to pursue.

Things begin to change.... Ishmail comes home late almost daily and sometimes reads his books or works on patient profiles and professional documents after dinner. They talk less and less...a haze forms around them, grows thicker and thicker—losing its way in the intrinsic web of an awkward façade.

The girls are rarely awake, and on some occasions if they are still up, they play with their father for scant minutes before falling asleep. During those times, life is back on a normal track. Sabaa tries to grasp onto this flimsy normalcy with eager attention.

"I'm so tired...so much work to do these days." Ishmail comes to bed sighing and complaining most nights. It's an indirect signal to Sabaa that he wants to fall asleep immediately. Sabaa has been waiting to catch up with him—talk and laugh to release the distress of the loneliness of the day. She is almost at a loss for words but has the common sense to push aside her disappointment.

"Go to sleep. You need rest. It may rain tomorrow. Patients won't turn up, so there'll be less pressure at work." Sabaa's voice hangs mellow in the air. He doesn't respond. She is resigned and lies down on her side of the bed. Ishmail snores faintly after a few minutes.

She stays awake beside her sleeping husband in a dilemma. It's a new challenge; she doesn't know how to handle it. Her thoughts keep running in different directions, speedy, reckless sometimes, breeding unnecessary doubts. Ishmail and Kamala have been spotted often—on their strolls to the riverbank in the evenings after work, possibly to discuss literature or philosophical views. Sabaa doesn't know the details. But she wants to believe that their interactions are innocent.

Some days they pass by the house and take Tara and Zahra with them. Sabaa politely declines their offer to accompany them, on each instance citing lame, vague excuses. The girls are used as a shield, probably, the presence of a third entity to rule out any indecorum, trying to justify the guiltlessness of their collegial relationship. Her mind grows tired...

~

The gossip gradually crosses over. People start talking about Kamala's association with Ishmail, dissect their time spent together, laughing and talking, even though they are in a professional environment mostly. It's beneath Sabaa to speak to Ishmail about this. No matter what she does, Kamala's presence feels like an itch on a mole in an unreachable spot on her back, irksome and uncomfortable.

Friendship, no matter how innocent, between a man and a woman isn't a commonplace thing in Bengalee culture. People don't trust such alliances. It's unusual and easily noticeable. Stronger gossip starts to form. In this tiny township, other people's business is considered one's own.

"Our doctor shahib is very busy these days. The other night I saw him in the pharmacy late," the police chief's wife sympathetically informed Sabaa, taking a bite on the cream biscuit and sipping the sugary tea to her liking when she came to visit last week. She paused and was intent on chewing the cookie as Sabaa remained silent. "Nurse Kamala is a very smart woman. She works well with our doctor. Nice...very nice," she murmured with a smile as an afterthought.

She is a kindhearted middle-aged woman, much liked by people, though there are rumors about her husband's corruption and unethical dealings by misusing his position. Sabaa

smiled back and nodded her head in agreement as she didn't
know how else to react.

"Doctor shahib has found a true student. He teaches Nurse
Kamala daktari matters, he told me," Sabaa uttered. "She is a
good person. I like talking to her. Our girls love her. I'm glad
to have her as our friend," she added, further trying to infuse
extra enthusiasm into her voice.

"Nice...very nice," the police chief's wife slowly repeated,
slightly at a loss for words.

This woman came all the way to visit Sabaa not to enjoy
her tea and cookies, for sure. She had a purpose—to alert
Sabaa about the ongoing chatter in a gentle way. Sabaa felt
she needed to stand up to protect her husband's reputation,
to save her marriage from unnecessary smearing by nosy,
silly talks. From that day on, she decided, no matter what,
she would defend her husband and her family. It gave her the
courage to thwart the cruel gossip hurled at her, Ishmail, and
Kamala for possibly no reason other than jealousy.

4.

Finally, Sabaa decides to join Ishmail and Kamala on their
evening walks. The girls are delighted and follow in their
wobbly gaits. But after a few times, she feels totally out of
place and forgotten, caught in the web of animated repartee
that the other two become engrossed in. So Sabaa opts out
of any further walking ventures. She is, however, extra careful not to hurt Ishmail's feelings when she politely refuses his
request. She even manages to smile at Kamala while saying a
gentle "no."

Walking is a pretense for togetherness...veiled under a
guise of propriety, Sabaa's mind utters voicelessly. Though she
tries hard, she is unable to totally brush off the uneasy ache
growing stealthily in her heart.

She doesn't understand whom they want to fool. Sometimes she feels like confronting them—by just being between

them to create an awkward situation for her own inward satisfaction. But she soon abandons this stupid idea. She can't find any joy in such wasteful, meaningless childishness. She feels dejected; emptiness consumes her.

In the late morning, as Sabaa is struggling to turn her uncertainties into constructive reflections, trying hard to keep away the poisoned thoughts twisting the insides of her rocky poise, her maid comes back from the pond with the washed laundry, laughing.

"*Buji*, do you know what I heard at the pond today?"

Sabaa pretends she is busy with needlework and looks up with an air of disinterest. This young girl is full of foolhardy tales, which she usually brings back when she frequents the pond on the pretext of some errand or another.

"You know what happened? Yesterday our Nurse Kamala went to see a patient at Gabtoli village. On her way back, she stopped the horse cart to rescue a pigeon from the roadside. It belonged to someone named Pinto," the maid panted. She has now fully captivated Sabaa's attention.

"So what? There are too many pigeons around." Sabaa tries to sound casual.

"Listen, listen, Buji, she refused to give it back! It was Pinto's pet. They quarreled, said bad words, really bad ones, Buji. Ruby's aunt told me so." She stops smiling to emphasize the graveness of the incident she's about to narrate further. Her upper lip quivers slightly, and she arches her eyebrows.

"Pinto and his friends blocked the horse cart and wouldn't let her go. No! Sat there on the road for one hour. Finally, our doctor shahib...he was coming back that way, spotted Nurse Kamala. He rescued her!" Now, this is really news.

Ishmail appeared as Kamala's knight in shining armor on the dot, at the right time! And he hadn't mentioned anything to Sabaa. There must have been a spectacle. Villagers must have gathered at the scene. Idle tongues are by now wagging all across the township and the outlying villages.

"Now, no more of this. You stop right there, spreading this nonsense all over the place. Always busy with silliness...no concern about pending work," Sabaa cautions the maid, irritated.

"It's not me, Buji. The whole town is talking. Why are you scolding me?" The girl moves away, crestfallen, somewhat shocked at being blamed.

That night, Sabaa waits to hear from Ishmail, but he says nothing. So she finally inquires. "What happened to Kamala? Some problem with a pigeon, I heard?"

"Who brings such tales to you? People have too much time to kill. Lazy good-for-nothing idiots! Nasty place! Gossip, gossip, empty brains! All nothing!" Ishmail is very annoyed and concentrates on getting ready for bed. Sabaa is taken aback at this forceful outburst.

She climbs into her side of the bed in silence and closes her eyes. Ishmail moves around the room, adjusts the window curtains, the light of the kerosene lamp that burns throughout the night in one corner in case the girls are scared and run in—all pretext to delay. Finally, he lies down beside her. As a stranger. No intimacy. No talk. An awkward, unknown silence invades the shadows and the stillness in the room. Faint sounds of crickets and nameless insects crawl inside with the vast darkness of the night.

Life continues, oddly uninterrupted. The light of day breaks at each dawn and each evening fades into the gradual depths of darkness. No major surprises or catastrophes unsettle the normalcy in this township and the villages on the outskirts.

5.

After the outburst, Ishmail seems to mellow. He asks Sabaa whether he can invite Kamala to their home. Sabaa agrees. So some evenings, Kamala leaves the hospital early to visit her and stays for tea. Sabaa encourages Kamala's visits to swat hard at wagging tongues. People see Kamala entering the house and Sabaa's warm reception. They see her as a welcome friend of the family. Some accept it as genuine. Some think they are being deliberately fooled. Some skeptics, seasoned in their wisdom, look beneath this cover for clues to unravel the deception.

Kamala plays with the girls, makes dolls, paper boats, and kites. The three of them run across the open ground under the trees, trying to fly their kites. Sometimes they play hide-and-seek. Their mirth and footsteps fill the house with warmth. For some reason, Sabaa feels awkward about joining them. On the pretext of work, she stays indoors. Kamala also reads stories to the girls to calm them down after the running becomes too intense. They adore her. At such moments, Sabaa doesn't dislike her either. The silent war with this woman has been created in her own mind, possibly. At the sight of Kamala with her daughters, it vanishes....

Ishmail returns from the pharmacy later than usual when dusk sets in. He pushes his bicycle as he enters the yard. Kamala's eyes seem to dance as she looks at Ishmail, Sabaa thinks. From the outside, there's nothing to accuse them of. They talk like any others who are acquaintances or friends. Is it Kamala being a woman that is creating such uneasiness? If only Sabaa knew the answers. Her mind stumbles and meanders over every instance she has found Kamala conversing with her husband, every time she has looked at him.

Sabaa hangs around with them in the initial moments, but as their dialogues become intense on the topics they discuss, she excuses herself to finish some work or to make tea. This becomes a routine. It's better this way. She is relieved to have them under her roof where she can keep an eye on them, become the face of decorum that they need, though deep down she tries to push away the suspicion that these visits are the result of a pact made by Kamala and her husband. Sabaa feels lowly, is disgusted at herself for even thinking this way.

At other times, Kamala follows her to the kitchen to help her prepare tea. Ishmail trails her in an instant. The discussion flows afresh as he stands near the kitchen doorway, Kamala seated inside while Sabaa listens in baffled silence, watches — powerless. But she is in a way glad that she doesn't have to spend time alone in Kamala's close proximity. She doesn't yet know how to handle that challenge, and generally when they are alone, their conversations are reduced to fragmented casual small talk about the girls or cooking, overburdened with meaningless polite observations. It doesn't flow with spontaneity as Kamala's world is so different, so unfamiliar to Sabaa.

Kamala should never be in her intimate household as she has no business violating Sabaa's territory, sacredly preserved only for her own family. But this woman is here because they share only one common interest — Ishmail. No matter how hard she tries, Sabaa can't bring herself to discuss her husband with someone who gives her piercing heartache, a nameless agony that claws mercilessly at her soul.

Sabaa wants to scream out, "Get out of my life! Leave Ishmail alone!" But she doesn't. Nothing changes....

6.

The girls don't need too much attention these days. Tara is free spirited. Zahra is surprisingly well coordinated in her speech and movement, unlike children her age. She is a thinker but follows her older sister blindly around the house, who is impulsive and an extreme risk-taker. Half of the time her rash actions have resulted in minor injuries for both sisters. So Sabaa has to keep an eye out to intercept Tara's mischief. Ishmail has less patience with Tara and her wildness. He's fonder of the thoughtful, observant, peaceful little Zahra.

The girls are happy to go about and play with mud in the yard by themselves. Sometimes, Sabaa joins them and tells them stories. They forget their mud cooking and jump on her lap with dirty little hands and feet, casting loving imprints all over her clean sharee. They listen to her attentively, with their innocent eyes following her every movement—lips forming the words, the rise of eyebrows as the climax builds, heart-beats in her bosom accentuated by breathing as the stories come alive in many shades—the monster is subdued and a happy ending assured for the brave princess.

Sabaa feels good at such times. She teaches the girls new words and rhymes. Her daughters have brought immense joy into Sabaa's life. But some people say she should have a son. Daughters can't give her what a son can. Deep in her heart, Sabaa doesn't care. She understands that her position as a woman is lesser as the well-wishers wait for a male child—the belief that Sabaa has yet to proclaim her dignity, her poten-tial glory in her fertility by producing a son, eventually. She knows Dhola is anxious to have a grandson and Ishmail longs for a son to carry on his name.

If Sabaa had been a son, she would be running the business with her father right now or be a doctor like Ishmail instead of drowning in the fathomless depths of impotent suspicion. She could have voiced her doubts openly without the shame of being judged and be released from the unbearable distress she is going through. A Bengalee woman is bound by societal norms, expected to compromise. Otherwise, she becomes an outcast, a shameless siren to be scorned forever.

People are indeed talking. Gossip travels at a reckless speed and has nine lives like a cat. It can be killed only with juic-ier gossip. What if Dhola hears about it too? That would be extremely vexing, wounding her dignity, the trust she has placed in her husband, the picture she has painted for the world to see, which she believes to be mostly true. She is con-fident about Ishmail's love for her and the girls. What if he loves another person simultaneously? She would rather die of shame than become the object of pity. She knows what her mother has endured in her marriage. She doesn't want Tota to suffer for her as well. She rehearses possible words she would say to Ishmail. A storm builds up, rages untamed in her mind. Fierce doubts and frustrations agitate her, smashing her peace. But she doesn't speak up. She doesn't know whether she is seeing too much in Ishmail's association with Kamala. She is aware that this town tilts without much wind in its sails. People have a habit of finding excitement where there is none.

Sometimes, in the middle of the night, she is awakened by Ishmail, his intense, quick breath on her face. Sabaa willingly accepts his nearness, welcomes his love. Her love for Ishmail remains unwavering, unchallenged. She feels warmth in the fold of his comforting arms. She knows he belongs to her, is committed to their relationship. The frenzied intimacy engrosses them with urgency, and then all quiets down.

She lies next to him, close, every night, his soft breath brushing the side of her face. She can't find her voice to speak, though her mind implores her to seize such moments to bring up her fears about Kamala's intrusion into their lives. But Sabaa remains frozen in her dilemma. Useless hesitancy prevents her from initiating an honest, long-deserved dialogue with Ishmail. She lets the opportunities slide by. In her heart she knows Ishmail is aware of the recent awkwardness between them. He does nothing to break it down. He pretends and evades any opportunity to smooth the wrinkles of unease.

~ɔ

The room feels airless, oppressed by the summer heat under the heavy blanket of the still, moonless night. Sabaa's eyes burn with sleeplessness as the moments keep building on. If she strains her ears, she believes she would almost hear the breathing of the trees standing motionless outside....

She gets up as the call for morning prayer breaks the silence of the night. She steps outdoors and strolls alongside the pond's borders. The new morning keeps unfolding, indolent in its elegance. The east sky dazzles in a blinding glow of the summer sun slowly stirring, caught in a cracked curtain of light and pale, sparse clouds. The grass is velvety soft and damp under her bare feet. She walks gently, avoiding the tiny yellow blossoms bursting out of blotches of green. At the edges of the bank, the palm trees and the wilderness of the morning glory shrubs splashed with light lavender flowers stare back at the new dawn. There is immense calm around her, overflowing in abundance. Sabaa swims in the water, floats with the water lilies' fragrance swelling in intense vivacity all across the pond.

On this amazing morning, Sabaa decides she will fight for Ishmail, for the life they have built together. Kamala shouldn't be allowed to ruin her happiness.

CHAPTER FOURTEEN

Whatever it takes

I.

As her world is in such turmoil, Sabaa discovers she is pregnant. Ishmail welcomes the news. He has always wanted a houseful of children, a stable family, glorious in abundant sibling affection. Being an only son, he missed the camaraderie of brothers, the joys of the bond of dependability, solidarity in shared pursuits.

Ishmail has felt alone all his life. His younger sister was long married off, lived an impoverished life with an undeserving man who brought trouble and heartaches into her life. Though of limited means, Ishmail tries his best to help his sister, always. She was a little girl when their mother died. He lived with Boro Ma, whereas his sister was shipped off to live with their father's cousin's family, not welcome in their stepmother's life. As the brother and sister were brought up in different households, Ishmail saw her on family occasions only. Due to their age difference and tradition, the emotional distance during their growing-up years created a gap that has been impossible to bridge. But he can sense her abandonment and has continued to suffer in silence for her. He has vowed to take away her pain as much as humanly possible under the circumstances.

〜つ

Sabaa feels tired all the time and depressed. The pregnancy exerts an extra burden on her. Her mind is unfocused, uninterested in the world around her. Even telling stories to the girls is a big undertaking. She longs to see her mother, her village, and bury her worries in the comfort of familiar faces. She wants an escape from this situation.

"I want to visit my mother. Dada is also anxious to see us... end of this month should be good to travel," Sabaa finally says to Ishmail.

"I'm very busy. Can't go, not now. But you should go, yeah. The girls miss your parents." He seems glad about her decision.

The overbearing weight of unspoken words, ever-consuming silences have become too disruptive and precarious, tilting the equilibrium in their relationship. Absence may bring healing.

"I'll be lonely without Tara and Zahra, I know, for sure. And you... of course. But you'll be able to rest there, Sabaa," he admits.

The ghost of the lost spark is unmistakable in his gentle voice, in the tenderness of his arms as he places them on her shoulders while speaking. Finally, they are talking—about normal things that matter in life!

That night, her sleepless mind races with unruly thoughts —fragments of numerous images of Kamala with Ishmail... flashes of memories of the days of frivolous joys long lost... the agonizing instances of uncertainties.... What strange turns life might take keep crawling into her mind.

2.

Travel to Harirampur by steamer boat takes about ten to twelve hours. Dhola has sent his most trusted elderly servant, Kadir *bai*, to escort Sabaa and her daughters. Sabaa has always treated Kadir with respect and as a family member. He has served in Dhola's household more than five decades. Kadir is ever ready to lay down his life for his master, benefactor, and the family. Regular strenuous work has given him a strong physique—iron-tough limbs. He's still extremely fit for his age.

Kadir knows well that he will be taken care of by Dhola and his sons when he will no longer be able to serve actively. Most of his family members are already employed with Dhola's printing press, household, or farming. Dhola is a good employer, committed to taking care of people who are loyal to him.

At six in the morning sharp, they board the steamer. The girls are excited. Ishmail comes to the jetty and stands there till the boat pulls out of the shallow depth and moves into deeper waters. They see him standing on the dock, a lonely figure silhouetted against the rising sun, surrounded by slim waves that encircle the wooden pier.

Sabaa has a cabin on the top deck. She has traveled in this boat before. It's large, oval shaped in the front, painted in a somewhat dirty yellowish-brown shade, with a huge propeller wheel at the back that breaks the water and pushes it forward. It has the capacity to accommodate up to five hundred passengers and has three tiers—the lower deck, which is the third-class level, mainly for people of limited means; the middle deck is the second-class level that has some sitting zones and open spaces, the canteen, and an area for the storage of goods being transported; and the top deck is the first class level that has two individual cabins. These are for wealthy travelers with families. Each cabin has two narrow wooden bunks—more like benches than beds—fixed to each side of the compartment walls. Four people can easily fit in one cabin. Sabaa got a cabin to herself.

More than half of the top deck is open. There are scattered steel benches in corners. Tickets for the cabins are expensive. Admission to the seats on this deck is costlier than the other two levels but cheaper than the cabins. Some travelers prefer it.

At the front of the deck is the captain's cabin, consisting of a big steering wheel and a hooter, enclosed by a large glass window that covers the entire front part of the ship and gives a full view of the river ahead. Just above the window in the middle is a huge searchlight that the captain uses at night to navigate the dark waters. At the farthest end of this upper deck are two tall chimneys that vomit black fumes constantly, stamping the sky with black mist, breaking the clouds with merciless precision. The steamer is run by coal. As Sabaa submits to a deep slumber, the girls get a quick peep of the coal room—hot and lit a bright orange red by the burning charcoal under the watch of Kadir, who holds them by their hands and gives them a tour of the entire steamer.

At noon the girls eat in the cafeteria with Kadir. He sends a canteen boy with a tray of food to Sabaa's cabin. It contains a large portion of steaming white rice, chicken curry drowned in a sea of mouthwatering spices, gravy and potatoes, a small bowl of daal, and a platter of overcooked mixed vegetables—greasy, slippery wet, sprinkled in liberal ladles of mustard oil.

The girls eat with their hands after washing up with soap and lukewarm water offered in a plastic bowl by the waiter. They sit on a long wooden bench adjacent to a table matching the length of the bench, fixed on the deck. Each girl picks up small bites of food with her little right hand and politely puts it in the mouth. Some rice escapes their tiny fists and falls to the ground. The gravy of the chicken curry trickles down to their elbows. The girls are learning to eat on their own. Sabaa encourages them to be independent while she keeps an eye on them. Kadir gently wipes the mess clean with the thin towel he carries on his left shoulder. Nothing misses his ever-alert eyes. The sisters like him and accept him as a co-conspirator to their world of adventure.

The steamer rolls through many villages and rivers, breaking the deep and narrow waves at a slow speed. For hours it surges ahead into the savage rivers, pumped with fierce currents at the height of monsoon. The receding shores follow and fade behind—far away, forlorn, lost to sight. The trees become faint, lose their green in the indigo sky on the distant horizon. The journey continues.

3.

It's almost dark when they reach the final destination. Sabaa and her daughters travel in a palanquin from the jetty, about two miles from home. Kadir accompanies them, walking beside it. Tara and Zahra are tired and fall asleep on the way. It has been a very exciting time for them. They behaved like angels on the long journey.

As darkness descends, the welcoming voices of crickets and nameless birds startle Sabaa with a sudden familiarity. The air and soil smell of pleasing care, wrapped in the dampness of the long-harbored rainwater.

The palanquin bearers' symphony of sweat and footsteps mingles with the songs they hum in muted, deep voices. The rhythmic sway and the evening breeze fan the lacy curtains of the palanquin. Silhouettes of houses, trees, and bamboo bushes come alive in the background and slowly recede into the blackness of the night. The men tread on higher ground and narrow paths along the edges of the shore of the Padma. The scent of sandy waves climbs inside Sabaa's lungs and fills them with cool freshness. Homecoming feels good.

Sabaa's body aches, burdened by long travel, and is on the verge of almost breaking when they finally reach home. The serene, welcoming light of hurricane lamps is tender, soothing. Dada, Tota, and the maids rush out as they hear the palanquin entering the inner yard.

Tota kisses Sabaa as she touches her feet, and she pulls her daughter close to her bosom. Dada is extremely happy to see her two great-granddaughters again. She helps the maids carry the sleeping girls inside to the bed already made up for the night. They will be allowed to rest till they wake up and then be fed, washed, and sent back to bed for the remaining night's sleep. Children should never miss dinner as food provides nutrients for their growth when they sleepis the common belief.

Dhola is glad to see them, also because Sabaa is with child again. He had a goat slaughtered in the morning for their welcome meal. The spicy smell of cooked goat meat mingled with the scent of the night encircles the house. The feast is ready. Sabaa's tummy churns in hunger.

4.

"This time I'll see a grandson," Dhola proclaims with pride as Sabaa sits down to eat. He likes his granddaughters but keeps a distance from them. He never displays emotions—he doesn't like it.

"Boys are pillars in a family. Girls are *shobha*—flattering, beauty to the eyes, to their parents. They leave as soon as they're ready to build their own nests." Dhola has very clear-cut ideas about gender roles.

"When you choose a daughter-in-law, make sure she's born of a noble mother, that her family is honorable, as she'll be responsible for the continuation of your dynasty. But when you marry off your girl, no need to bother so much because she'll not be in your family anymore," he declares.

Sabaa concentrates on the food on her plate as Dhola

smugly keeps throwing out his opinions. She finds his faulty ideology maddening, sickening, but she can't stand up to her father. That's not how she was brought up. That would be unacceptable behavior, obscenely disrespectful. Dada laughs affectionately in agreement with her son's views. And so do others, including Tota, the maids, and female neighbors who have come to see Sabaa.

~

Dhola, with all his limitations, in some strange way has also expressed kindness to Sabaa, ensured her wishes are respected. She especially remembers one incident that made her heart grow fonder for her father with all his faults, even today.

Right after she was married, Dada told the head servant to buy a sarong for Ishmail, which he did. The next day, Dhola found Sabaa in tears and Tota and Dada very angry with the servant. Usually a pair of sarongs is woven as one piece for convenience with markings in the middle, which later are cut and the pieces separated into two. The other half of the sarong that Ishmail received was kept by a farmhand and he had the audacity to wear it while at work in the field. Someone spotted the offense and reported it to Dada. This was a disgrace, insulting! The son-in-law of the house and a lowly born servant can't wear the same type of clothing, which would be scandalously above the servant's station. The maids were horrified; everyone in the household was outraged. Sabaa felt dishonored. This shouldn't have happened under Dhola's rule. Immediately, the servant's sarong was seized, and he was strongly reprimanded. Dhola was gravely displeased. He assured Sabaa that this was due to the ignorance of the servant boy and was not to be tolerated at all. His daughter's humiliation by a mere farmhand was unacceptable.

When Ishmail learned of this incident, he was highly amused. For years he has kept teasing Sabaa over her family's pointless vanity, their insufferable arrogance. Not to miss a laugh, he even shares this story with his daughters years later when they become adults. They understand their mother's predicament but continue to tease her no end.

At her parents' homestead, Sabaa is suddenly out of a job. The girls are taken care of by Tota, Dada, and the maids. Tota makes sure Sabaa gets a daily massage and proper rest. She also oils her daughter's hair adoringly and combs it to perfection. Her mother's touch is so full of loving comfort that Sabaa finally begins to relax. Her days are lazy, comfortable, and nights are endless, long. The thought of Ishmail and Kamala agitates her, often. In her sleep she hears their laughter distantly and wakes up disturbed. The baby within her also stirs and keeps her awake some nights.

Sabaa received a very short letter from Ishmail, but that was almost four months ago. No contact after that. She understands he is busy with work. He has written once to Dhola, a customary courtesy communication. There were a couple of lines at the end about Sabaa and the girls—a polite inquiry.

Dada sometimes looks at her quizzically. She has questions on her mind but avoids asking Sabaa point blank. Dada possibly thinks something is amiss this time. Tota doesn't say anything. She doesn't even mention Sabaa's life in Manikganj. Sabaa wonders if Ishmail walks on the riverbank regularly with Kamala now that he has more time to himself. Sabaa's heart feels hollow, and a chill clutches at it and continues to stab her mercilessly. She longs for Ishmail, the refuge of his arms. Another two months go by. Ishmail doesn't write or send any news. Her womb grows bigger with every passing day. She feels the baby kicking and coming more alive inside her. Then things change.

Sabaa wakes up at the girls' happy shrieks and looks out of the window. The evening is just nestling against the flickering lights of the hurricane lamps....

"Baba!...Baba!...Pick me up, up!"

Ishmail enters the inner yard, his daughters clinging to him while the servants carry his suitcase and the medical toolbox right behind.

That night after dinner, Sabaa faces her husband. The girls are sleeping in Dada's hut. Ishmail laughs awkwardly and touches her face with his right hand. Sabaa doesn't pull away but looks at him intensely with disdain.

"Why have you come?" she wants to know.

"You wanted me to come, no? I thought so. Maybe I'm wrong, but that's what Aba's letter said." Ishmail doesn't take his eyes off her.

Sabaa feels cheated, betrayed. She didn't know her father was so perceptive, had silently witnessed her sadness, was forced to invite Ishmail to visit his family. The emotions rise in her.

"I wanted to see the girls. See you. Anyway, don't bother about that letter. Now I'm here...happy I've come." He pulls Sabaa into his arms.

"You had no time to write to me, no time to find out about me," Sabaa whispers with an angry hiss. Ishmail holds her close. His arms have been affectionate frontiers where she always felt safe, but now she can't take it anymore. She pushes him away, asking, "What kept you so busy?"

"What is it, Sabaa?" Ishmail is surprised.

"Don't...don't touch me. I can't bear it anymore. You have all the time in the world for others," she pants as emotions get out of control and she moves away from him. Her tears start to roll down to her horror. All these months, she has done everything to prevent him from seeing her weakness, her raw pain.

"What do you mean?" Ishmail sounds surprised. "You know I dropped my work to be here. Besides, your father insisted that I visit." He's slightly irritated and changes his earlier stance.

Sabaa turns her face away, trying in vain to check her shameless tears, her bosom heaving in anguish at the humiliation of losing to indignity...to another woman?

"Sabaa, what's wrong? Why the tears?" Ishmail is uneasy, rather helpless. There's silence in the room. For many minutes, both sit in anticipation of something that could break this suffocating staleness. The reason for Sabaa's anger begins to dawn on him.

"There's nothing, nothing to worry about. You're building your pain on unfounded suspicions. Yes, I spend time with Kamala.... I talk to her. She has no friends." Ishmail pauses as Sabaa wipes away her tears, truly ashamed now.

"Just think of being alone, without family in a place like that. I haven't done anything improper. I have always been faithful to you," he adds. "I thought you understood my love for you and the girls," he utters again firmly but in a soft voice as he watches Sabaa in distressed frustration. "I always thought you were above pettiness.... "

Sabaa doesn't look at him. She sits on the side of the bed in stony disgrace. She has always prided herself on being above lowly prejudices—she's different, better than small minds bound by insecurities, baseless jealousies. She has always taken the high ground, unlike so many others who weave webs of gossip and idle, hurtful fibs to match their malicious delights. Did she see what wasn't there to see? Were Ishmail's and Kamala's interactions innocent, a trusting camaraderie in a difficult, alien work environment in that wretched township? How wrong was she? Surging doubts keep mocking her. What a fool she has been!

Ishmail stares at her for a long time in silence. Many thoughts cross his mind; images pop up. Finally, he lowers the flame of the kerosene lamp and slumps onto the other side of the bed. He falls asleep gradually, and so does Sabaa at some point.

Years and years later, when her daughters are all grown-up women and after many ups and downs in life, Sabaa finally is able to label Ishmail's relationship with Kamala—her husband was emotionally untrue to her, their marriage, though physically faithful during those turbulent times in good old Manikganj. She ultimately is able to release her pain....

5.

Ishmail spends the next days playing with his daughters and joking with Dada. The girls love to hang around and follow him. In the evenings, he takes long walks on the riverbank. The Padma River is at its fiercest. Waves hurl against the shoreline in deafening ferocity. At any time the banks will overflow, claiming land. Land erosion is every farmer's nightmare in this village. But they have no weapons to fight this enemy, to protect their homes and fields. The coast is outlined with the spectacular thickness of miles and miles of *kashphool*, or silver feather grass. The long green grass stems hold the snowy whiteness of the blossoms momentarily. Constantly stirred by the unruly breeze, the flowers release feather-like fluffy petals all over the blue horizon, the waves of the river.

Ishmail doesn't tell Sabaa about the date of his return to Manikganj. She has assumed his busy practice won't allow him a long vacation, but it seems Ishmail is in no hurry. Though he's not very close to Dhola and usually maintains a respectful distance, this time Sabaa finds him in deep conversation with her father. She doesn't know what they talk about, but Dada says it's related to a possible job in the military. They must be discussing Sabaa and the girls should he get an offer. He will have to leave his family behind in that case. So this was developing while she has been away all these months.

~

Ishmail doesn't try to talk to Sabaa again when he is alone with her. Very politely, he avoids any kind of physical contact with her as well. This is his way of protesting Sabaa's bad behavior, the mistrust, the unspoken accusations that she hurled at him, misunderstanding his friendship with Kamala. The awkward icy silence solidifies. Luckily, the privacy of their bedroom is out of reach of probing eyes, frank queries, and interested spectators.

Every night, Sabaa comes to bed quietly and tries to sleep. The rancid, sour air of uneasiness feels diseased, challenging her poise each second. During the daytime, there are too many diversions, too many people who have become part of their lives. Nothing stays private, which is a relief in the present circumstances. She would have liked to sleep with the girls, but that would mean lots of answering to Dada.

Sabaa is puzzled by what's happening to her marriage. It's hard to face Dada's silent eyes, weighty with concern. Dada is going to corner her, and soon. Sabaa needs some time to process her confusion—how to move her relationship forward with her husband. She wonders whether she has destroyed all chances to be happy, to have a genuinely decent, loving married life different from the mundane, stagnant expectations of a union between a woman and a man.

As the rooster crows the next morning, a guest arrives at Dhola's house. The maids have just stumbled out of their slumber, puffed off the flames in sooty kerosene lamps in preparation to begin their day....

CHAPTER FIFTEEN

One cup of worries, one drop of Manna

I.

People get out of their beds in curiosity as Kamala steps into the inner yard with a big, warm smile. Her small tin suitcase is beside her. Traces of her nightlong travel are visibly alive in her sleepless, tired eyes and loosely hang in the corners of her weary mouth.

"I'm on my way to visit my parents...thought I'd drop by on the way...to see how things are here," she says to the spectators, who watch her motionless, still owning their alertness to sleep.

"How's your health, Sabaa?" Kamala spots Sabaa on the veranda. She has stepped out, hearing the voices. Her legs are heavy. She can hardly move but somehow gathers enough strength and goes down the steps. Her bulging womb aches with the movement.

She takes Kamala's hands in hers and whispers, "So good to see you. The girls talk about you constantly."

"Are they sleeping?" Kamala adds with hesitation.

"Yes. Come inside. You must be tired." Sabaa leads Kamala as maids carry her luggage, under the others' watchful eyes that follow the two young women striding inside the house in friendly comfort. Ishmail is still in bed sleeping.

Looking back, Sabaa could never figure out what made her take that giant step that morning—her pride? Dignity? To keep her face to the entire household?... To right the wrong, pay the penalty of misjudging Ishmail? Or to proclaim her love, her trust in her husband?

~

During the day, Sabaa watches her husband intently and with caution. Outwardly, everything seems normal—his interactions with Kamala, herself. He joins them at breakfast, exchanges courteous casual pleasantries with Kamala. They share some information and laugh about work-related matters and people they know. Dhola briefly meets their guest, welcomes her to enjoy the hospitality of his home. All has been good so far.

In the evening, they have tea together with Dada. Sabaa makes sure to be present whenever Ishmail comes to the inner yard in the vicinity of Kamala's nearness. She doesn't want to give anyone any reason to talk about them. At dinner Sabaa makes attempts to steer the discussion towards Kamala's family, her village, in order to give her a background, an identity that's commonplace in all Bengalee households. The environment loosens up. Tota and Dada participate in the conversation.

That night, Sabaa initiates casual talks with Ishmail as she comes to bed. "It's really nice to have Kamala here," she remarks.

"Are you happy to see her? Really?" Ishmail is curious.

"Of course. We all are." Sabaa brushes away his doubts with a quick gesture. Kamala's bed has been made in Dada's room with the girls.

From time to time, they hear faint sounds of her laughter and Dada's coughing. Kamala is like a conjurer who has mastered the art of charming people, old and young. A consummate enticer! Ishmail seems to be slightly ill at ease, distracted. His ears are drawn to the sounds of the distant voices coming from Dada's room. Sabaa doesn't mind Kamala's presence at all. She isn't afraid of her anymore.

....The shadow in Sabaa's mind begins to lift.

2.

Kamala appears to be comfortable, carefree. She is enjoying her stay. She doesn't talk about her departure.

"You need a husband now, Kamala. A woman like you shouldn't be alone. The current of rivers and the age of a woman pass swiftly, so make haste." Dada is very forward with her advice. "Your parents should talk to a matchmaker before it's too late." Kamala giggles as she looks at the faces of the others around her.

"Dada has a point," Ishmail adds in a small voice. Kamala gives him a quick look and smiles.

"It's wise to have children while the body is still young and strong. A mother needs five years to recover after every birth," Tota chips in. An awkward silence grips the atmosphere.

"Try some more fish, Kamala." Sabaa changes the topic, rescues her. Tota quickly serves another steaming hot bowl of mouthwatering spicy fish curry.

Dhola's voice is heard from the outer yard. He eats early, right after the sun goes down, after the evening prayer. The frozen moments slowly kick back into normality. The conversation continues late as Tota clears the traces of dinner, tidies up the pots and pans. Dada mounts a fresh round of tobacco in her hookah. She loves gossip, and Kamala is good at sharing recent news.

Very early the next morning, Ishmail is up. He opens the windows, pulling away the curtains to let the sunlight in. The eastern sky is painted with a faint glow, heavy with the promise of a clear day. Only the early worshippers are seen doggedly going about in preparation to pray. Servants are getting ready for the fields. The chickens have not yet been released from the coops. The morning hustle is waiting to begin.

"Wake up, wake up, Sabaa. It's morning. Open the door." Ishmail sounds somewhat disheveled and restless as he tries to shake her awake by the arm.

He looks edgy, itching to go out of doors. Sabaa doesn't understand why she's being hurried. Her body is still in the grip of the lazy delights of the comfort of the bed after the late night.

As the morning rolls on, Kamala reads to the girls and plays with them after tea and a robust breakfast of handmade rice flour roti with sweet vermicelli cooked in thick milk, raisins, and brown sugar. Tota makes sure the visitor is well fed and properly cared for. Kamala is her son-in-law's colleague and a valued guest. The prestige of this house would be at stake if for any reason she found that the care offered to her has been inadequate, below standards. That would be a real shameful thing, unclassy. Tota can never allow that. The girls are too happy to sit beside Kamala and eat with her.

After breakfast, they all laze in the yard on a coconut-leaf mat under the big mango tree that lends its branches and shade to the inner yard, though it's rooted on the other side of the partition. The green mangoes sway in the wind. As some fall, the girls run to pick them up for their grandmother. Tota will later add these extremely sour-tasting fruits to the soupy yellow lentils to be eaten at lunch. On hot summer days, this delicacy is highly popular.

Ishmail hangs around, joking with Dada. From time to time, he speaks to Kamala. She is good at repartee. Saaba sits nearby in a wooden chair and is often dragged into the flowing conversation. She can't be on the floor anymore due to her heavy pregnancy. Everyone chips in now and then.

Ishmail and Kamala argue about surreal issues, ambiguous concepts. Sometimes they critique literary compositions in abstract terms. They oppose each other's views with animated passion, comfortable with playful antics. Sabaa watches their enthusiastic disputes, unable to understand the meaningless bantering. She doesn't know how to join in, to break this purposeless conversation that holds no plausible conclusion. She can relate to Khayyam and Tagore, Lawrence and Tolstoy, comprehend their agony and elation, but the line of hypothetical dialogues pursued by her husband and Kamala is lost on her. However, she stays close by, very much present in the background, a sentinel. She wants to remain a part of the deception she has carefully designed to display—that all's well.

Kamala is also good with Dada, makes her laugh at stories about her work in the community, about her family. As she listens, Sabaa rediscovers her as a friendly, agreeable person. Even in her bleakest moments, cast in doubts and low self-confidence, she never found enough grounds to be harsh to Kamala, convict her of anything concretely bad. She's surprised to find that she likes Kamala's brave, genuine, and open personality.

～つ

Later, Kamala is beside Tota, assisting her in cooking. Tota feels no hesitancy in opening up to this pleasant young woman. Kamala gives her a beautiful hand-embroidered handkerchief as a gift, which impresses her, no doubt.

"This is lovely. Where did you learn to embroider?" Tota gently touches the delicate needlework with her bristly fingers.

"When I was a nursing student, our matron guided me on some designs. A woman of many talents."

Sabaa is relieved that Kamala is so welcome in her family.

This gives her strength—sows more seeds of doubt about her own dubious assumptions against this woman. She rebukes herself for thinking the worst. She is now certain that Kamala is a friend, not a threat. She hopes none of the silly gossip has reached her homeland.

At lunchtime, the maid informs Kamala that Dhola wants to see her. So far, he hasn't adequately spoken to her. It's a common courtesy for the head of the house to inquire after his guests, ensure all comforts are extended. Kamala covers her head modestly and walks to the outer yard where Dhola is waiting for her. From the inner yard, they can hear Dhola's voice, faintly audible. A few minutes later, Kamala rushes back, totally distraught. Her face looks pale and her lips tremble as she tries to smile.

"What is it?" Ishmail is beside her in quick steps as Sabaa and Dada watch.

Kamala looks at him with momentary hesitancy, then in total disarray rushes into his arms, breaking into hysterical tears. Curious servants begin to peek. Tota looks on helplessly.

"I'll leave right now.... He insulted me...called me a prostitute.... Get me to a boat. I don't want to stay here another second." Kamala's voice is muffled as she buries her face in Ishmail's chest.

"I'll come with you.... I'll take you to your father's house." His face becomes ashen with emotion. Gossip did reach Dhola, no doubt about it now!

Ishmail tries to reassure her, faltering between words as the poignant moments unfold with lingering uncertainty. Sabaa is bewildered and watches, powerless, not able to intervene, to control the situation or console Kamala. Kamala is in hysterics in Ishmail's arms as the spectators wait for the next move. The melodrama begins to intensify. The highly charged few seconds feel like a lifetime.

Suddenly, a scream escapes from Sabaa's lips. Her body trembles like the bamboo branches tossed in high winds. Her water breaks. Excruciating pain tears through her body. She falls to the ground, clutching her belly helplessly. As all faces turn towards her, she hears Dada's urgent voice. "Quick! Help me, someone!...Let's pick her up. The baby is coming. Call Hawa's ma. Quick, quick! Get ready.... Move! Move!"

In a leap, Tota is beside Sabaa, trying to hold her in her arms. With the help of maids, she carries Sabaa towards the birthing hut that was built a few weeks ago, adjacent to the main bungalow. Kamala's howling stops as suddenly as it started. Ishmail releases her and tries to go near Sabaa. The women push him aside and slowly move ahead with Sabaa in their arms.

Luckily, all preparations have been in place. This time Sabaa herself arranged for wider windows and more space inside the birthing hut. She also told Dada point blank that right after the birth, she would be moving back to her regular living quarters. No more isolation with the new baby. No more of Dada's archaic, dictatorial rules to be followed this time. Dada had to give in to a more mature Sabaa's wishes.

3.

The next few hours are never-ending agony. As the contractions come faster, she gropes and screams while trying to push the baby out. She loses sense of time. The faces of Tota, Dada, and Hawa's mother become fuzzy. She can't isolate one from the other. The pain sits on her, breaks her body into a million pieces, consumes her senses. Her body is bathed in sweat, and she can smell the stench of blood flowing out of her. Her eyes search for the familiar face.

"He's waiting outside.... It's OK.... We have sent her home with a servant. Kamala is gone." Tota wipes Sabaa's face as the slow tears overflow gently.

Then the baby comes. It seems an eternity of waiting in pain and sweat and blood and the choking heat. She hears her body tearing apart amidst the throbbing, all paralyzing pain.

"It's a girl...a beautiful girl," Tota whispers as she picks up the tiny bundle in her arms. The chocolate brown writhing form with perfect fingers and toes, the petite face, small forehead laced with dark, curly hair is Sabaa's third daughter.

Images and thoughts race through Sabaa's mind. She feels a sense of sudden shame for letting down her father and her husband. It's not a son. Third time around, another girl. She feels defeated, exhausted. She wonders what they're thinking right now. Is she condemned? Is she belittled in their minds? Culturally, a woman is valued for the number of sons she produces. She remembers the old saying she grew up hearing: *a farmer is never content unless he has a bountiful crop every season; a mother's heart is never fulfilled unless she has many sons born out of her womb.*

In Bengal, lives are entwined mainly with land and crops. The more hands to work in the field, the higher the security towards a less impoverished life, the continuation of lineage, the guarantee that in old age there will be a roof and food till death makes the final claim. This cycle is considered sacred and has prevailed through ages. Women are looked upon as subsidiary tools to preserving this code of tradition, the talisman of honor, the stain of glory. They are to be present only in the background in assisting roles, subservient, abiding, and benign in the cancerous arena of the patriarchal monopoly.

As she turns away to the other side of the mat, Tota holds the baby up closer for Sabaa to see. Sabaa looks into the tiny, enchanting face. Covered in her blood and slime is the most beautiful living thing she has ever beheld! Gone are her doubts. Her mind soars with pride and elation at her amazing creation. The precious tiny bundle pulls her heartstrings in that instant and actually never lets them go, as she will fondly remember years later.

"Anushka. I'll call her Anushka," Sabaa whispers to herself as the tears well up in her eyes. Anushka is the heroine of a Russian novel she has read recently. She hears voices outside the door as she closes her eyes in fatigue.

Anushka steps into the world in the glorious summer of 1959 amidst the promise of uncertain rains and the sounds of the untamed waves of the Padma river that constantly break at the shores of Dhola's village.

CHAPTER SIXTEEN

A brother of standing

I.

Sabaa returns to Manikganj with her three daughters two months later. After Anushka's birth, Ishmail left them behind so that Sabaa could regain her strength. Taking care of three little girls isn't easy, so this time Tota and her youngest son, twelve-year-old Elias, accompany them. They will be staying three months till Sabaa gets a grip on everything.

Elias has been sickly since childhood. The doctors failed to diagnose the exact nature of his ailment. He constantly was fatigued, was out of breath if he ran around like any other boy his age. He went through many blood tests in Dhaka and was given expensive medication directly imported from England. Even then, he frequently suffered from fever, aches, and pains in his joints. Dhola spent a fortune on his son's treatment. The doctors finally advised that Elias should not undertake any strenuous effort and opt for a low-labor lifestyle because he had a weak heart.

So both Tota and Dhola are relaxed over his studies. He has

long and voluntary absences from school to manage the bouts of sickness he continues to go through. Unlike his older brothers, he isn't able to go to Dhaka to study. Dhola has recruited good tutors to home-coach Elias to ensure additional support so that he's able to catch up with his missed classes.

Elias is a shy, sweet-natured adolescent. As his outer world activities are restricted, he stays mostly in the house and continues to become an integral part of his sister's and mother's lives, unlike his two older brothers. As the boy is mostly sick, Dada doesn't mind him hanging around with the women. He has always been close to Sabaa and is dedicated to his nieces. He is overjoyed to learn about his upcoming holiday in Mankganj.

He likes Sabaa's bungalow bordered by the trees—the serene green of the compound. He spends time exploring the surroundings and playing with his two older nieces. He takes them around, teaches them to make paper boats, kites, and flutes with banana leaves. The girls in return adore their full-of-fun boy uncle. They call him *Mamu Jaan*. He loves to keep watch on the tiny sleeping Anushka when the women are busy or decide to rest. He fulfills his responsibility of guarding her with serious dedication.

"Buji, why doesn't Baba buy a house for you?" Elias asks as he watches Sabaa cook. Tota is busy stitching tiny quilts for Anushka outside on the veranda. The little one needs them as she wets frequently.

"Why? I thought you liked our bungalow." Sabaa hides a hint of a smile in her voice.

"I like your house. But Baba could buy you a bigger, better house with a big mango garden near our home. You could live close to us. Not here in this distant town.... He has money."

"Oh, my little brother! I know. But you're welcome to live here with me anytime." Sabaa pulls Elias into her arms.

"You mean it?...Always?" Elias's face lightens up.

"Always, always."

Sabaa is fiercely protective of Elias, mothered him when he was a baby whenever Tota left him with her. She never felt it was extra work but rather was happy to be in charge. Since he learned to walk and talk, he has been his sister's shadow. Even though mostly in ill health, he tried to be useful around the house as much as he could. He was the one to bring the first lily stems of the season to Sabaa. He took great pains to pick the green mangoes when, in pregnancy, she acquired a sudden taste for sour fruit and pickles, and to pluck the ripest blackberries from the highest, treacherous branches when she craved them. He was charmed every time Sabaa entrusted her little girls to his care in their infancy when she wanted to take sneaky breaks to walk around the backyard of the homestead, amongst the wilderness of trees and thick growth of creepers, colorful butterflies, and birds. She needed to get away from her unceasing motherhood.

As a young mother, motherhood wasn't all glory and smiles for Sabaa. Taking care of her infant daughters was hard work—sleepless nights, constant attention, and nursing were exhausting. Though she was helped by Dada, Tota, and the maids, Sabaa was expected to bear the maximum load. Her baby was her responsibility. Her own body was still growing. Her mind was weary, fragile, under so much burden. She felt trapped.

Motherhood added more restrictions. She was forbidden to venture into the backyard on her own, to prevent catching evil eyes or the bad wind that could potentially harm her and her baby. Sabaa didn't care two hoots about superstitions. They tired her out. Elias was her only ally. He kept watch as she went on her brief wanderings....

The best time was the hour before lunch when the entire household was busy with preparation of the meal. Elias sat at the edge of the bed where the baby slept and waved away the mosquitos and flies with a piece of cloth. If the baby wailed, he picked her up in his arms and slowly paced up and down the room so that no one was alerted. Sabaa usually returned within half an hour and took over from her brother. This was a common practice right after Tara, Zahra, and Anushka were born. It was a secret between them—no one ever found out.

2.

In Manikganj, Tota discovers new joys around Sabaa and her daughters. She swelters in the kitchen to cook their favorite dishes, washes and helps around the house so that Sabaa is able to relax. Soon Sanu joins her. She makes cloth dolls for Tara and Zahra, plays with them. Sometimes in the evenings, both Tota and Sanu sing popular folk songs to the delight of the girls.

"*Nana Buji, Nana Buji....*" The girls keep running to them with demands for one thing or the other.

"Tell me about your cows." Tara loves Sanu's stories. She's more interested in animals these days. She has been in close contact with cattle at Dhola's homestead.

"Make another doll, Nana Buji." Zahra is fond of Sanu's dolls.

"Sanu, you can't leave my granddaughters now," Tota teases Sanu.

"Sanu Ama, stay a bit longer with us," Sabaa appeals to her. "My daughters have grown too attached to you."

During the day, Tota and Sanu spend time taking care of Sabaa's family. At night they have a special mission. Under the dim electric light, they bend down to write verses from the Quran in small paper cuttings and keep them neatly folded. While in Manikganj, they intend to complete one million pieces. Their backs ache, fingers throb, but they continue. When all finished, these papers will be thrown at the foaming waves of the Padma to change its course to stop their parental home from erosion. This is Sanu's home now. She grew up here. She can't lose it now—lose so much in this life.

"Buji, what if this doesn't work?" Sanu's conviction wavers sometimes as she pauses in between writing.

"This will work.... Don't lose heart, Sanu." Tota is more optimistic, determined. Her fingers keep moving; her eyes are fixed on the paper. At any cost, she will try to protect her sister. She believes Dhola played a big role in shaping Sanu's destiny, possibly. So she has a greater responsibility towards Sanu.

"In the meanwhile, can we not hire laborers to move the homestead to our southwest farmland? It's miles away from the Padma," Sanu proposes cautiously.

Tota agrees and promises to be with Sanu when the move happens. She will have to somehow get Dhola to agree to her travel.

CHAPTER SEVENTEEN

Departure

I.

Ishmail gets the long-awaited offer letter from the military six months after Anushka is born. Since returning to Manikganj, Sabaa hasn't gotten a chance to see Kamala. Ishmail hasn't even mentioned her once. So she decides to avoid Kamala's name altogether. Sabaa has been apprehensive about the next phase of her relationship with Kamala after the infamous showdown with Dhola. She dreads a visit from Kamala, actually. But Kamala doesn't drop by anymore.

Ishmail is instructed to report to the Dhaka cantonment in six weeks to get his basic orientation and prepare for travel to West Pakistan. The base reporting camp is in Azad Kashmir, a small town situated in part of the disputed land of Kashmir controlled by Pakistan. The rest of the land has been under India's control, and the liberation movement of the Kashmiri people for an independent homeland continues through the decades. Politically, Kashmir through the ages has remained volatile, crucial to peace between India, Pakistan, and the citizens of occupied Kashmir—under constant military invasion.

Dhola reconfirms his generous offer to Sabaa and the girls to reside in his old Dhaka townhome with his sons. The eldest son has married recently. His son's wife is welcoming. Her life is lonely in the house as her husband is extremely busy and normally keeps very late hours. Dhola has almost retired and resides mainly in his village home unless he visits Dhaka. Now his eldest son has taken over the helm. The younger two sons are expected to follow suit eventually.

~∽

The day of Ishmail's departure from Manikganj arrives, slowly, definitively. All preparations have been made. The small township becomes crippled with sadness. In its own way, its people have loved the young doctor and his family. They know a replacement will be extremely difficult. They respected Ishmail and trusted him with their lives, valued his commitment and the good he did for the sick. Now it's time to say goodbye.

"Are you happy, Sabaa?" Ishmail genuinely wants to know as they start packing.

"Yes I'm. I'll always stand beside you…as I've done all these months." Sabaa's voice is unwavering and ripe with a message that is not lost on Ishmail.

People constantly drop in at the house to see them off and to learn about Ishmail's new career. Both Sabaa and Ishmail repeat the same explanations with patience, answering additional queries if anyone wants extra details. The elites organize a big farewell event for Ishmail, where he expresses his gratitude to the townspeople. Sabaa with her three daughters attends the function. She meets Kamala here for the first time after all these months. Kamala comes running as she spots Sabaa in the crowd. They hold hands for a long time without speaking. It's a silent goodbye—no words are spoken. Kamala wears a pinched, woeful look, like the summer sky laden with dark clouds promising fuller showers in store. Sabaa feels compassion for this woman, a twinge of mild sadness.

As a parting gift to Ishmail, Kamala gives him a compilation of Tagore's entire collection of poetry, a beautiful, expensive present with her handwritten tribute to Ishmail on the blank front page, her name signed at the bottom.

Later, though he gets transferred every three to four years in the military service, it always remains at Ishmail's household as a reminder of his life in Manikganj, his work, his struggles, and the complexities of his friendship with Nurse Kamala. His daughters' introduction to Tagore is through this book, and they grow up reading it. It becomes a part of their lives. They read the tribute on the front page but don't remember the person who wrote it, who remains a mystery forever.

~

On the evening of the final journey, Kamala stands on the jetty along with many to see them off on the Dhaka-bound motor launch. People have come all the way from the villages where Ishmail has provided home treatment. They have come to pay their respect. The townspeople garland Ishmail, hand over sweets in clay pots to Sabaa to snack on the way. As the moon glimmers in the eastern sky, the boatmen begin to pull the anchor.

"Doctor shahib, no one in this town ever understood you. They didn't know the real you. Blind, all are blind...you shouldn't have to leave." Kamala's voice is distorted with pain.

And then to everyone's horror, Kamala breaks down into uncontrollable tears and hides her face in her palms. The spectators and Ishmail, standing beside Sabaa on the deck, witness this young woman's agony without any words.

The boat gently backs away from the dock. The crowd begins to fade slowly into blurred outlines. Kamala's words keep echoing on the waves in Sabaa's ears. After that moment, ty*

she never brings up Kamala with Ishmail. They never see her again. This chapter in her life becomes immersed in the necessary present and the journey towards the unknown, imminent future.

⁓

Years later, while reminiscing about Manikganj, Sabaa tells Zahra about Kamala, every detail, all she can recollect. All there was in that story she pours out to her adult daughter. She doesn't hesitate to admit that the threat of Kamala in her life was possibly much more her own creation. After all those times have passed, Sabaa also realizes, though never mentioned, Kamala actually has never taken leave from her life. The memory has just been closeted in the furthest corner of Sabaa's psyche, inseparable.

2.

On reaching Dhaka, Ishmail moves to the officers' mess in the cantonment for a short duration. He is allowed to stay with his family only for the weekend before he flies out. Boro Ma arrives to see him off. His sister sends a tearful letter as she is unable to make it. Dada and Sanu come to Dhaka as well for the occasion, joined by Dhola and Tota. Isaq shows up with the intention to stay till Ishmail's airplane takes off. Relatives and friends drop by at every hour.

The girls resume their playtime with Sanu. There are many giggles shared as she continues to narrate funny stories.

"You're spoiling them, Sanu Ama," Sabaa cautions in mock seriousness.

"Granddaughters are meant to be spoiled.... I have only your girls," Sanu cheerfully responds. It's true as she hardly sees Mejo's children and grandchildren. They live too far away.

Sabaa receives a pair of silver bangles from Sanu as a parting gift. It reminds her of the closeted treasures she saw in the rooftop storage during her girlhood visits.

"Why...Sanu Ama...you don't have to. I'm not going away now, " she protests. She knows how important these jewels are in Sanu's life, a childless woman's last resource.

"But you'll be joining Jamai in two years. What if I'm gone by then? Anyway, I have so many...no one to give to," Sanu reassures her. It's an extreme sacrifice, hard for her to part with her possessions, but she wants to give a token to Sabaa as a remembrance. Sanu doesn't wear any jewelry. She stopped wearing it after she left Yusuf Ali. She doesn't even wear color-ful clothes. White is her only choice, proclaiming purity, irrel-evance, and stark emptiness.

"You're not going anywhere. Not so soon. Who's going to sing at my girls' weddings?" Sabaa affectionately hugs her aunt.

Sanu has become frail. Deep lines are visible around her eyes and beautiful mouth, ravaged by time. Struggling with lonesomeness, she still continues.

⌣

The house is in a festive mood. Goat legs and chunks of beef are bought from the local bazaar as well as large fish from the wholesale market. Chickens are killed. The kitchen be-comes jammed with vegetables, fruits, spices, and condiments of various kinds and shades. From dawn to dusk, Tota sweats with two maids in the roasting heat inside the small windless kitchen, constantly hovering over the stoves, stirring pots and pans. The house is vanquished by the dense, savory aroma of food.

From her girlhood, Sabaa has been extremely fond of this house. The residence quarters are on the first floor of a two-storied building. The ground floor houses the printing press. The constant humming of machines is actively heard from upstairs till late hours, snubbing the stillness of the night. There are two independent entrances to the house. A flight of narrow, rickety, steep stairs leads to the residence unit on one side, separating it from the printing press on the ground floor. Barred windows overlook the narrow road with mushrooming stores on both sides crowding the inadequate spaces for pedestrians. A constant stream of cycle-rickshaws festoons the street. Colorful paintings hanging at the rear of each three-wheeler on slim pieces of tin sheets catch the eye instantly. Each drawing tells a tale, mostly about lovers from popular folklore. Vendors swarm onto the streets trying to sell for their lives, announcing their goodies in loud singsong voices to attract the attention of busy housewives, bored children, interested onlookers, and the curious who hang around the streets in search of diversions.

The house is of old brick construction, consisting of two bedrooms with a huge open, roofless terrace in the middle that connects with the kitchen on one end and the bathroom on the opposite end. When it rains heavily, residents have to use umbrellas. During winter, it gets a bit cumbersome at night, especially if it's windy. Luckily, it never gets too cold in Dhaka.

In between the bedrooms and right after the staircase ends, there is a small space that's used as the dining area. A four-seater dining table set is squeezed in there. Female guests mainly eat in groups in the larger bedroom on a mat on the floor. Ishmail, Dhola, and some others use the dining table, taking turns depending on the number of eaters. Sabaa prefers to eat at the dining table with her daughters.

A second flight of stairs from the terrace leads to the spacious roof. There is an additional large room at one corner of the roof, where Saba's younger brothers reside. The printing machines keep whirring monotonously in the background. No one notices it after some time.

From very early morning, the persistent chanting of vendors

and the sounds of rickshaw bells, automobiles, and voices of commuters on the road filter into the rooms. Just opposite the house entrance, roadside makeshift food stalls sell breakfast: *poori*—deep-fried handmade flatbread; *haluwa*—sweet treats made with carrots, sugar, cream, and butter; *paratha*—roti fried in butter; and mixed stir-fried vegetables, potato curry, and egg omelets with onions, tomatoes, and coriander leaves. The saliva-triggering, syrupy-spicy, warm aroma rising from the food stalls hang over the surroundings, steadily penetrating the residences. Dhola prefers take-aways from selected stalls. It also gives the women a break in the morning. Sabaa loves the street food too.

The best thing about this house is that, sitting at home, women can do shopping anytime. The stores are on both sides of the winding street, selling almost everything that one could need. All they have to do is tell the security guard stationed at the entrance what they want—clothes, bags, cosmetics, sandals, scarves, trinkets, glass bangles, or any other products they fancy from any store. He informs the preferred store. Within a short time, an employee from that particular store brings an array of merchandise to the house to choose from. If the products do not match expectations, the store salesman is too happy to inform another nearby store to send a fresh supply. Sometimes the stores are paid right away after purchases are made. Otherwise, they take the bill later either to Dhola or his oldest son, who foots all bills.

⁓

The first two years will be challenging for Ishmail, away from his family in addition to embracing a different culture, stomaching rough military drills, and getting the hang of the work environment, but the promise of a better future dulls all concerns. Sabaa is both happy and sad. She is going to miss him.

Finally, amidst fanfare, feasts, and tears and hugs, Ishmail boards the plane towards his new destination—a world of uncertainty that he will need to tame and learn to live in!

Sisters for life

I.

When the stars are still awake, faint against the subdued night sky very early one morning, the girls are woken up by their grandmother. Today they are flying to Lahore, where Ishmail is posted. He is a commissioned captain now and has secured permission for his family to live with him. The sisters are excited and eagerly brush their teeth and wash their faces. Tota has very little difficulty getting them ready. The flight is at eight thirty. It's about a forty-minute drive to the Kurmitola airport from Dhola's old town residence.

No one in Sabaa's family has ever flown in an airplane. In fact, no one in her entire village and among her acquaintances has ever done so, to be honest. Though Ishmail has flown, he is a son-in-law, not a native of Harirampur. Moreover, he is a man. For a woman to fly is something more prestigious, a monumental triumph.

When the news of the travel became public and while the preparations began weeks ago, it became the talk of the village and among relatives and people they knew in Dhaka. For days no one spoke of anything but Sabaa's air travel. There were many disputes and information exchanges about what the aircraft looked like, how it was engineered, the duration of the flight covering thousands of miles in four hours, the altitude—high up in the air, piercing through clouds. Some enthusiasts searched for photographs in local dailies and preserved them as references when making a point. Older women had questions whether the plane would be able to go near the heaven that exists in the seventh sky, as Muslims believe. Some claimed that it was an act of sin to fly so close to the heaven reserved for the next life of only the pious, fortunate ones. Discussions and disputes heated up with the passing of each day. Sabaa's travel attracted more attention than Ishmail's. A woman flying thousands of miles alone in an airplane sounded more dramatic, definitely a sexy notion, stirring debate and endless spicy talk.

∼つ

People keep commenting on Sabaa's good fortune—a doctor husband with a desirable job, and now this glorious travel to a faraway land. It's a fairy tale come true! Dhola's luck has always been acknowledged and accepted with a pinch of envy by many. However, to date, in their minds Dhola still has one delinquency—he lacks a grandson. His own son's wife had a series of miscarriages. Sabaa has three daughters only!

Baby taxis, or the three-wheelers, have been summoned. All are lined up. Many of the relatives are going to the airport to see Sabaa and her girls off to a foreign land. They have been staying at Dhola's house for more than a week to participate in this rare occasion. Dhola will be paying the taxi fare, as is customary. He will also foot the bill for snacks and the miracle beverage—Coca-Cola—to be consumed at the airport while the relatives wait to see the travelers off. They will stay till the plane flies out of sight into the sky.

The excitement of getting up early and boarding the plane wears off. The girls are tired and fall asleep as soon as they are in their seats. It's a Boeing 720. Such a strong plane, and it flies so fast! Passengers are mostly men. There are also a few families. Sabaa is the only young woman with three little girls traveling without a male companion. Very rare, very courageous, indeed! People notice her immediately.

Sabaa has to wake up her daughters when lunch is served. On a lovely plastic tray, food is arranged in smaller dishes—*pilau* rice, chicken curry, bread rolls, butter, cheese, salad, and a chocolate and a lemon tart for each person. Tara eats by herself with a spoon. Sabaa feeds the younger girls. They love the food.

The cabin crew comes back with a food cart laden with soft drinks, juices, tea, and coffee. Sabaa tries coffee. The air hostess smiles pleasantly as she hands over a steaming cup to her. With a sip of the scalding drink, she begins to finally relax and enjoy her travel.

Sabaa has read so much about this magic drink in translated novels. In Dhaka, she didn't find anyone who drank coffee. No stores sell coffee. This is her first encounter with this beverage. She adds quite a bit of milk and sugar to subdue the bitter taste, but the aroma kills her! She decides she will promote coffee to Ishmail so that he buys it for their home. But first she will have to learn how to make it. Making tea is very easy, and she has been drinking it from girlhood. In some households, women are restricted from tea, though. The common belief is that it is addictive. It is *kharap*, or a bad habit-forming temptation for women. The fairer sex should be protected from such an evil because vice possibly becomes men much more.

The monotonous droning of the engines seems to go on forever. Finally, the air hostess announces the descent. The girls are now up, their little faces full of expectation and curiosity. They take turns to peep out of the window. The daylight is bright outside and cuts through floating clouds. The aircraft lands on the ground with a thud. Zahra is so scared that she keeps clutching her mother's arms.

The doors of the aircraft finally open. Sabaa climbs down the stairs with Anushka in her arms and the older girls ahead of her, trying to walk in single file, holding each other's tiny hands. She smiles fondly at them. It is a November day in 1961 and Sabaa and her three daughters' first travel out of East Bengal into a new universe. She finally has arrived.

2.

Sabaa fits into the new life very easily with her daughters. Ishmail is attentive to her needs and labors hard to keep the smiles intact on their faces. With a steady income, comfortable military residence, and other benefits, he can now afford selected modest luxuries as well.

Ishmail is an introvert. All the friendships he has made are mainly through Sabaa's contacts, apart from a handful of friends from his medical college days. In Lahore, Sabaa makes new friends and has a steady stream of followers who frequently visit and invite them to dinner or weekend get-togethers. Ishmail is ill at ease with outsiders, acquaintances, and in many cases even with relatives. He accepts Sabaa's friends and amicably manages to stay in the background as an invisible host or guest as the occasion demands. She overshadows him at social events; he is happy to be in the background. But he mostly enjoys spending time with Sabaa and their girls. To him, nothing is more important. He tries his best to provide a stable childhood to his daughters, a happy home to Sabaa.

The older girls are enrolled in one of the best schools. On most weekends, Ishmail rents a taxi for the entire day to visit the zoo, museums, or the many historical parks and monuments strewn all over the city. Numerous times they visit the Shalimar Garden, built by the Mughal Emperor Shah Jahan in 1642.

Autumn and winter are the best times for outings. In summer, they usually stay home because of the brutal heat. The sun's merciless fiery rays burn all the green into a deep brown. Schools and most offices close down from midday. The nearby shopping mall is a better place to hang out in the evenings, and occasionally Ishmail takes the family there to look around, spend a little bit on books, toys, or household stuff. Such evenings usually end with eating cone-ice cream.

On one of these outings, Ishmail buys a doll for Tara. The doll closes its eyes when it's laid flat on a surface. All three girls play with it, though Tara is the custodian. She is mostly gracious, but on occasion, when she wants to manipulate her sisters, she restricts their access to her doll. Zahra, blindly followed by little Anushka, is, however, careful not to evoke Tara's displeasure so that they all have stress-free playtimes.

~◞

Before Eid ul Fitr, the girls love to shop with their parents for new clothes, shoes, ribbons, nail polish, and whatnot for the festival. Ishmail is liberal in making them happy with anything they fancy and can be bought at a reasonable price. Once a year, such liberty is granted to them.

"Girls, when you're back home, you must keep ribbons, hairpins, bracelets, and combs in drawers as your mom told you. She doesn't like mess," Ishmail cautions as his daughters get ready for shopping. Anar Kali bazaar is their target.

"OK, Aba," the eager girls agree in unison. Sabaa has a hard time keeping their rooms tidy.

"Promise?"

"Promise, promise," the daughters pledge in one voice.

They are too anxious to go to the market to pick up their

goodies. They love red nail polish, which they are allowed to wear on only a few occasions. Eid is one of those. Their school dress code objects to such frivolities. No jewelry or any kind of makeup is allowed. With school uniforms, black shoes, and white socks, they are permitted to have braids or ponytails only. Unless it's bobbed short, keeping hair loose isn't permitted.

Anar Kali bazaar is famous for its exotic trinkets, cosmetics, and many other feminine attractions, alien to Ishmail. Its well-lighted, narrow alleys are bloated with dazzling paraphernalia, too alluring. Throughout the year, this place is jammed with shoppers from morning till late night as all possible fancy products are available here in one shop or the other.

The second Eid is celebrated by sacrificing a cow or a goat. A small amount is spent on luxuries.

On one occasion a day before Eid, Ishmail takes the girls to buy shoes. Sabaa stays back home to finish cooking. Good food on Eid is important to Ishmail. Meals, desserts, and snacks have to be prepared.

Anushka and Tara find what they want easily, but nothing meets Zahra's taste. So they keep exploring. Most shops are owned and managed by the Chinese. The huge stores flamboyantly smell of leather that one can sniff from a mile away. Shoes are stockpiled in thin hardboard boxes on wooden shelves inside, while some adorn the glass window displays to attract customers. The Chinese are three-to-four-generation immigrants to West Pakistan, own businesses, and speak Urdu with an accent. They work mostly in enterprises owned by their native clans.

The salesmen smile at the determined little Zahra as she tries on several pairs of shoes. Ishmail doesn't want to force her to settle for something against her wishes. Finally, in a big store, where the shoebox piles are stacked high almost touching the ceiling, the owner, a man in his eighties, comes over to serve Zahra. He gently shows her many different designs, always accepting her rejection with a smile, never questioning but encouraging her to explore further. He draws Zahra's attention to a black pair of shoes, simple in style, with micro-heels, slightly raised rather than being flat, a bow on the top. Inside on the sole is written, in sparkling silver-shiny color, *Little Lady*. This pair steals her heart.

"This little one knows her mind. She'll never back off from what she feels is right.... Mark my words, sahib," the old man predicts as he packs the shoes.

They wave at him as they step out, relieved. At home that night, she holds the shoes in her tiny palms, keeps admiring them. She has difficulty falling asleep because she has to peep inside the box several times to check on her shoes to make sure they are still there. At one point, as Ishmail is passing by the door, under the night-light he sees the girl kissing her shoes as she utters in a low voice, "What good luck.... I found you!"

From that day onward, for many years Ishmail calls Zahra "my little lady." Even her sisters tease Zahra with that name. She loves the nickname. It brings back the enthralling times of shopping with the family and a reminder of happy memories.

Zahra's shoe-hunting episode becomes a popular family story, narrated many times by her father and sisters over the years at festivities and family gatherings.

3.

Sabaa and Ishmail watch movies almost every Saturday. Sabaa is a cinema addict. If she has difficulty understanding the dialogues in English movies, Ishmail interprets to her in whispers. The couple is careful about the films the girls are allowed to watch. They don't want their daughters to be exposed to things that are not fit for them at an impressionable age. However, they permit the realities of life in tiny doses to the girls. So they are allowed to watch light kissing scenes in English movies, passionate embraces and villainous acts, romantic singing and dancing, and scantily clad women in Indian and Pakistani films.

When their parents watch mature films, the girls are left at home with their aya, the live-in Punjabi nanny who also assists Sabaa in the kitchen. Sophia Loren, the Italian-born Hollywood film star, is their favorite. Sabaa and Ishmail also like Cary Grant and Doris Day. From Indian movies they love Nargis and Dilip Kumar, legendary stars of all time.

Ishmail buys a popular Philips brand radio, the latest model, as his earnings are comfortable now. In the early mornings after the news, he listens to Hindi film songs on Radio Ceylon. When sleep begins to become lighter in the early hours, Zahra usually wakes up to the sounds of these melodies. As she hears the Hindi songs and her father shaving in the background, she knows dawn is breaking.

～つ

On Sunday evenings, Sabaa loves to listen to the radio drama program broadcast in Bangla from the Dhaka radio station at eight sharp. Ishmail and the girls listen with her as well. Dinner isn't served till the ninety-minute-long drama ends. Ishmail makes sure to maneuver to the right channel beforehand as Sabaa doesn't like to miss the beginning.

"Sabaa, girls, time for *natok* [drama]!" He normally raises the alert enthusiastically, though after some time, his attention wanders. He waits for it to end so that dinner can be eaten and he is able to read medical journals afterwards.

Tara and Zahra cram into the space in front of the radio with Sabaa, though sometimes they find the program hard to follow. But they don't want to miss this ritual. Anushka is too young to join in. By the time the drama ends, she is usually half asleep. But Sabaa holds off dinner till the end.

4.

After two years in Lahore, Ishmail gets transferred to Rawal Pindi in December of 1963. Their cantonment residence is on the outskirts of Islamabad. To escape the brutal hot summer days of Pindi, on weekends Ishmail likes to take his family to the nearby hilly town of Murree. The rental taxi cruises on the narrow, steep spiral roads for hours and finally takes them to a world of cool atmosphere for a day. Sometimes they stay an extra day to relax. The sisters run wild in the hills—their mouths turning blue with the juice of wild berries. Their arms and legs get scratched from thorny bushes. Laughing heartily, they chase each other in the idyllic landscape.

They stay at the same small motel in downtown Murree each time. The owner and his wife, a kind elderly couple, becomes very fond of the family. They serve special delicacies; some are meant for the girls' palates, which they immensely appreciate.

"This place makes me happy. I love it here," Sabaa remarks at every visit. So Ishmail makes sure to take them back to Murree frequently, though it taxes the purse strings. He likes to see Sabaa smiling. "I've never seen mountains before. They look so majestic! I wish my mother could be with us." Tota, as Sabaa recalls, has never seen mountains either.

"We must invite her, then...to visit us." Ishmail is true to his word, and Tota is brought to experience her first exhilarating exposure to the high Pir Panjal Range of Murree the year after....

In the evenings, they walk through the narrow, steep streets of Murree to buy inexpensive traditional trinkets, handicrafts, woolen scarves from the roadside stalls. Shopping is fun. So is haggling. They buy things they don't need. The prices are inconsequential, so they don't mind. At night, the stars shine through the windows. The houses spread all over the landscape at the foot of the hills look like an enormous garland, entrapped sparks of light in a long, never-ending circle. In the distance, silhouetted against the night, the mountains look mysterious in semidarkness.

Zahra stays awake for a very long time on such nights in Muree, peering outside. She's bewitched by the spell of silence drenched in faint glimmering moonlight, unaware how her life will shape up in the years yet to come. At these moments, she feels secure that her parents and sisters are sleeping nearby, and if she strains her ears, she will hear their heartbeats very close to hers.

The sisters like their school. They make new friends. Sabaa carefully ensures that they speak Bangla, their native tongue, at home so that they don't forget it altogether. They learn three additional languages simultaneously. When their friends come to visit, they chirp in a symphony of diverse dialects—Urdu, English, a little Punjabi, some Bangla by Anushka, still struggling to manage beyond her mother tongue.

Nanny screams only in Punjabi to restrain Tara and her followers, who keep jumping on the sofa to no end. She is afraid the girl will fall and break her neck or hurt herself really badly. Sabaa never steps into Nanny's jurisdiction when she chastises her daughters, which happens often to calm down Tara.

"*Ey kuri, Ey Kuri tu baith ja, ullu di pathi.* [Little girl, sit down, you silly daughter of a good-for-nothing.]"

Nanny's chanting continues. So does Tara's jumping....

5.

In January of 1969, Ishmail is transferred to Chittagong. Sabaa is excited. It's a port city in the south of East Pakistan. Though a few hundred miles away from Harirampur, it feels like home. Both she and Ishmail think it's good for the girls to be in their own culture now. Ishmail buys his first car—a four-door blue Fiat that Sabaa chooses.

The nation is politically volatile. The Awami League, the Bengalee nationalist party, spearheaded by Sheikh Mujibur Rahman, demands greater autonomy for East Pakistan under its six-point manifesto. Bengalees break into frequent protests and unite under the banner of the Awami League.

It's an uncertain time—a time of hope and a time of hopelessness. The status quo is challenged. Ishmail, Sabaa, and their daughters get caught up in this impossible time of desperation.

~~~~~

Tara is willful and temperamental. Sabaa looks at her daughter at times in wonder and is confused. She fails to understand what Tara really wants. But Sabaa knows that out of her three daughters, Tara needs her the most, though she hides behind a facade of toughness.

Tara is an extreme risk-taker, impulsive, but she has a heart of gold that is driven by genuine acts of compassion—mostly. People say she's the spitting image of her mother and has inherited Sabaa's striking looks. From childhood, Tara has grown up getting compliments on her beauty. To some, this has gone to her head, ballooned her pride. But her sisters laugh—riot—at this very thought and wave it aside with insignificant attention. They idolize her and adore her for who she is, especially Zahra. They are strongly tied in a friendship and sisterly love that is very special, very rare.

In the past, Ishmail didn't hesitate to discipline Tara whenever she scandalously crossed the boundaries. She was a child in age but a menace in action. As the teenage years hit, she becomes more daring and doesn't pause to thwart house rules meant for good girls. She hates to be nice, wants to play dirty, mean — to get what she at that point in time desires. Her parents grow frustrated but not much troubled as her behavior is guided by childish guile.

Tara cares deeply for the people she loves. Her loyalty for them is deep, unmatchable. Her sensitive mind is alert to detecting voids in others, and she is beside them in all sincerity. She is untamed, outrageous, but at the same time immensely compassionate.

Tara is more comfortable playing sports popular with boys and has strong fans loyal to her, following her in valiant ventures. They are awed by her daring and aspire to be like her, though her bold steering leads them into trouble at home at times. Her two younger siblings are sworn to sisterly secrecy, which they protect with their lives. So Tara's misdeeds are easily covered up most of the time with the diligent allegiance of her sisters, who guard her actions when she goes rogue.

Sometimes, when Tara's mischievousness soars to glowing heights, Ishmail grounds her by locking her in the bathroom. This is to bring some peace back into the house and basically teach her a lesson, not so much a heartless act. However, Tara's fiery free spirit remains unscathed, unafraid. She either tries to discover an escape route or defiantly ignores her defeat. The younger girls watch helplessly at such times. The moment their father is out of sight, they look for Sabaa to come to the rescue. Some days, Tara is lucky. Help comes faster. Some days, Sabaa is too fed up and thinks Tara deserves it. However, privately she doesn't agree with her husband's ways of chastising Tara.

"She's an adolescent now. Don't push her too much. She may break," Sabaa cautions Ishmail from time to time.

"She's too giddy-headed," Ishmail responds, or he says, "She needs to learn boundaries."

Tara likes to lead. Deep down, she has a hunger to be accepted and admired. She feels she deserves it more than anyone else. Being on top is important to her ego. Her smart, ever-restless mind constantly hunts for creative outlets to express ideas, ideals that charm people who get to know her. She never means to hurt anyone, but in her zeal to become the nucleus of any story, she does quite often.

At thirteen, Tara is almost an epitome of brilliance and bravery among her peers. Some are inspired to follow her; some have little choice, as crossing swords with her would ultimately mark them as losers. Others are simply attracted to her somewhat reckless defiance of everyday matters, especially norms.

Ishmail and Sabaa aren't overly concerned because she is doing well in school. However, they keep an eye on her from a distance, not to crush her pride at every mistake she makes but to extend a helping hand to pick her up before she falls heedlessly in the dirt, broken. However, Tara misjudges this support as restraint, criticism, and punishment.

Silently, she fumes into more rebellion by making choices oblivious of possible consequences. And this continues....

~

Tara considers Zahra her best friend, though they are quite the opposite in every possible way. From a young age, Zahra has known what she wants. Her choice is clear. She trusts people; her heart breaks each time that trust is misplaced. But she chooses to believe in people despite the disappointments, has conviction in their inherent decency rather than hold back in fear and the prejudice of suspicion.

Zahra lived in a world of her own till she was nine. Fantasies and daydreams resided together and came alive in her creative mind. Trees and flowers were her friends. She spent hours playing with them, speaking to them in her imagination. Reading was her escape from the pandemonium that bred around her. When others were running wild outside or climbing trees, chasing fallen leaves in a thunderstorm, she would find solace sitting in a corner in her room, reading, writing, or drawing.

Zahra composed her first poem at the age of five. It was about Tara—her sister, her best friend, whom she has never stopped loving and admiring. She can give anything to Tara, her heroine, at any time.

6.

A somewhat tiny resentment silently keeps brewing inside Tara since, from childhood, Anushka has been closer to Zahra than anyone else. She tries to brush away this low indignation and is successful most of the time. Zahra is Anushka's role model. She runs to Zahra in happiness and when in trouble. She holds Zahra in high esteem, admires her for her stubborn bold stands on truth. At ten, of course, she has a mind of her own—independent, astounding in creative feats. Anushka continues keeping faith in her sister all her life.

Anushka discovers beauty in everyday, humdrum existence. From an early age, she has almost stunned people with her courage to graciously smile with deepening dimples even at shocking absurdities. Disappointment never dampens her feisty spirit. She is a mender, a blender, puts others' priorities first.

In her heart, Anushka believes there is a story behind every action, that each person deserves a second chance. Even if they are complete and total "assholes," metamorphosis is possible. There is a kind of sweet innocence that gleams in the dark depths of her eyes. She's armed with warmth for everyone around her.

"Anush, you have such a beautiful mind! It's agonizing," Zahra has commented often, amazed at her sister's graciousness.

"Mother Teresa's post will be vacant soon. You can try for that, Anush...but you need to grow up first...maybe...." Tara never stops teasing her.

"For your information, I'm ten, Tara." Anushka fights back firmly to every bit of teasing Tara throws at her.

Though in her adolescence, Anushka is labeled a tomboy, later, she grows up into an amazing, attractive person, having admirably cruised through the early tumultuous years.

PART III.

1970S AND 80S

CHAPTER NINETEEN

We lived through the war!

I.

The girls smoothly transition to Chittagong to the delight of their parents. Tara has turned fourteen, and at thirteen, Zahra has her first boyfriend.

Zahra falls for Leo—somewhat. She isn't completely in love yet but is madly attracted to him. This is her first romantic awakening. Her emotions are still in the realm of adolescent confusion.

They start reading together...walking around the school grounds...eating tiffin in the canteen. Sometimes they hold hands while strolling on the quietest part of the school grounds, his palms sweaty while hers are trembling slightly the entire time clasped in his. Tara doesn't hesitate to win him over.

Tara is drawn to Leo the moment they are introduced. And then Zahra discovers they are sneaking out to the park, sitting under trees, spending time together without telling her. That's when she loses her boyfriend, and loses her sister and best friend. Though difficult, Zahra struggles with the pain and betrayal from those she trusted most. But she doesn't confront them. She decides just to fade into the background, keep her head high and focus on her studies. Her heart keeps breaking into millions of pieces. She doesn't want to become an object of pity among her friends and Tara's followers. She goes her own way. The heartbreak crushes her anguished soul.

Eventually Tara breaks up with Leo, simply out of boredom or maybe because she realizes how much she has hurt Zahra, whose love she holds very dear.

"Sis, can you forgive me? I know I have pained you." Tara is genuine. "I was mean, rotten. Not sure why I behave so badly at times," she whispers as she holds her sister close. Both weep long, silent tears of their insecure teen years. In tears shed in the weight of hurt hearts, they reconcile.

Zahra never looks back, though an ache stays inside her for months. But she forgives Tara. Tara is relieved. The refuge back into Zahra's heart feels good. The tears wash away all stains of bitterness, most remnants of pain.

They become sisters again, inseparable in their devotion to each other.

~

Time glides by, generally uneventful at home. Tara is mutinous sometimes, often lives through a mixture of happiness, anger, and bits of sadness. Her choice of friends doesn't meet Ishmail's approval. She wants to go out with them, hang around longer, but permission is mostly denied, causing constant friction and sparks between the father and the daughter.

Tara is consumed by teenage madness. Recurrent scenarios ensue; almost similar words are uttered over and over. It pains Sabaa no end, unsettles the smooth home environment. It's disturbing for Zahra and Anushka as well.

2.

The living room door is shut with a bang. Zahra hears her parents' voices as she bends over Anushka's drawing chart. This is her new project, and she needs Zahra's help.

Tara has gone off to a friend's house after school and isn't back yet. The last rays of the sun turn the hills and the trees golden before dipping into the twilight.

The girls hear more sounds—comings and goings in the living room. Ishmail's voice trails off; sounds of Sabaa's footsteps hover on the hard floor and continue. A car takes off somewhere close by. Anushka is oblivious of everything, totally focused on her project. The wall clock chimes, announcing the hours. It goes on and on, it seems.... All this while, Sabaa doesn't peek into their room even once. Zahra's heart knows something isn't right. It has something to do with Tara. What must have she done now to rouse her parents? Then a series of events takes over, fast. And as suddenly, everything returns to the way it was before—in the next twenty-four hours...as if nothing had happened. Zahra is relieved to see Tara sleeping in the bed next to hers with her face turned to the other side.

In the morning, before her sisters are up, as she tiptoes into the dining room for a glass of water, Zahra hears her parents talking in low voices.

"It's the best for the girls, Sabaa. I'll ask for a transfer...to Lahore.... My boss is going to agree...." Ishmail's voice is tender, almost a raspy whisper. He has his arms around Sabaa. Sabaa sniffles softly.

Zahra withdraws silently. Something has changed, definitely....

⁓

"Why are you always hateful? Cruel to me, Aba?" Tara's screaming echoes through the house. Zahra and Anushka hold their breath as the fight begins again. "Everyone goes out with friends. It's only me who is not trusted." Tara doesn't tone it down.

"You live in my house; you follow my rules." Ishmail is firm.

"Can you at least hear her out? You can't deny her every time." Sabaa tries to reason with him but is ignored.

"Tara, you have yet to learn to be responsible. You still can't differentiate good from bad." Ishmail remains unperturbed.

"You can't stop me.... I'm going to the picnic with my friends." Tara throws her notebook against the wall in protest.

"You know what you did...only a little while ago.... That stain still needs to be cleaned." Ishmail's cold voice cuts through. Tara halts in midair, inhales heavily. Her lips quiver, eyes flash.

"You're mean...mean!" Tara screams.

"Can you not be slightly lax with her?" Sabaa tries to negotiate again in a hushed tone.

"So that she can hang herself? Disgrace us more? You want that?" Ishmail spits out, loud enough for all to hear.

"I hate you! You're a mean old man!" Tara says whatever comes to her mind to express her fury. Her sisters watch helplessly. Then she runs to the bedroom and with a loud bang locks the door from inside, not allowing anyone to enter. She refuses to answer to knocks and declines food.

Tara cools down and picks up normal life the next morning, pretending nothing has happened. Ishmail has no reaction, remains nonchalant. But everyone knows this ceasefire is fragile, transitory, till new differences spring up. However, on several occasions, she goes out with friends without telling her parents. What they don't know won't hurt them. Zahra is aware, but it isn't her story to tell. She's extremely loyal to her sister. Anyway, Tara has sworn her to secrecy. Tara's rebellion continues, sometimes in silence, sometimes in volcanic proportions that rock the peace in the house.

Zahra understands Tara much more than anyone in the family. She pins all emotional deficits and delinquencies to life-changing events that simply happened to them, around them, and because at fourteen, Tara's life has taken a startling turn that remains a constant stab in her unhealed wound. That's something no one talks about at all in the family. That's something they will always live with as their very own, protecting and containing.... That's Tara's secret. Only hers.

Tara's grades begin to fall. This is her way to assert dissent. Amidst tantrums and agitation, she continues to disappoint her parents.

3.

On 7 December 1970, the first general elections are held in Pakistan. The Awami League wins a landslide victory, becomes the face of East Pakistan/Bengal. Bengalees are elated. They are finally successful!

A week following the election, after having served honorably for almost two years in Chittagong, Ishmail, along with his family, lands in Lahore. He was able to convince his superiors for this transfer. He believes this is best for his daughters. The extended family is dismayed, but everything comes with a cost. With many tears, Sabaa boarded the plane once more.

The Awami League's victory after a fierce contest with the Pakistan Peoples Party representing West Pakistan places the West Pakistani ruling administration in an impossible position, creates an unimaginable problem. They are simply not ready to hand over power to the elected representatives from East Pakistan....

On 25 March 1971, West Pakistan launches a genocide against the Bengalees...and the civil war begins.... It's the march for life for Bengalees....

4.

Historical background: *The seed of independence was actually sown with the Bangla language movement of 1952. And the discontentment grew over the years.*

On 25 March 1971 at midnight, the Pakistani army launched Operation Searchlight against the innocent people of East Pakistan to subdue the voices of Bengalees and delegitimize their elected representatives, who had won by majority vote. The leader of the Awami League—the father of the nation, Sheikh Mujib-ur-Rahman—was arrested. The killing began right away.

While under occupation, East Pakistan was renamed Bangladesh on 27 March 1971, formally proclaimed by a Bengalee officer who had deserted the Pakistani army to join the freedom fight—Major Ziaur Rahman, the commander of the East Bengal Regiment. On behalf of Sheikh Mujib, he also declared himself the interim head of the republic. Later, a second elaborate declaration was broadcast from the independent Bangladesh radio station Shadheen Bangla Betar Kendra, which operated from Kolkata.

The genocide perpetrated by West Pakistani forces against its own defenseless citizens of the Bengalee race over the duration of nine months claimed millions of lives (the total number is disputed) and destroyed families and infrastructures. Bengalee military officers, soldiers, and police were killed ruthlessly. An estimated ten million refugees crossed over to India (UNHCR 2000, 59), and thirty million were internally displaced.

About two to four hundred thousand (exact numbers are disputed) girls and women were raped by the Muslim West Pakistani soldiers in the name of fighting a holy war against infidels, the term they used to label the moderate Muslim Bengalees. It was a Nazi–Hitlerian strategy. Bengalee women were declared as Hindus, as enemies. The soldiers were rewarded for their atrocious acts committed against them.

∼⌒

East Bengal is crisscrossed by countless rivers, streams, and lakes and by the fierce Bay of Bengal in the south. Over generations, Bengalees mastered the language of the waves to survive, decoded the savage signs of typhoons to persist. From time immemorial, the fury of the monsoons, intensified by the inexorable tropical cyclones born in the womb of the Bay of Bengal, has been tirelessly lashing the inland with destructive force. It is a commonplace phenomenon that the Bengalees wrestle with from the day they are born. Some dominate it; some learn to live with it; while others succumb to its inevitable lethal grip. No one can mess with the harsh wrath of nature in Bengal. The storm- and rain-swept land transforms into a thousand islands when the swelling waves cross over infinite distances, discharged from the fiery folds of their sources of origin in the mighty Himalayas to vanquish the vast, flat landscape—challenging the invincible Bengalee spirit.

The Bengalees belong to a brave race. They duel with nature and disease and haven't been subdued through the ages. The Mughals failed, and so did the British, to fully subjugate Bengal, which historically remained unconquered or quasi-independent all along. Though the British took control of the region in the late eighteenth century after the infamous Battle of Palassey in 1757 and the Battle of Buxar in 1764, uprisings continued throughout the colonization period to overthrow them, piercing holes in their rule.

Pakistani soldiers were engaged in a senseless battle with the fierce Bengalees in their own homeland and finally defeated. On 16 December 1971, General Niazi, leading the West Pakistani forces, surrendered with 93,000 soldiers in Dhaka to the Indian commander, General Manekshaw, and the Bengalee freedom fighters...and the people of the newly formed Republic of Bangladesh.

∼⌒

It is a totally new environment in Lahore as the citizens of the same country are openly at war with one another. In the office, Ishmail can detect the shadow of suspicion in the way his colleagues, the West Pakistani officers, look at him. News of killings of Bengalee military officers, soldiers, and police, along with innocent civilians, is no secret. Every Bengalee family is affected.

In school, the girls also face passive animosity from some of their classmates. The three sisters are the only Bengalee students in their school. There are whispers behind their backs. Many of the fathers or older brothers of their classmates are in the military and are now deployed to crush the civil war in East Pakistan. In their own country, the girls are treated as aliens.

By August, the atrocities launched by the Pakistani army become a global concern. The superpowers begin a dialogue, and some show support to Pakistan while the others voice theirs for the Bengalees. But one thing is clear—Bengalee freedom fighters, the *mukti bahini*, are holding their ground and beating the West Pakistani-trained soldiers. India openly assists the mukti bahini. America and China stand by their ally, Pakistan. Senator Ted Kennedy leads US congressional support for independence for Bangladesh. The French minister André Malraux vows to fight along with the mukti bahini.

Rumors spread that a merciless fate may be waiting for families and Bengalee forces now serving in various duty stations in West Pakistan. Though the senior officers try to instill a spirit of solidarity, trust is totally broken. Ishmail decides to send his family back to Dhaka. His friends caution him that this may trigger alarms. He could be marked as a flight risk, suspected of preparing for desertion, to join the freedom fight back in the homeland.

"There are things more painful than death. I'll stay here, take my chances. Nothing is more important to me than Sabaa and my girls. They'll have a better chance of surviving back in our village." Ishmail's voice is firm.

5.

With a heavy heart, on a rain-drenched day in September of 1971, Sabaa lands in Dhaka with her three adolescent daughters, having again traveled alone without a male chaperone. Her co-passengers are overwhelmingly Pakistani soldiers in civilian clothes. Their cropped haircuts and stiff body language give them away.

The city is choked in a foreboding silence, often pierced by faint sounds of machine guns in the distance. Military convoys dominate the roads. Smoke owns the blue skies as houses are ablaze somewhere. It's a different Dhaka, bizarre, broken.

Sabaa's life has taken yet another turn. She doesn't know if she will ever see Ishmail again, whether it was a goodbye, an ultimate farewell this time. She left him behind—in enemy land all alone. It was a tough decision, an impossible choice to make.

It's a strange war. Unnecessary...

"The world is watching as we are butchered. The superpowers are deep in political games." Like all Bengalees, Elias is angry.

"Russia favors India, Mamu Jaan. And India supports us." Tara is more optimistic.

Everyone in the house is glued to broadcasts by the BBC Bangla service, Shadhin Bangla Radio, operating from Kolkata, and Radio India. News is important. They also listen to Radio Pakistan to check what lies it's spreading.

India fortifies the Bengalee freedom fighters. Its interest is political, its long-standing hostility to Pakistan. Breaking up Pakistan would cripple its strength forever.

Zahra is reading Karl Marx these days. Elias bought her a book on socialism. "America is antisocialism, against Russia...so it favors Pakistan," she chips in to the discussion.

"Yeah, America is threatening to steer its Seventh Fleet into the Indian Ocean, flexing its muscles," Elias mutters. "No one is thinking about the massacre of Bengalees."

A bigger war is imminent. The cost of freedom is high.

⟶

The house where the girls and Sabaa are now staying is in the newer part of Dhaka. Dhola bought this house in a posh neighborhood a decade ago. It filled a need to feed his status as the business flourished. The house in the old town was rented out right afterwards, though the printing press continues to operate from the ground floor.

The evenings cast dismal shadows as blackouts and curfews are imposed. The mornings are bleaker and stuffed with horrors. Every day, alarming inhuman stories of brutality are revealed. Pakistani soldiers raid houses randomly, making arrests, especially males between the ages of thirteen and fifty whom they then put in military trucks to unknown destinations. Only a handful of fortunate ones return. The rest are shot dead and dumped in unmarked ditches. Dhaka is covered in a sinister shroud adorning a pervasive smell of death. Dread hangs in every corner.

The United Nations, as fearless as ever, condemns the killings and human rights violations but fails to defuse the situation politically. In every family, someone has been killed or gone missing. Most families also have someone who has joined the mukti bahini.

Bengalee mothers live in constant terror. Young men are lined up and shot in front of their grief-stricken parents and families, who are forced to watch the atrocities. Torture is used as a weapon of intimidation. But the resistance begins to grow, and it grows bigger every day.

Sabaa's cousin is shot dead by the military in broad daylight in Mymensingh. He was Tota's sister, Mejho's son. He leaves behind a bereaved young widow and minor children. No one is safe under the fascist military.

～⊃

There is no news of Ishmail. War with India has broken out in the western part of Pakistan as well. Ishmail is positioned near the Lahore border with the field ambulance hospital. Sabaa tries to hide her worry from the girls and goes about with a brave face.

"Zahra, I've been so mean to Aba. What if he doesn't come back? He'll never know how much I love him," Tara says quietly as the night sky is pierced by orange flames in the distance. The army must have raided that area and set fires. The constant roaring of machine guns breaks the silence of the night under curfew.

Zahra has a cold and fever. Tara lies down beside her on the bed.

"He'll come back. You know that," Zahra tries to reassure her sister. "Now, move away or you'll catch my cold."

"I really don't mind. We can snuggle under the same quilt and have the same kind of fever." Tara moves closer.

～⊃

Tara starts writing her journal. In a sprawled hand, she tries to express her pent-up adolescent emotions...

I don't know why I become so mean sometimes. I make Ama cry, Zahra sad. She is my best friend, but I hurt her, especially when Aba favors her—he agrees to everything she says, but he refuses to listen to me. I get angry. I fight with Aba over little things, say nasty words. I want him to see me, treat me as he does Zahra and others. No one understands me—except Zahra. Sometimes I don't understand myself. I am not a bad person. I know I have broken the house rules, created many problems…shamed Aba, Ama….

This war is scary. What if the Pakistani military comes for us? I don't want them to shoot Ama and my sisters. I hope they take Nana, actually. He is an angry old man. I don't like him. I know I should not say bad things about Ama's father. She wouldn't like it. But Dhola Kazi has a heart of darkness!

I love you, Aba. Please don't die in this war. Ama's pain would be unbearable. I want to prove to you that I can be a good daughter to you. If you die without saying goodbye to me, I will die of a broken heart myself.

Years later, Tara shows her journal to Zahra. It makes her cry.

6.

The final stage of the war begins with the bombing of Dhaka by the Indian air force on 3 December.

"Buji, India is alerting everyone about more bombings in Dhaka…. Shadhin Bangla radio is broadcasting it," Elias tells Sabaa as they crouch on the kitchen floor to eat breakfast. "We need to leave soon."

"How are we going? Is it safe?" Tara, like her sisters, is excited, not afraid.

"Try to hire a boat by tonight," Dhola advises his sons. "No need to delay anymore."

When the bombing starts the next morning, Bengalees mostly are jubilant. Many fearlessly climb on rooftops, waving and shouting their support of the Indian air force every time their aircraft appear in the skies of Dhaka. They want to see the Pakistani forces crushed.

Sabaa's brothers manage to hire a big boat to travel to Hari-rampur. Several friends and relatives join them. Women sit under the scanty roof while the girls huddle outside with Tota at the back, the unhooded part, where she sets up a kerosene stove and begins cooking. Twenty-four people are on board, including four boatmen. Dhola discusses politics with some men at the front of the boat; some young men climb on the roof while bombs hit Dhaka. A festive mood befalls.... The sounds of bombs are received with cheers. The BBC reports that the Pakistani military is now morally crippled and holed up in bunkers in the Dhaka cantonment. All other cities are falling to the mukti bahini. This is the first time Zahra sees the body of a dead soldier as it floats facedown in the Buriganga River, bobbing up and down with the rising and breaking waves. She isn't shocked or sad; she is devoid of any emotion by then.

In thirty minutes, they cover eight miles. They see villagers carrying Bangladeshi flags, crowding on the banks to wave at them. The passing boats wave to one another and exchange greetings. The countryside is as unperturbed as before, unviolated by the war. Tota generously serves lentils, chicken curry with potatoes, and rice to all. They stop near a bazaar to buy snacks and take bathroom breaks. Zahra and her sisters along with other females walk into the fields, followed by a crowd of children. They are a novelty! Tota shoos them away.

There aren't any toilets, so they squat in a jute field with the tall, leafy plants serving as cover. The squatting requires precision and patience. It's difficult, but the absurd situation is laughable. The girls giggle a lot while relieving themselves. For the first time in months, they are free from fear. Tota accepts their rowdiness with patience. She's glad that her brood has managed to flee the burning city.

Back on the boat, the war in Dhaka seems unreal. On the radio, victory songs and announcements stimulate the euphoria. It is a feeling that is very different, extraordinary, and unique. Bangladeshi flags hoisted on bamboo poles dominate the landscape, dance with the wind everywhere, with their motif of the rising sun on a green background breaking boundaries....

West Pakistani forces have undermined the stubborn courage of Bengalees who wear the dust of paddy fields as an armor of pride, ignoring their fanatic devotion to their land and heritage. In the overpowering scent of the moist soil, surging waters, and brutal climate, life-threatening diarrhea and the fierce resistance of the people, the highly trained Pakistani military is defeated, emasculated for its arrogance. In indignity, they surrender after facing heavy casualties. Their ego is castrated, their machismo destroyed forever.

Bangladesh is born on 16 December 1971 after a fierce battle of nine months.

~~

Right afterwards, Bengalee forces serving in West Pakistan are arrested as prisoners of war with their families. They are forced to live under harsh conditions in captivity and indignity till the new sovereign government of Bangladesh and Pakistan come to an understanding to repatriate these trapped citizens. Ishmail is taken as a POW. Though extremely stressful, he tolerates the hardships in the concentration camp knowing his family has been spared from cruelty....

And the war changes Ishmail forever!

CHAPTER TWENTY

Salad days and
re-awakenings

I.

After being a POW for almost three years, Ishmail is repatriated to Bangladesh in 1974 and reunited with his family. He rejoins the Bangladesh military. All his savings and personal effects are left behind in Lahore. Sabaa counts every penny. Ishmail bicycles to his office. They start afresh in Bangladesh in an environment of political and economic instability. The girls pursue their education.

⁓

While she is waiting for admission to the university, Tara has a crush on her music teacher, Ripon. They start talking one evening after class. Everyone has left by then. That's when it all begins. Zahra is worried, horrified—if Ishmail finds out, he will be very upset. Tara is too young to make a commitment, and the music teacher is far below their social status.

Tara's new madness continues for six months. Ripon is in

his early twenties — a vocalist and composer with an amazing voice. Music is his life. He wants to be famous one day. And Tara suddenly seems to glide from heaven into his content, small life, splashing with the colors of warmth and beauty, opening his mind to a fantasy he never dared to think of. He falls for her heavily.

It's an all-consuming love that burns inside, driving him to the edge of sanity. Tara is taken aback at the intensity of his emotions, his forceful reactions. What she started lightheartedly becomes weighty as an anchor that pulls a ship down into steadiness against rocking waves, keeps her home. Tara doesn't want to be tied down in safety.

Ripon can't sleep at night and walks the streets around Tara's house — under the lonely sky on barren roads, breathing in the glow of decayed, feeble lampposts. He composes hundreds of songs during his nocturnal wanderings in the silent hours. At dawn back at his room, he jots down all his creative ideas. He sends them to Tara.

Tara gets nervous. She feels smothered under the burden of this newfound love that is truer for him than to her. The novelty wears off in the tension over being found out by her father. It becomes worrisome. She decides to call it off and drops out of music class.

"I need some space...to think. Let's stay away for some time," she proposes. He labels her as cruel, irresponsible, cold, and calculating.

He can't accept it and constantly phones Tara. He knows the best time to call — when Ishmail is busy with his private medical practice. Ripon doesn't have a phone at his tiny one-room residence. He has to depend upon the mercy of his friends to make a call or pay cash at shops to use their phone. It's difficult in a noisy public place where others are listening. But he doesn't give up. Tara never picks up the phone. It's always Zahra who informs him, as instructed, that Tara isn't home or has gone to bed early. Finally, the calls become too frequent. The possibility of Ishmail finding out becomes a reality, so Tara hatches a plan and tutors Zahra.

Zahra asks Ripon to meet her at the bookstore opposite her college and indicates Tara will be there. As agreed, Zahra finds him waiting in one corner of the small, stuffy bookstore, looking anxious, pale, with signs of sleepless nights etched on his tired eyelids.

"Where's Tara?" He swallows hard, in pain. His Adam's apple moves up and down. It's fascinating to watch. Zahra has to forcibly keep her eyes on his face.

"Aba has sent her away to Sylhet town...to prepare for university admission tests," Zahra lies. "She'll stay there at my aunt's for some time." Another neat lie as coached by Tara. Sabaa doesn't have any sisters. They have no relatives in Sylhet.

"What?... I need to see your father. I will tell him everything. I can't go on like this," Ripon says, desperation in his voice.

Now, this is something the sisters had not anticipated. They thought the news of Tara's departure from Dhaka would put him off her scent. He is a gentle soul, not a fighter. Tara has made a mistake in reading his personality, for sure. Desperation makes him daring.

"He has a gun," Zahra suddenly mentions. She has become emboldened with her lying by now. She needs to protect her sister at any cost.

"Who?"

"Aba. He'll shoot you if he finds out about you and Tara.... He's a very angry man. He fought in two wars," she warns.

"What?" Ripon is taken aback. "But there are laws. He can't escape...police would catch him." Beads of perspiration break out on his upper lip, dampen his sideburns, a slow, gradual emergence as his mind races, questioning the prospect of such an insane action. Tara has always talked about her father's temper, the need to be secretive.

"Well, he'll definitely kill himself after he shoots you if I know him well. The family name is very important to Aba." Zahra watches the nervous movements of his hands. Then he sits down on a nearby chair, perplexed.

"I have to go now," Zahra says. "You're a good musician. Maybe one day you'll be famous. Aba wouldn't mind you so much." She leaves him with this consolation as Ripon tries a weak smile, harboring terror in his eyes.

Later at home, the sisters giggle as Zahra narrates the meeting verbatim. They are not heartless; they are teenage girls, unprepared for such demonstrative devotion from a temperamental young man of little means. The phone calls stop. They never hear from the musician again.

2.

University days start with new promises for Tara. She loves literature and is delighted when she gains admission into the English Department.

"I'm very glad you made it, Tara." Ishmail expresses his appreciation.

Finally, Tara is taking the first steps towards reaching her goal despite her rocky journey through life so far. She wants her father's admiration like he has for Zahra. It means a lot to her. She hates to be lesser to her sister. Though she deeply cares for Zahra, Tara fails to understand this pointless rivalry that she knows exists.

Tara changes totally. The professors and the courses offer her the motivation and novelty she has been searching for. She becomes truly interested in her studies. She works long hours at the library; interpreting the minds of literary talents grabs her concentration. Recognition from her professors brings her spirit to new heights of gratification. Ishmail is relieved; Sabaa takes her mind off of Tara and moves on to other things.

Tara meets Amin through friends at a university function. When it ends, she's unable to find the classmate who is supposed to give her a ride home, so she asks Amin to walk with her up to the main road to catch a baby taxi. It's quite late and starts to drizzle. There are no three-wheelers in the vicinity. Amin offers to drop her at home in a rickshaw. On the long trip, they sit huddled in the narrow back seat of the rickshaw under a plastic sheet as cover from the rain. They sit too close; the warmth of his body burns against her skin. She talks loudly, outdoing the sound of the deafening rain on the dark street, more to break the awkwardness, while he listens. Then something happens. He takes a brave step. He very suddenly grasps her hand and holds it till the road reaches her home.

The next day, she goes to the Philosophy Department, as Amin is a student there, and stands outside his classroom. He spots her as soon as class is over. Tara's face has a rare glow. In her light pink organdy sharee with an ink-blue tie-dye border, she looks elusive, unreal, somewhat delicate, and stunning. That day they eat lunch at the university cafeteria. Their story begins from there.

Tara falls in love again. She is in her second year of undergrad. It spells disaster from the very start. Amin is a frail, not so tall, somewhat insignificant, shy young man. He has a face that would go unnoticed in passing. His subdued personality doesn't instantly create interest to provoke any curiosity—a person tolerated but ignored.

Tara's ebullient nature is a contrast to his quiet demeanor. He rarely talks, smiles mostly when with Tara and agrees with everything she says. He is poor and struggles to meet the costs of fees and books. No one in his family has ever graduated from high school. The smell of paddy fields is fresh on him. Tara finds love in his simplicity, his inconsequential existence, his odd kind of silence.

"I'd love to see your village. Will you take me?" Often she

chides the fellow who offers a dry, tortured smile in response.

"Tara, Amin is so different from you. Are you sure about him?" is Zahra's reaction after meeting him. "Do you think Aba will agree? Accept him?"

"He's the one, sis. I love him. When does our father ever like anything I do? Just remind me of one instance. This time I'll do what I want to." Tara is defiant. Only a year or so ago, she got rid of the musician. "Aba judges me for one mistake I made.... Is he never wrong?" There is lot of unresolved pain in Tara.

Zahra doesn't want to remember Tara's secret. It's off-limits to this family.

⁓

Zahra is charming in more ways than one, according to her sisters.

"Sis, you could sell an igloo to an Eskimo," Tara adamantly maintains and deep down thinks her parents' partiality towards Zahra has something to do with her charm.

"You can market hopes...sell them as well?" Anushka is more playful. Zahra laughs at such compliments, doesn't fight them, though.

"You use the Zahra magic on Ama and especially Aba. I've never seen him so gentle with anyone." Tara holds this against her in half jest, half seriousness.

"Smitten, you mean?" Anushka thinks the same.

Zahra is the adapter, the accommodator in the family. "Our savior," as Ishmail named her early in life in genuine admiration of his daughter. She is ready to jump in with eagerness, to help with a smile, sincere and mesmerizing. Even total strangers can't escape. She wears empathy like her skin.

Anushka labels this as kindness, whereas Tara thinks it's an art, though harmless, that Zahra uses to get her way. Especially in their adolescent years when it was difficult to get Ishmail's permission to go to the movie theatre or outings with friends, the sisters nominated Zahra to face Ishmail with their plea. In most cases, their strategy guaranteed the expected outcome. Though Zahra laughs at these accusations made by Tara, she does believe that she has got some extra leverage with her parents as compared to her sisters. She uses this to keep peace in the family, in fact mainly to protect Tara as she always has issues with their father. Despite everything, Tara and she are best friends.

Zahra's mind is relentlessly engaged in innovative actions, though small, sometimes outwardly inconsequential, that she champions with the faith that they have the potential to preserve harmony in life and nature. So she continues to advocate for the rights of the plants, animals, and birds. She even feeds crows daily on the rooftop, emphasizing the need to be kind to these unwanted birds. Sabaa listens to her ideas with a smile, but Zahra can't escape from her sisters' teasing. They all agree the crows create a nuisance on the roof but tolerate it.

Through her growing years, Zahra was called shy. People labeled her as an eclectic from girlhood, in attire, looks, attitude. Early on, she had an idiosyncratic style that intensified with the passing years, adding to her appeal in adulthood, somewhat wacky but definitely enigmatic. Heads turn when she steps into a room. Unlike Tara, she is not a classic beauty, but there's something about Zahra that kills indifference.

Zahra loves to wear vibrant colors, surprisingly mismatched, carrying them with ease in her stride. This erroneous calamity adds to her personality, intensifying her charm. She has an immodest collection of stone-studded silver jewelry, gathered over the years. She wears her chunky trinkets meticulously, unabashed at all times. The gems sparkle in a unique symphony, creating an image that's enchanting, sort of surreal. No matter what, she has a fierce free spirit in every possible way.

Anushka learned singing and sings almost like a professional vocalist. She took real pains and worked hard through the years to perfect her talent. Ishmail likes to wake up in the morning to her husky, enchanting voice as she continues to practice daily. The magic in her voice soars through the house, touching every corner, the balcony, the windows, and fades into the green and blue of the outside world getting ready for the day.

"Your voice is so sweet, Anush, like sugary honey-crunch ice cream. Ummm...." Tara admires her singing to no end. She can be generous when it suits her mood.

3.

For the next two years Tara is pulled to Amin with a bizarre attraction, though he doesn't make any promises for a joint future. He has a widowed mother and a younger sister in school back at his village who he has to support eventually and is duty bound to make them his priority. Tara is a distraction whom he loves but is unable to accommodate in his future life.

Ishmail and Sabaa are on the lookout for the right match for Tara. The pressure at home to get married intensifies. Several young men with strong credentials and their families are introduced to Tara, but she always finds some reason to reject them. Her parents don't want to force her but expect her to agree to a sensible proposition eventually. That's how most marriages happen in the Bengalee culture — arranged, with the blessings of the parents. They know nothing about her romantic liaison. Tara keeps it a secret.

Tara lives much more in a make-believe world and is in denial about hard realities. She hasn't yet figured out how she will tell her parents about Amin. She has no plan. She and Zahra discuss some options, but nothing seems realistic.

However, at one point, Tara gives an ultimatum to Amin—to either choose her or walk away. Amin walks away—two long years of romancing given up so easily, without any hesitation! It meant nothing to him. This breaks her heart. It's a rejection extremely hard to accept. After many months of grieving, anger, and futile despondence, she decides to forget him. Her studies become her only concern....

4.

Sabaa watches Tara navigating through life with many stumbles and hard climbs, reaching emotional plateaus and then elegantly striding into her new life. Her daughter's transformation amazes her. Tara's self-esteem and confidence soar. With eager sincerity, she completes her master's on time. Her focus is to begin her life without any hesitancy or unnecessary delays. Life hails her.

~~~○

At twenty-eight and living in Dhaka of 1984, Tara looks at the world with very different lenses. Now she teaches English literature to her students at a renowned college. She opens the door for them to infinite passions that possess the potential to create unbridled rainbows to touch, untraveled trails to trek, with possibilities to harness dreams that breathe beyond the trappings of the mundane. Her students admire her and try to follow her as she bounces in confidence, as she's the emblem of the new, so different—an enigma. Her youthfulness and vigor shake up the lurking cobwebs of doubt about their own limitations, liberating their spirits.

Her parents continue matchmaking for Tara with new enthusiasm. They want her to get married, have children. Now is the right time for her to take the next steps towards a stable future.

Tara understands her parents' wishes. She laughs and keeps

pushing aside the potential suitors and their families. She isn't ready. She hasn't yet met the man who could sweep her off her feet, hold her tightly in the comfort of his arms, and walk beside her firmly into the unknown future. She waits with optimism.

Then, suddenly, things turn around, and she finds herself wrapped up in a life-changing drama—a NASA scientist working in America finds her most suitable as his life partner. Tara agrees to this match. By then, Zahra has already left the country.

CHAPTER TWENTY-ONE

The kingdom
in the clouds

I.

Zahra has always been studious and completes her law degree with distinction, to Ishmail's pride. Dhola, her grandfather, is long gone by now. He wanted her to be like Indira Gandhi, the famous first female and second-longest-serving prime minister of India, the daughter of the legendary leader J. Nehru. A woman of grace and beauty, Indira took the world political center by storm.

Sabaa basks in the glory of her daughter's achievement—a lawyer! Zahra has taken after her grandmother, Ishmail's biological mom, whom neither Sabaa nor any of the girls had met. There isn't even a single photograph of his mother to be found. But from his foggy memory of her, Ishmail can see Zahra's striking resemblance to Nadiah Bibi, the shy young woman who allowed her older sister to become Ishmail's Boro Ma, the real mother, while she faded into the background without any complaints or demands. Nadiah Bibi passed away one fine morning, still in her youth, without any preamble, any drama, or causing any problem for anyone. Ishmail was in seventh grade at the time, away from home, studying in Darjeeling. In life she was deeply humble—in death more unassuming.

Ishmail wishes he had paid more attention to this mother while she was alive. He begins grieving for her loss much, much later, after her body has returned, earth to earth, ashes to ashes, dust to dust.

2.

Zahra now works in a law firm. In the Dhaka of 1984, her job is pretty exciting compared to others. It has been quite a journey to get an insight into people's needs and desperation—criminality, punishments, and resurrections. Each dawn brings newer challenges, but she is ready for it.

She admires her bosses—a couple in their midforties, both fiercely committed lawyers, educated in the United Kingdom. They encourage and guide her but at the same time give her immense autonomy to grow. Her job entails processing cases on violence committed against women and girls. The sad faces, fear-filled eyes, and façade to maintain the status quo in a traditional society, manifested in anguish, shadow Zahra's every waking moment as soon as the case files are handed over to her. Navigating through heartbreaking testimonies of cruelty and deception hasn't been easy. She processes several groundbreaking cases on sexual abuse, penetrates legal loopholes, persists, and wins them all. In a short time, she becomes a rock star champion for women's rights.

Even in the modern 1980s Bengalee culture, it's not always easy to be independent, to project clear views as a woman. In the Dhaka milieu, she has already been defined by many as aggressive, a feminist who loves to throw men under the bus for the sheer joy of destroying them, a common misconstruction of the term and its inherent lost potential. Bengalees consider *feminist* a bad word, but it's used without scruples to define Zahra, a sparky young woman, one with sensible audacity. Even many women find it hard to defend her. Zahra, indeed has obscenely undressed a truth in public that's so vulgar, so immoral that people don't want to recognize it — vehemently reject the existence of sexism and discrimination. The tall and short of it is, Zahra is labeled as only trouble by some. Her sisters and parents persistently stand up for her, though she wants them to ignore the futile criticism. She doesn't need any protection. A woman who pushes boundaries to initiate new trends has less sympathy in a culture that thrives on denial. She understands, doesn't give up.

The law firm offers her a temporary posting in Kathmandu for six months, initially to assist a project jointly funded by international human rights organizations. She would be working in collaboration with the Nepali government. There's a strong possibility of an extension up to two years, subject to funding and the government's willingness to stop human trafficking. After four years of hard work as a junior lawyer, this is recognition, a solid promotion. Zahra is elated. However, Ishmail finds it hard to let her live alone in a foreign country. It's easy to convince Sabaa. She has great faith in her daughters. She persuades Ishmail to agree.

Zahra accepts the offer.

⌒

The Nepal project focuses mainly on social justice issues for the poor with special emphasis on empowering women and their protection. Zahra's role as a consulting legal associate is to assist Nepali initiatives on preventing trafficking of girls and women to brothels in Bombay. Zahra has been fascinated by the stories of Nepali women's struggles for their rights, fighting a rigid patriarchal system and a culture of discrimination. She begins to investigate the historical background further with new enthusiasm....

～⁀

In 1984, Nepal, the only Hindu kingdom in the world, out-wardly looks like a friendly, harmless culture. But women and girls have been targeted by a myopic male-controlled heritage with brutal consequences for their health, development, safety, and survival. The caste system, cultural frameworks, and extreme gender discrimination are at the base of all development challenges.

The history of the women's movement is simply intriguing. The National Code of Nepal (Mulki Ain) of 1963, which codifies the inheritance system, derives from the Hindu system of belief emphasizing patrilineal descent and a patrifocal residence system. Some of the provisions severely limit economic options for women; 303 acts, including the constitution, identified 103 discriminatory provisions and 92 schedules in various acts and regulations that discriminate against women, notably in nationality, marriage and family relations, sexual offense and property rights, and legal and court proceedings.

Attempts at reforms against gender discrimination have long been a quest in Nepalese and international history. In the 1850s, there were attempts towards gender reform in Nepal when Jung Bahadur Rana (the founder of the Rana dynasty who ruled Nepal for thirty-one years) decreed laws to prevent and discourage the "sati" (practice of widows being burnt alive with the dead bodies of their husbands on cremation pyres). Though Rana was considered to be successful in preventing the wives of his brothers from committing sati, it's recorded that his own wives embraced sati upon his death.

The women's movement in Nepal dates back to 1814 to the Nalapani War, when women struggled against British imperialism. They marched beside men in the civil rights movement of 1948. Nepali women also took an active part in the democratic revolution of 1951, which overthrew the 104 years of dictatorship of the Rana family. In 1948, the first women's organization, the Nepal Woman Association, was established. It worked to indoctrinate political awareness among women. From the 1960s onwards, the partyless Panchayat system banned all political parties and independent women's organizations. The political system of Nepal from 1960 (to 1990) was based on self-governance, historically prevalent in South Asia.

However, the declaration of 1975 as the International Women's Year, followed by the declaration of the United Nations Decade for Women (1977–1985), marks the change in the UN's focus on women. In 1975, Nepal actively participated in the International Women's Year and the first UN World Conference on Women in Mexico City. In the same year, Nepal amended the Muluki Ain (the national code) to grant inheritance rights to daughters if they remained unmarried up to the age of thirty-five. In 1977, the Women's Service Coordination Committee (WSCC) was formed at the Social Service National Coordination Council (SSNCC) with an objective of expanding development and welfare activities for women. In 1979, the women's study conducted by Tribhuvan University highlighted Nepali women's significant contributions to and role in the national economy. These findings were instrumental in sensitizing policy makers to recognize women's productive roles and inclusion of a separate Women in Development (WID) chapter in the next five-year plan (1980–1985). As a result, in 1980, the women's development section was established at the Ministry of Panchayat and in local development. A plan of action on women in development was formulated by the WSCC and SSNCC in 1982.

Nepal has made specific policy declarations to integrate women in development since the early 1980s. Successive five-year plans have made appropriate policy declarations for improving women's status. Such efforts have focused on credit and employment generation, education, and health.

A *few women's mechanisms were set up, including the Ministry of Women and Social Welfare (MWSW), the Women's Division in the National Planning Commission, and the WID Division in the Ministry of Local Development.*

Both multilateral and bilateral external funding agencies have played a positive role in making (women) gender an issue in development since the mid-1970s. Their efforts have evolved over time, passing through various phases focusing on women's development and empowerment.

During the 1980s, participation by women in Nepal's political and economic sectors was very low. The UN's declaration of a Decade for Women (1975–1985) started discussion and debate on women's rights and issues impacting women's protection. However, the role played by women in the development of the country remained insignificant. The nation has yet to realize the importance of eradicating discrimination against women. Most women, especially in rural areas, are incapable of fighting for their rights.

⌁

Zahra reads about the story of the Nepali girl Tulasa Thapa and many others like her that made news headlines. She starts researching such cases, investigates all the material, any piece of news available with fresh vigor.

At twelve, Tulasa was kidnapped from her home village on the outskirts of Kathmandu in 1982. She was smuggled to Bombay and sold into prostitution. Tulasa was tortured, beaten repeatedly, and raped to break her. It's reported that she was sold to three different brothels in Bombay at prices ranging from 5,000 to 7,000 rupees. As she comes across more such stories, Zahra knows she has made the right decision.

On a cold, foggy day in February of 1984, Zahra lands in Kathmandu.

3.

The office in Kathmandu is small, a mixed construction of brick, asbestos with plywood walls, and tin roofing. A small garden of wildflowers and roses, in bloom around the year, in the front adds color to the worn-out office structure. The office has big curtainless windows opening onto the mountains. From every spot, the distant Himalayas dazzle to captivate. Though in the heart of the city, the office compound is at the dead end of a narrow street that opens to a hilly terrain, overgrown into wilderness. Its rugged rare loveliness is hard to ignore, claims instant attention.

Zahra rents a two-room apartment on the top storey of a rickety old brick building with wooden floors, within thirty minutes' walking distance from her office. She is alerted that running water may be a problem. But if she agrees to pay an additional one hundred rupees monthly, the landlady would make sure to have enough buckets filled up for her use. Zahra pays the extra bucks. It's a small price for the luxury of securing a regular supply of water. The house is close to the sacred Buddhist shrine Baudhanath.

The Baudhanath, commonly known as Baudha, the holy shrine, dominates the skyline of the Kathmandu Valley. It's one of the largest Buddhist *stupas* in the world and was built shortly after the death of Lord Buddha. As of 1979, Baudha is a UNESCO World Heritage site. Refugees from Tibet have seen the construction of over fifty monasteries around Baudha. This stupa is on the ancient trade route from Tibet that enters the Kathmandu Valley. Tibetan merchants have rested and offered prayers here for numerous centuries. When refugees entered Nepal from Tibet in the 1950s, many decided to live around Baudhanath. It's a holy temple for Buddhists around the world and a tourist attraction.

The Baudha can be seen from Zahra's apartment, a five-minute walk down the road. Zahra is drawn to it and loves to hang around the stupa whenever she has free time. It's surrounded by street shops of arts, crafts, and Tibetan jewelry, and cafés and eateries that serve local, Western, and Chinese food. Pizza and meat dumplings locally called *momo*, are popular on the menu and are dirt cheap. Tibetan cuisine and the local *tody*, an alcoholic drink, are sold freely. Heinz and Indian-brewed beers are easily available alongside steaming coffee and tea. Zahra eats at the restaurants frequently to avoid cooking at home.

Buddhist pilgrims and monks are always present at the site, praying and meditating in corners, squatting on the dusty ground, even through entire nights. On moonlit nights, the site is transformed into ethereal beauty. The atmosphere is calming and sacred, charged with the rhythmic sounds of the soft chanting of *mantra*—prayers by saffron-color-clad monks—the whirling of the giant prayer wheels, the exotic scent of butter lamps and holy Tibetan incense sticks mixed with the aroma of strong coffee and tea. At nighttime, the pale moonbeams blend with the dim streetlights to create magic. Zahra loves to hang around the shrine at such times.

Two weeks after moving to her apartment, one evening, though a bit late, she walks to the stupa to clear her head. She finds it easier to think in this peaceful atmosphere, the protective open grounds alive with ceaseless rhythmic motions, compelling smells and sounds, but not distressing. Zahra's mind is laden today. Her office secured reports of three more cases of trafficking in one week. It was heartbreaking to read through the pages. All were adolescent girls, innocent victims tricked into a sinister trade they knew nothing about.

The wind is high. Watery moonlight spreads over the site, on the tip of the dome and snuggles it with a mellow silvery brightness. It's a dreary night. Zahra feels lonesome as she listens to the chanting in the background. An overpowering sadness starts rising inside. She lights three butter lamps in memory of the lost girls, possibly traded into brothels in Bombay by now, far away. The flames flicker swiftly to life and sway with the breeze. She offers her prayers, in solitude and silence, eyes closed.

"There, be careful of the lamps. The wind is against you," someone cautions in a deep Western voice and in a flash pulls her shawl away with a sudden jerk.

She turns around startled and is horrified to find that the loosely hanging bottom portion of her wrap has caught fire. It's almost charred in seconds as she looks. The flames lustily lick it with deadly greed. She was too engrossed and didn't realize the imminent danger. In a split second, the flames rioted. The fire is put out by the owner of the voice, a total stranger, as quickly as it started—by beating the sparks and stamping on the shawl, now lifeless on the ground. All happened too swiftly before she could even feel the heat.

She takes a closer look in his direction and is surprised to come face to face with a Western Buddhist monk smiling at her reassuringly. His deep blue eyes on a tanned face, very cropped hair, almost bald, and rosary beads around one wrist reveal his identity. He was stooping earlier, now straightened up to tower over her five-foot-three-inch frame. He must be way over six feet, with an attractive face and broad frame, she notes, the first things that come to her mind in the midst of her small trauma. She stands still.

"No harm done. It happens often. The wind some nights gets out of hand, becomes a risk with such lamps," he says, still smiling, trying to help her out of her shock over the suddenness of the incident. "Many house fires start with unattended butter lamps. Sorry about your shawl, though. Had to act fast. I am *Bhikku* Arthur O'Connor. *Namaste*." The monk presses his hands together, slightly bows in a humble gesture of greeting. He then shakes off the charred remains of the shawl, folds it, and politely hands it over to Zahra.

"You're a monk?" With renewed attention, Zahra takes in his maroon and saffron robe, dusty bare feet sticking out from beneath the attire. Her voice bursts with disbelief.

"Yes, I'm a monk. I'm with the Shanti Temple, on a mission in Kathmandu. I was born in Ireland. Many years ago, of course." The peaceful, friendly smile continues, adding to his charm.

"Sorry.... Thank you, thank you so much for saving me from the fire, Fath—" Zahra falters, abruptly stops in mid-sentence, confused. She doesn't know how to address a white man turned Buddhist monk, and so friendly on top of that.

"You can address me by my first name or as *Bhante* or *Bhikku*. Whatever you're comfortable with," he gently assures her, realizing her bewilderment. "People are puzzled initially. You're not the only one." He tries to ease her awkwardness.

"I've never met a white monk. I think I owe my life to you. You saved me from being almost cremated." Zahra presses her hands together as a response to his greeting.

"That's a bit overboard." Now he laughs with a pleasant sound coming from his heart, she thinks. It touches her heart instantly.

"I'm Zahra. Working with a project on trafficking. I'm a lawyer."

"Wow! Impressive credentials. First time in Nepal?" Arthur asks.

"Arrived two weeks ago," she says. "How did you know I'm new here?"

He smiles, doesn't respond right away.

"A young woman alone lighting butter lamps late at night, lost in thought.... I can read the signs." He glances at her. They both laugh.

She falls in step with him. They walk past the giant prayer

wheels and reach the line of cafés towards the entrance of the shrine. Zahra shivers involuntarily as the wind chills her afresh.

"It gets a bit cold at this time of the year. Care to have a cup of hot coffee?" the monk inquires. He is kind. "I can walk you to your house after that."

"OK, in that case. It's a bit late. People are going back home," she observes.

He orders coffee for her, black tea for himself. In the light inside the café, she gets a good look at him. Slight lines around the eyes that appear to be much deeper blue now. A pleasant mouth, a bluish head as his dark hair has started to grow back, fighting the recent shaving or cropping. He looks like Yul Brynner in *The King and I*, kind of attractive. He catches her watching him.

"It's OK to look at and wonder about me. Many do. No offense taken." He smiles as Zahra tries to quickly glance away.

"None meant. This is my first time socializing with a monk. Sorry if I'm too curious." She smiles back.

"Sizing me up?" He winks.

Zahra laughs out loud.

"I'm harmless. A bhikku." His voice has a hint of mischief, mock modesty.

Over the next ninety minutes, they talk and order another round of steaming sweetened drinks. Arthur narrates his life story—an honest, frank portrayal. He was born in a small town in Ireland and lived with his five siblings till he went to college. He has turned forty-one. From childhood, he has been attracted to theology, the mystery of life and death, and how the enrichment of the spirit has the potential to conquer physical needs, desires, and pain—to be liberated from earthly bindings and discover the taste of being free.

Arthur has a postgraduate degree in theology and religion

from London. During his undergrad years, he came in touch
with Buddhist teachings, deliberated with monks, and regularly attended meditation classes off campus. He was drawn to
Buddhism. He began to join Buddhist pilgrimages regularly.
The conflict in his country started brewing, mainly political
and nationalistic in nature, fired up by historical events. His
soul, burdened with this political violence in Ireland, was tortured and broken, like many. Peace was the only magic path,
the philosophy that was needed to heal the extraordinary suffering inflicted by human beings on their own kind.

Bloody Sunday in Bogside in 1972, with the shooting of
twenty-eight unarmed civil rights marchers, killing thirteen,
marked a new era of violence and counterviolence. Most victims were young. In addition, 470 people were killed in the
same year in Northern Ireland, followed by almost 2,000
bombing incidents all over the country. It was a desperate
time, and everyone was hurting. Arthur was affected deeply.

Arthur visited Europe's first Tibetan Buddhist monastery in
Scotland while in college to learn *dhamma*, or *dharma*, which
means *cosmic law and order* in Buddhism and is also applied
to the teachings of Lord Buddha. In the past, he had been to
Nepal for short visits on pilgrimage. This time he has come for
a year or more to confer with the monks of the recently established Shanti Temple.

Zahra listens, mesmerized as a new world unfolds. This dis-
arms her. In return, she shares about her personal life, her
work in the past and at present, while sipping coffee. Though
still somewhat guarded, she tells enough to give him a good
narrative about herself, her family and heritage.

The monk keeps his promise and walks Zahra to her apartment. It has been easy to pour out portions of her life to this
stranger she met only over an hour ago. An unknown emotion
stirred inside as she talked about her work, the pain and misery that she witnesses regularly. Her voice held a sharp sad-

ness when she related the case of the three trafficked girls and the reason for her being at the stupa, to calm her distressed mind. She also tells him about her own fascination with Buddhism, some teachings she has been casually following from college days.

"Thanks for listening to me. I needed a good listener tonight.... But as we stand here, three girls remain lost to this universe," she remarks on reaching the main entrance of her building and quickly looks away in an attempt to hide the tears slowly creeping into her eyelashes. It has been too much. She is exhausted by the day's undertakings. She is also missing her mother and her sisters on this lonely planet.

"You're hurting. You do a tough job.... Try to breathe in and out, slowly. Walk back a little from the concerns and contemplate. There's always some solution to problems...some closure to suffering," he says quietly. He pauses, giving her time to compose herself.

"I'm usually at the stupa after dark to pray, and I like the walk around the shrine. It helps me to think. If you're too burdened and need to talk, you'll find me there." He presses his hands together in the gesture of namaste and walks away into the night. She stands there and watches him vanish at the bend of the road.

4.

The next few days are extremely busy. With her project head, Zahra meets with a group of journalists, border police, and UN officials. She works with other lawyers from partner agencies to prepare for additional budget proposals, policy documents, and reports. More unreported stories of trafficking come to light as the investigation continues. Zahra tries to gather updated information:

The sex trade is very extensive in Nepal. The girls are usually brought from the countryside into the cities to work in bars, restaurants, massage parlors, and other places that attract tourists into the country. Many are trafficked to India, especially to the brothels in Bombay. The trafficking of girls through Nepal to India for forced prostitution is one of the busiest slave trade routes in the world. A large number of young women and girls are smuggled into India every year (approximately 5,000 to 10,000). Crossing the border is easy as there are about eleven hundred miles of open landscape between Nepal and India. Moreover, there are no immigration control checkpoints between the countries. India is not only a destination country but also a transit route for Nepalese and Bengalee women and girls to be further trafficked to Pakistan, West Asia, and the Middle East, as well as for women from Russia to Thailand.

Girls from Nepal are very desirable as sex workers because they are considered more attractive due to their lighter skin tone, and they are believed to be virgins who make men more virile and pose less risk of contracting STDs. The majority of trafficked victims are poor, uneducated, and belong to a low cultural status. They come from all parts of Nepal, but the most vulnerable are from the lower castes, or the untouchables, and ethnic minorities.

Poverty-stricken families are lured with hopes of false job opportunities or suggestions to innocently sell their daughters under the guise of marriage in many cases. The victims are threatened physically and mentally and get little or no payment for their work. They are often held in debt bondage as sex slaves by their captors.

Sometimes trafficked girls escape or are rescued by police raids, but reintegration back into a normal life is difficult because most victims suffer from depression, anxiety, drug addiction, post-traumatic disorders, and sexually transmitted diseases (in addition to social ostracization in some cases).

Historical and cultural factors contribute to trafficking.

The Hindu caste system has a code for prostitutes. In Southwestern Nepal, the Badi caste were traditionally entertainers who sang and danced for the wealthy. They also offered sexual services to local kings, religious leaders, and landlords. Prostitution is a social norm among the Badi, a disadvantaged untouchable caste.

In general in the Nepali culture, girls are often considered to be a financial liability because their parents have to pay a dowry at the time of marriage, which is a huge burden on poor families. Additional factors contributing to human trafficking are the lack of jobs in rural areas, as well as an increase in demand for cheap labor in the carpet and textile industries.

Zahra hasn't been to the stupa since the day she had coffee with Bhikku Arthur. As the sober chanting from the shrine drifts in regularly through her open windows at night, she can smell devotion, the flavor of piety, encircling the hollow shadows hidden safely in the dark corners of the humongous construction. Her feet are restless. She is tempted to go out there to breathe in the cold of the night, but she has been totally exhausted under the pressure of work the last few days. She also needs time to calm her distress before facing the monk if she happens to bump into him. It was embarrassing to display her frustrated tears the other night. She felt young and naively unprofessional.

A week later, she is brave enough to take a tour of the shrine area and strides through the thinning crowd towards the somber Baudha standing solemnly under the softness of the moon. The streetlights reflect a subdued brilliance against the shrine's white outer walls. She cautiously passes by the butter-lamp-lit spot as a low breeze whizzes around. She stops at the prayer wheels to offer prayers and then walks around in the hope of finding Monk Arthur. He's nowhere to be seen. A strange desperation overtakes her. A round of the entire stupa takes about twenty minutes at a moderate pace. It's longer for her as she stops to check out from a distance the worshippers, spread out in corners, praying silently. He's not here tonight. She's a bit surprised at her disappointment.

As she nears the main entrance, Zahra hesitates and decides to go back to the same café of the previous night for a quick cup of coffee. It was actually good coffee although slightly on the sweet side. She will request the waiter to bring sugar separately…. The young waiter instantly recognizes her, greets her with a big smile.

"*Didi* Namste. *Kosta honun cha?* [Sister, how are you?]." In Nepal, women are addressed as *didi* to show respect.

"*Mo thik cha* [I'm good]," Zahra responds, smiling back. She has picked up some Nepali.

"*Ewuta Coffee leye anoos. Chini na rakhney* [One coffee, no sugar]." She tries her broken Nepali, well received by the warm, smiling waiter.

In a minute, he is back with a steaming cup of white coffee, a heap of sugar lying limp in a small saucer. As she stirs the hot drink, they strike up a conversation. He speaks reasonable English, a courtesy to foreign tourists. He tells her that Bhikku has been here every evening since they had coffee last week. He hasn't been here so far tonight. Zahra is interested to know more about him. The waiter is a talkative, friendly guy and doesn't need much encouragement. He tells her that Arthur is very well respected by everyone at the temple and in his village, which the monk frequents to distribute malaria medicine and vitamin D to children. He gets the supplies from the local UN office and hospital. He even takes care of the sick, helps mothers to give cold sponges to children in high fever, and collects water for them from the well when there is sickness in the house. He is considered a saint in the village. Children especially like him as he always has candies for them and gives free rides on his bicycle around the village.

"Didi, Bhikku is a white man, but his soul is like the color of his robe, pure Buddhist, *ek dom* Nepali, *pakaa* [totally Nepali]." The young waiter is full of respect and adoration for Bhikku Arthur. Zahra pays for her coffee and walks out of the café as the night deepens.

"*Pheri Bhatula,* Didi Namaste [Will meet again, sister]."

"Pheri Bhatula, Namaste," Zahra says in response.

5.

The next day, after exhausting work, Zahra takes a break to stroll in the backyard of the office building to recharge her brain. Most of her coworkers are out at various meetings and on errands. So she is alone in the office except for the receptionist and the Gurkha guard. He is a good man, middle aged, extremely loyal, and friendly. Most of the time he is surrounded by a tiny crowd that persistently forms around him every hour—people who stop by while in passing for a chat or to smoke with him under the lazy sun. Personal safety is not an issue in Nepal. The Gurkha is just a symbolic presence, a formal requirement for the office, actually. The office gate is usually kept open. The staff don't bother about locking up their cubicles or any materials often left on the tables.

Besides Zahra, there's a Swedish woman who is the project manager and her boss—single, pleasant, and in her late fifties; three Nepali lawyers—two females and a male; one male administrator who's the jack of all trades and manages HR, accounts, and every problem that crops up; one female receptionist; and the Gurkha. He lives in a tiny shed at one corner in the back, as his job is round the clock, 24/7. Zahra is not sure how he manages to have a family since he hardly ever leaves the office compound. However, she was told that the Gurkha is blessed with seven healthy children ranging from six months to sixteen years, a lovely wife, and a happy life in a village on the outskirts of the Kathmandu Valley.

It's slightly cooler today, breezy. Tiny feathery puffs of

lonely clouds drift in and out of the office through open windows, constantly—very light and within Zahra's grasp if she really wants to touch them! She has never before lived with such amazing clouds that walk inside houses. The mountains in the distance are blurred somewhat as a fog is forming, slowly enveloping the distant landscape in the blink of an eye as she watches. Every hour the entire scene changes in spectacular loveliness. She begins to breathe in, breathe out, and slowly unwind.

"Didi, Didi!" She sees the Gurkha hastening towards her. He doesn't speak one word of English. His Nepali is colloquial, making it difficult for Zahra to communicate with him, even mere necessities, and vice versa. It's a no-win situation. With his outstretched right hand, he gestures towards the reception area. She follows him smiling, unsure of what awaits. His all-toothy smile covers his face with gentle affection. This man likes her a lot.

Zahra pushes the screen door. The pleasant, soft, airy sound of the chime follows. The interior of the reception area appears darker as her eyes adjust.... Instantly she sees him.

"Namaste." Arthur gently springs to his feet and greets her before she can fully acknowledge his presence.

"Namaste, Bhikku. What brings you here?" She fails to banish the surprise and joy from her tone.

"Gani...ah...the waiter at the café in Baudha...said you're looking for me," he explains, sensing her puzzlement.

"Oh, I...had coffee there last night." Zahra blushes now. She didn't imply very openly her desire to see Arthur again. The waiter is smarter than she thought. "We were just chatting. I'm sorry you had to come all this way."

"Don't be. I meant to come this way." He tries to smooth out her embarrassment.

"The office is quiet today. Colleagues are attending conferences...traveling." Zahra wants to reassert the importance of her agency.

"Nice office." He appears to be interested. Zahra doesn't know what to say next.

"The sun is back again," he remarks in an attempt to fill up the awkward silence. The fog has lifted from the mountains; the clouds have wandered away, allowing the light to crash inside through open windows.

"It's almost the end of your workday, I think? I'm walking towards the Shivapuri Mountain Range, about four hours' walk round trip. If you're interested in joining me, I could show you the trek."

Zahra had mentioned her passion for walking the other night. She loves a good stroll, especially in the tranquility of the forlorn trails around the mountains. His memory is sharp.

"We can talk. If there's anything you would like to discuss ...." He stops to look at her reaction. His kindness touches her heart.

"Yes, I'd love that," Zahra agrees hastily. It's Friday and most offices close down early, after lunch break is over. There is no pending urgency. "The walk and the talk," she adds. He nods.

"It's a lovely trail close to the range. I walk there quite frequently. Let me see what kind of shoes you're wearing." He looks at her feet.

Laughingly, she sticks them out for him to inspect the rather sturdy pumps, bubbly red, size five.

"Quite tiny...." Both laugh. "Hmmm. Women love to wear high-heeled shoes. No disrespect. I understand the sentiment even as a bhikku...but for safety and comfort on this walk, your pumps make sense." The mischievous smile is back on his face, kindling his eyes in amusement.

Zahra picks up her handbag from her workstation. She leaves the knapsack and documents behind. She is determined to take a break from work tonight. She can always come back tomorrow morning, even though it's the weekend. So best not to disturb the papers....

~⁀

They walk side by side. Arthur walks slower than his usual gait so that Zahra is able to keep up with him. He explains that this short trek will take them through Budhanilkanta, a small township, the connecting point where the valley ends, about two miles from her office. They will be taking the much shorter, easier trail used by locals, not the regular established trek. By seven thirty they should be back to Budhanilkanta. Zahra can get back to her apartment in a *tuk tuk*, a three-wheeler auto—about a forty-minute ride from there.

As the trail gradually inclines uphill, she tries her best to cover up her panting. Thorny grass pricks her legs, shielded by her clothes. Nameless tiny blossoms break the dark green idle strips with an array of colors. She is struck by the vivaciousness that follows them. Arthur is unperturbed, shows he is true to his claim of frequenting this terrain regularly.

The Shivapuri Mountains loom up ahead, magnificent, a sprightly presence that commands the entire landscape. Lively patches of wilderness are casually thrown over intermittently, adding vibrant palettes of countless shades to the foot of the mountains. The sun's rays sit softly on the highest peaks, reflecting and glittering on the treetops and lower mounds. They stop at bends and edges of the spiral muddy path to admire the colossal beauty that unfolds at every step. Arthur points out rare flowers, trees, and best views. He lends her his hand when they cross over narrow ledges and rugged stones in some spots. His grip is firm, steady, and warm. She feels comfortable and safe. He is quite unconventional for a monk. Zahra thought they shied away from a woman's touch.

"Your hair looks like a halo," he says as she stands with her back to the dying sun.

"What do you expect when rubbing shoulders with holy souls?" she says and immediately stops. "I'm so sorry! Oh! Apologies...didn't mean to be rude." She turns red to the roots of her hair in embarrassment for taking a jab at him. Arthur starts to laugh aloud. The situation turns comical. The hearty, heavy sound of his laughter echoes into the mountain crevasses and hits back like a boomerang. She joins in the laughter, hesitant at first, then haplessly, unable to control herself. The echoes are invigorated.

They sit on a slanting large black rock to enjoy the view from above and break the hard climb. Zahra needs it more than Arthur. He looks fully composed. Monks are well trained and practiced through breathing exercises and meditation, possibly.

"Being a monk, how different are you from commoners like me?" Zahra wants to know.

"Hmm. Easy to ask, difficult to answer. Are you testing me?" He glances at her in mock seriousness. Zahra shakes her head.

"We don't possess anything; nothing belongs to us. No matter how hard it is, nothing is ours to keep. That's the first step. Any action undertaken free from greed, hatred, and ignorance is the cause of happiness," Arthur says. His voice is devoid of any playfulness now. "Renouncing suffering is the field of all joys. Forming attachments is the core of suffering. I have renounced the world."

"Do you miss normal life in your holy pursuits?" she asks, equally sober.

"No I don't. I have taken the vow voluntarily to dedicate my life to serve others. I believe it's unethical to walk back. We're not really holy. We keep trying to be free," he adds.

"Zahra, I had a hard life. I saw how people suffered in Ireland through decades of conflict, brutality...torture. I found the path to inner peace when I fully embraced Buddhism. I understood pain...to heal. There was no other way for me." The humility in his tone is astounding, fiercely modest. They sit in silence. She senses a strange camaraderie developing between them. Arthur's body language feels tranquil, affectionate.

She examines the half-buried stones scattered all over the landscape and wonders if these have been here for hundreds of years. So much history and culture may be hidden under this land. The sun starts to vanish. Arthur looks up at the sky. A black cloud is forming; the wind begins to become harsh and cold within moments. The scenario has changed suddenly. He gets up and helps Zahra to her feet.

"The wind is strong. A thunderstorm may be brewing. It's so unlike this time of year. Let's try to walk faster to reach some shelter before it hits us." Arthur doesn't sound worried but has a hint of hurriedness in his voice.

Over the next twenty minutes, they walk in silence, faster, jumping over half-buried stones and thorny bushes. Progress is slow on the rough terrain. Zahra's arms get scratched, but she doesn't want to stop. Her hair is blown over her eyes constantly as the wind gains strength and pushes them forward. Then the rain starts in tiny drops.

"We're almost there. We'll reach the foot of the road in Budhanilkantha in about thirty minutes...but the rain and wind may be faster. I have a small cabin up on the left-side path. If we hurry, we can get there soon," he shouts over the rising wind trying to drown his voice. Thunder crashes somewhere with a deafening sound. Zahra is startled; she is really scared now. Rain comes in full force and splashes against them. She shivers at the touch of the cold drops on her skin.

"Take my hand. Hold it tight. Let's run," Arthur suggests. The next few minutes, they run furtively amidst the harsh wind, and rain, and thunder pursuing them. Finally, they reach a makeshift tiny hut half hidden among dense creepers and overgrown trees and plants, almost falling off the edge of the muddy path into the roaring stream below. She could have never found it on her own had she not been led here by Arthur.

"Come inside. This is a log cabin I use for meditation during weekends and on sacred days." He opens the timber door for her. He gropes around in the dark, finally finds the matches, and lights a candle.

Surprisingly, the cabin is quite spacious. The floor is made of wood. Some patches are still jagged and could do better with a bit of scraping. There is a big window covered by a sloping bamboo top to prevent slanting rain from gettin in. In one corner is a local mat made of dried leaf, rolled against the wooden wall for use when necessary. A small door leads to the bathroom on one side. In a rattan basket is a plate and an earthen mug, placed with care. A clay pitcher stands beside the basket. In another basket are some neatly folded saffron-colored clothes, possibly a change of robe. A rope is secured across the wall nearby, and a quilt made from colorful scraps is slung over it. Arthur fishes out a piece of saffron cloth from one of the baskets and hands it to her to dry herself. This is kind of a monk's towel, Zahra assumes.

"It's clean and dry," he says. The room is in languid darkness with the light of one tiny candle, though he has opened the window slightly to allow the air from outside. It drags in the smell of wet soil and the fragrance of flowers and leaves while squeezing inside. Gusty wind keeps raging, followed by thunderclaps almost every minute. The vibrant blue of the sky is neatly choked away in the grip of frozen pitch-blackness. The glow from the lightning brightens up the hut for a second at a time now and then.

"This is a very basic place...my refuge from locality. Villagers constructed it years ago out of kindness, before my time. It's bare," he explains.

"It's OK. I'm glad we're not out there...terrified of cyclones and thunder," says Zahra, unable to control her teeth chattering in the cold. "Though we have cyclones almost every month, I'm not immune to thunder. I was so afraid. I thought it was going to fall on my head any second." She expects Arthur to say something light, tease her, but he's somber, thoughtful.

"You're cold. I'm so sorry. I have an extra robe, but I can't offer it to a woman," he says, faintly uncomfortable.

"But you can change. Why are you suffering in wet clothes?" Zahra suggests genuinely.

"I don't want to change while you're so wet and cold." He looks at her over the flicker of the candle. He wants to suffer along with her, a comforting thought. The monk in him knows no other way.

"I can wrap the quilt around you...will give some warmth." Arthur gets up and brings the worn-out quilt. She smells his nearness as his hands gently go around her with the quilt. A loud thunderclap crashes somewhere nearby. The hut shakes at the sudden forcefulness of the sound. The candle flame leaps up and dies. Before she realizes it, Zahra jumps into Arthur's arms, startled, trembling violently, and clasps him tightly.

"Oh my God!" A scream escapes her as she buries her face against his chest.

"It's OK. Our cottage is not hit. It fell somewhere outside." His voice is gentle as he holds her, trying to soothe her fears. Zahra doesn't remember how long she has sat like this, with Arthur's arms around her, holding her close against him. She feels his warm breath on her forehead. The sound of rain is incessant outside, but the thunder stops at one point.

"You'll catch your death of cold if we go out in this rain. I don't even have an umbrella," Arthur pronounces.

Then it happens. She has no recollection.... She refuses to take responsibility for it. In the dark, she tilts her face upwards to look at him, and her cheek accidentally touches his lips, warm and soft. She feels his body stiffening, and then he lowers his mouth and kisses her on the lips. It's gentle at first and then forceful and lingering. She doesn't pull away, kisses him back. They don't utter any words; in silence and in the folds of darkness in the room, they cling to each other. His fervent kisses cover her face. As he holds her, his hands tremble in the unexpectedness of pent-up emotions. His embrace is maddeningly tight and firm. Zahra stops shivering—not cold anymore. The darkness around them provides sanctuary, emboldens them in an embrace. A liaison to be questioned, condemned in the light of the day—between a Buddhist holy man of the cloth and a naïve human rights activist.

Many moments later, he releases her and is up on his feet. Her right foot went to sleep long ago, but she dared not move in his arms, fearing the spell would be broken. He looks out of the window to the night outside, subdued and thoughtful. He searches for the matches.

"Let's try to go now. The rain has almost stopped," Arthur says, concentrating on lighting the candle. He avoids looking at her. His face appears extremely pale, as if sucked out of blood.

"Bhikku, I led you to sin," Zahra says, downcast, with a sob in her voice, repentant now.

"No, it's not you. It's me." His voice is low. He listens to the sound of the rain. "Let's go" is all he says after a while.

He doesn't utter another word as they walk in the drizzle. He marches ahead of her in the narrow, overgrown dirt path, swallowed by darkness, in total silence, never glancing back at her. She walks hastily over stones and puddles, following him in a trance. After about fifteen minutes, which feels like an eternity to Zahra, they reach the main road in Budhanilkantha at the bottom of the temple of Lord Vishnu. In the hazy stillness, the rain falls steadily. People have taken shelter; no trace of life is evident anywhere. As Arthur looks around for a tuk tuk on the deserted road, a passing truck brakes beside them. A man juts out his head from the cracked window of the driver's side.

"Bhikku, what are you doing out here in this rain? Where do you want to go?" the driver asks. He knows Arthur.

Both Arthur and Zahra squeeze into the passenger seat beside the driver as the back is hoodless, meant for carrying goods. In the small space, their bodies touch. His sturdy thigh brushes against hers for the next forty minutes. Though he tries to keep his arms close to his body to avoid any physical contact, it falls slightly against her soft shoulder, touches her wet hair loosened around her face and neck, tumbling in a heap beneath. She is so much conscious of his nearness, of his presence—she panics.

"Namaste" is all they say to each other when Zahra gets down at her apartment.

In a daze, she climbs the stairs to her apartment. Once inside, she switches on the light, and gets out of her wet clothes. A hot bath is all she needs, but she has no energy to heat up water on the stove now. Instead she splashes her face with cold water. The warmth of Arthur's kisses lingers on her cheeks, lips, and forehead. She is unable to wash away his caresses, his touch.

6.

Zahra tries to bury the incident at the log cabin and focuses on work. Only work can save her mind in turmoil, her rattled nerves. She knows she has been complicit in allowing a holy monk to break his vows. It's a discomforting thought. But paradoxically finds it difficult to forgive herself for engaging in her outrageous behavior on that night of thunder and darkness. She is uncontrollably attracted to him, she knows now. Though Arthur started it, initiated the intimacy, she didn't object or pull away.

For days she avoids the stupa for fear of bumping into him. Every evening, it calls to her through the endless sacred chorus of chanting, the scent of the butter lamps and lighted incense sticks, the sounds of footsteps of the worshippers and tourists, along with the silvery moon. The stupa stands erect in somber glory, commanding devotion and bliss, silhouetted against the night sky, blotting out any other view from her living room window. Every object, every motion tries to beckon her, entice her back to the shrine.

She hasn't heard from Arthur. There's no need for him to contact her, though. Somewhere deep in her heart she keeps expecting to see him, hear him calling her name. But he has totally vanished into the thin air, in the folds of the mysterious distant mountains. She decides to keep the window closed, though it chokes her tiny sitting room, isolates it from the presence of the stupa it is so spoiled by. An unknown emotion keeps rising and rising inside her. She tries to push it back, bury it somewhere far away. She doesn't dare analyze it. Too difficult to handle!

Zahra walks over to Thamel in the evenings after office hours to avoid the Baudha. Thamel is a traditional market crammed with hundreds of tiny shops full of local artifacts, crafts, beads, silver jewelry made with semiprecious stones, pashmina shawls, woolen garments and carpets, books, and cassettes as well as restaurants, cafés, and bars. There are offices of trekking and tour agents intimately sandwiched among the stores and eateries. Every color is trapped in the crevices of this street. It is blatant and brazen in its archaic setting, immersed in the scent of incense sticks, Tibetan Buddhist *tankas*, and prayer flags. The stores are on both sides of a narrow, winding street that's about four to five miles long. It twists around the grandeur of the artistry, tiny sporadic impromptu roadside altars of worship of Hindu gods and goddesses, splashed with marks of sindoor—a vermillion hue—and flowers, mainly marigolds and red hibiscuses, offered by devotees. Nepali heritage comes alive at every bend of this street snaking through the heart of the valley.

Lately, Zahra has been reading about Buddhism, the philosophy and way of life prescribed for monks. She has picked up rare paperbacks from the renowned Pilgrims Book House in Thamel to widen her knowledge, to fathom what creates selfless, unwavering devotion and the courage to renounce earthly pleasures, love, and joys.

In order to understand Arthur, she has to know what Buddhism is all about, the doctrine that inspires the commitment to embrace sublime wisdom, sets the soul free of the worldly bondage of misery.

~

Weeks slide by. The trafficking cases continue at a snail's pace. Misinformation, gaps in reporting, and corruption override any glimmer of a breakthrough. It's frustrating. Meanwhile, Zahra visits an Indo-Nepal border town on the other side of Sitaraganj with her boss and a Nepali colleague, Binita. Sitaraganj is a famous hunting ground of traffickers of girls. It's depressing to witness the utter poverty of the people, the ignorance about trafficking, the silent resignation to a dismal fate and acceptance of the wrongs done. They meet with families of some victims—parents bereft with sadness as they wait to hear from their daughters. Most villagers are nonliterate and survive on meager, unsteady incomes. Opportunities are limited, scanty chances of regular employment. They are hounded by pervasive sickness, destitution, and desperation—easy prey to perpetrators who feast on young flesh.

On moonless nights, the village sinks into complete darkness, as there is no cash to buy kerosene for the lamps. The small huts are crowded, bleak, and stuffy. Meals are sparse, basic. Some nights the villagers lie down hungry. Battling the odds constantly makes them brittle, forcing them to succumb to the gleam of better times as created by the crooked vultures. Families unknowingly hand over their daughters to escape this dreary life.

Zahra travels back to Kathmandu with a heavy heart and loads of guilt for being so fortunate to be free, to soar into a life of her own choosing.

~ͻ

On her return, Zahra takes a half day off and hikes towards the Shivapuri Range. Fresh air and exercise can be antidotes to a dampening spirit, can lift the sadness. She takes the regular longer route as advised by her colleagues. She has nothing to be worried about as the entire day lies ahead, plenty of time to explore, even get lost, and find her way back before dusk sets in.

The summer days have become longer. She packs a light lunch, water, and an orange to eat under a tree—a lone picnic in the wilderness. A slight breeze and the sun wrapped in drifting shiny clouds uplift her mood. She walks for a long time with occasional brief stops to admire the breathtaking views, ecstatic in their uniqueness, sacred like truth.

After lunch, Zahra lazes underneath a tall tree on a grassy spot between half-buried dark stones. The sun plays on her face through gaps among the leaves as the wind stirs them gently. In the background, the ice-kissed, frozen Himalayan peaks dazzle in the daylight. She wanders around another hour and then turns onto the return trail.

The walk back is much easier because it's mostly downhill. From every turn on the trail, the majestic Himalayas shadow her. She feels good at their unwavering companionship. It's calming. At least she is not alone in this vast terrain. Through the bramble bushes and overgrown patches, she comes to a bend that seems familiar. She ventures forward and recognizes the twin trees beside the muddy path and the feisty growth of nameless wildflowers. A few steps ahead and she is certain it leads to Arthur's log cabin. She follows the path. In ten minutes, she finds the cabin buried under trees, wild plants, and creepers. Silently, she takes the last few steps to the cabin. Arthur must be in the valley. Today is a working day.

Gently, she pushes the timber door. It opens at her slight touch. She peeps inside. It's dark because the window is tightly shut. The room is filled with the incense of wildflowers, the earth...some smell of emptiness. She leaves her shoes beside the door and sits on the wooden floor in the dimness. It's cool and comfortable. She wants to stay longer—but there's no need to risk bumping into the monk if he heads this way for some reason, breaking his routine. While leaving, she remembers and takes out her umbrella from the knapsack. She leaves it on the floor, closes the door, and steps out. In half an hour, she reaches Budhanilkantha.

At the foot of the road is the temple of the Hindu god Vishnu. She crosses the threshold of the temple. A huge statue of Vishnu etched out of black stone lies sleeping on his back in the coils of a stone-curved serpent, placed in a large pool. Heaps of flowers and traces of vermillion powder on the statue indicate the worshippers' devotion to this deity. People believe in a popular legend that states that one of the monarchs, King Pratap Malla (1641–1674), had a prophetic vision that any Nepali king, if ever he visited Budhanilkantha Temple, would die in a mishap. Royals after King Pratap have never visited the temple in fear of the prophecy. During the months of October and November, thousands of pilgrims attend a festival at this temple for the awakening of Lord Vishnu from his sleep. Only Hindus are allowed to get close to the statue.

Back at home that night, Zahra reads from the book of Buddha she bought recently. Buddha's stand is clear on controlling passions and emotions:

So one, always mindful, should avoid sexual desires. Letting them go, he will cross over the flood like one who, having bailed out the boat, has reached the far shore. "The flood" refers to the deluge of human suffering. The "far shore" is "Nirvana," a state in which there is no sexual desire.

She fully understands Arthur's plight, feels sorry for him, sad for herself. This should have never happened. In the whole world full of billions of deserving men, she could find only a monk to fall for? Awareness hits her like lightning.... She's in love with Arthur. How insane is that? She has met him only twice! It was love at first sight, as she has read in romantic fiction. It's now futile to deny her feelings. It's indeed very frustrating and exhilarating at the same time. Now she understands the reason for her despondency. Arthur is somewhat nonconventional, unlike other monks, but he's deeply committed to the teachings of Buddha. He had no qualms reaching out to her, assisting her over the steep rocky path prior to the kissing incident. He didn't try to avoid her proximity. She doesn't know whether this was due to his Western upbringing or outlook. But a monk is a man of the robe. Did she force him to break his vows? He must be repenting now and finding a way to cleanse his soul. She wonders whether he despises her. The thunder led them to the mess, the consequential behavior. So she must not harbor any appalling thoughts of intimacy with him.

"Back off.... Back off now, Zahra.... He's not for you," she repeats over and over. She calls herself hopeless many times before finally falling asleep.

7.

Two days have passed after her solitary hike. She comes home late in the evening, following the lengthy staff meeting towards the end of the day. She was actually glad about the long hours in the office, a good distraction from her personal problems. Over and over in her mind, she has analyzed the situation all this time and decided to find a new place to live closer to Thamel, which is alive even on its worst days. A change of environment may help her to start afresh, the best way to wipe out the stupa and Arthur completely.

She thinks of speaking to the landlady on the weekend and give notice. She has to forget Arthur, move on with her life, as this is not going to work even in the craziest place on earth. She can't knowingly allow the monk or herself to indulge in further sinful acts. Even recollection of the incident, reliving the pressure of his lips on hers, is indecent, grossly wrong. She's finding the memory difficult to banish, though. At most inopportune moments, the scene pops into her head, turning her knees to jelly. Constant taunting by the stupa is also becoming unbearable. She shuts the window with vehemence.

Music usually distracts her from the chanting outside. She switches on her tiny portable cassette player and makes coffee. If she's not too tired after work, her new routine is to take a walk to Thamel or the Durbar Marg, where the royal palace is. The translation of the words in English is *King's Way*. History cites that the rulers forcibly seized lands from farmers and monasteries, and demolished existing structures to make the road. This is the first time she has been sharing a city with a living monarch and a royal family. The palace looks exotic from the outside. She has peeped through the gate to get a glimpse of the garden, the fountain, and the pebbled path leading towards the main mansion. The Gurkhas on guard outside allowed her innocent curiosity, didn't rob her of the chance to become awestruck. In fact, they enjoy such reactions from foreigners.

⌒ɔ

The closed window mocks her as the scent of incense sticks infiltrates through the cracks. She sips coffee and listens to songs. She doesn't feel sorry for herself anymore. Yes, she is lonely, and she has deliberately blocked the view of the stupa. She has nowhere to go tonight, doesn't feel like cooking, but so what? Still she has the freedom to decide to do what she wants. It's her choice to be alone, not a compulsion. She will forget Arthur ever happened.

Someone knocks. Zahra opens the door to find the landlady's nine-year-old son standing with a smile in the semidarkness. She notices the figure beside him only when he points with an outstretched hand in a gesture of respect. Arthur stands right there, towering over the narrow space at the top of the stairs.

"Namaste," he says. "Can I come in?" Then he turns to the boy and thanks him. Zahra stands aside to let him in. "I got your umbrella. Very thoughtful."

She is at a loss for words.

"Please sit down, Bhikku. Would you like some coffee?" Zahra finally utters, tidies the cushions on the small two-seater, making room for him.

She has a good look at him. His face is pale, rigid, unsmiling. He returns her gaze with eyes cast in a coolness she fails to understand. Gone is his friendly demeanor, his ease. He sits on the edge of the sofa, uncomfortable, as if it's made of thorns. Zahra doesn't sit down. She stands between the small side table and the settee, slightly puzzled. She gives him time to regain his poise. He must have come to lecture her or to advise her to make a confession of her sin committed at the log cabin and ask for forgiveness at the temple. She doesn't know what happens in Buddhism.

"Yes, coffee would be good. Thank you." He glances directly at her now with a hint of a smile on his lips. A tiny bit of his former self returns for a second.

"Give me a moment. I'll make coffee." Zahra strides into the kitchen with her half-finished cup.

As the water boils, she takes down a mug from the kitchen

cupboard. She doesn't remember how much sugar he takes. She doesn't know anything about this man. She is ignorant of the ways of a monk. She is angry with herself now because the moment he stepped into her apartment, all her resolutions vanished, her defenses against him crumbled, her heart started to race recklessly. One look at that face and her love struck back full force—tripled, actually. She turns around at a slight rustling noise. Arthur steps into the kitchen. She watches him approaching closer and closer, unable to move. It seems all her bones have melted into water inside the wrapping of her skin. He doesn't talk. He takes her in his arms.

Hours later, as they lie squeezed in her small bed, Zahra wonders what just happened. Arthur is softly snoring beside her—in a pleasant way. The warmth and nearness of his body against hers make her feel safe, loved. She lies still so as not to wake him. She wonders what time it is. They will have to eat something, but there isn't much in the house. She doesn't even know what he eats, possibly only vegetarian food. He is a Buddhist monk—can't kill any living being as far as her amateur knowledge goes.

Arthur had carried her into the bedroom after the first fervor of kissing. He made very little sound, only faint moaning as he called her name over and over again—"Zara, Zara...."

"I didn't know you were a virgin. I'll be gentle," he whispered into her ears as he loved her. All was lost to her during those moments of ecstasy. It was she and Arthur and the love that overflooded her heart, dissolving all caution.

She wonders if her father knew what she was doing, would he be upset? Very disappointed, for sure. One doesn't mess with a monk. And an unmarried woman doesn't have sex in Bengalee culture. She keeps herself only for her husband and offers herself on the wedding night, pure and chaste. That chance is lost to her forever...but she wants only Arthur, no one else. Nothing else matters anymore.

⟨⟩

"Hungry?" Arthur wakes up and in the small space, turns his face to smile at Zahra. He has to maneuver his large frame in this small den.

"Yeah. We'll have to go out to eat. Sorry," she says.

"Don't be. I was thinking the same. I just barged into your place."

"I don't cook...a bad cook, actually." She wants to be on the clear. Arthur laughs at her honesty.

"I know a lovely place close to here," he adds.

"Good. I was considering two options before you arrived. Either starve or walk over to a roadside restaurant," she offers.

He laughs again and springs out of bed. She follows him to the living room. He opens the window, and a gust of fresh air fills up the room. The chanting, the incense, the many voices and sounds return immediately. He looks at her quizzically.

"I didn't want to look at the stupa anymore. Reminded me of you." She smiles, guilty.

"You tried to block me out by refusing to look at the holy shrine? It's a sin." He kisses her and holds her close.

"No it isn't. You're a good liar for a monk."

"I'm a good sinner if you think about it," he says teasingly as he plays affectionately with her long, dark tresses.

"But you came back for me . . ." she says dreamily.

"Yes." He's definitive. "Listen, Zara, it will be difficult to meet here regularly. What about you pack a bag for the weekend and meet me at Budhanilkantha at the foot of the temple? We can walk to my cabin together," he proposes. "Tell your landlady you're going away with a friend. Otherwise, she may

get worried. Here, people take care of each other like family."
Zahra likes the way he says her name—dropping the *h*. She's
Zara to him.

As they climb down, they meet the landlady at the bottom
of the stairs, talking to a neighbor. She becomes alert, noticing
Arthur, and bows humbly with hands pressed together. Zahra
has a hard time subduing a giggle.

"She got a whiff of a holy monk!" Arthur says after they
are a safe distance away from the landlady.

"With so much reverence in her heart!" Zahra matches his
words. Both laugh out loud. Luckily, at that time of the night,
there aren't any passersby to be shocked at their mirth.

He takes Zahra to a rooftop vegetarian restaurant inside
the stupa grounds. The view is astounding. The moon glows
over the white dome of the shrine and soaks the landscape in
a faint glimmer. The waiter brings a candle, though the streetlights lend enough brightness. Arthur orders vegetable fried
rice, Malaysian tofu curry, and a salad. The taste of the food
is exotic. The cost is minimal, inexpensive.

"I fell in love with you the moment you smiled on the first
night...under the night sky, surrounded by the lights of butter lamps," he confesses. "You stood like an angel trapped in
a garland of light, trying to find your way."

"I'm fully absolved!" Zahra lets out a mock sigh of relief.

"What about you?" He's eager to know.

"Ah, when I saw you in my office. I knew you were feeling something too. I fell in love instantly. I realized it was destiny...had to happen." She is truthful, all seriousness.

Arthur's eyes follow the way the words form in her mouth,
the tilt of her lips as she smiles, the radiance in her eyes that
look straight back at him. They sit feasting on every line, every
expression on the other's face.

"Zara, here's the money to pay for the food." He hands

over Nepali rupee bills, breaking the silence. "The restaurant won't accept money from me. Normally, I'm not even supposed to have any," he says.

"Why?" She is surprised.

"Because...I'm a Buddhist monk. A sinner monk." He straightens up and mockingly beats his chest with his hands. Zahra breaks into laughter. "Do you know how beautiful you look when you laugh?...so spontaneous." His eyes soften. He keeps staring at her.

"Bhikku—"

"Arthur. Only for you. Bhikku for others," he interrupts.

"Can I pay?"

"Nope. I may be a monk, but I'm still a man. I brought my girl on a first dinner date. I pay." He is adamant.

The waiter appears with the bill. He bows with great respect every time he looks at Arthur. They tip him well.

As they walk down the street to her apartment, he turns around to glance at her one more time.

"What am I doing? I'm so much older than you. And a monk." His voice is hoarse, barely above a whisper.

"Yeah? You're my monk, and I don't care." Zahra crosses the narrow road. Arthur laughs at her defiance.

"Namaste," he says from the other side and quickly walks away.

Back in her room, Zahra holds the pillow where Arthur had lain and sniffs his smell to fill up her lungs. The room has new meaning. This is where she has found true love. This is where a monk gave up his vows for her. She offered her virginity to him. What does that tell her? The euphoria of love casts a spell, grows bigger and bigger, fills her tiny room. She sails on happiness—doesn't want to think of consequences, not now, not anymore. Image after image float through her mind.... It takes a long time to fall asleep.

8.

Zahra hails a tuk tuk and gets off near the temple at Bud-hanilkantha. She has lightly packed the knapsack with necessities. Arthur is the architect of what happens next. The last three days have been never ending. She has been happy but nervous, waiting for this day anxiously. What if Arthur came back saying it wasn't a good idea? Changed his mind? He is married to his vows, actually. Every footstep outside her door was a torment as she waited to hear him knock to give her the bad news. In the office, she stiffened each time the Gurkah came inside on an errand. When he smiled at her, she assumed he would tell her Arthur was in the waiting room. At night, sleep escaped her. She looked at the stupa from her window, fully aware Arthur was down there somewhere chanting. It was nearly impossible to fight the impulse to see him. Separated by a five-minute walk from her, he was breathing the same air as she.

She paces slowly. Her eyes keep searching for Arthur in the stream of people going towards the temple and coming out of it. He can't be missed. The saffron attire always stands out.

"Namaste." She turns around to Arthur's beaming face. He looks killing. The robe is neat and fresh, the saffron of the attire brighter than ever. Maybe holier, she wonders.

"How are you?" he says cheerfully as he closes the gap between them in quick, easy strides. "You look beautiful, as always," he adds in a more subdued whisper, keeping the smile on his lips.

"You look holier.... I'm alright. Was busy and missed you." She smiles back. His eyes dance in amusement.

"I can't carry your bag in public view. Limitations of a monk," he says playfully.

They fall in step together and take the side street lying widowed beside the temple. When they are beyond human eyes, he holds her hand as they walk side by side. He carries her knapsack on his back.

"A monk with a purple knapsack. An image to remember," Zahra teases.

"I love your colors. Whenever I think of you, I see you mobbed by vivacious tints, enigmatic blends, a riot of conflicting shades. Striking results. Becomes you." He stops, turns around to kiss her.

The sun is about to set, melting in its red hue. Some color spills over the mountains and onto the green as far as the eye can see. Flocks of birds circle high over their heads, homebound after finishing the day's play. The silence is impenetrable. An unbroken blanket of calm covers every nook and cranny in its folds. They can smell the scent of stillness dropping down to embrace the approaching dusk. They watch the sunset together, motionless, engrossed. Arthur's steady arms are around Zahra.

They reach the cabin in the twilight, following the fireflies. Darkness falls suddenly. The twin trees rustle in the breeze as they pass. They step inside when the night sky in the east begins to host sparkles of the stars, one by one.

"I have fruit, biscuits, bread, and milk. Hope you don't mind?" Arthur asks. "Life with a monk isn't easy." He releases her hair from the claw hairclip she uses to tame its unruliness against the wind. The escaped mane bursts out and swells over her shoulders, covering her back. "I love you. Love you, Zara," Arthur murmurs in her ear.

In the candlelight, they eat dinner. He opens the window to allow the moonlight in. Zahra feels the star rays sneaking in, hiding inside the creases of the moonbeams. She tells him about the fascinating night sky of her grandparents' village, all about Dhaka, stories of her conspiratorial sisters sworn to protect sibling secrets, her beautiful mother who loves to wear jasmine in her hair, her decent father and his easy anger, her fun friends loyal to their last drop of blood, the streets and rickshaws...and her life of twenty-eight years so far.

She tells him about her first true crush. She was sixteen. He was a young man who had fought in the war in 1971. The first time she met him at her grandparents' house, he came with his rifle slung over his shoulder, long hair, eyes burning with a fervor to make things right, heart filled with impossible dreams. The newly liberated Bangladesh was in a downward spiral, drowning in nepotism, famine, floods, sickness, political insanity, corruption, and an epidemic of violence. Young men, especially vocal against the lawless chaos, were targeted both by the government and opposition factions. Killing and vengeance became the new normal.

Zahra never got a chance to share her feelings with the young man. He was shot at point-blank range one night. His crime: he was disillusioned, vocal against corruption. He and his friends were planning to launch a new revolution that would guarantee equality for all, and accountability of the immoral political leadership. So he was framed, killed, and defamed as a traitor.

Zahra saw his photograph in the newspaper afterwards—the burning eyes cooled forever, lying lifeless, lined up on the ground with six others. For months and months, she mourned alone, in secret, in silence.

She pours out every detail. Arthur understands and holds her close. His country's brutal political strife drove him to seek solace in a way of life that has healed him. It turned him to Buddhism. Zahra has turned to law, to fight injustice.

They lie beside each other, bodies touching on the scanty mat, and fall asleep gazing out through the window at a slice of the night sky bursting with a million stars.

When she opens her eyes at the chirping of birds outside, the night sky has gone from the window, replaced by the glow of early dawn seeping in, hesitant. The sun is yet to rise. She sees Arthur's profile in the opposite corner from her, meditating in a lotus position, eyes closed, body steady and relaxed. She watches him for a long time, unabashed. He looks peaceful. Last night he loved her intensely, held her close. That face was next to hers. She doesn't know what twists of destiny are ahead of her. There is an ache inside that she refuses to acknowledge. She has no answers, no solution. It's going to be a desolate, heartbreaking, uphill emotional journey. The penance of falling in love with a monk, possibly.

Buddhist books she is reading denounce sensual pleasures, desires for another as forbidden....

In Buddha's first discourse, he identifies craving (tanha) as the cause of suffering (dukkha). He then labels three objects of craving: craving for existence, craving for nonexistence, and craving for sense pleasures (kama). Kama is identified as one of five hindrances to the attainment of a state of perfect equanimity and awareness (jhana).

Throughout the "Sutta Pitaka" (teachings of Buddha, containing more than 10,000), Lord Buddha often compares sexual pleasure to arrows or darts. In his teachings, he explains that craving sexual pleasure is a cause of suffering. If one, longing for sexual pleasure, achieves it, he is enraptured at heart. But if such longing for pleasures diminish, he is shattered, as if shot with an arrow. It takes concentration and insight to extinguish desire.

Arthur opens his eyes. The first thing he looks at is Zahra. He smiles with love in his eyes. She notices his fresh robe. In some places, dark patches are visible, still wet where the water met his bathed body. She didn't hear him waking or bathing as she was deep in sleep.

"When you're ready, I'll bring in water for you. I waited for you to wake up," he says, a sense of soothing emanating from his voice.

"I was lost...didn't hear you." Zahra sits up.

"I bathed outside. Didn't want to disturb you." He smiles again. "I can't heat up the water here. It's cold."

"I don't mind, really," she says.

"Sure?"

"I'm sure." Zahra is definite. Arthur goes out and in ten minutes is back with two buckets. He takes them to the bathroom carefully, without spilling a single drop of water.

"I'll take a walk while you wash up. There's some milk...and bananas. No tea or coffee. Sorry. I'll be back in an hour."

"What about your breakfast? You've eaten?" Zahra wants to know.

"I don't eat anything before noon." He steps out of the cabin. Zahra has yet to learn much about a monk's ways, she thinks. His footsteps fade on the muddy path.

She finds Arthur's washed robes hanging outside on the line. She explores around, looking for the source of water, and finds the feisty brook throwing up cold, fresh sprays from the crevices of a high stone wall, which she assumes is a part of the mountain range. The stream below the cabin is too far down and can be reached only by taking a precarious path, barely inches wide in places. Arthur returns after Zahra has bathed and tidied up the cabin.

"There you are! Fresh as a morning glory flower." Arthur finds her. He has picked a bunch of fragrant wildflowers— white, turquoise, and lavender. He touches her wet hair gently, holds a strand close to his face, and inhales, eyes closed.

"Let me dry your hair; otherwise, you may catch cold. The water is icy in the morning." He starts to rub the wetness out of her hair with a loose end of his robe.

~⁓

For two nights and two days, Zahra loses herself in Arthur's love, sleeping in his arms in the stillness of the night, waking up at new dawns beside him. It has been like a honeymoon-time.

As they walk out of the cabin on Sunday noon, her heart aches to leave it behind, all alone in this wilderness, crying for the loss of their presence. He understands her feelings.

"We can come back next weekend if you want to have another rustic picnic with this monk," he says.

"Yes. I want to," Zahra agrees in a quiet voice. They kiss and hold tightly one more time before stepping onto the muddy path.

When they reach the temple, Arthur lingers behind as Zahra walks ahead. She calls a tuk tuk. Before climbing in, she looks for Arthur. He stands at the foot of the temple, staring at her direction. The tuk tuk speeds up.

9.

Zahra goes back to the cabin the next week and again the week after and every weekend after that for the next three months. Neither of them wants to stop living the secret life—blissful, matched with longing. The cabin comes alive in domesticity with her presence, her lone strands of dark hair shed on the wooden floor, the wildflowers she wears, and the scent of her, their moans and laughter. They don't talk of the future. They don't make any plans for joint lives. They live only in the moment.

Zahra understands the daily conflict that Arthur goes through since he secretly broke the vows. She senses his pain over the deception he has owned up to because of his love for her. As they lay on the grass under the starlit sky one night, Arthur wept in silence, holding her tightly in his arms. She felt his desperation and kissed his tears dry.

"I follow the Tibetan *Vinaya* lineage. I have taken the bhikku vows. I'm meant to practice celibacy," he whispered and then drew her close. Under the night sky as their witness, they made love, ardent, passionate.

"I love you. Arthur, Arthur," Zahra repeated over and over again. They didn't discuss anything that night.

~

It's not easy to fathom Arthur fully. In one moment his love is at the height of crazy fervor, and then he is aloof, withdraws from her. Lying beside him, she realizes he is not with her anymore; he has retreated somewhere she is unable to reach. He constantly struggles. She counts every moment from Monday to Friday, to the end of office hours. Then comes the frenzied weekend when she totally loses herself, her grip on reality.

"What's up, Zahra? You look lost these days," her colleague Binita remarks one day. She has noticed the changes in Zahra for some time.

"What do you mean?" Zahra tries to evade.

Zahra often pairs up with Binita in court for case processings. She provides support, sitting at the lawyer's table as Binita argues the cases. She's friendly, easygoing, newly married to a wealthy businessman, and shares some lineage with the king. Zahra has spent many wonderful evenings after work at her house, where she lives with her in-laws. It's not far from the office. In a short time they have become friends, and Binita has been too generous opening her door to this lonely foreigner.

"...Like someone dancing on the clouds. See those out there? Touching the Himalayas? Can't be traced.... You can watch only." Binita doesn't give up easily. "I can taste your oozing joy with my eyes. What am I missing?"

How can Zahra tell her friend about her secret life? It's something best not spoken of. She may be judged for breaking solemn rules, crossing the thin line of tradition. She isn't sure how much she can share and buries herself in work. She avoids invitations to evening outings with Binita for fear of being found out. Binita's mom has Buddhist lineage while her dad is a Hindu.

Also, she needs time to adjust to her new love life. She pretends to be overly busy, carries big piles of documents to read on the weekend as a bluff to put off speculation. Binita winces at her antics, believes them to be true. To her landlady, Zahra explains her regular absences as official field missions. She has to be ready with deceptions to hide her secret. No one should ever find out.

Sometimes Zahra is weary, sad, and anxious. She wants to have a life with Arthur, a regular, normal, genuine partnership that's up front, not tainted by secrecy and duplicity. But she doesn't know how that can happen. She is aware that no matter how much he loves her, wants to be with her, at every encounter with her he is tortured. She can't think of the time when he may decide to walk away. She tries to bury this fear as she goes about her daily life. But the thought haunts her, doesn't give her a moment's peace. Arthur has said nothing about their future.

Zahra's boss wants to extend her contract by an additional year. New funds have come through at the last minute. Her current contract will be expiring soon. This news comes as a pleasant surprise. She has been debating the idea of talking to her boss to request an extension even without pay if nothing worked out. She heaves a sigh of relief—couldn't think of a separation from Arthur. Not now. They haven't yet spoken about what happens when her assignment ends. She has dreaded bringing it up. Now she sees some light...enough time to plan. For sure, Arthur would consider thoughts of a life together. Her happiness is important to him, she knows in her heart. Their relationship has grown extremely fast. One day with Arthur feels like more than a month. She doesn't mind a humble life with the basics if she has him beside her.

She is amazed at the speed with which the time has passed. Almost five months have gone by with Arthur, as if in the wink of an eye! Now a year's extension has changed everything...is a godsend at this critical period in her life. She wants to give him the good news.

She will have to find a way to discuss Arthur with her father. First, she needs Arthur's assurance. She wants Ishmail to understand and endorse her decision. He will be disappointed for sure. Her heart aches at the thought of hurting him. He will have difficulty accepting a monk, no doubt.

She looks for Arthur at the stupa in the evening. They will both be traveling during the coming weekend as already planned. He will be leading a faith-based congregation while she will go back to Sitarapur to dig up more information on trafficking routes. Meetings have been set up with local influential leaders, communities, and the police. The entire village needs to be roused to assist in the crackdown on traffickers.

The only way to catch Arthur is at the shrine. Zahra wanders around, searching. Darkness begins to gather. The corners of the dome look mystical in the semidimness. The streetlights flicker on weary wooden poles, swaying with the wind. Finally, she spots him speaking with two other monks at the foot of the dome in the farthest corner. He walks up to Zahra when he notices her and politely greets her. In public he is careful not to show any signs of intimacy.

"I'm glad for you, Zara. I'm sure your office recognizes the value you add to their work," he says with a civil smile, with noticeable aloofness as she gives him the news.

"You have to excuse me. I'm in consultation with our fellow bhikkus. I have to go back to continue. Namaste." He bows respectfully and returns to his colleagues. He doesn't give her a chance to engage him further. Zahra smiles weakly in an awkward response and walks away without another glance.

Back in her room, she is restless. She wishes there were some way of contacting Arthur later that night. The aborted conversation earlier makes her apprehensive, dejected. Something was amiss...Arthur wasn't pleased to see her, for sure. His body language was wooden, stiff, devoid of any emotion. It seemed she had interrupted something. There was a forced politeness wrapped in steely caution in the way he met her, unwillingly drawn out to acknowledge her presence. She could see his eyes were disturbed and uneasy, the shadows of old struggles back in them. She is mad at herself for hounding Arthur at the shrine, forcing her presence. She burns in shame. A strange hollowness grips her soul.

She finds it difficult to fall asleep. The stupa looms outside her window. Its long shadow falls on the narrow lane, stamping out the dim streetlights. She opens a book to take her mind off Arthur. It's getting late, but tonight her mind is turbulent. She reads the same page five times without grasping the meaning and then gives up.

She hears a soft knock, a faint sound. At first she thinks it may be the landlady's tomcat chasing his female friends. Then she hears it again and opens the door. Arthur is outside at her doorstep.

"As I was leaving the stupa, I looked up and saw the light from your window." He enters, closing the door behind him.

She stands in the middle of the room, incapable of any reaction, undecided whether to sit down or keep standing or to ask him why he is here so late. She is elated, confused, and troubled all at the same time, making her dizzy. Before she can do anything, Arthur comes to her rescue. He lunges forward and carries her to the bedroom. They begin all over—where they had left off on the weekend. He loves her again and again.

"I saw the hurt in your eyes. I couldn't stay away," he whispers as he kisses her ears.

"You did look at my window?"

"Nope. I lied. You stood against the light at the stupa, the breeze wrapped in your clothes, hair. Couldn't take my eyes off...lost my mind. Wanted to hold you in my arms right there and then." Arthur is solemn.

"What happened to the other two bhikkus?"

"I got rid of them. I have become good at lying...made mistakes in my prayers after you left." Arthur draws her closer.

"You broke my heart. You were so distant. I felt I didn't know you," Zahra whispers.

"You know me. The deception. My struggles being a monk and your lover." His voice sounds broken. "But believe me, my love for you is true," he says forcefully and kisses the top of her head. Zahra nestles in his arms and shuts her eyes. "I'm human.... I forgot before I met you," he sighs, extremely saddened.

He holds her tightly with desperation, as if afraid that if he loosens his grip, she might run away. She knows he is questioning his behavior in his thoughts right at this very moment while he is holding her, lying next to her, uneasy about being disloyal to his vows. She doesn't want to think anymore, not now. She will have plenty of time to analyze the situation tomorrow morning and while on the field mission for the next seven days.

He stays the night. Very early the next morning, while the stars are still awake in the dying night sky, he leaves stealthily. His footsteps are so light that the stairs do not make any sounds as he climbs down.

Woke up on the wrong side of your love

I.

Zahra has been expecting to hear from Arthur after returning from her trip. He must be back from his discourse by now as well. She has missed him every day, even while working and with her busy schedule. The happy memory of the night at her apartment kept coming back. In all the time she has been with Arthur, that was the night she felt the bond between them was strongest, unbreakable. She is confident of his love, the strength of their relationship. All doubts are left behind. She has no more fear about losing him, about telling the world, including her family, that he exists, is the most important person in her life.

A week's separation seems long. She waits for him to contact her as two more days pass. *Monks have many responsibilities, and maybe he got busy with additional work. Who knows?* she reasons, pushing her anxieties away.

Zahra gets fidgety as the weekend approaches. She will have to know by Friday morning if the plan to meet at the cabin is still OK. When Arthur fails to contact her, she walks to the stupa. Arthur isn't there.

She stops at the butter lamps. So many brightly ablaze tonight, lighted by faithful devotees as prayer offerings for loved ones. She lingers a bit longer. This is where she had met Arthur months ago on that fateful night. She walks around aimlessly, makes another round of the shrine. The huge eyes painted on the stupa have a religious meaning—symbolizes the wisdom of Buddha. Zahra looks up at the eyes, searching for a sign for guidance. The occasional lonesome wind brushes over her, giving a chill she can't shake off.

She is sure that if Arthur shows up at her apartment and doesn't find her, he will come here looking for her. But in her heart she also knows he isn't there. She feels an icy emptiness.

"I was here. I waited for you under the stars as the eyes of wisdom watched me beside the fires of the butter lamps…so that the darkness around me is lifted. I can see," she says softly to herself, pushing back the tears.

"Didi, namaste." She hears a familiar voice as she is about to leave the grounds. It's the young waiter.

She decides on a cup of coffee and to send a note to Arthur through the waiter. He is too happy to do her errand and brings a pen and paper as well as an unused, crumpled envelope. She writes only six words, no greeting, no closure. It says, *Bhikku, need to consult you. Zahra.*

~~~

After a restless, difficult night, Zahra feels better in the office, is able to drown her personal problems, her unrestrained thoughts and worries in work. She also signs her new contract. Her boss arranges tea and snacks to celebrate the occasion. She opens the floor with nice words, praising Zahra. All her colleagues, including the receptionist, have some words of appreciation and kindness for Zahra. It touches her, makes her unnecessarily weepy.

Later, she calls Dhaka and speaks to her mother on a faulty line, screaming at the top of her lungs most of the time. Sabaa is happy for her but also informs her that Tara's wedding talks have progressed. The date will be fixed soon, she assumes. Ishmail isn't home, but Sabaa promises to give him the news as soon as he returns.

The day plods on. Still no news of Arthur. She wonders if he is back or whether he is unwell. She is sick with worry. She decides to pass by the café again on the way home to find out the fate of her note. At that point, the receptionist comes looking for her. She has a call waiting on the line. Zahra takes it from her office. Her heart leaps in anticipation.

"Namaste, Zara. How are you?" It's Arthur, familiar, comforting, as always.

"I sent you a note, Bhikku." Zahra keeps up the pretense immaculately. Her heart continues somersaults.

"I got it. That's why I'm calling you. We need to talk." He pauses. "Now...." His voice is distraught.

"Can't we meet at the cabin later?" She whispers.

"Ah, no. I won't be there. I'm going away on a solitary meditation to do some thinking," he says.

"About what?" Zahra is numb.

"My vows. Can't go on like this. Not anymore. I'm a monk, Zara," he says. He sounds steely cold. Aloof.

"That's all you have to say?"

"Zara, I have to leave Kathmandu, otherwise.... I think...go back to Ireland or to some other place. It's very difficult for me. You understand?" Her ears pick up a faint hint of pleading or exasperation; Zahra can't figure out.

"What about your work here? What will happen to that? You can't leave."

"At this point, yes.... That's my only option unless I can overcome my problems...disturbing emotions. I have nothing for you." Arthur's voice seems to be coming from very far away. Zahra has difficulty concentrating on his words, attaching meaning to them. The words swim in front of her eyes.

"Nothing for us?" she repeats as if in a trance. "And you've to say this over the phone...?" Zahra's heart breaks...and breaks into dust at each word she utters, but she regains full control of herself immediately. She doesn't want him to sense the intensity of her pain, the destitution lurking in her longing for him, the immense hurt tearing at her heart, grief over the only love she has found and lost.

"Zara, I'm sorry. I am. Earnestly. For causing you pain." He pauses again, coughs to clear his voice. "Can you forgive me?" he says in low, hoarse notes. Zahra doesn't respond. "I don't know how to explain my behavior to you...all this time. Will you be OK? Zara?" he asks again, his sadness very distinct now in the way he calls out her name.

"Don't worry about me, Bhikku. Go well on your way. Namaste." She hangs up, cuts him off. It doesn't make any sense to continue the conversation further. It was too distressing. She didn't want him to smell her desperation.

Zahra packs up her bag and leaves the office right afterwards. She is angry for stupidly falling for a monk, and her anguish is almost annihilating her soul.

2.

In the deepest end of her heart, in the tiniest crevices of drops of blood, hope remains alive. In the evenings she stays at home in case he comes over, is up late at night expecting to hear a knock on her door. She keeps her living room window wide open so that the light can be spotted from the stupa site. He may find his footsteps in that light leading to her doorway. In the office, whenever the phone rings, her heart stops as she thinks it might be Arthur, calling to take back every word he said, sorry for hurting her. He doesn't call. He doesn't stand outside her door. He avoids any chance meeting with her on the street. She can't cry. The heavy ache stays frozen, doesn't melt.

A silent storm has been brewing in Arthur's mind for some time. Forced into the conflicting position of being her lover and a man of vows tortured his mind, challenged his integrity. Zahra has been aware of it all along, could feel it right from the beginning of their relationship. He tried to break away but was drawn back to her on the rebound each time with a fiercer intensity. It frightened her. Maybe he sensed it too. She feared that he would despise her someday for the love he had for her, that compelled him to violate the vows he was committed to, to betray his faith he considered precious, vital to his identity. He couldn't exist in the shame, the pain of losing it. She understood the consequences, the cost of her love for him, but it was so true, so soul wrenching that she couldn't keep away. Her love was so condemned but so dear. It burned her with a vigorous strength, and she was reborn into a new life every time she was with him. Without him, she wasn't herself anymore. Her heartbeat stopped. In his arms, she found the meaning of her existence. It was madness from the beginning to the end and possibly doomed.

Arthur denounced earthly pleasure and desire, the luxury of comfort voluntarily for a life of humility, piousness that heals, that liberates, to be true to Lord Buddha's teachings, to avoid any attachments sure to end in suffering. He strongly believes life is a transitory passing phase, and true faith in Buddha's principles is the passage towards Nirvana, the emancipation of the spirit from earthly bindings. Zahra's presence has no place in it.

In Buddhist ethics, one should neither be attached to nor crave sensual pleasure. Arthur feared his frailty in committing both. Everything now becomes too clear to Zahra as she examines every moment, every word they exchanged, everything about her relationship with Arthur, over and over again. She has never been so happy as she has been with Arthur, though it was brief...and has never experienced so much grief because she has lost him. He loved her intensely but has hurt her the most.

Zahra keeps reading about Buddhism...

In Japan, Buddhist monks and nuns can marry after receiving their highest ordination. The marriage of monks can be found as early as the Heian period (794–1185). Apart from certain schools in Japan and Tibet, most who practice Buddhism as ordained monks and nuns choose to live in celibacy. Sex is seen as a serious monastic transgression.

Within Theravada Buddhism, there are four principal transgressions that demand expulsion from the monastic sangha: sex, theft, murder, and falsely boasting of superhuman perfection. In the case of monasticism, abstaining completely from sex is seen as a necessity in order to reach enlightenment.

Arthur is a follower of Theravada Buddhism.

The hurt is so overpowering, it keeps bruising Zahra's soul and pulls her into a deep canyon of despondency. Like a zombie, Zahra moves around and works and works more for months without any break. She accepts Arthur's departure from her life. He has left her finally, but she is unable to despise him. She can't be angry with him either. She despairs, wonders how she is going to spend all the time left on her extended contract. Work becomes tiresome.

She gets a phone call from Ishmail. Tara's wedding date

has been fixed, and Zahra is wanted back home to assist with preparations.

3.

It's not easy. It's sudden for when so many plans have been made, so much enthusiasm garnered. But family comes first. Her boss understands that. Zahra was looking for an escape route, and she has found one, and in time before the weariness consumes her entirely. She promises to forward some deserving names of potential candidates to take over her work.

Zahra doesn't want any fuss. The girls cry as they all gather for a final cup of tea and the last piece of cake together. They put a *sindoor bindi*—a vermillion spot—on her forehead, adorn her neck with a garland of marigolds, roses, and jasmine flowers, and present her with a *tanka* so that she has a safe trip back home. The Gurkha adds another red spot on her forehead and says, "Namaste, Didi"—one last time. She will definitely miss him. With love, they send her away.

It has been difficult to make this decision, hard thought out. Finally, she came to the conclusion that a clean break would be good to recover from the mess that's sinking her in a dark quagmire of misery. Her drastic resolution hasn't lifted up her spirit, though. But she deserves another chance. She has to heal in order to be functional. So she resigned.

Her flight is in two days. She has to pack, buy a few things, pick up gifts for the family and her friends before she travels.

All the neighbors come to say goodbye and see her off as she gets into the taxi with her two suitcases. The Kathmandu Valley falls behind; she heads towards the airport as the automobile speeds on the uneven tarmac road. Her love for the valley, the mountains, the temples, and the tea shops quietly climb into her heart.

The night before, she visited the Baudha one last time. She strolled on the grounds and stopped to light three butter lamps—one for Arthur, one for her, and one to celebrate their love, for the life with him...short, sweet, but never meant to be. As she was leaving the shrine, she hesitated in front of the café. The friendly waiter wasn't around. She would have liked to say goodbye to him.

The Himalayas keep following her, faithful as ever as the taxi navigates the narrow roads. A piece of herself she leaves behind, forever spread over the wilderness of the mountain slopes and the silvery lines of each cloud.

Tribhuvan Airport is quite informal, lax. The flight is delayed, she is told, as she struggles with her suitcases amidst the crowd of passengers and their families who have come to see them off. People fuss with their belongings, saying some last words before traveling, share some momentary laughter. Zahra tries to find a place to sit down, tugging at her baggage.

"Let me help you. Allow me, at least with your bags."

That voice she waited to hear every moment of each day since the last phone call—she waited the longest six months of her life for him. She turns around. Arthur smiles, holding out all the love he has for her to take.

"Bhikku? Why are you here?" Zahra asks in naked surprise.

"I called your office yesterday afternoon and was told you were leaving today. I traveled on a bus the whole night. Missed you at the apartment by five minutes." He looks at her, the deep look that has the power to disturb her senses, wreck her completely. His face is pale, somewhat awry, and exhausted, dry lipped. "I couldn't let you go without seeing you. One more time.... My last phone call couldn't be our final conversation."

Zahra's legs seem to have grown roots in the ground. She can't move, pull them out.

"Let's have coffee at the café across the street. One last cup?

It's safe to leave your luggage here," he pleads. How to say no to a holy Monk when an entire crowd is watching? Zahra gives in.

They sit face to face across the narrow table, two feet of distance between them, their knees touching underneath. Arthur doesn't move away from the touch; neither does she. He leans forward. His breath touches her face. His nearness is insanely close. She finds it difficult to look at him directly. She doesn't want him to see her tears stealthily welling up. So she stares beyond him, towards the mountains. The Himalayas are everywhere in Kathmandu. Always fascinating, always spectacular!

"Your office said you resigned. Why? I thought you were keen on taking the extension." Arthur forces her to look at him now. *Because you broke my heart!* she wants to scream out for the world to hear. The wound is raw and threatens to bleed.

"I wanted you to be true to your vows, complete your mission here. It matters to you more than your life. I didn't want to jeopardize that," she says instead. "I thought I would be a distraction, always. Mess you up again. I couldn't do that to you." A faint sob escapes her.

He moves forward and takes both her hands in his. Her tears begin to fall now. She sits facing him in stony silence, doesn't move, doesn't try to pull away her hands. The warmth from him flows into her heart, and it's calming. Somehow he reaches into her soul in an instant. The clotted pain begins to soften, finally. She knows she can never love anyone in the impossible way she loves this man. The coffee comes, but Arthur still holds her hands. The waiter puts down the cups on one corner of the table and moves away. Arthur releases her hands.

"I couldn't trust myself anymore, wanted you so badly. If I stayed here, I would have knocked at your door, your sanity,

I know…so I quit." She wipes away each tear, almost talks to herself. Her fingers leave faint smudges on her cheeks as he watches her every move intently. His gaze is fixed on her face, troubled. Zahra stares at her hands, the colorless steam from the coffee cups.

"Zara, I love you. I love you so much it hurts. I want you to know this."

His eyes look blurry. The blue in them turns washed out, so faded it's almost difficult to detect the color in them anymore. She doesn't recognize whether it's her tears or his. It strikes her that he's talking about his love for her in the present tense. He still is in love with her. She smiles weakly through the weight of her tears.

"The last six months, I subjected myself to rigorous regimentation. Meditated, fasted, searched my soul after we spoke. I have found harmony at last. My life belongs to a different course." He holds her eyes in his.

"If there were any other path, I would have taken that to be with you. The pain of losing you will stay close inside my heart. Always. My love for you lives, Zara," he says.

But you didn't choose me. The words keep pounding with harrowing intensity inside Zahra's head.

They sit in silence. She forgets to ask him why he had phoned her office.

Guru Zasep Tulku Rinpoche advises, "Don't think your practice is no longer worth the effort just because you have broken your commitments; don't abandon your commitments and daily practice; just pick up where you left off…. If you forget to eat breakfast, you don't give up there and then. The next day, you go ahead and eat breakfast. Simple." The words she had read hammer in her mind.

~

He waits as she checks in. She turns around to see him standing as she goes through the immigration. One last glance, a brief smile, and she enters the security area. The walls bar him from her eyesight. She wonders how long Arthur will be standing there, whether he is leaving now or will wait till her flight takes off to the sky, above the towering Himalayas, reaching for the clouds. She will never know because they didn't discuss keeping in touch. He didn't ask for her address in Dhaka.

4.

The flight from Kathmandu to Dhaka takes about three hours. Zahra decides to push away thoughts of Arthur. She must move on. He has. As she closes her eyes, she visualizes him chanting sacred mantras at the foot of the dome, eyes shut, the handsome face in earnest concentration, night after night, the magical moonlight caressing him in a soft embrace. Will he ever glance towards her apartment window? Will the stupa be the same after what happened between them? After he transformed her life so much, and she his? How will he wash away the warmth of their love from the log cabin, the scent of her presence buried deep in its spirit, engraved in his soul?

The plane inches towards Dhaka. The new memories need to be replaced by the old precious ones—to seal the vacuum she carries inside. Life lived with Tara and Anushka, Sabaa and Ishmail begin to tiptoe back into her thoughts. Her growing-up days were complicated but content, for sure. All seem like yesterday—the ecstatic, happy moments, big worries over small things, countless differences, disappointments and difficult heartbreaks, bittersweet tears and incredible laughter.... An existence is made up of so much! Snapshots of the past flood into her mind, a speedy slideshow in a flash, precious memories stored unspoiled in the crevices of her soul.... She waltzes into the memory lane, a two-way street of many flavors, salty, sweet, spicy—of the magical times!

The plane enters the skies of Dhaka.

"Ladies and gentlemen, we'll shortly land..." the pilot announces over the monotonous buzzing of the plane's engines.

She is finally returning home! The home that she has missed so much. She tries to break out of her wasted sadness. Very soon she will be seeing familiar loving faces waiting to receive her. They matter more than anything. She will have to pretend to be cheerful, eager.

Zahra is glad that pain is colorless, can be deceptively hidden in the folds of the soul. She knows her sisters' keen sense of sniffing out distinct shades of sorrow. Anushka is supposed to be at the airport for sure, but will Tara be there? Her heart racing, Zahra descends from the plane after almost eleven months of separation from her sisters.

As she walks out of customs, Zahra sees Anushka waving at her, smiling, exuberant....

CHAPTER TWENTY-THREE

"Will you make me something beautiful for you?"

—*a Native American prayer*

I.

Singing has been a passion and also a refuge for Anushka. It's a hobby and a habit. As she struggled with the daily frustrations, the overwhelming pressures of her postgraduate medical studies and residency, singing provided a blissful break. Though she didn't want to, she has become a doctor in the end like Ishmail. She finds a bizarre kind of joy while striding through the long, dim corridors of the Dhaka Medical College Hospital, where her father studied. Ishmail is very proud of her, as she has followed his profession.

Finding her way wasn't easy, didn't happen effortlessly. Like many of her friends in the unsettling days of the teen years, she wasn't sure about anything, what she really wanted. She sought *something* more from life, inexplicable but meaningful.

Many, many aches and joys shaped the life of today's Dr. Anushka, who aspires to take away others' pain.

2.

Anushka was extremely naïve, impressionable, like any other eighteen-year-old while in twelfth grade. She was still in love with physics in those days. Flirtations with quantum theory, the laws of thermodynamics, and Newton's law of gravity excited her, but she wasn't sure about the field of education she wanted to pursue further. She was also drawn to philosophy, anthropology, and psychology. Human minds and actions interested her.

Anyway, she had enough time ahead to prepare adequately to decide further. Of course, her father would have a big veto power, "as strong as Russia or China at the Security Council," as Tara pronounced repeatedly, if he disagreed with Anushka's choice. He expected her to follow in his footsteps, take up medicine, a noble profession. Sabaa was easy on the girls and believed they should be allowed to choose.

Ishmail encouraged his daughters to be independent and smart, and he nurtured their intellectual growth to be free spirited. To him, the sensible choice of an educational path would result in solid professional opportunities in the future, ultimately solidifying confidence and emancipation, both essential for financial and emotional stability.

His views had clashed with Tara's openly, numerous times since her adolescent years. With Zahra, the disagreements were steered much more diplomatically, in degrees, as by nature she possessed a tendency to avoid insensitive exchanges of words. She believed unnecessary uproar and antics left behind traces of scars that last a long time. Though never compromising principles dear to her, she was open to dialogue, to listen to opposing perspectives. Ishmail respected that, and somehow Zahra could get away with her ideas, though he didn't always fully endorse them.

Ishmail was more lenient with Anushka as she was yet to gather her wits to contradict him stridently. Though she didn't fully agree with his stands or views entirely, she maintained a safe distance, evaded word wars with her father, unlike Tara.

~~⌒~~

On some days after class, Anushka studied with her friend Maya. They had chosen the same subjects and were good support to each other. Maya lived with her brother and his wife in a huge, beautiful archaic house in the same neighborhood. The house was separated from the main road by a big emerald-green lawn in the front, shadowed by tall ancient trees blooming graciously throughout the year. The mild scent of flowers roamed the place like an elixir of affection. One had to step on a patch of grass to enter the house. In the rainy season, shoes got mobbed by puddles of water and resulted in an ungainly sight. Even then, the grassy spot remained, bold and a nuisance, but no one thought of putting a tarmac strip to ease entry to the house. It was their parental home.

Maya's parents died when she was in primary school—cancer and coronary disease. The girls had been friends for years, and the families were somewhat acquainted; otherwise, Ishmail would have never agreed to this arrangement of after-class studying. He didn't feel comfortable with the idea of his daughters spending too much time away from home except when they were attending classes.

Propelled by the simplicity of young minds, the girls vowed an everlasting friendship, never to separate, even when they became professionals or got married. They would sit on the lawn on the soft grass under the trees and study, giggle, and gossip as many lazy middays and evenings progressed. At eighteen, the world seemed to be shouting out countless possibilities.

Maya's brother Ibrahim was a renowned architect, his wife, Lily, a practicing lawyer, an activist who had been working with policymakers for women's rights for decades. Both were much older than Maya, in their early forties, childless—a happy, pleasant couple, open-minded and modern. They led intense, busy lives, and Anushka often saw them in and out of the house during the time she spent there. In some instances there were brief exchanges, some information and laughter shared. They were pleased to have Anushka as Maya's friend and felt less guilty for their sparse presence at home, slaving away at their schedules. The cook had actually been Maya's nanny in the past, which made things even better, and their trustworthy guard was a longtime employee, so Maya was in a secure environment during their absences.

Maya was a menopausal baby, as people liked to whisper behind her back. She was born when her mother was in her late forties. Her mother didn't think it was possible to conceive again after a gap of so many years after Ibrahim's birth. There were miscarriages, though, in between. Maya was a miracle. Ibrahim was almost like a father figure to her, twenty-three years older. In her childhood, she was more comfortable when her brother turned up for teacher–parent meetings at her kindergarten. Her elderly parents were often mistaken for her grandparents, which even at that early age embarrassed her.

3.

The rain came in heavy torrents as Anushka entered Maya's house on that Monday, the first day of the week after holidays, to thrash out the almost unbreakable equations. The assignment was due in class by Thursday. Sweeping rain generously showered her from the curtainless windows as the automobile took speed. Today, she had taken a three-wheeler baby taxi from college. Almost every drop of rain found refuge in her hair and clothes.

She stepped into the unsuspecting puddle at the door. That was the final straw—and walked into the living room with soggy sandals, hair plastered on her face, some stray strands clinging to her shapely bosom. At the sound of her footsteps, Ibrahim looked up and found her in subdued misery. Maya started to giggle, noting the pitiful sight as she climbed down the steps, which spiraled down from the upstairs living quarters to the ground-floor family room—a novel architectural feat for such an old house! Maya wasn't heartless but just a teenage girl overwhelmed by the absurdity of the situation. Anushka looked weirdly funny, drenched, and wretched.

"Look at you! Ha...ha....What happened?...Grand entry of Madam Scarecrow!" Maya teased as always, good-naturedly bubbling with laughter. Anushka was forced into giggles.

"Hey, young lady, mind your manners." Ibrahim glanced at both girls.

"It's OK.... I look bizarre." Anushka tried to brush off the raindrops and Ibrahim's reprimand of her friend at the same time. Between them, they were used to such teasing. It wasn't unkind. It was simply funny.

"You're all wet, Anush! You'll catch a cold. Fetch a towel for her, Maya." He looked again at her, up and down, slightly amused. He had come home early that day as his meeting had been canceled. Lily was away from Dhaka to attend a case processing hearing and would be back the next day.

"No worries. I should be fine. I have totally spoiled this place." Anushka shook off mud from her sandals and was embarrassed at the dirty puddle she had created on the sparkling white mosaic floor of the family room.

One side of this huge rectangular room was occupied by a four-seater sofa, an ancient comfortable rocking chair, along with a large television on a low wooden table, smugly standing on a Tibetan carpet, paled by age in spots. And on the other end were a collection of rare creepers, ferns, and potted plants—lots and lots of them, creating a spontaneous in- house jungle. On the margin of this room, fading into the dining room, hung a rattan swing, secured with strong ropes from a beam. The entire wall of this room on the opposite side was made of French windows that opened onto the backyard, another piece of terrain exploding with robust blossoms—jasmine, marigolds, wild plants, and roses. The room had a unique character, was consuming in a pleasant way. This was Anushka's favorite spot in the house.

Ibrahim didn't leave immediately. He settled down on the rocking chair with a newspaper as Anushka toweled the rain out of her dark hair and face.

"We're having tea with *samosas*. Want some?" Maya threw the question to him.

"Would love to," he mumbled with eyes glued on the newspaper.

As they sipped tea and ate the freshly fried crispy samosas, the homemade deep-fried wheat flour patties with potatoes and pea stuffing, they chatted about their classmates, upcoming exams, politics, art, literature, and of course some social gossip. Ibrahim heartily joined in the conversation, providing additional facts, pieces of news unknown to them. It was an endearing discussion that Anushka really enjoyed. Ibrahim was more into facts. He evaded gossip with a lenient smile. After an hour, he vanished upstairs, leaving the girls to study.

Maya was a balanced person overall, but she did miss a normal life like Anushka's and others of her age. She wasn't unhappy with her present life. Being an orphan wasn't easy, alienated her from others her age. Though Ibrahim and Lily truly cared for her, she felt an emptiness inside that pulled her into gloomy moods sometimes. Anushka's empathy, warmth, unquestioning friendship, and love helped. They could talk about anything for hours without restraint. There were no secrets between them. They were like true sisters.

The rain continued. It was getting late. Normally, Sabaa would send the car to pick Anushka up. Their driver on that evening had gone home early with a fever. She phoned Maya so that she could arrange for their driver to give a ride to Anushka instead. Ibrahim volunteered. "You stay in, Maya. No need to hop into this maddening rain. I'll take Anush home."

Both Ibrahim and Anushka tried to huddle under the one and only umbrella that could be found and stepped out of the door into the rain-swept grounds.

A pleasant masculine smell hit her nostrils in that close radius of the umbrella. He held it over her head, trying to give her more room as they carefully avoided the deeper puddles. Anushka was quite tall for a Bengalee woman. Ibrahim was almost a six-footer, lean and well built with a kind, smart face. She became more and more conscious of his proximity as he tried to keep her close, shielding her from the merciless shower. She wasn't feeling any awkwardness, though. They moved together. He lightly held her with his free arm. The umbrella folded up as a strong gusty wind stumbled over them, spraying the cold of the sharp drops in harsh suddenness.

"Wow...umbrella's gone. Let's run to the car before we're drenched to our bones." Ibrahim laughed helplessly, trying to talk over the sound of the rain and the wind.

"What a tragic adventure! But it's a good tragedy. I don't mind getting wet in the rain anytime," Anushka said as she tried to be comfortable in the passenger seat with the dampness clinging to her clothes.

"You're a delightful, interesting girl, Anush." He started the car as he glanced sideways to catch her eyes.

"Well, I'm not a girl anymore. When you were not looking, I grew up."

"Yeah?"

"Oh yeah! My mom had two of us at my age." She was serious.

"You're smart, not just beautiful," Ibrahim mused.

"Give me a quantum equation and you'll know," Anushka said smugly. Ibrahim laughed.

The car reached her house. It took less than ten minutes on the traffic-free road.

"I liked the teatime with you today," he said. She smiled.

"Thank you for the lift. Bad weather but charming." She got out. She waited for him to reverse the car and waved.

"Go inside. Rain's going to kill you." He rolled down the window and then in a minute was back on the main road, speeding away.

4.

Anushka walked by the general bookstore to pick up some stationery and the new edition of *National Geographic* magazine. This store sold new and used books and every educational item that a student might need. It was one of the largest in the city and well regarded for its good collections. Maya was still in the library trying to finish her assignment when she left the college. Shopping alone without her was no fun, Anushka realized, flipping through the books.

"What're you buying?" She heard Ibrahim's deep voice from behind.

"Oh, I'm just looking at some stuff. What're you doing here? Isn't it office time?" She hadn't seen him for over a week after that rainy evening. "Please, could you get that yellow book down from the upper shelf for me?" she said in the same breath, pointing to the bookshelf.

Ibrahim's lanky frame loomed over her as he grabbed the book, reaching with his long arms. He pushed back his bushy hair from the forehead and smiled at her, handing over the book.

"Why are the shelves so high? They don't think about us women!" Anushka's voice was laced with exasperation.

His witty, intelligent eyes, caged in thick glasses, were amused. His soft bristles seemed almost bluish, hinting at a robust growth of beard ready to burst out soon. He looked good in his white full-sleeved shirt, deep blue denims, and greyish Hush Puppies.

"I didn't know you were allowed to wear jeans at work," she noted.

"Umm, today's casual, no meetings. I'm the boss, by the way. I make the rules in my office. The boss is always right, you know?" He smiled teasingly with a friendly shrug. She shook her head, either in agreement or dissent. She wasn't sure.

"You're rather observant," he reflected.

"My head is tightly secured on my neck, and my eyes see without additional gadgets," she said comically. He laughed out aloud.

"So, what have you been doing since I saw you last?" he inquired casually.

"Mmm, not much, apart from studying." She was noncommittal.

"Care to have a cup of tea? There's a good café two minutes from here. I would kill for a cup," he added. Before she could make up her mind, she found herself walking in step with him.

"I can't stay too long," Anushka said with faint hesitation.

"Just a cup of tea, Anush...not proposing marriage!" He threw in the widely used common line. Maybe overused and not funny at all, but still he said it.

"You're already married!" Anushka snapped back.

"I am. Very true," Ibrahim looked at her directly, laughing at his own joke, then added quietly, "Pity I didn't meet you when single."

Anushka was bewildered, didn't know what to say. Another of his jokes, possibly...

She liked the tea shop, styled in a trendy décor—rattan chairs, low tables, authentic handicrafts, and a handful of original paintings by local unknown artists displayed on the thin plywood walls. It yelled *cozy* from every angle. Subdued sounds of old English songs filled the background.

The tea was great, steaming hot, heart-wrenching amazing aroma. They also ate vegetable cutlets with a spicy sauce. The tea burned the lips, smudged on the remnants of the hotness of the sauce.

"You didn't buy anything, I noticed," Anushka observed.

"I'll send our intern to pick up the items I identified there. Nothing serious. You didn't buy anything either," Ibrahim remarked.

"I was window-shopping, actually...on my way home," Anushka lied. She noted the blurry, faint finger marks on his glasses. It bothered her. *For God's sake, why doesn't he clean them?* she thought as she toyed with the teaspoon, curbing an overwhelming desire to snatch them from him and wipe them clean. They chatted some more, on inconsequential matters.

"I thought you said the other day...you enjoy art exhibitions. A good one is starting at the end of the month at the national art college. I can join you if you're interested," Ibrahim said as they got up to leave, fingering back his bushy hair encroaching on his forehead, touching the frames of his glasses dirty—one more time.

"Yeah, I would like that."

"I'll call you to confirm the time. Got to check my schedule," he added.

"OK. I'll tell Maya."

"Of course," he agreed readily.

Ibrahim waved as he crossed the road to the car park. He was returning to the office. Anushka didn't feel like going back to the store anymore to pick up the magazine she wanted. She saw his car amidst many others—slowly vanishing onto the busy road.

5.

A certain sense of elation followed Anushka around, stayed with her till she fell asleep very late that night. She was wrapped in an unknown, bizarre emotion that was frightening and at the same time astoundingly refreshing, very new. A topsy-turvy tossing inside her continued leaving her weak in the legs. Her body seemed weightless, ready to rise up to the sky like a feather. She lost her appetite, lost sleep.

"You look like the sinking *Titanic*, Anush. Aimlessly drowning in your own whirlpool." Tara laughed saucily with a quizzical glance towards her, trying to measure her up. Anushka squirmed away quickly as Zahra came to her rescue.

"Study pressure? Anything I can help with? You look pale." She was concerned.

"Nahhh...all good." Anushka picked up her bag and walked out of the room as her sisters exchanged looks. She didn't know what to say.

She was counting the days...wished the end of the month would arrive today!

Anushka resumed studying with Maya some days when she had time. She didn't come across Ibrahim or Lily. They were overwhelmed with new projects and keeping late hours, Maya informed her. The girls loved to have the house to themselves and enjoyed its unrestrained comforts, oblivious of the universe around them. The two friends sweated over physics—equations and formulas—discussed popular songs, love stories of classmates, with a dash of politics in between, as was customary.

"Anush, you're not yourself these days. What's up? Want to talk?" Maya observed one day.

"Hey...pay attention to your unsolved angular motion equation rather than me," Anushka fired back teasingly.

They took turns on the swing and the rocking chair, ate bowl after bowl of popcorn, courtesy of Maya's nanny, while laboring with their studies.

Though she would have liked Anushka to be more forthright, Maya backed off. She knew her friend too well to pester her further. From time to time she glanced at Anushka's pale face, sparkly eyes that rather stood out on her smooth sandalwood complexion. The thick ponytailed hair high up on the back of Anushka's head bounced as she dived into the pages of her notebook, meticulously jotting down the formulas, fervently trying to break them.

Memories of the chance bookshop encounter and teatime with Ibrahim faded into the background.

⁓

As Anushka entered the house after classes were over, Sabaa informed her that Ibrahim had called and left a message for her. "He said to meet him at his office tomorrow at noon. Why are you seeing him?" Sabaa asked casually, concentrating on the chore at hand.

"It's kind of a project, Ama. Not to worry," Anushka reassured her instantly. She didn't know why she lied to her mother.

"How will you go? Want your father to send the car? Will Maya be with you?"

"I'll take a baby taxi. It's close. I haven't talked to Maya yet. She'll definitely be with me." Anushka was being truthful now.

"OK. Be careful on the road. These baby-taxi drivers are crazy. Always speeding. No respect for traffic rules. And take

Maya with you. Your father wouldn't like you to walk into an office by yourself." There was a hint of caution in Sabaa's tone.

Anushka was relieved to find that her sisters weren't around as she talked to Sabaa. Less explaining to do. She decided to inform Maya of the outing. It would be fun to have her join in. Or would it? Her mind hesitated, but she shrugged it off. Anyway, Ibrahim wanted that as well. She dialed Maya in the evening.

"Maya isn't home. She went out an hour ago," the nanny's sleepy voice answered.

"Do you know what time she'll be back?"

"She didn't tell me. I was napping on the balcony when she left." Anushka smiled as it was obvious what the woman had been up to.

"Any idea where she went?" she asked further.

"She has a toothache. She went with Lily." The woman threw some specific light now.

"She was OK in class only a few hours ago when I saw her last," Anushka mentioned.

"It comes and goes. Started again when she came home. It was bad."

Anushka left it at that and hung up. She would check with Maya tomorrow in class.

⟿

"Where are you heading? Special occasion? Anything I should know?" Tara asked. Anushka caught Tara's eyes in the mirror as she was getting ready the next morning.

She had picked up a deep blue outfit splashed with traces of faint lavender artistically interwoven into the fabric. She dressed with care that day, touched her eyes with mascara that highlighted the deepest, mysterious dark stored in them, added a light brush of pale, soft pink on her lips to accentuate her pure marble-white gorgeous smile whenever she dimpled.

"Off to the college. Why?"

"You look different in a strange, sweet way, little sister. You're blooming this morning." Tara yawned, but her searching eyes lingered slightly longer on Anushka's face.

"Tara, please! Don't crack into her privacy. At eighteen, a woman is entitled to an embargo from sibling harassment," Zahra threw in her legal punchline.

"You're going to be a brilliant lawyer, Zahra. Glad you're studying law to protect helpless civilians from hapless privacy persecution." Anushka smiled as she walked out.

"Overruled!" Tara shouted in jest, ducking from Zahra's flying pillow targeting her face.

6.

Maya didn't turn up in class. Well, nothing Anushka could do about that, she thought. As the morning rolled on, she kept tabs on her wristwatch, somewhat anxious. The hours moved maddeningly slowly. She couldn't concentrate; her mind didn't register a single word that the professor harped on. Unlike most other days, she had no questions to ask.

Finally, the morning class was over. She was going to skip her afternoon class. It wouldn't take her too long to reach Ibrahim's office. There were some nice shops a block away from his office building. Instead of showing up too early, she could hang around the shopping complex. Better not to be late. Anushka directed the baby-taxi driver.

She walked around the shopping center. There were eye-catching collections of bags, shoes, and expensive perfumes. It was an upscale place and a haven of imported goods. From time to time, she checked on the time. She was fifteen minutes early on an almost traffic-free road. Who would think fifteen minutes could feel like a lifetime?

On the dot, Anushka gave her name to the pleasant, pretty young woman behind the reception desk. The receptionist spoke on the phone, and in two minutes Ibrahim appeared. The faint scent of his expensive aftershave cologne filled up the space, declaring his presence. Unlike the other day, he was wearing black pants, a full-sleeved white shirt, and formal shoes. Even his glasses looked clean and gleamed, reflecting the daylight.

"I thought you were not coming. You didn't confirm," he said.

"Oh, I'm here now." Anushka was confused. What was there to confirm?

"Yeah, glad you made it. We'll take my car. It's not far from here." He said something to the receptionist. Anushka fell in step with him.

"Maya has a toothache," she said.

"So I heard. I don't see her much. She usually avoids me unless she needs something." He smiled.

"She's going to miss this." Anushka didn't explain that she hadn't even told her friend about today's outing.

The art college was in a large, old building close to Dhaka University, half hidden amidst trees, multicolored flowers and greenery leading to a small lotus pond and sitting area in the front where art students and visitors liked to hang around. The spacious continuous balcony wound around the main building. On the ground floor, the galleries were packed with canvases of various sizes of oil paintings and watercolors. Captured forever, frozen in time were portraits, landscapes, abstract expressions in interesting uses of color by reputable and unknown artists. Several sculptures and figurines in brass and metal were also displayed. On one side of the wall, the paintings and handiwork of famous artists and sculptors were exhibited—Shikdar, Abedin, Qamrul Hasan, warriors of the Bengalee art movement. A world of extraordinary creative amazement unfolded right in front of Anushka. For hours they went from one piece of art to another, trying to absorb the offerings of passion, without talking, in deep concentration, awestruck by the human capacity to create revolutionary beauty, tossed out in magnificent excellence.

By the time they completed the rounds of the galleries, it was almost early evening. The sun was dim, and the breeze was breaking the heat in pleasantness. Anushka walked towards the lotus pond.

"Let's sit here for a few minutes? But if you have work to do, you don't have to wait," she said.

"No, I have time. This is nice." He sat down opposite her in the grass. They had nothing more to say. The colors of the canvases were in their minds. "The paintings were raging spectacular," Anushka mused softly.

"Would you like to eat something? Early dinner before we head back?" he wanted to know.

"I don't mind. Yeah." Anushka for some reason didn't want this evening to end. He helped her to her feet with a firm grip of his hand.

"I'm hungry. Missed lunch today," he said. "By the way, blue becomes you." He glanced admiringly at her attire as she stood up.

"Blue is my favorite color. I never get tired of wearing it." She smiled. Her dimples cascaded across her face. He looked away.

They crossed over to a small eatery. Anushka wanted clear vegetable beef soup. Ibrahim ordered fried rice and sweet-and-sour prawns. He made her laugh by teasing the waiter with absurd questions. The young man was perplexed and ran to the kitchen to get clarifications from the chef each time. Anushka had to look the other way to stop from laughing out loud while Ibrahim used his antics on the unsuspecting, naïve waiter. He winked at her as she struggled to be serious.

"Come on, no more. Poor guy!" she exclaimed between giggles. He watched her, amused.

"I made you laugh, at least." There was a hint of mischief and something more in his eyes. She didn't understand it. His eyes lingered longer on her face. Anushka blushed faintly and prayed that it went unnoticed.

The food arrived. The waiter eagerly placed the dishes on the table and explained the contents. Ibrahim listened attentively, very serious, eyebrows knitted together. All traces of fun-making totally evaporated. Ibrahim waited till the waiter retreated into the background, then served food on her plate. In a strange silence of camaraderie, they continued to eat. The food tasted good. Chinese cuisine was for all weather, all times.

"How's exam preparation?" Suddenly he was the parental figure, Maya's much, much older brother—a somewhat formidable fragment of an authoritarian image.

"We're good," she mumbled through a mouthful of fried rice and coughed as a tiny particle of rice ended up in her windpipe.

"Here, take a sip." He smiled and passed her a glass of water. His face softened. They ate without another word.

"I'm done." She pushed away her plate.

"Let's go," Ibrahim said in a small voice.

He paid the bill. They walked outside. It was less humid, windy, and kind of nice. They found Ibrahim's car. Bird droppings decorated the roof as it had been parked under a tree for a long time undisturbed. They laughed at the sight.

Anushka was out late. Sabaa had strict rules and might not be amused with her today. The car sped through the thin traffic.

"Anush, I'm glad we went to the painting exhibition today," Ibrahim said as the car entered the street near her home. He turned his face sideways to look at her searchingly. "I enjoyed it much more because of you," he added as she listened. Her heart raced, reckless. She hoped he didn't hear the sound of her heartbeat. It was too loud.

"There. Your house! You OK?" he asked gently.

"I loved looking at the paintings. I wanted to tell you...all day long," she said. The words sounded childish in her ears. "And also the Chinese food." She got out.

"And the waiter?" His voice held light jest.

"Yes, all of that."

His soft, familiar laugh followed her. He didn't pull away immediately, waited in the car till she opened the gate and stepped into the yard. She turned to wave to him. The ignition still running, his hands on the steering wheel, he looked back at her. Through the thick glasses, she thought she saw a trace of sadness in his eyes. She wanted to say something, but before she could utter a word, he accelerated and was gone.

Her parents were out to attend a wedding and would be late. She was relieved. She found Tara and Zahra at the dining table eating dinner. There were two kinds of fish, vegetable curry, salad, mango chutney, daal, freshly steamed rice spread on the table. They were talking and laughing over something while eating as she entered.

"Anush, join us. Take a plate," Zahra said.

"Not hungry. But I can wait till you finish." Anushka pulled a chair and sat beside her sisters. A sense of warmth enwrapped her immediately as she joined in the giggles. Tara pushed an empty plate towards her. Zahra dumped a ladle of rice and a dash of vegetables. Sisterly affection won over. Anushka slowly started with small nibbles, resigned to the comfort of the food offered. It tasted like the feel of love in her mouth. It fed her emotional hunger.

7.

"When are you going to tell me about the art exhibition escapade, Anush?" Maya inquired as Anushka entered with books and notepads, geared up to study together a week later.

"Yeah. I...I wanted to...wanted you to come, but you were down with a toothache." Anushka didn't understand why she stammered slightly and hoped Maya hadn't picked up on it. "It was really good. I wish you were there. I phoned you," she added as an afterthought. Maya gave her a hurt look. "Who told you?" asked Anushka.

"My brother, who else?...Last night at dinner. You should have been the first one to tell me. You went without me and didn't say anything afterwards." Maya's voice still lacked the usual warmth.

"I was so busy with assignments, things at home, I forgot. Believe me, Maya. And then you were absent most of last week." Anushka's voice was troubled. She realized their friendship was on the verge of taking a hit.

"I had a toothache, remember? Wasn't absent out of pleasure." Maya tried to make a point.

Nanny entered at that moment with tea and a plateful of chocolate cookies and cream rolls, freshly baked but bought from the bakery across the road. It served as a good diversion. Maya stole a glance in Anushka's direction while pouring tea. As they sipped the tea and bit into the crispy, sweet cream rolls, the tension began to disperse gradually. Anushka flipped the pages of the physics book. The girls bent over it with frowns. The equation to be solved looked beyond comprehension. It would take hours to break it. They were fired up now.

They fell into easy conversation in between studying. Anushka was relieved. A part of her had been asking herself about the reason for keeping the outing a secret from her best friend. They shared everything. She understood Maya's hurt and accepted her reaction. Being an orphan from an early age, she depended on Anushka as a sibling, someone who would stand beside her as a sister, in affection and loyalty. This faith in their relationship had been breached.

"Maya, I'm so very sorry to have caused you pain. I won't do it ever again," she said before leaving, genuinely remorseful. "Next time, you and I will go together. We'll buy a painting and hang it in our study area, right here," she added.

"Anush, I have only you. You're my best friend. And will always be."

⌒⌒

Preparations for exams kept Anushka busy. There had been guests in the house and so many things to do. She had missed her study time with Maya. However, they were studying together in the library and spent time in the college as usual.

After almost about a month, Anushka came face to face with Ibrahim as she and Maya were hanging around. Lily was busy clipping potted plants, cleaning and watering them. This was her one hobby that even in her busiest professional engagements she made time for.

"There you are, Anush. Haven't seen you...since the art gallery. What have you been up to?" he said in a cheerful, casual voice. Was it laced with a hint of joy, or was she reading too much into it?

"Anush promised she'd go with me to the next art exhibition." Maya spoke before Anushka said anything.

"Who's your favorite painter, Anush?" Lily asked, focused on her plants. "I know I love Qamrul Hasaan.... His paintings of Bengalee women are so amazing...but he has a questionable moral character," she went on without waiting for an answer.

"Come on, Lily! He's an artist. Give the guy some slack," Ibrahim interjected with mock protest.

"Huh! When is a man ever wrong? Pity!" Lily threw back. Maya laughed out loud. "Artistic talent shouldn't push one to be immoral.... Don't make excuses, Ibrahim," Lily added lightly with grave intention, Anushka thought. After all, Lily was an activist and a lawyer.

"Agree! Agree!" Maya chanted.

"I love several famous painters. Also the upcoming new artists," Anushka managed to squeeze into the discussion, finally picking up the thread of the conversation. Nanny surfaced with a tray laden with cups, plates, and snacks.

"Tea is here." In strides, Ibrahim was beside the teapot.

"Who wants some? Shall I pour for you?" He looked in Anushka's direction.

"I'm afraid I have to go now. Can the guard call a rickshaw?" She was ready to leave. Best to get home before it got dark. Ishmail had taken the car to visit a sick friend.

"Stay, have tea. Ibrahim can drop you off later," Lily chipped in.

"Yeah, no need to take a rickshaw," Maya voiced.

"OK. I can also run you girls to the ice cream corner if you behave. Maya, you'd better change. I'm not taking you out in these rags," Ibrahim added jovially.

"Come on.... She's fine. Men!" Lily waved him aside.

"I need to drop off an envelope at my partners' house on the way. You'll have to sit in the car in that case. Can't take you in. Your choice. Want to join us, Lily?" he added.

"No, I'm happy as it is. Got to finish with the pots."

Finally, they were in the car in less than twenty minutes. Maya had changed. She took the passenger seat while Anushka sat in the back. As he started the ignition, Ibrahim briefly caught her eye in the rearview mirror. The moment was as quickly gone. She thought she imagined the look.

⁓

A fortnight later, Lily got four concert passes from one of her clients and invited Anushka to join them. Anushka's love for music was no secret. Since the girls would be chaperoned by Lily and Ibrahim, Ishmail consented.

It was an enthralling experience. Both friends were elated. As the lights were dimmed in the large performance hall, the music and vocals of famous performers began spinning magic. Anushka was glad she could attend the show. There weren't many opportunities like this for her. Tickets to such programs were expensive, and Ishmail wasn't a great fan of live concerts. He was more comfortable with his radio or being in front of the TV.

At intermission after two hours of the performance, buffet refreshments were served. It was part of the package deal. They lined up in the slow-moving file to fill up their plates. The spread was appealing with finger food, fruit, confectionery, and hot and cold beverages. Ibrahim pointed out the tastier items to them. It was fun. Each of them heaped up their plates. Unlike teenage girls, Anushka and Maya weren't ashamed of robust appetites.

Later, as Lily and Maya went to the ladies' room, Anushka was alone with Ibrahim. He took her around the lobby of the concert hall where beautiful decor, craft pieces, and paintings were displayed. He pointed out the history of some of the artwork. Standing close beside him felt good, heartwarming, as she listened to the sound of his deep voice.

That night back in her room, Anushka struggled with sleep. She had wanted the evening to last forever, but it didn't. The tint of the evening wouldn't rub off easily from her overtaxed mind.

8.

Exams were over. After a break of four months, fresh preparations would begin to get into the university for undergrad. Physics enticed Anushka, but she remained as undecided as ever. Ishmail was pushing her to get into a medical college. He believed at least one daughter should become a doctor. Acceptance to any of the faculties would be a deciding factor in determining her future.

Anushka felt lonely. College had kept her busy till now.

Maya had gone to Sylhet to visit relatives with Lily right after the exams were over. Sylhet borders with Burma and is endowed with lush green mountainous terrain—a beautiful city famous for its tea gardens and the shrine of a highly esteemed Sufi saint, Hajrat Shah Jalal. People believed that prayers offered for any wishes at this shrine usually got granted. Hindus, Muslims, Christians, and Buddhists all alike visited this place with hopes in their hearts.

Ibrahim, she heard, had been in Stockholm for months, working on a new business deal. He came back briefly during the exams, but Anushka didn't get to see him. Lily also took a break and joined him in Stockholm for some weeks. Maya couldn't go because of the exams, so the current visit to Sylhet was Lily's attempt to compensate Maya for leaving her behind.

Anushka read about Sweden, the fourteen islands and over fifty bridges on the Baltic Sea archipelago, the thirteenth-century architecture, the cobblestone streets, the Royal Palace, museums, and cathedrals. She wished she could be in Sweden. She longed more to be with Ibrahim, walking beside him on cold starry-bright evenings; unearthing the magic of the lost centuries embalmed forever in stone castles and medieval buildings, memorable historical paintings in art galleries; tasting the famous cinnamon buns with glogg, the Swedish traditional drink mixed with orange peel, cinnamon sticks, and cardamom seeds, with almonds and raisins floating on top.

Meanwhile, Sabaa was caught up in an emotional situation, an intense family dispute. Elias, with his wife and daughter, had moved into their house as differences with his older brothers escalated. Dhola was offended and perceived it as a direct insult, a point-blank rejection of his authority, but Sabaa couldn't turn away her sick brother. He was dying. Anushka and her sisters, along with her parents, got pulled into this row, so distasteful. Dhola's ego was too big to respect choices that didn't include him or secure his approval. Her brother's sickness and father's uncompromising pride created a heartbreaking roller coaster for Sabaa. She was immensely distressed as the family feud deepened.

"You're breaking up my family," Dhola accused her. "Elias should be with us, his brothers. Don't fill up his head with ideas."

"Elias is very sick, Baba. How can I not let him stay?" Sabaa asked her father.

"You're disloyal to us. You're not a good daughter to me, Sabaa." He was harsh, uncompromising, shifting all blame onto Sabaa.

Tota by then was fading in her ailment, losing her mind and trapped in her bed.

~

"Ama, don't cry. You're doing the right thing for your brother." Zahra suffered with her mother, as did her sisters.

"Nana is such a disgusting, egoistic, pig-headed, stubborn . . ." Tara exploded. She had some exceptionally stronger names for Dhola that she uttered only in her sisters' presence.

"He'll come to his senses. Don't be so sad, Ama," Anushka said consolingly. "Where else can Elias Mamu Jaan go?"

Anushka wanted to race out of the house. She didn't want to be in this family drama anymore. It took her energy, her sanity away. She already had too much on her mind. She wanted to run away to Stockholm, to discover the footsteps of the weary travelers on the stairs of the centuries-old cathedrals buried in mystery and untold stories of the past.

9.

Dhola kept hurting Sabaa with harsh words. She needed her mother at that time much more. Tota had never been overtly expressive about her affection for Sabaa. Her declaration of love had been neatly camouflaged within the care she gave to her children, the fierce protectiveness with which she stood beside Sabaa whenever she detected a crack in her daughter's life. Her rock-solid silent presence in the background was the proof of her love, saying it all.

Sabaa wondered whether she could have tried more to communicate with Tota, tried harder to express her love, confirmed that she was important to her. In Dhola's life, Tota was an auxiliary domestic workforce, not for a moment valued, an accident, something unavoidable that simply happened. Sabaa was aware of that, and it pained her. Comfort and care were guaranteed to all family members, servants, and outsiders under Tota's foolproof watch. She worked in the background, invisible mostly, weaving warmth, handing out boundless solace to every need, each wound and teardrop.

Early on, Sabaa recognized her mother to be somewhat complex in nature—a proud woman but resigned to her inferior status in Dhola's life. Her stubborn acceptance of a subservient position kept her marriage and family intact. She didn't fight for Dhola's love, but she fought to prevent him from taking a second wife. Though she constantly bickered with her mother-in-law and disliked her profoundly, she never engaged in malicious or vengeful acts to harm Amina Bibi.

Tota was frugal and counted every penny when the destitute borrowed money or grain from her or pawned goods in exchange for cash. She was very cautious and wouldn't forgo a single penny in her business of land and cattle leasing. Paradoxically, she was also extremely generous. At any time, she lent money even without any collateral, fully trusting the word of the borrower. The desperate knew Tota would never say no and never remind them to repay their loans. She knew she would get her money back when the time was right for them, and she waited in faith.

Sabaa visited her mother regularly at the hospital, now lost to the world....

"Ma, Ma, I still sleep under the quilt you made for me...years ago. The designs and stiches feel like your hands touching me," Sabaa gently said, taking Tota's hands in hers, withered and coarse with years of hard work and age. The dim light in the hospital cabin seemed too bleak, masking the pain on Sanu's face, who sat sentinel at the foot of Tota's bed.

"You taught me my first stitches. Where did you learn?" Sabaa's voice was hoarse with tears. Tota was beyond listening.

Sabaa knew Tota had limited time to spend on crafty, delicate pursuits, to perfect her needlework. All her efforts were to feed into necessity, in the moment, hurriedly delivered. Her handiworks were criticized for being common, crude because she knew only a few basic stitches.

On many occasions, Sabaa had heard Dada's rebukes. "This is as terrible as the way she does everything." Dada vomited out harsh words at every opportunity. At every instance, she undermined Tota's ways—"organized chaos," as people called them, including her sons but with kindness.

In one instance, before they finally moved to Manikganj, Ishmail came on a short vacation. Tota had spent the entire day cooking the food he loved. In her eagerness to please him when serving his favorite rice pudding, she ladled a large portion on his plate, spilling it over the sides. Ishmail couldn't hide his slight aversion to this clumsiness as the heap slowly started trickling from the plate onto the table.

"What are you doing, woman? You're serving my son-in-law, not a farmhand. Move it, move it, change the plate," Dhola observed, and was sharp. Dada laughed out loud.

"That's how she does it. Knows no better!" Dada's voice was a mix of rebuke and amusement.

Ishmail was extremely embarrassed. He didn't mean to be rude to his mother-in-law. Beads of sweat showed on Tota's forehead at this humiliation. Her face burned in indignity.

"I'm bringing a new plate," she stammered and fumbled with the dishes.

"I'll eat from this plate," Sabaa said, coming to Tota's rescue, handing out a lifeline to her mother.

"Eat what you can. The rest Elias can finish." Tota was relieved, her prestige saved somewhat.

~⌒

Tota never asked anyone for anything. She had her own means. When her sons took over the family printing business, she wanted them to buy her six gold bangles. She asked them constantly, each of them separately. They smiled and ignored her. The first signs of sickness were invading her body at the time. She complained to Sabaa about her brothers. Sabaa was saddened but couldn't count on Ishmail's limited earnings to give such an expensive gift to her mother.

After that, Tota kept on talking about her desire to go on pilgrimage—*hajj* to Mecca—while her health problems kept escalating. Again no one listened to her wishes. That's when she slowly started losing her mind.

One night she locked Dhola out of their bedroom. No matter how much he knocked, she refused to open the door. The sons and their wives woke up and pleaded with her. That night Dhola slept in the small extra guest room. He was much humiliated, exposed to the entire household as they witnessed his powerlessness.

"Your father has bad eyes. Always looking for young bodies. I don't want him near me," Tota whispered to Sabaa later. There was a trace of subdued paranoia in her eyes.

"That's not true, Ma. He's an old man. He has taken to religion now," Sabaa argued.

"No, no, no.... Old or young, men are men. Did you not notice how he looks at the servant girls?" Tota's eyes were doused in venom. It was a false allegation. "I don't want him in my bed. Not anymore."

A month later, Tota had a stroke. Servants, friends, and relatives lined up outside the hospital cabin door. Everyone came to pay their respects. They felt they owed it to her, to give back for the numerous kindnesses she had extended, the many free meals and alms she had offered to them and their families.

"Ma, Ma, can you hear me? Elias is staying with me.... Baba is very angry." Sabaa's hushed tones bounced against the silent walls of the hospital. Sanu's tears kept falling. Tota's parched lips moved wearily in silent gestures, didn't form any words as she stared with vacant, lost eyes. Her grey hair was tangled on the white pillow; the wrinkled face looked limp, erased of all recollection. Sabaa remembered the times at the zoo, visits to the famous Howrah Bridge and Gonga Ghat, the numerous fun-filled horse cart travels on the streets of Kolkata crisscrossed with tram lines, bursting with pedestrians, motor cars, buses, and bicycles. Those were good days.

Tota had frequently sneaked money into Sabaa's hand so that her dignity remained unfractured under the pressure of many wants when Ishmail had just moved to West Pakistan. He was shouldering many financial responsibilities. Tota was the bearer of everything that was happiness in Sabaa's life. Sabaa never forgot the ecstasy and pride of looking at her newborn's face as Tota held the tiny Tara in the folds of her arms the very first time after a grueling twenty-four-hour labor.

"She's yours, Sabaa. Hold her firmly. Don't let her fall," Tota's voice had guided her as she gently eased the infant into Sabaa's arms. Simple words, vastly meaningful. Sabaa always remembered, never gave up on her daughters.

10.

Between Tota's and Elias's sicknesses, time seemed to stumble. Sabaa and the family tried their best to cope and continue with their lives. Since there was no college, Anushka mostly stayed home, assisted Sabaa in entertaining the guests who visited Elias every day, almost at any hour. It was tiring, but she had to do her part. It's an accepted norm for Bengalees to visit sick relatives to express their concern, solidarity, and prayers. Her sisters were busy on weekdays, so they were spared. On weekends the duties were equally distributed.

The phone rang while Anushka was trying to figure out how to kill the boredom. "It's Maya for you, Anush." Zahra drew her attention.

It was so good to have Maya back in her life again! She missed her friend. They chatted and laughed for almost an hour. Luckily, Ishmail wasn't home. Long phone conversations annoyed him. To him, telephone calls were meant to connect on important purposes, not for flippant chitchat.

"Maya's back? You can visit her in the afternoon . . .car will be free." Sabaa knew her daughters very well. She had seen how edgy Anushka had been lately.

"Ama, you're so great! I'm dying to see Maya." Anushka was ecstatic. "She's been away for weeks...was so bored without college, without her."

"Don't be too late. Your father doesn't like to have the driver wait," Sabaa cautioned.

Sabaa remained an important part of each girl's life as they were growing up. They found it easier to communicate with their mother, and even when they didn't, Sabaa knew what was happening. She had a way of knowing. She didn't intrude or advise unnecessarily, but if she felt she needed to be the parent in a situation, she spoke up, gave her take on the matter. She was always with them, present in their pains and joys. That's what they liked about Sabaa and found it difficult to be untruthful to her. They knew she had their back.

Anushka found Maya on the front lawn, sitting under the shade of the tall teak tree. The fragrance of its white blossoms was in the air. Maya waved at her. Anushka made herself comfortable beside Maya on the grass and took a helping of the peanuts that she was nibbling from the bowl.

"Anush, I have something to tell you."

"What is it? Say only the good or hold thy peace forever," Anushka uttered in a theatrical voice to make Maya laugh. But she didn't. She looked serious.

"We're leaving. Soon."

"What? What do you—?"

Maya cut her off. "We're going to Sweden. All of us." Anushka's face reflected arrested shock.

"Please, please, don't be upset. Be happy for me...." Maya pleaded with a catch in her voice, childish and naïve.

She informed Anushka that Ibrahim had accepted an offer to work as a senior architect in a reputable firm. Great salary, generous benefits. For that reason, he had been shuttling between Stockholm and Dhaka for the last few months to weigh the pros and cons. He had been considering the proposition seriously for about a year, actually. Lily's trip to Sweden was to take stock of everything, assist, rent a house, and make arrangements for the move. The paperwork was complete. In four weeks, Lily would move there and rent out this house. Maya in the interim would stay with a cousin in Sylhet, whom they had visited recently till her travel documents were ready. She would be joining them right afterwards and take admission to Stockholm University. Lily had explained all the details during their Sylhet trip, as both she and Ibrahim didn't want to disturb her peace while exams were going on.

"Stockholm University was founded in 1868 as a college. In 1960 it became a full university. It's very good," Maya said quietly.

"Are you happy?" Anushka had been listening without interruptions so far.

"Yes and no. I will miss you, Anush. This house. Everything about Dhaka."

"I'm so glad for you. I'll miss you, too, but you're going to be happy there." Despite trying hard, Anushka's voice didn't sound very upbeat.

She was puzzled why Ibrahim had never mentioned about the move. He'd had so many opportunities—the day they spent at the art gallery or the other times he'd dropped her home. The planning had been going on for months. She could have kept his secret from Maya. Her mind raced back to every instance they'd met, every word they'd said. Suddenly she felt an intense, overwhelming sadness, let down by someone she trusted so much.

"Anush, let's go inside the house. I bought a book for you. It's on the tea gardens of Sylhet. I know you're going to like it." They stepped inside together, arms linked.

The family room was strewn with papers, boxes, markers. Flowerpots were pushed into one corner. Gone were the faded carpet from the floor, the TV, and the rocking chair—the comfort of the room. The swing remained, in the passive silence of isolation. Lily was busy with two handymen sorting, packing, storing. She smiled affectionately at them.

"Anush! Good to see you. Maya told you everything?"

Anushka nodded. She stood bewildered in the middle of the confusion of packing boxes, useless scrap paper, plastic tape, and the messy furniture in the room. Maya found a low stool for her to sit on.

"I know it's too sudden for you. We didn't tell Maya till all was finalized, her exams were finished. We decided to migrate, as it's best for Maya.... Sad, Anush? So sorry." Lily was genuine. "You can always write, you know?"

Anushka watched as Lily noted down the numbers on the boxes. Each one had a different caption—*kitchenware, glasses, shoes, books*. A large pile of boxes...Anushka wondered whether their entire life could be contained in such little spaces.

Lily told her about their new house on the lake. From the balcony, the old stone buildings could be spotted in the distance. Ibrahim's office was only a fifteen-minute walk away. Most people walked or biked to work. Public buses were easily available, inexpensive to ride, and reliable. Lily would initially be working with a legal firm on a part-time basis until she found a permanent position.

"Maybe you'll come to see us? We'd like that," Lily said gently.

"When are you flying out, Maya?" That was all Anushka could manage. She was afraid that if she talked too much, she would expose her pent-up agony, which had been killing her since she heard the news. It might have looked like exaggerated emotions, too much. That wouldn't be of any good to anyone.

"Exactly six weeks from now. My ticket has been booked." Maya's eyes were dancing. "I'll be going back to Sylhet end of next week."

"We need to pack. Empty the house. Most of the furniture will be gone by this weekend. I'll stay with my sister after Maya leaves." Lily kept numbering the boxes while she talked. "You'll come by to see us off, right?"

"Of course she will!" Maya stressed.

"Yes, yes, I will," Anushka said in a small, passive tone. The maid informed that her car had arrived to take her home.

"Anush, one second. I have something for you." Lily hastened upstairs. She returned with a small gift bag, shiny black with a silvery lining and the name of the store embossed on both sides. Lily handed it over to her. Inside was a soft, beautiful silk scarf.

"Ibrahim bought it for you from a boutique in Stockholm that specializes in hand-painting and dyeing. He said you'd like it." Anushka listened, her feet glued to the floor. She couldn't move. "He chose blue because it's your favorite color."

On the way home, Anushka's eyes kept moistening. It seemed as if her heart was being crushed under tons of steel—heavy, suffocating. At the bottom of the gift bag was a card with a painting of a bird flying over Lake Malaren. *Hope you like it—Ibrahim, Stockholm.* That was all it said. The words created havoc inside her, tossed her world upside down. That was all he had to say.

II.

Tota languished in the hospital bed for months in semiconsciousness. She never complained about bedsores, pains, never spoke a word, and early one morning silently died as Sanu sat vigilant at her bedside.

Elias died in a hospital in London two weeks before Tota. He had flown to the UK with the hope of a miracle. Dhola survived them by only twelve months and died in his village home on a rain-swept morning as the waves of the Padma crashed on the emerald shores.

~

Maya still writes sometimes about her new life, trifles about Lily and Ibrahim, and how they all have become a part of the Swedish culture.

Anushka now thinks maybe everything was in her imagination—the way Ibrahim looked at her and how his eyes lit up when they spent those very brief times together, how his face softened whenever he smiled at her, the sadness in his eyes. Maybe she had grossly misread more than there really was. He had never made any inappropriate advances, for sure. He had never concealed their meetings from Lily or Maya. He was forthcoming in each instance. The expectation and pain were Anushka's own creation—she was too gullible to differentiate between an honest friendship and an attraction, platonic affection and romantic love.

Ibrahim didn't try to contact her after he left Dhaka. Anushka waited every day to hear from him, every week, for months. The hurt deepened. The anguish of not hearing his voice was unbearable; the bitterness of his silence was torture. Slowly, all her tears halted inside, stayed buried for many, many years.

At eighteen, her universe crashed in a headlong collision that she wasn't prepared for—she had an incurable crush on Ibrahim.

PART IV.
CONCLUSION—
JANUARY 1985

CHAPTER TWENTY-FOUR

Silk sheets and diamonds

I.

With arms linked, Zahra and Anushka walk out of the airport. The driver puts Zahra's luggage in the car boot.

"So glad you're back, Zahra." Anushka beams. "Eleven months was like a lifetime." Zahra is already quite lighthearted now. Dhaka feels good.

"You came directly from work? How's residency going?" Zahra's voice holds affection.

"Work is good.... Aba is in chaos." Both sisters smile. A part of Zahra feels sad for Ishmail. Sometimes they had given him a hard time, especially Tara. During her growing-up years, they locked horns even on trifles.

"You know, Anush, to be honest, we never really expressed enough appreciations for Aba. We were too busy picking at his frailties. So often missed seeing his love for us."

"Yeah...he gave us a marvelous childhood, really," Anushka agrees.

"War is a terrible thing to happen to anyone. We lived

through the worst war! It left scars," Zahra says, thinking of what Ishmail had endured, his long imprisonment as a POW in a desolate fortress in Pakistan. On several occasions, somehow he had survived by fractions of seconds from being shot dead, caught up in coups and countercoups after rejoining the Bangladesh army. Fellow officers had died while he continued to live, spared. The stress of such burdens could be enormous.

"We can still make amends...," Anushka adds softly.

"Yeah.We must be more receptive to him." Zahra vows.

Zahra is glad Anushka hasn't asked anything about Kathmandu so far. The car cruises through heavy traffic, overtakes swarms of rickshaws and commuters, and finally pulls into the driveway of their home.

⁓

Life begins in Dhaka again right in the heart of Tara's wedding preparations. Tara is excited and shares too many things that pass over Zahra's head. Amidst many giggles, the sisters continue from there.

Zahra is sucked into the mayhem with urgency and has no escape in the upcoming weeks....

2.

The house is in disarray, a totally festive mode. A constant flow of people coming in and going out has an element of organized chaos, an orchestra gone rogue on reaching the tempo. Voices, a clattering symphony of noises in the kitchen, cluttered boxes of different sizes carelessly scattered across the living room floor, crammed spaces in the dining room...and a monstrous mountain of shoes at the entrance can't be ignored. It's like a shoe war.

The backyard terrace is under Sanu's occupation along with a group of elderly women. They're busy making several kinds of spicy and sweet delicacies, shocking culinary miracles. Mounds of rice flour are being kneaded, shaped into triangular and circular forms to be filled with stuffing. Children are banned to venture near them.

The telephone has been ringing intermittently. People pass by, ignoring it completely. Everyone is running in haste for some unexplained purpose and on errands only known to them. Anushka hears someone shouting her name, so she comes down the stairs, searching for the source of the voice.

"Phone call for you," says a voice belonging to a face she doesn't recognize. Anushka is surprised that she is known to this unabashed girl.

"You're sure it's for me?" Anushka asks.

"Asked for Anushka. You're her, right?"

Anushka takes the receiver. "Hello?"

"Hello, Anushka?" A familiar voice on the other end, warm, keen as always, from the past. A voice she thought was lost to her forever.

"Yes?...I'm listening," she says again after a second's hesitation. Stunned. Unprepared.

"I'm here for four days. Landed yesterday afternoon. We're selling the house. Maya wanted me to give you a package," Ibrahim says, his tone quieter now. He may have possibly detected the faint aloofness in Anushka's voice.

"Can we meet sometime? At your convenience?" he says.

"Of course. Tara's getting married end of the week. We're a bit busy.... Does tomorrow afternoon work for you?" Anushka tries to sound normal. "I finish early at the hospital," she adds further. They confirm a place to meet close to the Dhaka Medical College Hospital, where she works.

Her heart feels strange. It's not pain, not ecstasy. Just slight discomfort, a cocktail of civil curiosity and anxiousness. She didn't inquire how he was. Neither did he. Trying to be matter of fact, they both dived into awkwardness. But possibly natural—under the circumstances.

～

Anushka carefully maneuvers her steps over heaps of loose objects lying on the floor. In one corner, a group of teenage girls are busy preparing festoons and decorations, comfortable amidst steaming cups of tea, plates laden with snacks, half-filled glasses with lipstick stains and blurry with greasy fingerprints. Wrapping paper, scissors, glitter, and bottles of glue are strewn carelessly all over the place. It's hard to recognize the comfortable family room with the upheaval these girls are committing. They have transformed it into a crime scene.

Finally, escape into her room...in solitude to examine the long-lost threads of thought. Memories buried in the past begin to scramble out from the realm of banishment. Eight years have elapsed.... She was only eighteen when her life had plunged into an emotional, all-consuming black hole. She had been embarrassingly green, stupidly impressionable, hopelessly touchy—that's how Anushka rates her irrational teenage self. Now she is a confident doctor who strides the hospital corridors with poise and purpose, checking on patients, trying to keep her promise to the sick and the broken, bringing hope and continuity to lives so loved.

She doesn't know how to connect with Ibrahim, not anymore. Once she had so much stored in her heart to share with him. But that was years ago. That time has passed, claimed by many moments of urgency, trifles, laughter, and tears. All of that is less relevant, a past no longer significant in today's reality. Now they live in a different universe altogether.

She has almost the entire night to think through tomorrow's meeting with Ibrahim.

3.

"What's wrong with the electricity? Why can't a wire be pulled from the main circuit?" Sabaa's voice, full of irritation, is heard from downstairs.

The illumination of the roof and the outside walls has not yet materialized despite many attempts by the electricians. Lights are associated with festivity, especially to announce a grand occasion like a wedding.

"They're trying, Aunty...for the last two days now," a man answers.

"This contractor isn't experienced enough, it seems," a female voice adds. "During my niece's wedding, my sister contracted the Gulshan decorators. They're expensive but the best, you know. If you need good service—"

"Come on, Lena. Stop bragging about your wealthy sister and her snooty-tooty ways," another impatient male voice cuts her off.

"Don't always try to stop me when I speak. I'm your wife, so you have no patience with me.... If you don't like it, go somewhere else. Don't butt in." Lena fights her husband back.

Sounds of giggles mixed with footsteps drown the squabble. Nerves are delicate, tempers running high as people hustle and bustle, flexing their importance around the house. Everyone's trying to participate. Each presence is significant, contributing, and useful, possibly.

"Who's in charge of flowers? Anyone knows?" someone keeps asking loudly.

"The flower man has vanished. No one has his contacts. Don't blame me if the flowers aren't delivered on time," a woman responds.

"Who wants tea? Lunch won't be ready before three," someone announces.

Tara hears the stream of the hue and cry coming from downstairs, the fabric of a faceless chorus of many sounds.... It's too noisy, giving her a headache. The house is swelling with stay-over guests. Some have traveled from other cities, some from Sabaa's village. It's the first wedding in this house, and almost every relative has been invited. The list is long.

People consider an invitation to the wedding of a relative as their birthright.

Tara hasn't seen Zahra since morning. She needs to find her soon. Something very important has come up, and Zahra must know all about it. It's so good that she has returned from Kathmandu after quitting her dream job. Quite a surprise!

Zahra hasn't discussed anything in detail yet, but Tara has a gut feeling there's more to it. In time, her sister will share the story; she is confident about that. But now she must find Zahra because time is running out. Four days left to her wedding. The *henna-holud* celebration will be taking place three days from now. With every passing moment, Tara's anxiety keeps building up.

⁓

"Sabaa, the wedding venue called. They said there were some last-minute additions made? Why? Who did that?" Ishmail asks. He is losing his cool too early in the morning.

"Relax.... It's taken care of." Sabaa tries to calm him.

"Who's overseeing it? What changes are we talking about? Do you know how much extra it's going to cost?" Ishmail mumbles.

As she heads out of the house, Anushka bumps into her parents, conspiratorial in their discussion on the menu or something regarding the wedding preparations, she guesses.

"Where are you going?" Ishmail asks. "It's only seven thirty." He glances at his watch, surprised.

"I thought you'd taken leave for the wedding," Sabaa says.

"Yeah, I have a half day off today...a week's leave from tomorrow. I have to be at an urgent morning surgery. Couldn't get out of it." Anushka is apologetic. "I'll be back by three, latest."

"The car is busy. Someone has taken it to chase the flower man," her father says with an annoyed face and a hint of subdued agitation.

"I'll take a baby taxi from the main street. Don't worry so much." Anushka dashes out, leaving her parents somewhat disturbed.

"Be careful. Those auto drivers are psychos." Ishmail doesn't give up so easily. He is irritated with many things. The chaos has been taxing his patience for the past weeks.

"Aba, this is 1985. I'm twenty-six! A doctor like you, and on call," she throws over her shoulders without looking back, trying hard not to be harsh.

It's a beautiful morning. She walks half a block and spots a three-wheeler waiting to be hailed, under a tree. The driver, leaning against the automobile and chatting with a passerby, is visibly relaxed. They always are, making the best of their time while looking out for passengers.

It rained last night. The trees and flowers seem to be sparkling in the sun, clean of winter's heavy layers of dust. Colors on plants and flowers hide under the restraint of a film of dirty brown during this time of the year. December and January are the dry, dustiest months but the best time for weddings.

It doesn't usually rain in January. Rain before a wedding means good luck for the couple to be united in matrimony. So the female wedding guests are pleased. Rain in Bengal is associated with fertility and the prospect of a good crop, good luck for the farmers. Rain is a sign of cleansing, positivity. The myth has now become a part of the culture. It's also cooler after a shower.

The three-wheeler speeds into traffic. Anushka is nervous about meeting Ibrahim in the afternoon. She needs to be calm, poised to make him understand that she is mature, confident, and in full control of the game.

～⁓

Zahra sneaks to the rooftop to have a few minutes free of chaos, running around on errands, or making nonstop phone calls. If anyone spots her, she will be dispatched on yet a newer task. It's been hectic since she came back from Kathmandu as piles of invitation cards had to be distributed, shopping done, home visits made to ensure certain relatives craving special attention feel included and welcome. In essence, they are troublemakers but have to be appeased. In Bengalee weddings, some folks need to be stroked differently so that they are made to feel important. Otherwise, disharmony and unhealthy gossip create futile tensions and dampen the fun. Families are careful to sincerely avoid unpleasantness if they can on such happy occasions.

Along with Sabaa and Anushka, Zahra has been busy, making herself useful so far in every matter that has demanded her assistance. So much has to be followed up on to make sure nothing slips through the cracks. It's a humongous affair—a Bengalee wedding!

She finds the electricians working on the roof, swearing under muted breath. The three men have been very busy for days but unsuccessful so far in illuminating the house as contracted. Their reputation is at stake. People have volunteered numerous suggestions, unsolicited advice, and are even making jokes about their skills. As of now they have tried every trade trick. It seems there is a problem at the main electrical circuit, which is disrupting additional flow of power up to the roof as needed. A wedding house must be decorated with lights so that people can recognize it from afar, and also to boost the festive mood. There is a special budget kept aside for decorations and lighting at most weddings.

Zahra chooses the opposite side of the roof away from the sweating men, which luckily is still vacant of any human presence. The evening sky has a brighter glow as the streetlights reflect on its blue. The path from their house merging onto the main road is quiet now. Traffic is trickling down to sidetracks from the main road. All seems to be orderly, following a subtle pattern. She doesn't feel calm at all. There's too much on her mind. Kathmandu feels like a fantasy now, another lifetime. She is already missing her work. The most difficult part lies ahead—explaining to her parents about her sudden resignation from the job she had so adamantly accepted, refusing to listen to Ishmail's initial reservations. She will have to find a convincing story. Her father is an exceptionally smart man and may see through the thin words unless she crafts them well. His overt concern borders on prying, which he doesn't realize most of the time. In his generation, this is considered normal, caring. Sabaa is easier to handle. She is much more noninterfering, and her faith in her daughters is unwavering. She won't press for additional information if Zahra doesn't voluntarily provide any. Her sisters know she has quit her job but not the details. Sooner or later she will have to tell them all. Not many secrets can be kept among sisters. That's the sibling code.

It seems as if it was only yesterday when she landed at the Tribhuvan Airport in Kathmandu. The air was cold, soft against her face as she climbed down the stairs from the plane to embrace the new phase in her life. In the distance, wrapped in a haze, she could see the outlines of the regal Himalayas, unstoppable in pride. She had to wait a moment on the aircraft's steps to catch her breath as her eyes embraced the spectacular view. All comes back to her now in a flash. Her lungs suddenly seem to inhale the familiar air; her face feels the touch of the mountain breeze.... She is shocked to discover that thoughts have the power to provoke fantasies reborn as real!

Tomorrow is another day—maybe will hold more hope than today. She climbs down the stairs as the wind drops and the mosquitos start the chase.

4.

Tara received a phone call a while ago today. The phone had been ringing constantly since daybreak and through the last two weeks of insanity. It rang again as she was passing by.

She was the bride-to-be and not expected to attend to calls. But there was no one around, so she picked up the receiver. She listened. This call was for her. Slowly, the color evaporated from her beaming, eager face. Her eyes gazed afar, aimless, at the leaves of the eucalyptus across the street, unfocused, dazed. She kept listening. A light bead of perspiration slowly formed on her upper lip and forehead, right above her beautifully sculpted arched eyebrows.

"Yes, I understand," she uttered in a small voice, barely above a whisper. "I'll be there. Yes, I got that." She hung up and kept staring at the black telephone, not believing the conversation she just had. In the span of two minutes, a mountain of emotion surged and tried to drown her in a mist of uncertainty. She had been torpedoed, unaware. She would have to think calmly amidst the endless waves of pandemonium hitting her coexistence with the preparations moving at full-steam.

Ninety minutes have already elapsed since the call. Tara steps over the callous mess carefully and walks around the house purposelessly, oblivious of the minutes tickling by. Her eyes keep searching for Zahra. She is nowhere to be seen.

"Tara, not yet bathed? Get inside a bathroom before it's taken. The house is overflowing with guests. My goodness!" says a woman, a total stranger passing in a hurry, trying to balance a huge package in her arms. Too big for her fat, tiny arms. Tara smiles politely and knows she isn't expected to respond.

"Tara, Tara, upstairs! Now! You've got to see this." Someone is looking for her. A loud shriek and the sound of laughter follow.

"Who has kept the tap running? It's flooding.... These damn children! No one is keeping an eye on them! Where are their mothers?" An angry male voice echoes through the house. Again, no one responds; no one pays any attention.

Tara walks in sort of a trance. She doesn't see anything. The voices around her have no meaning.

The tailor is waiting upstairs for a fitting, a pile of blouses to be altered, Tara remembers now. Her friends sent a masseuse a while ago, who is also waiting in her room. This is their treat for her, to relax her, prepare her for the upcoming life-changing event. They are on the way to spend some exclusive time with her—her three best friends. All married, two are mothers already. Tara hopes they are delayed in traffic or whatever. She needs some time to compose her thoughts before they arrive, prepared to launch hawkish indulgences of frivolity expected to cheer up a would-be bride.

Tara steps onto the balcony without being noticed. She has had enough. She wants Zahra. Her sister appears to be lost, sort of sleepwalking since her return from Nepal. She is different...not sure what has changed her so much. They haven't been able to talk heart to heart so far in this crowded madness. She now hates every moment of this rowdy influx of people invading their house. It's becoming toxic. The dining table is always overloaded with dirty plates, dishes, and glasses after every meal; bathrooms are messy, toilets blocked; unaesthetic heaps of damp used towels are endlessly hanging from the rails of the balcony, a torment to the eyes. Voices are becoming increasingly louder and stronger with the passing of time. Children are running in and out of the house, banging at the entrance screen door, in danger of falling apart at any time. Ishmail will have a fit soon. All so much out of control. No one can have a moment of peace here.

Tara tries to retrace every word of the conversation she had on the phone. Was she calm, casual in her response? Did she convey the significant impact it had on her? She wonders if she sounded too submissive, too eager in her acceptance. It's almost three p.m. She has exactly three and a half hours to decide the next course of action.

She watches Ishmail standing on the lawn, instructing the handymen on arranging chairs in the corners for guests. He is almost breathing down their necks. From the upstairs balcony, she can actually see the top of his head—the faint impression of balding peeping from under the thinning grey hair of a silvery sheen in the middle of his scalp. But the hair is robust around the front and temples. Unless someone towers over him, his secret is safe. Men feel emotionally impotent when they lose their hair, especially when they are younger or at middle age, she has heard. That's when the midlife crises spring up to avenge for a dissipated youth and prompts men to take a chance on life. Ishmail has hit his sixties, so he should be OK—not wretched or mourning his vanishing strands to dash into the arms of embarrassment. Her father is an honorable man.

The decorators are setting up a huge tarpaulin that covers half of the large grounds. This is where her henna-holud party is supposed to take place in three days. A lot may happen actually before that.... Tara winces thinking about it.

She keeps watching the preparations below.... A beautiful handmade floral rug is spread to cover the plastic mat underneath, thrown over the grassy floor. Flowerpots are positioned circling the stage where she will be sitting during the ceremony. So far, no one has been able to trace the flower man, she heard this morning. Maybe he has run away, unable to meet his contracted commitment. Who knows? Anything is possible in this culture. Ishmail wouldn't be amused. Because of his military training, he is regimented to follow rules, face up to pledges, and in every instance tries to ensure plans are not disrupted. He is already festering much with the electricians, the unruly presence of a large number of houseguests, screaming children. He is struggling to be civil as he is the host, the father of the bride. Any lacking on his part won't be forgiven, or accepted with sympathy.

A big van cruises up on the street leading to the house and stops outside the gate. The handymen join the driver in unloading the cargo, taking a momentary break from Ishmail. Two large covered copper cooking pots are carried into the kitchen. From the look of it, Tara is sure it's *briyani* being catered for the guests. Briyani is a mouthwatering exotic cuisine popular in South Asia, served especially at festivities. The recipe includes *basmati* or *kali jeera*, a kind of fragrant rice cooked with mutton or goat meat, potatoes, heaps of butter, and a concoction of special spices and herbs. Tara loves briyani.

Wedding guests are constantly hungry and don't follow specific lunch or dinner times. The maids have been melting in the heat of the stoves for days feeding the guests. So Sabaa must have ordered this food. There are more packages, big and small, as well on the van floor, possibly sweet yogurt and grocery items.

But where is Zahra? Tara is sick with worry. She needs to discuss the phone call with her sister. She can't do it alone—the burden is killing her....

CHAPTER TWENTY-FIVE

A good plan,
ripples of revelations

I.

It has been an extremely busy day so far. The surgery took longer than Anushka expected. After that, she attended to several patients as the duty doctor had made a sick call. Today of all days! His patients were distributed among others. Only the urgent cases were handled. The rest were referred for the next day.

Anushka's whole body is aching in exhaustion. She checks her watch. Ibrahim must be waiting. It's almost noon. She rushes towards the street for a rickshaw.

Anushka notices him first as she enters the small café. It's an eatery mostly frequented by students from the medical college and nearby Dhaka University. It normally offers fast food, snacks, canned juice, cold drinks, tea, and coffee. Fried rice and egg noodles are popular with vegetable samosas and chicken sandwiches, slightly on the expensive side, added on the menu page under the heading "Special of the Day." She has been here several times in the past. A cloud of smoke and the aroma from the food form an extra-thick shroud beneath the low ceiling, hovering in the scanty space packed with armless wooden chairs and narrow tables.

Ibrahim has more grey hair now. Still looks robust, neatly combed. He is immaculately dressed—white full-sleeved shirt, black shoes, formal pants, but no tie. He stands up as he sees her approaching. His chair makes a faint mechanical sound on the tiled floor.

"I thought you were not coming." He smiles.

"Sorry I'm late. Last-minute patients, long surgery." Anushka is apologetic.

She notices faint lines around his mouth holding his pleasant smile, sparkling white teeth, a few lines around his piercing eyes, as always. He is clean shaven. His glasses are clean as well; they do not cuddle smudges from his fingers anymore, to her relief. He has not put on any weight, stands tall and straight, seems to be lankier than she remembered him last. Her alert mind notes volumes in the fraction of a second.

"You're an elegant professional now." He pulls out the chair for her. "And beautiful," he adds softly. His eyes betray genuine admiration. Anushka smiles back somewhat nervously. The initial awkwardness is broken, though.

"You look the same.... Anyway, surgery tired me out, " she says quickly.

"Impressive. "

"My work? Or me?" she teases. He smiles in response. His eyes light up.

Anushka is a mature adult now. Long gone are the days of gawkiness. She meets diverse kinds of people daily and has learned to navigate the caveats that life offers. In the process, she has become sophisticated—quick to replace shyness with pleasantness. She finds it easier to beat nervousness with a smile.

"Both.... I can vouch safely," he says as an afterthought.

"How are you? Maya wants a full account of you. I have to report back." He keeps his stare unabashed. Maybe this is a pretext to reconnect?

"You don't have to use an excuse to see me." Anushka doesn't cower.

"Guilty as charged!" Ibrahim doesn't deny it, teases her back.

His eyes carry care as they linger on her face. She doesn't avert his gaze either and looks straight back at him. He orders tea for both of them. Then he tells her about Maya, Lily, and their lives in Stockholm, the city of cobbled streets and museums, theatres and parks. How the very thought of it wrecked her heart, how much she wanted to visit it once. Almost a lifetime ago, Anushka thinks.

Maya works as an art dealer and is dating a Swedish artist, quite famous, much older than her. But she is happy. Lily still pursues social justice issues and is working with migrant populations. She is extremely busy. He works at the same firm, chasing similar dreams as before. They still live in the same house that overlooks the lake. Anushka takes in all the news, attentive.

Anushka hasn't written to Maya for over a year now, she realizes. She has been too much wrapped up in her own life, work, competing priorities. There hasn't been a single vacant moment to store away for a break. Those days of college life, filled with carefree happiness, are all lost in the whirlwind of present commitments. And Maya hasn't written to Anushka either during all this time.

"She has given you a package." Ibrahim hands over a small gift bag.

Anushka finds a book on contemporary art and a greeting card. As she opens the book, a tiny chip of paper falls out. Maya's note—imploring her to visit Stockholm. She has her own apartment, and it's an invitation to take a vacation.

"Are you seeing anyone in particular? Any thoughts of getting married?...I shouldn't be asking this. Too personal?" He has too many questions, too much enthusiasm to find out all about her.

"Oh no!...Too parental, perhaps...but you can ask me anything." Anushka is half serious. "Remember, you have to report everything back to Maya." She sounds amused, makes it light and easy to breathe, thwarts unnecessary disquiet.

"Our attending surgeon is sweet on me...but he's my boss. We haven't expressed our feelings or anything openly yet. Just had tea together several times. We meet at the OT, often. He's also training me," she adds, slightly shy now.

Anushka tries to think what more she could say, how much she can safely inflate about the sparse teatime experiences with her boss. She may not be totally lying. This mutual liking has the potential to develop into something much more beyond the collegial cups of tea together. Occasionally, they catch up briefly to shake away hours of fatigue in the OT, discuss patients. If she allows this to grow, of course it will. There's interest.

She did have a fling, a brief harmless, sweet platonic relationship with a classmate in the first year of medical school, though. He was funny, smart, engaging, and quite a looker. But by the end of the year, he got a scholarship to Moscow and left abruptly before she could properly warm up to him. It was just the initial phase of more than liking him but a far cry from missing a heartbeat or messing with her sleep and appetite. That's how it felt at the time. However, after his departure, she did miss him and detected an emptiness for months. They exchanged a few letters, which took weeks in the mail...then everything cooled down gradually, though a tiny stab remained for a while. Anushka didn't want to discuss him with Ibrahim at this moment.

Tara's advice at the time was simplistic, frank. "Anush, don't be blind on just one kind.... Look around. You'll heal faster.... Not worth a cry over this silly dude, li'l sister."

Zahra was more understanding and maddeningly optimistic. "Just wait. He may be feeling the same for you and decide to come back. Long-distance relationships can work," she had said cautiously. But it died a natural death. Anushka thought she was jinxed on matters of the heart....

Anushka still remembers the day she came back from Maya's house with the blue scarf. Zahra was in their shared room studying. Very casually, months before, Anushka had told her about the outing to the art exhibition, some excerpts of her interactions with Ibrahim. It appeared to have been harmless girlish chatter at the time. Her sister listened attentively, didn't advise her on anything; neither did Anushka seek any. As she stood in a stupor in the middle of the room clasping the blue scarf, Zahra got up and just held her in a warm hug for a moment longer. Zahra didn't ask any questions but shielded Anushka from Tara and also her parents that day. Anushka didn't know what Zahra had told them.

Later at night as she drowsed on and off, trying to drown the blunt, hollow feeling inside. Zahra woke her up and gave her a sleeping pill and a cup of warm milk. After that, they never referred to that night again.

She is glad to have a special bond with Zahra, who is always looking out for her — always safe to share things with her that are best left unsaid.

"What an interesting place for courtship, the operation theatre!... Oh, you're lost in thought. I'm boring, right?" Ibrahim's voice brings her back to the present.

"No, no. Nothing like that," she tries to protest mildly, sorry now.

"Anush, sometimes I wonder whether it was the right decision to leave Dhaka just like that. Should I have stayed back?"

There is a forlorn catch in his tone. It's unmistakable, not her imagination. His eyes are troubled, shaded in sadness. She doesn't know what to say. He waits to hear from her.

"It was the right decision at the time," she says cautiously after a minute of silence. Her brain keeps rummaging, drawing out the memories from the past. The mummified feelings are safely strapped somewhere inside, comatose.

"Did it hurt?" Ibrahim asks.

She looks straight at him, faintly smiling now. The deep dimples transform her face, accentuating her charm. She pushes back a loose strand of hair. "That was another time. In another life, lost in time. It's not relevant anymore." Anushka pauses. "I was a chit of a girl. Barely eighteen. The world looked different then," she adds.

He smiles back affectionately and nods, possibly is walking back into those days right now in his thoughts.

"I've to go. Tara's wedding. It's a crazy time. So much has to be done," she says distantly. "Also drained now.... My morning was exhausting."

"I understand. I'm so glad you agreed to meet me today." He stands up. Together they walk out of the door. "I left without saying goodbye. It bothered me. A lot. It's good that I got a second chance to correct the wrong," he says again.

"I'm glad you came back to say goodbye. No wrong is to be righted. All's OK."

He takes a step towards Anushka, places both his hands on her shoulders, and looks straight at her. Some strands of hair fall over his forehead, threatening to shield his eyes. He's dangerously close.

"Take good care of yourself. Send me a card when you get married," is all he says.

"You're not going to come back for my wedding?" Anushka laughs, breaking the uneasy spell in mock surprise.

"I'd like to believe I deserve to be invited to a very important day in your life." He smiles back. "I'm staying with a friend close to our old house. I can give you a ride home."

"Nah. I have to pick up something on the way for Tara. I'll

take a rickshaw. You get going." Before he can say anything more, she hops into a rickshaw and waves at him.

Ibrahim stands transfixed on the roadside as the rickshaw paddles away into the traffic stream. She looks back and in the distance sees his figure slowly receding. Anushka needs time to process the meeting, the words exchanged. In the next thirty minutes on the way home, she will be able to recover from this blast from the past, banish all the ghosts far, far away.

She had determinedly put the past behind her, and so should it remain.

2.

"There you are! Found you! Hiding?" Finally. Tara turns around to the sound of Zahra's voice. A surge of relief rushes through her.

"Oh, Zahra! Zahra! I was looking for you too.... Something serious has happened. Not sure what to do," Tara whispers ominously as she hugs her sister. "I'm finished, Zahra. Done! My life is so over, sis!" Tara cries out, panic in her tone.

"Tara, Tara, listen to me. Is it the wedding jitters? Fears? You've just begun living your life.... You're stunning, smart, you have an amazing job, and you're only twenty-nine! You're ... " Zahra tries to reassure her, speaking gently as she puts her arms around her very nervous sister.

"He knows...everything. What shall we do? Aba will kill me or die first. The guests...the arrangements...oh my God! Oh..."

Zahra interrupts her sister's lament. "Hold on. Who knows? What? Tell me everything, from the beginning,"

"Hey, girls! We're finally here!" The sisters look down to see Tara's two friends waving from the lawn below. Lucy and Ava, Tara's best friends, have arrived. Gigi, the third one, isn't with them. Her two-year-old has a fever, they learn later.

Both women are Tara's college friends, loving and loyal—stood by her through rain and hail. All gather in Tara's bedroom. Anushka joins them. They listen attentively to Tara. Her fiancé had called and asked to meet her to discuss a damning rumor about her.

"He knows.... What he knows is true. He said he couldn't go ahead with the wedding unless I clarify...." Tara pauses, helplessly glancing at the bewildered faces of the onlookers. They wait for the details, don't want to pry. "Two days ago, I also received an anonymous hand-delivered note." She struggles to hide traces of tears in her voice.

"Where is it? What did it say? Why didn't you tell us?" Anushka wants to know, as do the others. They all have the same unspoken questions.

"I panicked. The maid brought it in. I flushed it down the toilet. It said, 'I know every detail of your shocking secret. I will tell your would-be in-laws. This marriage is a farce,'" Tara says in a small voice.

They don't know who this person is, whether it's a ploy to blackmail her or a sinister prank, what she or he stands to gain.

"Was there a postmark?" Ava inquires.

Tara shakes her head. "I didn't notice."

Finally, Tara talks about her secret, the load she has been carrying for many years, unable to share it with another living soul. The women listen in silence. The imminent damage control is to make sure it doesn't leak out further. They discuss various options. They vote on some, veto others. In less than three hours from now, the meeting is set with Tara's fiancé.

"Go and slap him hard and say, 'Look at my face, you rich bastard.' One glance at your beautiful face and the battle is over," says Lucy. They laugh, even Tara.

Lunch arrives. Chinese fried rice with kebab. Interesting intercultural combination of cuisines. Iced Coca-Cola and pickles on the side to spice up the food. More ideas are voiced and examined. Time is running out.

They all agree that Tara should meet her fiancé as planned at the restaurant he suggested and try to convince him that this matter isn't important enough to pull out of the wedding. That's plan A—if the meeting goes well. Plan B is to run away—totally, to Ava's uncle's house in Chittagong. If Tara wants a clean break from her existing life, she has two options there. She can teach at the orphanage school in the interim, patronized by the family, or assist in establishing a girls' college that's in the pipeline and become its principal after its inaugural in the next six months. Tara is a credible professor, and her experience would be invaluable.

Ava's uncle is a well-known former politician, a reputable philanthropist, and has done a lot of charity work for the underprivileged. Ava agrees to talk to him, pull strings. Tara is welcome to stay with the family till an alternate place can be arranged. Ava's eighteen-year-old younger brother would travel with her to Chittagong tonight in that scenario.

Tara restlessly paces the room. "I think it's best to go away for a longer time. Let the talk die down first. Not going to happen overnight. Gossip has many lives. Can't face anyone, my students, colleagues.... This scandal...I need time."

"You can also apply for a long leave of absence without pay," Zahra suggests.

"Yes. Take a sabbatical," Lucy agrees.

"Rejoin only when ready," Anushka adds.

"Well, he may be a total gentleman and take you to the altar, Tara. Who knows?" Ava tries to be optimistic.

"Or he may turn out to be a total jerk," Anushka intercepts. "Most Bengalee men have huge egos...inflated chastity code for women." She has seen enough instances in her profession.

"Only fairy tales have happy endings. But I'll be open, positive, try my best. Can't drag Aba and Ama into this scandal," Tara mumbles. The pinched look on her face doesn't go away. But she's more confident now about the upcoming ordeal after unloading her problem.

"Deny everything. Honesty doesn't pay." Lucy is dismissive while others look thoughtful. It's not an easy situation.

"No." Tara is firm. "Can't start a new life built on lies." This gets a majority vote.

"Very little time is left on hand. I'll prepare everything for plan B. Make calls...arrange your travel to Chittagong tonight should things go bad. I'll be back soon," Ava promises as she leaves.

Lucy decides to stay and divert Sabaa so that she doesn't become suspicious. Zahra sends the tailor and the masseuse away. Tara isn't in the mood anymore to deal with such trifles. Her future is on a lifeline at this moment.

~~⁀⁀

Finally, the three sisters are together in the room after many months. They have an hour to kill before Tara has to get ready for her meeting. The house surprisingly is less noisy. People are out and about their errands, possibly. Tara is calm. The burden has been shared, and now a decision has been reached to deal with the damning secret that has gnawed at her, drawing blood for years.

Tara and Anushka focus on Zahra. They want to hear about the lost months in Kathmandu. She doesn't know how to start. Tara makes it easy for her, saying, "Sis, you've been different since you came back. Something must have happened."

"Tell us.... This will keep Tara diverted for some time," Anushka adds eagerly.

Zahra avoids their gaze, toys with her bracelets she is wearing bought from Thamel during the days she stopped going to the stupa to avoid Arthur. Somewhere in her mind she hears the faint whirl of the prayer wheels, the sound of the footsteps of the worshippers, the chanting around the dome gleaming under the moonlight, magnificent and sacred.

"Something bizarre happened.... I fell in love with a Buddhist monk," she says suddenly and successfully subdues an imminent sigh. The pensive note doesn't go unnoticed by her sisters.

"What?" Tara can't believe her ears. Forgotten are her own worries at this surprising revelation.

"You always manage to pull the trump card...start the theatre from the beginning, not at intermission, sis." Tara's old self is back, her tone lined with soft jest.

"Zahra, what happened?" Anushka is earnest.

"He made his vows before he met me. So had to let him go. But I know he loves me. Truly," she adds as the sadness slowly takes over.

Tara and Anushka pull her into a hug. She rests her head on Tara's shoulder as she clasps Anushka's outstretched hand.

"Holy cow!" Tara whistles softly as she holds Zahra in a tight embrace.

"How are you now? You kept it to yourself all this time?" Anushka's eyes echo her sister's pain. Zahra has been back home for weeks, never has spoken a word about Arthur.

"Too difficult to share...but glad I'm back.... Not sure what to tell Aba about quitting my job.... My heart is so broken...." The light shines through her tears.

Zahra tells them some odd crumbs of her life in Kathmandu—the wonderful times of truly and fully being alive for the first time in her life at the log cabin. The hikes into the heart of wilderness with Arthur on those many extraordinary moments lived together. Lying under the starlit silent skies. Finding the way following fireflies on dark nights. The taste of love on her lips.... The footprints of so many more moments treasured in her heart.

"What'll you do now?" Tara wants to know.

"My old office contacted me last week. They asked if I'm available for a project at Bandorban...to investigate human rights violations against our tribal population," Zahra replies.

"You'll be so far away from us. I'm sure Aba won't object," Anushka comments.

"Is it safe to work there?" Tara is concerned.

"I want to get out of Dhaka. Can't breathe here. I'm considering the offer. Sounds interesting." She knows at the end she is going to accept it.

"If I take plan B, you and I will almost be neighbors, Zahra." Tara sounds dramatic, and despite all odds, they break into laughter.

3.

Tara chooses a teal-colored silk *kameez* top to wear with black jeans and ink-blue moccasins. She fashionably drapes a tie-dyed blue and purple-splashed folded silk scarf on the left shoulder, exposing outlines of her taut bosom. Her silky hair falls loosely on her shoulders. The dark of her eyes appears deeper as uncertainty is mirrored in them. Her face glows with subdued excitement and anxiety. She is all set for the rendezvous. "Absolutely fetching!" her sisters remark in unison.

This is the first time Tara is going to meet her fiancé, Akand, in person. The marriage has been arranged, as is common in Bengalee culture. In a flash, all the memories of the engagement and the events that followed float through her mind....

Akand's mother saw Tara at a college event and liked her. The next step was to find out more about Tara and her family. After all queries were answered favorably, she met Tara's parents with a proposal of marriage. Before accepting it on behalf of his daughter, Ishmail, through his network of friends and relatives, did a quick background check, as much as possible from afar, to find out basic facts about Akand—moral character, education, job, his family's background to rule out any scandals, as is customary. When all was satisfactory, her parents asked Tara's opinion. She consented.

Tara's photograph was shared, and Akand agreed immediately. Usually good sons rely on their mothers. In this case it was no different. The photograph was a formality, icing on the cake.

Akand was still in America when his mother arrived with sweets, flowers, an expensive new red silk sharee, and an engagement ring—one solitaire Indian diamond of humongous size set on a gold band. It had belonged to Akand's paternal grandmother, a family heirloom Tara learned. Her family, the guests, and the domestic help were equally charmed at the sight of such aristocracy.

Ishmail hosted a modest engagement party to celebrate the occasion that included mainly close relatives and friends, and Tara was officially engaged to someone whose photograph was given to her a day before the event, more as a done deal than a matter to dissent from. Everyone said it was a good match.

Tara liked the photo, and there was nothing much to object to about Akand. Her friends said she was very lucky. The chance of becoming the wife of a NASA scientist, to live in the US in the future, was no joke. Anushka was more in favor of a face-to-face meeting to get to know the man before becoming his wife, which couldn't be arranged as Akand was far away. Zahra was in Nepal and so unable to give her opinion. It happened too fast.

After the engagement, her fiancé was nice enough to call Tara once from an unfamiliar city in the US. This was the first time Tara had ever received an international call, a call from thousands of miles away especially meant for her. Ishmail passed the receiver to Tara after the operator asked for her by name, stating that a call was waiting from America. Her father advised her to speak slowly as the voice from this part of the world would require slightly more transmission time to reach the other side.

"Speak loudly. Otherwise, he won't hear. It's not a local call," Ishmail kept guiding her.

"Doctor shahib, let's go. We should let our daughter speak freely." Sabaa intervened and literally dragged Ishmail by the arm out of the room.

Tara tried to lower her voice as much as possible while she spoke as the entire household was listening from the other room, she guessed. She could sense even the maids were lined up against the door with tremendous inquisitiveness. Such a big thing was happening in this house, and they wanted to be a part of it.

She could also hear the operator breathing away silently somewhere on the line, possibly too curious to listen to this long-distance budding romance. Normally, they were supposed to connect callers and leave the link. But such kinds of telephone calls weren't routine phenomena.

Tara didn't know this stranger at all to start an immediate romance, though she already belonged to him. It was a funny notion, but she liked it. He belonged to her too! He was nice, asked her about her work, her hobbies, what kind of house she would prefer to live in as he was buying a property. Tara was simply thrilled. No one had ever sought her advice or preference on such important matters. She was excited and nervous. After she hung up, she forgot most of the things they talked about and couldn't satisfy Ishmail's queries. The call lasted twenty minutes and was extremely costly. It felt like hours, though.

"It's good to be attentive when talking on the phone...especially such expensive calls," was his frustrated remark. Tara almost giggled in his face. Her mother saved her.

"Come on, Doctor shahib. Go easy on her.... We've never received a call from America before. Come, tea is ready."

Anushka was at work when Akand called. Later in the evening, she got the full details from her sister, which were in essence what happened before and after the phone call, mainly Ishmail's reactions, with many giggles. Though Tara had forgotten most of the phone conversation, she clearly remembered every word of one bit of dialogue:

"Do you prefer grey or loud green?" Akand had asked.

"I love both colors." Tara didn't know what else to say about such opposite shades. She wasn't sure why it was important for him to know about her choice of colors.

Zahra missed the engagement party because she couldn't take leave from the office. But she called regularly to stay abreast of the wedding preparations and progress, though she was going through a rough emotional patch at the time.

~

Akand had landed in Dhaka a week ago, but the families forbade any contact between him and Tara prior to the wedding. As they had waited for months, one more week wouldn't make any difference was the ruling. The joy and surprise of the first meeting on the wedding night would be compromised otherwise. Since his arrival, the first phone call he made to Tara was in the morning today.

4.

Her sisters and friends are in the car with Tara. Before leaving the house, they told Sabaa they would be at the salon and would be back soon. Ishmail wasn't home yet, so leaving the house was hassle free, no questions asked, no prying. They drop Tara at the restaurant where Akand is waiting for her while they step inside a nearby gallery that sells paintings of new artists. Easy to pass time in a place like this. They have deliberately arrived ten minutes late to keep him checking his watch. It's a trick to make the opponent nervous, according to Tara.

"Listen to him and agree. Don't be rash," Lucy advises.

"I think you should decide what's best for you," Zahra says as Tara gets out of the car.

In a minute, she vanishes through the designated restaurant's door. There are no proper cafés in Dhaka for young people to meet in the evenings. Chinese restaurants are the only reputable places where a respectable woman can meet a man alone without the fear of being criticized or even ostracized.

Tara looks through the faces of the people seated inside. It's early for diners. A handful of people are scattered all over the place. In an hour, the dinner crowd will begin to appear. She spots Akand as he gets up, observing her walking his way down the narrow aisle between the lined-up tables. It's him as in the photograph, in white shirt, light blue jeans, taller than average Bengalee men. The snapshot didn't reveal his height, though. His mother did proudly mention that fact, she remembers now.

"How are you, Tara?" he asks politely, glancing at her head to toe. He was watching her keenly as she was approaching.

It feels awkward for both but is much more pronounced in him. He has been drinking Coca-Cola but doesn't offer her a drink or anything. The checkered tablecloth looks damp around the spot where the bottled beverage stands.

"Thanks for coming." He speaks again as they sit down.

"What did you want to say to me?" she asks in a low tone, eyeing him.

The man has a pleasant face, sharp eyes behind a pair of smart glasses, looks older than his forty years, slightly plump in a comfortable, agreeable way. One crooked tooth on the left side adds an extra charm to his smile, she notes. He's better looking than the photograph. She can't dislike him. She could work this out. Her earlier hostility towards him begins to evaporate instantly.

"Well, as I said, this guy phoned me out of the blue...told me about your elopement. He says he has all the proof." He notices the slow blush creeping into her cheeks. A very slight bead of sweat begins to break out on her forehead. *Shit*, she says to herself without vocalizing. She doesn't want him to see through her.

"Did he say who he was? Why he is doing this?"

"Does it matter?" he wants to know.

"No, it doesn't. What do you want to do about it?" Tara asks back, flatly.

"Is there any truth in this accusation?" He looks directly at her.

"Yes. It's one hundred percent true." Tara returns his gaze, daring him. She forgets Lucy's advice. He's taken aback, falters slightly, coughs to subdue his uneasiness.

"My mother will return from Kolkata tomorrow morning." He pauses deliberately to see her reaction. Her palms are sweaty now. "She's still shopping for the wedding, in fact. Right as we speak, I understand. I have to tell her.... She will want to call off the wedding. I know her too well."

Tara understands he's not bluffing. Any Bengalee mother whose only son is a physicist at NASA in America, is filthy rich, and possibly leads a glamorous life would walk away from an association that smells of dirt, damning secrets, and disgrace. But Tara wants this marriage to happen, more for her father's sake then hers. All preparations have been made— guests invited, venues confirmed, food ordered. Too late to cancel this wedding. The humiliation would kill Ishmail. He doesn't deserve this shame. She can't let that happen. He's an honorable man, proud of his daughters. He wouldn't be able to show his face anywhere, the reason she panicked and decided to have this meeting. She waits for Akand to speak.

In her mind, she prays and hopes he has the courage to go through with the wedding.

"Our family has a reputation. If this story leaks out, we'll be damaged forever. Have you considered how tongues will wag...the gossip? Oh my God!" He shakes his head. He shakes it from side to side several times. His face looks almost comical, petty.

As she listens, her mind races. Surprisingly, the threat of calling off the wedding seems much less dreadful, doesn't feel so ominous anymore. She continues to watch him.

"You're beautiful," he abruptly says, sounding dazed. Tara smiles. His eyes are fixed on her face. He is softening. What a relief! Ava's prediction is coming true after all. Ishmail doesn't need to know anything about this drama happening right now. All is saved.

"What if I don't tell anyone about your elopement? We go through with the wedding.... But I need to know what happened exactly."

"What do you mean?" Tara is baffled.

"You were gone with this guy for over twenty-four hours?" He leans forward on the table and looks hard at her. He wants a confession of her innocence.

"For God's sake, I was only fourteen! So was he. Before I realized anything, my father brought me back home. What's there to know?" Tara snaps without raising her voice.

"What damage was done? Before I marry you, we need to be clear," he demands.

"Nothing happened," she says. Her eyes flash as she looks at him directly. Her thoughts are running faster, along with her heartbeats.

"Are you still a virgin?" The filth is finally out. The pretense of decorum, decency falls apart.

"You have no right to ask that."

"Yes! If I'm to be your husband!"

Tara halts, as if he has slapped her. "You're not. Fortunately! Listen, I can't marry you. No! Even if I tell you every detail, in your mind you've already convicted me. You're assessing your losses and gains. Whatever I do, there'll be a shadow. I'll always be lesser in this relationship." Tara is sure now what she wants. She gets up.

"Sit down. Don't be foolish. Think about the humiliation...." Tara keeps standing. She's not going to be dictated to by this prig of a man.

"I was thinking only of my parents...my father, actually.... That's why I'm here. Tell your mother to find another bride for you," Tara spits out. "With your credentials, it won't be difficult."

He looks bewildered at his defeat, his failure to handle the conversation to his advantage. He isn't ready to be overthrown like this. Suspecting Tara's vulnerability, he came with the expectation to win this round.

"Tara, you'll regret this." His voice contains suppressed anger. He's not used to rejection.

"I don't want you. No, not anymore."

"You're damaged goods. No decent man will want to marry you, or even your sisters if your disgraceful story comes out." He's insulting, repulsive.

Tara's refusal has hurt his ego badly, shaken his manhood. He feels he can't accept a rebuff from a woman, especially one who has a dishonorable past—a woman with a tarnished character.

"You're so wrong!" Tara is ready to go.

"Listen, Tara..."

"No, you listen now. You're despicable, arrogant. Even if you kiss the ground I walk on, I'm not taking you back. Go now, hurry.... You may not even have to cancel the venue or any arrangements. Three days are enough to find a Bengalee wife. One more thing. You're too old for me...and not my type. And I don't like your name. So obnoxious!" Tara can't resist throwing it all in his face.

She walks out as he watches, stupefied.

～つ

"Plan B!" Tara shouts, a weight off her chest as she joins the others.

Tara drives off with Ava. Her light night bag is already in the boot of the car. They head towards the railway station, where Ava's brother is waiting. Together they will board the night train to Chittagong city. Something different waits for her there, something bigger. Nothing can dampen her now—not the gossip, not the smirks left behind in Dhaka.

Zahra and Anushka hail a rickshaw. They have a bigger challenge ahead—to inform their parents, tell them about the next move. The taillights of the car vanish from sight as the rickshaw takes a turn into a side alley. Familiar shops and houses on the borders of the street slowly emerge as they continue to cruise.

Zahra is glad for Tara. She had the guts to make a decision that she wanted—not to please anyone, to stand up for her own good. All these years Tara has been trying to break out of a shell, an invisible ceiling that has kept pressing her down, squeezing the very spot she was standing on, smaller and smaller, trying to rob her of her power to rise.

5.

Zahra remembers that night fifteen years ago very well—the ominous night when it all happened. She was studying for exams. Tara hadn't returned from her friend's house. She had phoned and told Sabaa that her friend would drop her home. It was past ten, a windy, dark night outside. Ishmail was pacing in the living room. Anushka was fast asleep after she had completed her school project.

"Where is she? Tara's becoming so rowdy, unmanageable

because of you. You can't control her," Ishmail lashed out.

"How was I to know she wouldn't be at her friend's house? I trusted her," Sabaa responded.

"You're too soft on her. Spoiled her totally," he blamed Sabaa.

"You're unnecessarily rough with her, so she rebels," Sabaa fought back.

The phone's shrill sound pierced the silence. Ishmail talked into the receiver.

"Hello? Yes, yes. Alright. I understand.... Yes." Ishmail listened, his voice hardened when he spoke. The rest was inaudible from the girls' bedroom.

Zahra could hear the hushed tones of her parents after he hung up. Then the doorbell rang. Sounds of footsteps echoed in the hallway. There was some discussion, at one point an argument with some people, and then Ishmail's clear voice penetrated through the house.

"My Tara is five times better than your three sons put together!"

Zahra slid beside Anushka in the bed and pretended to be asleep while Ishmail went out with the visitors with whom he was arguing. She was panicked and knew something bad had happened to Tara. Her body trembled in fear, but she didn't have the courage to ask her mother anything. Sabaa remained in the living room.

~⁓

"Where's Aba?" Zahra asked in the morning before going to school. Sabaa looked as if she had been awake all night.

"He'll be back soon. Keep an eye on Anush and eat your tiffin with her." Sabaa was incoherent.

In school Anushka always ate with her own friends, and after classes the three sisters came home on the school bus. That was the routine. Zahra knew something was very wrong. Tara wasn't back yet.

Tara still wasn't home when they returned from school. The day dragged on. They showered, played in the garden in the afternoon, and had an early dinner. Sabaa looked as if she would break at any moment. Her eyes were bloodshot due to lack of sleep or crying. Her lips looked parched. Possibly she hadn't eaten anything since last night.

Sabaa paced the living room, from time to time looked out the window to check. The hours wore on. Her nervousness was infectious. Zahra got caught up in it and couldn't concentrate on her studies. Luckily, Anushka was busy practicing math for her test and wasn't paying much attention as she was hell-bent to get a better grade than her longtime rival, the snooty popular girl in class who happened to be good in math as well.

The sun went down. They all sat in the living room. Sabaa wanted them to stay close to her. She was a wreck. Anushka was surprised but didn't object. She usually preferred her own study room.

The phone rang, finally, once again. After she hung up, Sabaa smiled for the first time in many hours. She looked relieved.

"Your Aba is bringing Tara home. Soon." She beamed at the girls.

"Where was she? You let her stay overnight at her friend's, Ama? If Tara can stay overnight, I can too," Anushka told her mother. At eleven, she was exhibiting the first signs of her adolescent defiance.

"Anushka, shush, shush!" Zahra stopped her from pestering their mother and walked out of the room with her.

Ishmail returned with Tara after dark. Actually, it was only eight in the evening, but it was an intense moonless, gloomy night. Even the stars were covered by a thick coating of dark clouds. Tara didn't go to see her sisters right away but stayed in the living room. Sabaa and Tara talked in low tones for several minutes. Then Tara flung the door open and marched into their room. All three sisters slept in the same room in those days—Tara in a single bed while Zahra and Anushka shared a double bed. The room was vast, with a big attached bathroom with a tub.

"Where were you, Tara?" Zahra wanted to know, visibly on the verge of crying in relief to see her sister back, well and unharmed.

"What do you care? Best daughter of our parents!" Tara lashed back, unfriendly, defensive.

"Ama was worried about you. She didn't eat or sleep the entire time till you returned."

"Oh, shut up, Zahra!" Tara slammed the door of the bathroom. Anushka was baffled and decided not to participate in any of the flaring temper play.

For almost an hour, Tara didn't come out of the bathroom. They could hear the sound of running water inside. Sabaa came looking for her twice in the meanwhile.

Then there were those dialogues Zahra couldn't help overhearing sometimes—made her extremely uncomfortable.

"Ask her, again... again. We need to know what happened," Ishmail urged. "This girl is out to ruin herself... drag us all down. Mark my words," he said again.

On some nights, she had heard sounds of Sabaa's subdued crying while Ishmail consoled her gently. She had seen her parents holding onto each other in desperation.

⁓

"Tara, talk to me. Did he touch you?" Sabaa asked. Zahra heard their mother speaking in a low voice. Tara didn't respond. "Where? How many times? What did he do?"

"I already told you. Stop pestering me!" Tara's voice was loud enough for both Zahra and Anushka to hear.

"Keep your voice down! Shameless! Tell me again." Sabaa was angry. "Did you undress? Did he? Did he touch your breasts? Tell me, tell me!" Sabaa was desperate.

"No, no, no!" Tara screamed back. "Ama, get off me! Stop!"

Then she ran out of the room and shut herself in the bathroom again, slamming the door with a loud bang. Tara didn't eat her dinner that night, though Zahra softly knocked and called her several times. Sabaa let her stay there.

~~⌒~~

"Keep an eye on whether she has her period," Ishmail suggested to Sabaa.

"She says not yet. End of the month," Sabaa's response drifted in. Zahra didn't mean to snoop but couldn't walk away.

"Don't trust her. She's lying. When she bleeds, tell her to show the pad," he said again.

"OK, now, stop it. And don't shout at her. She's a little girl, after all. She's hurting.... She's afraid of your harsh words." Sabaa was more empathetic.

"She's stupid enough to run away and you're blaming me?" he roared in suppressed anger. Sabaa didn't answer back anymore. Zahra thought she was crying.

"You never tried to understand her. Look what happened! We need to mend her now. She's all broken." Sabaa sniffled.

"We've to be careful. This can ruin her. Forever. I've requested my boss for a transfer. There are posts vacant in West Pakistan," he added later in a kinder tone.

At some other times, Zahra saw her parents huddled together, Ishmail's arms around Sabaa with care.

"We'll be far away before gossip begins.... Time will bury whatever happened.... We have to think of our younger daughters as well," he muttered. Ishmail was so wrong. Bengalee society doesn't forgive a woman so easily.

In December of 1970, Ishmail arrived with his family from Chittagong at his next duty station—Lahore....

The secret that Tara has lived with for so long is finally out to haunt her mercilessly. A mistake made impulsively in adolescence has shadowed her throughout her entire life. Zahra is proud of Tara for taking a bold step tonight. Difficult? Of course, but rewarding and inevitable....

6.

Tara rests her head against the car seat as the automobile speeds up. Streetlights pass by in a flash. She feels calm. Though drained, she is relieved now, finally. She has made her choice. She knows there will be struggles; the present euphoria will begin to fade under challenges. But today she won! At fourteen, she ran away from home in rebellion, returned defeated. Today she is running away to create a new future. She is in full control.

"How do we tell Ama and Aba?" Anushka wants to know as the rickshaw inches towards home.

"Best to make an honest pitch. We tell them everything," Zahra suggests.

"We need to distribute the work. Aba can call the not-destined-to-be-the-groom's snooty momma to inform her the wedding is off." At this, both sisters begin to laugh. The tension lifts immediately after the hearty laughter. Their hearts feel lighter. "She's a character." Anushka makes a face.

"We're two grown-up women. We can do it. You and I will call our relatives...cancel the venue, caterers...decorators. Those are the most important," Zahra says on a serious note.

"The flower man is all yours, Zahra. He's absconding, the last I heard."

"Sustained!" Zahra tries a mock-serious voice.

Both sisters laugh again, beating the background noise of

the traffic. The young rickshaw puller turns his head to check and laughs with them as well without understanding the real cause of the mirth.

"OK, the idiot electricians are yours, Anush...to hold and to cherish and box their ears off. Latest update—they're still on the roof struggling without success."

The rickshaw stops in front of the gate. To their surprise, they find the house finally alight, sparkling with gorgeous multicolored bulbs hanging from the roof in loops, beautifully garlanding the front walls. Now it really has the air of a house of wedding! Guests must be pleased. Tara would have loved it. She is possibly nearing the railway station by now.

"My God! Look at this! Your guys have proved they have balls...as Tara would have liked to say," Zahra comments. Both sisters giggle. They enter the house, arms linked.

~

Sabaa and Ishmail listen to the sisters intently. They had initially thought it would be an extremely difficult challenge to handle Ishmail. He would pull the house down in anger. They find him very mellow. He looks exhausted. There's defeat in his eyes, but he doesn't lose his temper. He agrees to their plan regarding calling off the wedding from their side before the other party can make a move. That's going to save whatever little pride is left. In people's memory, they will be remembered as rejecting the wedding, not being rejected. Sabaa starts crying. She had put her heart and soul into organizing the event. She had been praying for years for Tara, for her happiness. No one talks for several minutes, each lost deep in thought.

"Hmm. In a way I think Tara was wise to walk out," Ishmail says, still subdued. "This marriage wouldn't have worked in the long run. Don't be sad, Sabaa." He puts his arms around his sobbing wife.

"I wanted Tara to be loved and admired for who she is, have children, keep smiling. But I'm with her. She's my daughter." Sabaa's voice is broken, holding many tears in it.

"I agree, Sabaa. Don't worry. Tara is a fighter. Let me now think what I should say to Akand's mother. I'll call her soon." Ishmail gets up. "I know Tara won't take my calls, but if you talk to her, tell her I love her, and I'm proud of her," he says on his way out to the balcony to the surprise of everyone.

The lights start blinking at that moment, and then some parts of the illumination die down with a big popping sound.

"What a nuisance! It went off again!" Ishmail shouts from the balcony. "Can you kick out the electricians first thing tomorrow morning, Anush? They're your responsibility, right?" he says as they all start laughing.

"These guys are totally hopeless. Spent so much money for their low-quality service." Sabaa is fed up.

The sisters are relieved that she has found something to focus on. It means she will recover faster from the hypershock.

CHAPTER TWENTY-SIX

Shadows and mirrors

I.

Back in their room, they miss Tara. The sisters have quarreled, wept, and giggled so many times in this room. Tara has a separate bedroom with an attached bathroom on the other side of the balcony, though — the prerogative of being the oldest among the siblings. Her room is maddeningly quiet tonight. No sudden bursts of music, no lights. In its muted presence, it boldly is declaring Tara's absence.

Anushka pulls away the curtains from the large windows. The compound walls outside are back to darkness, as they are used to, the result of the failed illumination. All signs of the wedding house hubbub have been snuffed out abruptly. No more hurried footsteps in the corridors, on the stairs. No gleeful shrieks in the balcony, on the lawn. The clattering in the kitchen is discreet tonight. Ishmail has made the phone call and announced the news to the visitors. The house is gripped by stillness after weeks.... It's not the sound of sadness, though, Zahra thinks.

Moonlight leaps into the room through the open windows. The sky is ablaze with fiery stars. Anushka has switched off the light, as they often do on such nights. In the dimness, the sisters sit in silence, their backs resting against large cushions carelessly thrown on the rug. Right at this moment, Tara's train must be speeding ahead, piercing the darkness of the night, touching unknown tiny stations in its snaky gait, inching towards the distant coastal seaport city. In hours, she will be miles and miles away. Anushka plays a cassette that Zahra brought from Kathmandu, a farewell gift from her colleagues, a song collection by Nina Simone.

"Tara must be asleep by now," Zahra says as the songs play in the background.

"Zahra, would you have stayed back if your monk had asked you to?" Anushka wants to know.

Zahra thinks. The images come back—the first touch, the fervent intimacies, soft incense of the wild blossoms, melting of hearts, sleepless nights...the cost of tears....

"I don't think so, no. I let him go...though couldn't release him from my heart," she says aloud. *Every fiber in my body is crying out for him.* Her mind is voiceless.

"Do you miss him?"

"Every second." Zahra's whisper is soaked in a sob.

"Would you have gone to Sweden?" Now it's Zahra's turn. She has never been so direct. Silence. No one speaks or moves.

"No, I wouldn't have. He's married," Anushka says after some time. "I was only eighteen.... And he never asked," she adds as an after-thought.

They listen to the songs in silence. Both lost in thoughts.... So much has happened to all of them. They aren't like others, they realize.

"Do you remember Nana Buji Tota, her Amazonian sisters...their matriarch mother?" Zahra asks suddenly.

"They were so different." Anushka nods. "Somewhere in our veins, in our bodies...traces of DNA of those very brave women may be alive?"

"...Endowing us with exceptional strengths? Enriching our existence...to brave the life we want?" Zahra matches Anushka's thoughts.

"Do you think years later you will change your mind and contact Arthur?" Anushka is such a romantic.

Zahra doesn't respond right away. She smiles. Her thoughts go back again into the past, the life lived—and is history now.

"Life can be strange, Anush. Who can tell what will happen? The future isn't within our reach," she says finally.

Acknowledgments

My sincerest thanks go to:

My son, Syed Shabab Wahid, a Public Health Professional and an amazingly sensitive person who encouraged me to write this book; my childhood best friend Nasrin Murshed Ava, a literature graduate, the first one to read my book and give a thumbs up; my niece, Rubaiyat Khan, a smart software Engineer employed with Facebook as a product manager who usually reads about fifty to eighty books a year. She made me believe in myself. She also painted the book cover. My heartfelt appreciation also goes to my friends and well wishers: Tasmia Rahman, Nahid Kabir, Nadiah Khan, Taslima Lazarus, Shamima Ahmed, Rachel Carnegie, Juthi Ahmad, Sanjeeda Islam, Adrika Lazarus, Najma Hasib, Mansur Hasib, Maruja Salas, Lazeena Muna McQuay and Neill McKee. I am ever indebted to them for their faith in me. My special thanks and gratitude are for my content editor, Jennifer Hager who guided me, challenged me, engaged me in countless discussions and inspired me; the ProofreadingPal for their professional assistance; and Sara DeHaan, my book designer, who I trust to create magic with her professional expertise.

About the Author

 Nuzhat Shahzadi is a creative writer. She is a Bengalee American — grew up in East Bengal, initially a part of Pakistan that emerged as an independent sovereign nation in 1971 following a violent civil war. In her adolescence she got a first hand taste of living through a horrific genocide.

She authored and co-authored numerous entertainment-education materials and directed animation films on social issues honing the power of story telling to influence behavior. Her work with the United Nations took her to the heart of unchartered territories marred with armed conflict in Asia and Africa—from the war torn landscape of Afghanistan, Sri Lanka, Nepal to the shores of Angola, Cote d'Ivoire...the slopes of Rwanda, Uganda and Mozambique that borne the scars of civil conflicts. She travelled extensively to many other regions that offered her the opportunity to work closely with the most marginalized grass roots communities. In one of her international assignments, she was based in a remote island for several years in the south Pacific where the idea of this book was born.

Shahzadi holds two post graduate degrees: a Masters in Public Health, and an MA in English literature. At present she lives in greater Washington DC area in the US.

CPSIA information can be obtained
at www.ICGtesting.com
Printed in the USA
LVHW041158300920
667477LV00001BA/28